Nightmare Series
Books 4 - 6
Written by David Longhorn
Edited by Emma Salam

ISBN: 9781797937311
Copyright © 2019 by ScareStreet.com
All rights reserved.

Thank You!

Hi there! I'd like to take this opportunity to thank you for downloading this book. I really appreciate it, and to show how grateful I am to you, I'd like to give you **a full-length horror novel in 3 formats (MOBI, EPUB and PDF) absolutely free!**

Download your full-length horror novel, get free short stories, and receive future discounts by visiting www.ScareStreet.com/DavidLonghorn

See you in the shadows,
David Longhorn

Nightmare Resurrection
Nightmare Series Book 4

Nightmare Resurrection

Prologue: Stranger on a Train

Cassandra Bradley looked out of the train window as it pulled out of the small Welsh station. She had lost count of how many obscure places they had been through. There were two stops to go, if she had calculated right. Then, although she knew them by heart, she again consulted the list of instructions on her phone. She would have to get a taxi, chargeable to expenses, to the coastal village of Maldwyn's Bay. There she would, apparently, be met by a boat and taken to her employer's private island, Holyhaven.

'Prepare to have your personal ID checked by security before you are admitted to Mountfalcon House.'

She checked her ID again, frowning at the photo.

It doesn't look much like me, she thought. *Well, it might be mistaken for me in a bad light. I look so vacuous, and those teeth!*

Shoving the ID back into her bag, she picked up a copy of a tabloid newspaper that someone had left on the adjacent seat. The front-page headline was guaranteed to draw in the casual reader.

FARM FAMILY MURDERS – POLICE STILL HUNTING 'MANIAC'

Cassandra immersed herself in the lurid account. It was truly horrific. A week earlier, a couple called Murray had been found horribly mutilated at their farmhouse a few miles from a small town called Machen. The news, however, had been pushed off the front pages until now. The big story had been the chaos in London caused by the Hobbs Lane incident.

And nobody seems able to explain that, she thought, *so they're moving on to more familiar horrors.*

After a search, the bodies of the couple's two missing children were found in a flooded quarry nearby. Police were asking anyone with information to come forward. According to the report, detectives still had no real clues to follow. And there was some confusion over the children's bodies, as they were 'badly decomposed' despite the boy and girl only being missing for a few hours.

So many terrible things happening, she thought as she scanned the columns of newsprint. *So much chaos and suffering in the world. I shouldn't worry about starting a new job, now should I?*

Despite her best efforts, Cassandra found that the news was not sufficiently distracting. She was still nervous about the upcoming interview with Sir Charles Lanier. She flipped through to the horoscopes page, and for the twelfth time she read what her stars supposedly had in store. 'Beware of new projects or relationships – now is not the time for a major change'.

Great, she thought. *Just what I need. But these newspaper astrologers, what do they know? They just churn it out for the masses. Not like getting a proper natal chart from a professional.*

"Do you mind if I sit here?"

Cassandra started, looked up to see a tall, friendly-looking woman pointing at the vacant seat opposite.

"Of course!" she replied.

It was only after the woman had sat down that Cassandra glanced around the carriage and noted that there were plenty of vacant seats.

Maybe this woman just wants to chat, she thought. *Oh well, that might take my mind off things.*

"You seem a little nervous," the woman said in a surprisingly deep voice. "If you don't mind me saying so."

"No not at all!" Cassandra replied. "I am starting a new job, you see."

"Ah, I see," the woman said. "That is always a somewhat stressful experience."

Cassandra felt slight puzzlement over the way the stranger talked. The woman pronounced English words clearly, precisely. But there was no hint of a foreign accent, which could account for the rather mechanical way she spoke. The depth of her voice might be down to smoking.

"I am from Eastern Europe," said the woman. "My name is Katya. And your name is Cassandra, is it not?"

Cassandra gasped.

"How did you know my name?"

"It is not difficult," said Katya airily. "I have a gift for such things."

The woman leaned forward into the dull winter light, and Cassandra saw that her eyes were very dark against her pale skin.

"You see," Katya went on, "I am – what you call a psychic."

"Oh, that's totally amazing!" Cassandra exclaimed. "I went to see one in Brighton last year but she was terrible. You could tell she was guessing most of the time. One of those who just says things like ''I have a message from a spirit who has the letter A in their name.'''

Katya nodded wisely, and they talked about the realm of the paranormal for several minutes. Then they moved on to Cassandra's worries. The woman seemed so sympathetic that Cassandra felt much better about her situation already. Katya listened intently as she explained that she had been recruited from an agency to look after a rich, elderly man.

"But I'm not even supposed to say that much!" she said, suddenly alarmed by her own chattiness. "I signed an agreement, it was pages of legal jargon. Please don't say anything to anybody about this!"

"You have not told me his name, or where he lives," Katya pointed out. "As for me, I am living in a small village on the coast, where I give psychic readings. That is no secret!"

"Oh, then you must be going to Maldwyn's Bay just like–" Cassandra began. "Damn, I did it again! You must be one of those empathic types. People open up to you. I suppose it's part of being psychic."

"I suppose it is," agreed Katya. "People do tell me things. And I tell people things. And sometimes I manage to help them. Perhaps I can help you with your troubles?"

"Are you a Gypsy?" Cassandra asked, then put a hand to her mouth in embarrassment. "Oh God, did I say that? It's very rude. And anyway you're far too pale-skinned for – oh God, there I go again. Sorry!"

"I am not a Gypsy fortuneteller," Katya replied, shaking her head and smiling. "But I am a member of a lost tribe, in a way.

My people see things that others do not. We can sense the aura of those who are troubled, nervous, afraid – yes? We walk in the realm of dreams. That is why I sat next to you. Fate brought us together, I think, Cassandra."

This is just what I wanted, Cassandra thought. *I so need to be told what my path in life should be. She's right, it is fate. If she is the genuine article, of course.*

The tall woman reached over and took one of Cassandra's hands in hers, ran a finger over the palm. Normally, Cassandra would have flinched from such uninvited contact, but not now. She knew, without being told, that it was part of the mystical process.

"This man you are going to work for," Katya said. "He is Sir Charles Lanier."

"That's right!" Cassandra gasped. "You are so genuine – my coming here was a total secret. He doesn't–"

Cassandra stopped herself again, and Katya smiled.

"I see it all," the pale woman said. "He does not want it known that he is frail, infirm – in need of a nurse. A permanent career. Not an easy job, even when one's employer is a pleasant individual."

The woman frowned, and closed her eyes for a moment.

"What do you mean?" Cassandra demanded. "Is something wrong?"

Katya took a deep breath, exhaled, opened her eyes.

"Oh, Cassandra, this is not good," she whispered urgently, leaning even closer. "This man, Lanier, he is – not so nice. He will make you do things you do not want to do. Rich old men, they treat women like us as things, objects to be used. You do understand me?"

Cassandra's mind reeled at the implication. She had always put more faith in psychics, mediums and fortunetellers than she cared to admit to others. But part of her still resisted the implication of Katya's words.

"Surely," she protested, "I could just complain to my agency? They frown upon that sort of thing. They have a zero-tolerance policy for all forms of harassment!"

Katya shook her head.

"Perhaps in normal circumstances you could complain. But, Cassandra, you are going to the private island of a very rich man. It would be your word against his. Who do you think they would believe? How would you prove anything? These policies you talk about – they are often simply for show."

Cassandra felt her world collapsing around her. On the one hand, she could not ignore Katya's warnings. Not when the psychic was so obviously genuine. Katya had offered such insights into her life, her past, her destiny. On the other, in her bag she carried the agreement she had signed, and the contract of employment.

"Whatever can I do?" she asked.

Katya released her hand, sat back, shrugged.

"I can only reveal a few hidden truths in this way," she said. "A full psychic reading, that would take longer. And these conditions are not ideal."

Cassandra looked out at the landscape rushing past. The train was reaching the end of a valley, and she could see a distant view of the sea beyond. Soon they would be at the coast, and she would have to choose.

"Please help me!" she begged, reaching out to seize Katya's hand. "You can't just tell me these things and then walk away."

Katya looked at her for a moment, her expression blank. Then she smiled, and to Cassandra's troubled mind it was as if a sun of new-found friendship had emerged from behind clouds of doubt. A speaker crackled to life and the guard announced that the train was reaching its final stop.

"All change," he added.

"All right," she said. "I cannot simply abandon you to such a fate. Let us share a taxi to the coast. I have rented a little cottage in Maldwyn's Bay. There we can hold a proper psychic reading, and you can decide how to shape your destiny."

Cassandra almost wept with gratitude. A small voice in the back of her mind told her she was placing a lot of trust in Katya. But there was something about the woman that banished such skepticism.

"You're so kind!" she said. "I can't afford to pay you very much now, but–"

Katya held up a slender, white hand.

"Do not speak of money. There are far more valuable things."

When the train pulled into the small station, Cassandra got up and started to take her luggage down from the rack. Katya helped without being asked, easily managing the bulky bags, carrying them down the carriage to the door.

"You're a lot more fit than I am," Cassandra said admiringly as she trotted behind the taller woman. "You must work out."

The taxi ride to the coast took nearly an hour. They talked all the way. Cassandra, who did not make friends easily, felt that she had known Katya all her life. The pale woman always seemed to know exactly what to say, and how to say it. When they arrived, Katya insisted on paying half the fare, although Cassandra pointed out she could claim it all on expenses.

"We are friends now," Katya said, putting her arm through Cassandra's. "My home is a short walk from here. Please, let me carry that heavy case."

The village seemed deserted as they walked through the cobbled streets. Now and again Cassandra caught a glimpse of someone at a window, but whenever she looked directly at them, they darted back out of sight.

"The locals are very shy with strangers," Katya remarked. "But once they got to know me, they took me to their hearts. So generous."

Katya's home was a quaint, white-washed cottage near the small quayside. In the harbor, Cassandra saw a few fishing boats bobbing on the gray, wind-lashed waves. However, there was no sign of the boat from Holyhaven Island she was supposed to meet.

"Come," Katya said, opening the door. "I will make some tea, yes? And then reveal your future."

Inside, the cottage was surprisingly Spartan. Cassandra had had some vague expectation of bead curtains, dreamcatchers, statues, oriental rugs. Instead, she saw a cheap carpet, basic furniture, a television, a few books, some newspapers. There were no ornaments, pictures, or houseplants. The place looked like it had been deserted for months. The only sign of habitation were some clothes drying on a radiator. The clothes were small, certainly not big enough for long-limbed Katya.

"Do you live alone?" Cassandra asked.

The pale woman glanced at the clothes, then shook her head.

"My little niece and nephew, they are staying with me. They are playing in their room, I think. They will not disturb us."

At Katya's invitation, Cassandra sat down at the kitchen table. Soon she was sipping lemon tea from a glass and watching her hostess close the curtains against the weak December light.

"Now," said Katya, sitting opposite her. "Give me your hands, and we will consider your destiny."

Cassandra reached across and felt the woman's strong fingers enclose her smaller hands. As they did so, she heard a slight noise. It sounded like someone opening a door. She wondered if, despite Katya's assurance, the children would come out. It would be natural for them to want to see their auntie, she reasoned.

"Cassandra," Katya said, her voice lighter, softer than before. "I need you to open your mind. Think of happy memories, from your childhood. When you are happy, you are truly yourself. It is that true self I wish to contact."

Cassandra, keen to oblige, duly thought of the enjoyable times she had had with her parents, her little brother, her school friends. She recalled beloved toys, her first crush, a wonderful birthday when the pony she had always yearned for had appeared, complete with a shiny red bow in its mane.

"That is good," breathed Katya. "That is very good."

Again, Cassandra was struck by how high-pitched the psychic's voice had become. Then she was back amid her childhood memories. But this time things were not quite so pleasant. She struggled to recollect incidents, places, even people. Her grandparents, for instance – why could she not recall what they looked like? Two benevolent figures looked down on her, but their faces were blank. She felt other memories start to disintegrate, slipping away from her, melting into a sea of nothingness.

"I can't – I don't – what's happening?" she stammered. "Why can't I remember?"

"That is good," sighed Katya, almost crooning the words. "More, I need more."

The other woman's pleasure only upset Cassandra more. Far from showing her future, Katya seemed to be erasing her past. She tried pulling her hands away, but the larger woman held her in a vice-like grip.

"No!" she yelled, hurling her entire body backwards, tipping over the chair and crashing to the bare boards.

In the gloom she saw Katya stand up and begin to stride around the table. Cassandra scrambled upright and ran into the living room. She was making for the door when two pale, naked figures leapt out from behind the threadbare sofa. Their faces were rudimentary, mask-like, with small dark eyes. Instead of mouths, they had muzzles fringed with razor-like teeth. They were the size of young children, but there was nothing child-like about the way they bounded toward Cassandra.

She screamed, tried to dodge away, but the nearest creature had already fastened thin, wiry arms around her legs. She fell headlong, hit the floor hard and was too badly winded to keep struggling. The other small monster landed on her back, grabbing her by the throat.

She flinched in anticipation of an attack by the inhuman teeth. But instead the creatures simply kept her down until Katya's boots came into view. Then her captors simply stood up and walked away. Cassandra looked up, scared and puzzled. Katya crouched down by her, the tall woman's face in shadow.

"We are nearly finished," she said. "You already know it does not hurt."

"Why are you talking like that?" Cassandra demanded. "Is that your real voice? I don't understand?"

Katya reached down and lifted her easily, then held her upright. With the touch of the woman's hands Cassandra felt her memories start to flow away from her again. She struggled, feebly this time. In response, Katya casually lifted her off her feet and swung her round so that Cassandra's back was to the living room window. Now the tall woman was facing the light.

"Oh my God!"

Cassandra stared at her own face. It was paler, the eyes a little darker, the mouth a little fuller perhaps. But she had seen so many Instagram pictures of herself that there was no doubt Katya had somehow become her near-double. She was looking at a vastly more beautiful, confident version of herself.

"Yes," said Katya, in a voice Cassandra suddenly recognized as her own. "Soon all you have ever known and felt and thought will be mine. Then the young ones will dispose of what is left. Do not worry. You will feel nothing. Your body will be merely an empty shell. Less than an animal."

Cassandra could not even try to struggle, merely moan in despair as the last vestiges of her personality were leached away.

"Don't be sad," said the false Cassandra, letting her victim go to slump onto the cheap, dusty sofa. "I will be far better at being you than you could ever have been."

***

"This is worse than being in the bloody army," whined Phelps, kicking a stone up the beach.

Murphy looked over at his subordinate, gave a wry frown.

"Care to explain how?" he asked. "We are enjoying a nice bit of fresh air, walking by the sea. And we're getting paid. Many a poor soul would see that as a very cushy job."

"Yeah, but it's so bloody boring, innit?" Phelps continued. "Stuck on this friggin' island, nothing ever happens. No booze, no birds, no decent grub."

"Whereas when you were in the army it was just one long Roman orgy," Murphy said, with mild sarcasm. "Wine, women and song, day and night."

"You know what I mean!" retorted Phelps. "There's nothing happening here. All you can do is watch telly, sleep, or wander up and down like this, maybe chuck rocks at seagulls. Enough to send you off your rocker after a while."

Murphy sympathized with the younger man. He himself was bored much of the time. He would have much preferred guarding Lanier in London, or New York, or Dubai – anywhere else, just as long as there were people around.

"Never mind," sighed Murphy. "Let's get down to the jetty, we've got to bring this new nurse over."

"That's more like it!" exclaimed Phelps. "God, wish I had a live-in nurse. Sexy little uniform, naughty giggling, plenty of bed-baths."

"You really are quite disgusting," Murphy said. "I hope she turns out to be a lesbian with a black belt in karate."

"I could live with that," Phelps replied with a leer. "I like a challenge. Point is, she has to have a nice pair, and a fine, peachy bum. Those are my minimum requirements."

Phelps continued to reel off his specifications for the perfect woman as they crossed the narrow strait to the mainland. The village that lay opposite Holyhaven was almost deserted outside the tourist season. There was nobody waiting on the windswept dock for the security team.

"She's a no-show," Phelps complained. "Typical woman. Wasted journey."

"Stop moaning, she was coming by taxi from the station," Murphy pointed out. "She might be late."

They had tied up the boat and jumped onto the dock when a young woman appeared, carrying two large suitcases. As she walked across the quayside, hips swaying, the security guards exchanged astonished glances.

"Private healthcare is clearly the way ahead," remarked Murphy.

"God almighty, look at that figure," Phelps drooled. "Even better than the face."

Murphy was about to tell Phelps to shut his mouth when he realized that his own mouth was hanging open.

"Good afternoon," said the young woman, in a pleasant contralto. "I am Cassandra Bradley. Do you want to check my ID now?"

"Yes please," said Phelps immediately. "Also, we need to conduct a full body search, for weapons and that sort of thing."

"Get the lady's cases, Phelps," said Murphy, shoving the other man aside. "I'll handle this. I'm sure everything is in order."

Cassandra smiled as she handed him her agency ID, passport, and a sheaf of other documents.

"These seem to be in order, Miss," said Murphy. "Though I must say not one of these photos does you justice."

"Flatterer!" she said. "And please, call me Cassandra. I just hope everyone on the island is as friendly as you boys. I've been a little worried that Sir Charles might not find me … acceptable."

"Oh God," muttered Phelps under his breath, as he heaved the luggage into the boat. "The lucky old bastard."

We are all lucky bastards, lad, thought Murphy, taking his time to help Cassandra aboard. *Things around here just got much more interesting.*

Nightmare Resurrection

Chapter 1: Unwanted Gift

"For God's sake, Charles, will you just listen?"

John Scoresby felt his heart-rate increase, and began to become breathless. He leaned against the mantelpiece of his Georgian farmhouse's dining room as his head swam. He had been worrying so much he had barely eaten that day. A sense of impending disaster had killed his appetite.

Calm down, he told himself. *You're not a young man any more. Remember what the doctors keep telling you.*

The man on the other end of the phone was, technically, Scoresby's boss. But he had long considered Charles Lanier to be a friend. And in the past, appealing to that lifelong friendship had made a difference.

But not today, it seems.

Lanier continued to talk, explaining in measured tones just why he wanted LanCorp to pivot one hundred and eighty degrees on a key issue. Scoresby could hardly believe his ears. He held the phone out, stared at it, listened for a few moments' longer. Eventually he could tolerate no more.

"Jesus Christ, Charles!" he erupted. "What the hell has happened to you? This isn't like you at all. Are you going senile?"

For a long moment there was silence. Scoresby wondered if he had gone too far, if this would trigger the boardroom meltdown he had long feared. A few financial journalists had been predicting a split at the top of the Lanier Empire for years, but until now Scoresby had not believed it possible.

But why should it happen because of some internet claptrap about government conspiracies, of all things?

When Lanier started speaking again, however, his voice was still polite, even mildly genial.

"I really think it's for the best, John," he repeated. "But of course, if the board is with you, you could oust me as chairman. That's the only way this policy change could be stopped, old friend."

Scoresby felt a terrible sinking feeling. It seemed he had no choice but to put it to a vote of the other directors. He could swing a majority, he calculated, and dethrone Lanier. It was the nuclear option, as it would upset the markets for a top CEO to lose his position too abruptly.

"I don't want to do that, Charles ..." he began, trying to sound calm, conciliatory.

"Oh, don't sweat it, John," Lanier cut in. "Look on the bright side. I'll have to retire sometime. And if I retire, I'll have more time to spend with Cassandra."

Cassandra, Scoresby thought, gripping the phone more tightly in his frustration. *That bloody woman again. There's no fool like an old fool. Marries his nurse because she's got a nice face, long legs, and big boobs. Even worse, why does he have to take her vacuous ideas seriously?*

"Does Cassandra," he said, keeping his tone level, "really have the experience to dictate policy to three national newspapers and a global TV news service?"

"She's awfully bright and creative, John!" replied Lanier. "You'd like her, you really should pop down and visit. She's so keen to meet you both. Oh, and by the way, did you get the gift she sent?"

Scoresby looked at the brown cardboard box on the sideboard of his living room. He had begun to unwrap the parcel, then paused in bafflement and a little disgust.

"Oh, yes, it arrived safely," he said. "I was just – admiring it before you rang."

"Isn't it amazing?" Lanier enthused. "She's so creative in so many ways, I don't know how she does it."

"No," Scoresby said, sincerely, "I don't either. What on earth did she make it from? I thought it would be cool and hard, but instead it's yielding and – sort of warm."

"I know!" Lanier replied. "Such a clever girl. And she produces all her little works of art with local materials – stuff she just finds lying around, or so she tells me. Anyway, the point is that we'll discuss editorial policy and a few other little matters when you come down. Now I really must go – Cassandra has made quite a wonderful quiche, and one must feed the inner man, you know!"

"Charles!" Scoresby cried, but the CEO had already hung up. "Bloody hell!"

Scoresby flung the phone onto the table, not caring that it scored a furrow on the polished oak. At that moment Dolores, the maid, looked around the dining room door. Scoresby glared at her, then essayed a fake smile. He recognized that he had many faults, but prided himself on treating his staff decently.

"Mister Scor-ezbee?" Dolores said tentatively. "Is it okay if I dust in here now?"

He beckoned the young woman in, and she began to dab at his wife's collection of fine china ornaments with a feather duster. He watched as Dolores worked her way along the sideboard, then paused at the parcel from Lanier. She looked round at her boss.

"This is a new ornament maybe?" she asked doubtfully. "Or is it a chocolate Easter Egg? But Easter, it is gone now, yes?"

"Yes, long gone," he grunted, going over to join her. "Here, what do you think of it?"

He lifted the supposed work of art out of the box. For the first time he saw the object as a whole – egg-shaped, reddish-brown, with a knobby surface. It was about twelve inches long and half as wide. Scoresby guessed it was made of some dense substance, as it was too heavy to be hollow. He suspected it was a rock wrapped in fabric and then covered with some kind of resin.

"Here," he invited. "Feel it."

Dolores reached out a tentative hand, jerked it back when her fingers touched the leathery shell. Scoresby smiled at her reaction. He, too, found the slightly moist object unpleasant. And, as he held it in his hands, he was again puzzled by the fact that it seemed to be warmer than room temperature.

"It is not nice," Dolores said firmly. "Senora Scor-ezbee, she will not like this among all her nice things!"

"No," he agreed. "She has taste. Unlike some people."

He replaced the object in the box. If he unseated Lanier at the next board meeting he could chuck the thing away. But if he did somehow manage to be reconciled with his old friend he might be expected to display the artwork prominently, at least when the Laniers were visiting. He decided to put it in the roomy attic of the old farmhouse.

"When you're finished, Dolores, you can go," he said, as he packed the egg back into its box and jammed the flaps down. "No need to wait around, it is the weekend after all. The cash is in the usual place. And there's a hundred extra, as Christmas is coming up."

"Thank you, sir!" she said, flashing a bright smile at him. "Will the senora be back tomorrow?"

"I hope so," he replied, pausing in the doorway, "her father seems to be on the mend. I'm sure Margaret will be glad to be home again."

Scoresby deposited the box in the attic among a clutter of junk, most of which struck him as more useful than the so-called *object d'art*.

"No fool like an old fool," he muttered as he climbed back down the ladder. "Seventy-eight, and he falls in love with some vapid bimbo. And the whole business goes tits up."

After lunch, Scoresby tried to work. But despite the long list of emails that needed his attention, his mind kept wandering back to the gift in the attic. It was odd, but for some reason the image of the boxed egg sitting amid the cobwebs and dust bunnies disturbed him. The ability to focus intensely on a given matter was one of his trademark skills. He was famous for his eye for detail, a skill that complemented Lanier's sweeping, strategic visions.

Now Charles is buggering about with details while I can't focus at all, he thought disconsolately. He closed his laptop and went to make himself a drink, settling on neat Scotch. He sat on the couch in the television room, but as soon as he flicked on the news, he saw the crawl along the bottom of the screen refer to 'New Monster Claims'.

"Monster bollocks!" he exclaimed, turning off the set and hurling the remote at the screen. The black box connected and cracked the bottom left corner of the glass.

"Bugger it all, I give up!"

Scoresby fixed himself another treble whiskey, wishing his wife was home so he could talk over this latest, biggest crisis. Instead he was alone, half-drunk, and miserable. He decided to go for a walk to the village, a couple of miles through winding lanes, simply to get his thoughts back in some kind of order. It was a crisp, clear November day.

Scoresby paused to throw his unfinished drink down the sink before leaving.

"Balls to work, I'm rich enough. Maybe I'm the one who should retire."

As he was putting on his walking boots he heard a faint thud that seemed to come from above his head. He looked up, but the hall ceiling was of course unaltered. He wondered if the box from the Laniers had somehow fallen over. Or, he reasoned, perhaps bats or birds were roosting up there.

Yes, that makes more sense.

When he returned from the village he felt refreshed and energized. Convinced of his own rightness, he worked far into the night, marshalling support for the forthcoming board meeting. By the time he felt too tired to go on it was nearly two o'clock and he had his majority. A narrow one, but it was enough.

All I have to do is turn up, he thought, with grim satisfaction. *Maybe if I simply tell Charles I can stop him, he will back down?*

The thought lingered as he got into bed, hoping for instant oblivion. But, not for the first time, tiredness failed to bring sleep. Instead Scoresby lay gazing up at the ceiling, wishing he was back in their London apartment.

Too quiet in the country, he thought. *Idyllic for some, dead for me. And isolated. Nearest police station is, what? Ten miles, fifteen? And the nearest hospital, more like twenty. Still, Margaret had her heart set on a place in the country.*

With a sense of isolation came memories of his lonely, often miserable childhood. He had learned self-reliance, but never forgotten the way warmth, love, comfort were withheld. Scoresby dozed, but fitfully, waking every few minutes. Uneasy thoughts whirled in his head, and eventually one particular memory pushed itself to the front.

Mister Snaffles.

"Bloody hell!" he moaned, turning over, punching the pillow.

Nightmare Resurrection

Of all the bloody stupid things to remember. Perverse way the subconscious mind works, dredging up the thing most likely to keep me awake.

Mister Snaffles had been a kind of goblin in a children's book young Johnny Scoresby had received for some birthday or Christmas. Scoresby could not remember the occasion, or even who had given him the book. All he could remember clearly about it was the picture of the supposedly comical protagonist, a pale, spindly creature with an oversized head.

Mister Snaffles had had tiny, evil eyes, a hooked nose, and a pair of rat-like front teeth. Scoresby was recalling more about the book now, as if someone was going through his childhood memories, selecting the most unpleasant. Mister Snaffles had spent most of the story sneaking into naughty children's bedrooms and tormenting them in various petty ways. Mister Snaffles' hair pulling and ear-tweaking was no doubt intended to be funny. But the appearance of the little monster had left little Johnny in no doubt that the intruder could do far worse.

"Ugly little bastard," Scoresby muttered into the pillow.

What kind of lunatic thought that was suitable in a children's' book?

There was another noise from the attic. It sounded like a small creature, scuttling across bare boards. Scoresby froze, then sighed. It was winter, when bats and other wild creatures hibernated. It would be natural for them to seek out a relatively warm attic. But whatever the local fauna might be doing, he would put money on it keeping him awake.

Then he had a brainwave. His wife used earplugs to block out his snoring. He found them in her bedside cabinet and stopped up his ears. As an afterthought he borrowed her sleep mask as well, as a pale hint of moonlight was visible through the curtains.

Right, you little furry or feathery bastards, feel free to have a hoe-down up there. I'm off to the Land of Nod.

With all sound and vision cut off, Scoresby found it easier to doze. This time no unpleasant memories surfaced. Soon he lost all sense of time and place, and dreamed of a tropical sky, waving palm trees, and gentle waves breaking on white sands.

Nightmare Resurrection

The pain stabbed deep into his throat, causing Scoresby to jerk upright and lash out. As he tore at the sleep mask he felt a gush of warmth flow over his chest, soaking his pajama top. Something pierced the back of his hand, and he heard himself howl in rage and fury, the sound muffled by the earplugs. He flung the mask aside and flailed at whatever was attacking him. He could not see it in the gloom, but felt the creature leap off his torso to dodge his blows. The pain from the bites in his throat and hand was distracting, but he still managed to focus on the problem.

Identify your enemy, he told himself. *Assess his strengths and weaknesses, judge your moment to attack or retreat.*

Holding up a pillow in the direction he guessed the animal would attack from, he quickly shuffled sideways and switched on his reading lamp. He gasped in horror at the amount of blood that soaked the front of his pajama jacket, staining the royal blue silk black. Then the attacker appeared, leaping around his improvised shield to stand glowering at him.

"Mister Snaffles!" he screamed.

The grotesque creature stood just over a foot high. It was as pale and spindly as he remembered, its face even more nightmarish that he recalled. The creature chittered at him, and he realized it was laughing, mocking, enjoying his terror.

"You're not real!" he shouted, but the person shouting was a boy of six, not a man in his seventies. Panic erased decades of adulthood, and with it all judgment, all confidence. He was a little boy again, and the world was no larger than his bedroom, and his bedroom suddenly a dark and terrifying place.

Scoresby hurled the pillow at the little monster. Mister Snaffles easily dodged it, and bounded toward him again. He threw his reading lamp, missed, heard it shatter. Scoresby screamed, threw himself out of the bed, struck his head on the corner of the bedside cabinet. The stunning blow added to the pain from his bite wounds. Squealing in triumph, Mister Snaffles leaped onto his back, sank vicious needle-sharp teeth into the back of his neck. Scoresby was terrified.

It's trying to bite through my spinal cord!

"Help!" he screamed, losing all sense of time and place. "Mummy, help!"

Another pain impinged on his fraying mind, a gripping agony that embraced his chest. He felt the frenzied biting, the blood, the terror all begin to fade away. The last thing he heard was a high-pitched, hateful voice.

"Mummy's not here. It's just you and me, Johnny!"

***

Dolores arrived at seven, ready to make Mister Scoresby his special coffee and lightly-browned toast. She added a glass of orange juice to the tray and carried it through to the bedroom. The door was ajar, which was unusual. When he did not reply to her knock, she went inside. The first thing she noticed was that he had left a light on. Then she noticed some other things, and dropped the tray.

It took her nearly ten minutes to recover from the shock and call the police.

***

The Reverend Herbert Bullingdon was opening up the church. It was Sunday, but he did not feel particularly enthusiastic about the service to come. The congregation at St. Wystan's had dwindled to the point where Bullingdon had seriously wondered if he should encourage people to bring their pets.

A few cats and dogs, he thought whimsically, *the odd rabbit, perhaps a carp in a bucket. Would get the numbers up. Please the bishop.*

The priest unlocked the side door, and then went through the ancient building to the main entrance. He unbolted it, eased the big slab of oak inward, then stepped outside to survey the village. Then, as part of a daily routine, he took a few more steps forward, turned around, and glanced up at the church tower.

No sign of erosion, he thought, examining the ancient stonework. *Nothing about to drop off. Good!*

Bullingdon was about to go inside again when he frowned, paused. While he had discerned no damage to the tower, he still felt something was not quite right. He shook his head, smiling at his own confusion.

Old man getting a bit dotty, he thought. *Forgetful, imagining things, generally a bit confused. Oh well.*

It was only later, as he was preparing the communion wine and wafers, that it occurred to him to wonder about something that should have been obvious. The church porch was topped by some badly-worn medieval decorations, including a row of small gargoyles. Bullingdon had always thought there were two, one on each corner. If anyone had asked before this morning, he would have stated the number as fact. But now he recalled seeing a third grotesque figure. It had been in the middle, grinning down at him, black against the cloudless spring sky.

But surely, I would have noticed it before now?

He left his preparations and went outside. Gazing up, he shielded his eyes against the blue glare. There were only two gargoyles. He had been right all along.

Start doubting your own senses and you might as well give up. Faith is all very well, but we must bow to commonsense in everyday matters.

Just as he was going back inside, he heard sirens in the distance. He thought of troubled souls in need of aid, and said a quick prayer for them under his breath.

***

Denny Purcell sank back on the sofa switched on the news, caught the tail end of an item about a media executive being found dead in mysterious circumstances.

"Might that be one for us?" asked Frankie Dupont, as she walked into the room carrying a tray. "Here, try this."

"Filet gumbo?" Denny said, half-listening to the news report. "As in the Carpenters' song?"

"The very same," Frankie replied, smiling. "My first attempt with British ingredients. But, hey, London's a foodie kind of city, so this is more or less authentic."

Denny nodded at the screen.

"Probably not interesting," she remarked. "Old rich guy dies. Maybe he was having some kinky fun time behind his wife's back."

A picture captioned John Scoresby appeared briefly. The crawl along the bottom of the screen read 'Lanier said to be 'devastated' by friend's death'.

"Lanier?" Frankie said. "Oh, well, if that guy was one of his pals, I hope he caught his dick in a rusty threshing machine."

Denny, with a mouthful of gumbo, laughed and spluttered.

"If you ever open a restaurant," she finally managed to say, "maybe you should stay back of house while somebody else handles the customers. And this is delicious, by the way."

"Thanks!" said Frankie. "I managed to edit that poltergeist story into some kind of shape, but I think it needs your magic touch."

"Of course," Denny said, holding up a forkful of food. "I'll do my best 'awe and mystery' voice, say all the right things. But we both know it was the kids throwing stuff, right?"

Frankie nodded.

"Nine times out of ten," she agreed. "We'll have to at least hint at that. You'd think kids today would have something better to do."

Denny shrugged.

"I've given up trying to make sense of the younger generation," she said in a fake old lady voice. "You're over thirty these days, you're obsolete."

They ate in silence for a while as the news gave way to the weather. Out of the corner of one eye, Denny saw Frankie scratching the back of one hand.

"Does it still give you trouble?" she asked quietly.

Frankie shook her head.

"Not really," she replied. "Mild irritation, like a rash that keeps recurring, you know?"

How can I know? Denny thought. *I didn't get plumbed into the metabolism of an alien monster for a few days.*

"I still dream about it," Frankie admitted. "Me and all the rest of them, still trapped in that great mountain of flesh. But I guess that's only natural."

Denny nodded, deciding to drop the subject. Nearly a year had passed since the so-called Hobbs Lane Incident. Official explanations as to what happened on the London Underground were widely challenged, not least by Lanier's media empire. She and Frankie were widely considered to be charlatans, cranks, or part of some wild conspiracy. The bizarre events had cast a long shadow over their careers.

"You'd think a guy like Lanier," Frankie said slowly, "would have been more interested in our story. He started in British tabloid journalism, for Christ's sake. They'll publish anything."

"'Nazi Bomber Found on Moon'," said Denny instantly. "Your turn!"

They started to laugh as they played their old game, mixing real and fake tabloid headlines, seeing if they could fool each other.

"'Elvis Found Alive in Glasgow'," said Frankie, with a suddenly straight face.

"False!" Denny shouted. "Way too normal! It should be something like 'Elvis Found Living on the Moon – With Hitler.'"

Frankie held up her hands in mock surrender.

"You got me. One point."

Denny thought carefully, then said, "'Drunk Killed During DIY Head Transplant'."

"False!" Frankie responded, then looked confused. "No, true!"

"Cheater!" Denny accused. "Anyway, it is true. The headline, I mean. Not the head transplant. That's just – well, I mean it's too ridiculous – isn't it?"

There was another pause. When Frankie spoke again she was looking at the screen, no longer smiling.

"Just like our story, right?" she said sadly. "We're a down-market tabloid headline. 'Journos Claim Attack by Monsters from Another Dimension.'"

Denny shuffled along the couch, hugged her friend.

"Hey, we both know people have short memories! Give it a little more time. We're getting a lot less attention from the crazies. That means we might get more legitimate work. With a bit of luck."

Frankie smiled up at Denny, put her bowl down on the floor.

"Sure," she said. "And in the meantime, we put our stuff online and showcase our many talents. While investigating obvious bullshit UFOs, hauntings, Bigfoot, Nessie–"

"At least we got to monetize the channel," Denny pointed out. "We've got enough followers to pay the rent. And don't diss Nessie, I'm pretty sure she's real."

They talked a little longer, then Frankie got a call from her mother in Louisiana. While the two caught up, Denny went into the kitchen to work on editing their poltergeist story. First, though, she checked the comments feed on their YouTube channel.

Amid the usual torrent of abuse, sneering, and illiterate nonsense were a few interesting items. One that had been posted just a few minutes earlier caught her attention.

> 'Why don't you investigate the moving gargoyle at St Wystan's Church? I was out jogging and I saw it move! Just got my phone out in time. Weird!'

There was a link to a photo of a quaint old English church in what looked like early morning light. Denny enlarged the picture, thus blurring it slightly. She could make out the gargoyles the commenter seemed to find so interesting. The church porch had two of the grotesque little statues at each side. But then Denny looked again at a blur she had assumed was a bird in flight between church and jogger. It could, if she squinted a little, be a small, humanoid form racing up the lead-tiles slope of the church roof.

"Lame," she said, and closed the window.

But as she edited the poltergeist video, the image of the alleged gargoyle kept intruding on her thoughts. Eventually she gave up trying to find a euphemistic way to say that two kids were pranking their parents and went back to the comment link. She copied the picture, enhanced and enlarged it. The result was a blurry, pale gray form that might have been a spindly monkey.

"Whassup?" Frankie asked, crossing the tiny kitchen behind her.

"Probably nothing," she replied. "Somebody thinks a gargoyle on their church has come to life."

Frankie chuckled, then fell silent. Denny felt her friend's small hand clutch her shoulder.

"Oh my God," breathed Frankie. "It can't be. Can it?"

At that moment Denny gasped at her own foolishness. She suddenly put together disparate bits of data. There was the overall shape of the blurred form, the trailing strands of black hair, the pale flesh, the hint of a muzzle-like visage, the way it ran head down, arms almost trailing on the roof tiles.

"But it's so small!" she protested.

"We start small," Frankie said quietly. "Come on, we're both thinking it. That's a Loper."

Nightmare Resurrection

Chapter 2: Demons and Bureaucrats

"So, let's be clear about this," said the committee chairman. "Just so that we're all on the same page."

Ted Gould felt himself becoming tense, but tried to keep his expression neutral.

Here we go again, he thought. *The very British, very polite trashing of all my ideas.*

"Your request for funding is interesting, certainly quite detailed," the chairman went on, glancing at the sheaf of documents arrayed on the table. "But ultimately it is based on the bold assertion that beings from some kind of – well, let us call it what you do, another dimension – attempted to invade our world last year. Would you say that is a fair assessment?"

"Interlopers," said Gould, keeping his voice even, "beings reported by many reliable observers in this and other countries. And there are related entities, large and extremely dangerous, all entering our continuum from a realm where different physical laws apply. And I didn't say invade, I said they attempted to migrate here as their own world was dying."

"How did they get here?" asked a committee member, a distinguished physicist. "How can anything travel from one universe to another? I am not clear about these portals you refer to."

"My hypothesis," replied Gould, "is that the portals may be Einstein-Rosen bridges. Rips in the fabric of space-time, giving entry to a parallel universe. At the Romola Foundation we called the Interlopers' realm the Phantom Dimension."

"And, as you spell out in quite exhaustive detail, it was full of monsters," said the chairman. "Creatures that can read minds and take on horrific forms based on our subconscious fears or desires. A bit outside the realms of mainstream science. One finds such entities in science fiction, in fairytales, in horror films. But in the laboratory, one looks in vain for any real evidence of their existence. What do you say to that argument, Doctor Gould?"

Gould felt himself reddening with repressed anger.

Every bloody time, he thought. *They always make it sound like comic-strip stuff, never accept the solid evidence.*

"I think that abundant evidence of a strange and significant phenomenon, as presented to you, at least deserves fair consideration," he said carefully. "Bear in mind that something undeniably happened at Hobbs Lane. And in other parts of the world. Reliable witnesses saw bizarre organisms appear out of nowhere, then disintegrate. That is a lot of data to dismiss."

Gould looked from one member of the three-man committee to another. The third person facing him, a statistician, had not spoken yet. At first, Gould had thought the expert was deep in thought. But then he caught sight of the reflected blue glow on the mathematician's face and realized the man was simply on his phone.

"Data, yes, hmm," the chairman murmured. "Much of this data was gathered by two journalists, while working for a so-called charitable foundation whose chairman has disappeared."

"Blurred video of yet more monsters, taken by a couple of American journalists who have repeatedly been accused of faking footage," put in the mathematician, with a marked sneer. "No accurate figures, readings, measurements. Just gosh wow stuff."

Gould took a deep breath, looked past the committee chairman's' left ear. He found that if he looked the man in the face, he felt like punching it.

"There are also a number of eyewitnesses who returned from the Phantom Dimension," he said. "People who were abducted and subject to bizarre, cruel experiments by the Interlopers."

"And whose testimony is no more reliable than the video footage," said the mathematician. "Some of these people supposedly vanished in the distant past, but no verifiable records exist. Most are exhibiting signs of psychosis."

"Those witnesses include my own sister, Lucy," Gould pointed out, still keeping his voice under control.

The chairman looked down at his folded hands in embarrassment.

"Doctor Gould," he said finally, "a small child was found among a disparate group of undocumented – people. Not one of them has been identified with any degree of certainty. A mystery, certainly. But to introduce the element of time travel..."

Gould sighed.

"I have tried to explain that time flowed faster in the Phantom Dimension. My sister was abducted nearly fifty years ago, but has only aged about four years. And of course she is confused, given the terrible things...the terrible things they did–"

Damn, he thought. *I can't do this anymore.*

Gould pushed his chair back and stood up.

"Gentlemen," he said, making for the doorway. "I came here without any great hope of a fair hearing. I expected to be mocked, dismissed, not taken remotely seriously. You have at least proved me to be a competent prophet."

"Really, Doctor Gould," said the chairman in a reproving tone. "There are correct procedures–"

"Stick your procedures up your fat, pimply arse," said Gould, and slammed the door behind him.

In the corridor a dark-haired woman rose from a chair, started to put her phone away. She peered at Gould's expression, and her face fell.

"I take it they're not going to be funding your research?" asked Harriet Zoffany.

Gould, still fuming, strode past her without speaking. They were in the car park of the research institute before Zoffany spoke again.

"They're just conformists, Ted," she said. "These days, for every real scientist doing cutting-edge research – pure research – there are a dozen guys with brand new doctorates climbing some corporate ladder or other."

Gould did not look at her, instead continued to stride towards his car.

"They'd have turned down Galileo, Newton, and Einstein as well," Zoffany added. "Not that you're in their league, we both know that, I just thought I'd point it out."

Gould stopped, looking down at Zoffany with a rueful smile.

"I'm sorry," he said. "No call for rudeness. Well, there is call for it when I'm rude to those purblind buggers. But not to you."

He stooped to kiss her.

"Let's have a pizza, a bottle of wine, and discuss our futures," she suggested. "And in the future, please walk more slowly when you're furious. I've only got little legs and these heels are already killing me."

"Sounds like a plan," Gould said. "The pizza, I mean. And I promise to massage your poor aching tootsies this very evening."

"Now that's the man I chose to shack up with!" she exclaimed, as Gould unlocked the car.

"Proves I don't get everything wrong," he said. "But if I have to be a kept man much longer, I'll go barmy."

"You're not a kept man, you're a man taking a career break," she insisted. "This is me being supportive, by the way. And I'm far too tired to fake it, so you know it's genuine."

Zoffany had returned to the National Health Service after the Romola Foundation had collapsed. The NHS was so desperate for trained staff that few questions were asked about her earlier career. Her salary had taken a nosedive as a result, and she was working far longer hours. Meanwhile, Gould tried and failed to win funding for some research into inter-dimensional physics.

"Okay," he said, as the buckled up. "Consider me supported. I just wish–"

Gould was interrupted by a blast of 'Highway to Hell' by AC/DC. As he took out his phone Zoffany rolled her eyes.

"What about something lighter?" she suggested quietly. "Bit of Monterverdi, maybe?"

"You kids today, with your Renaissance opera," he shot back, grinning.

Then he frowned at the screen of his cell, mouthed the word 'Denny', and took the call.

***

The Reverend Bullingdon took his duties seriously. He had few regular churchgoers, but if one called upon him for help, he went. Today that meant driving his antiquated Ford Fiesta along winding roads in grim winter weather. He was on his way to see an elderly farmer, Josiah Larkin. The man's wife had called him, saying that Larkin had experienced some kind of shock that morning.

"He was mucking out the cows," Liz Larkin had explained. "And he must have had a fall."

Bullingdon naturally asked if they had called the doctor.

"Oh, he won't have no doctors," Mrs. Larkin had said. "He just keeps asking for a priest. Do come, Reverend! It will do him good just to see you."

The Larkin farm was on the far edge of Bullingdon's territory. When the priest drove into the farmyard, Liz was standing outside, wringing her hands anxiously. Before Bullingdon had even got out of the car she was tugging at his coat sleeve.

"Oh, Reverend, I think he's dying!" she wailed. "I think the shock will carry him off, I really do!"

Again, the priest urged her to call an ambulance, but she brushed the suggestion aside and hurried him into the small living room. The farmer, who Bullingdon guessed was in his late seventies at the least, was lying on the couch under an old tartan blanket.

"The Reverend's here!" said the woman, unnecessarily. Her husband was already reaching out a quivering hand for Bullingdon.

Oh dear, the priest thought. *The poor soul does seem to be in a bad way. The Larkins really should seek medical help.*

"Hello, Josiah," he said, taking the man's hand and sitting by the couch. "I hear you've had a little mishap."

"Mishap?" croaked the farmer. "No, Reverend! It wasn't no accident!"

The priest looked up at Liz Larkin, who looked even more unhappy.

"He's wandering in his mind, I reckon," she said in a stage whisper.

"I am not wandering in my mind!" responded Larkin. "I am not barmy! My eyes might be weak, but I know what I saw."

Seeking to calm the man, Bullingdon leaned closer, took Larkin's hand between his own.

"And what did you see, Josiah?"

"It was a demon, Reverend!" gasped Larkin. "I saw it suckling at the teats of one of my cows!"

The priest smiled benignly.

Larkin is known to like a few beers, he thought. *Perhaps he's started seeing things.*

"I'm sure that it looked like one, Josiah," he said. "But one can take some things in scripture too literally. Now, why don't you let me call nine-nine-nine?"

"I'll die here, not in a hospital!" protested the old man, gripping the priest's wrist. "And it was a real thing I saw. And not a natural thing, not natural at all. Not after what it did."

Bullingdon had not taken any courses on counselling for a while, but he felt that contradicting Larkin might only over-excite the man. So instead, he put on what he thought of as his 'sensible, listening face'.

"And what exactly did it do, Josiah? You can tell me. You know I will not mock you or dismiss your words."

The farmer seemed about to speak, but then he looked over the priest's shoulder, and spoke to Liz.

"What are you thinking of, woman?" he snapped. "Get some tea for the vicar!"

After a few fretful protests, Liz Larkin allowed herself to be sent out. Then Larkin beckoned the priest closer, lowered his voice.

"When I saw that thing, Reverend, I picked up a pick-handle I keep in case of burglars," he explained. "And I took a swipe at the little bugger!"

"Did you hit it?" asked Bullingdon, deciding to humor the man further.

"Took it by surprise!" Larkin said, with a flash of pride. "Knocked the little sod into the corner of the barn. Had nowhere to run. So I decided to finish it off. That's when it–"

Larkin paused, looked past the priest again. Bullingdon glanced around, saw Mrs. Larkin looking on from the kitchen doorway. Behind her a kettle began to whistle shrilly, and she turned to quiet it. Larkin spoke again, his voice low and intense.

"That's when it changed," he declared. "And it wasn't a little monster any more. No, it was our Georgie, like he was just afore we put him in the ground, in the cold clay, sixty years ago. And him unbaptized. That upset the old lady no end, but the vicar at the time, he was a stern man."

For a moment Bullingdon was confused, then he recalled parish gossip. The Larkins had no children. There had been a stillbirth, back in the days when such things were not spoken of out loud, and hastily forgotten.

They buried unbaptized children to the north of the church, he recalled. *Along with the suicides.*

"Oh, my son," he said. "I am so sorry. So very sorry."

Tears were streaming down Larkin's age-ravaged face. The old man's grip relaxed, his hands fell away.

"I killed it, Reverend," Larkin whispered, in a horrified tone. "It was wounded and crying and all twisted, and I knew it must be a devil's imp that was deceiving me."

Larkin began sobbing uncontrollably.

"Never a day goes by when I don't think about our little boy. Never a day, Reverend. We never talks of it, like they all say you should. That's not our way. Old-fashioned, we are. But I could never forget that poor little body afore the midwife took him away. And so, when I saw that imp of Satan mocking him like that, I saw red, and I brought that pick-handle down and I smashed – I smashed–"

Bullingdon leaned forward to embrace the farmer, who was now moaning in despair. He felt the bony frame of a once-powerful man quivering with emotion. Then he heard the tinkle of a spoon on china, and gradually let the old man lie back. Liz Larkin brought in the tea tray as the priest dabbed tears from her husband's cheeks.

"I think it was a rather upsetting experience," Bullingdon said to the old woman. "And Josiah here obviously needs a little rest. Now, I know you don't hold with doctors..."

It took six cups of tea and nearly an hour of slow, persistent negotiation, but Bullingdon eventually persuaded the Larkins to let him call an ambulance. He decided to wait and offer moral support on the journey to the hospital. Then he asked discreetly for 'the little boys' room' as his bladder was overfull with strong tea.

The Larkins, predictably, had an outhouse rather than an inside toilet. After he had used it, Bullingdon decided to take a quick look inside the barn. He did not believe for a minute that Larkin had seen a 'devil's imp'. But something about the description troubled him. He could not quite figure out what, and felt that looking at the scene of the mysterious incident might help.

The barn was warm with the heat of the Larkins' small herd. Cows mooed pitifully, still waiting to be milked. He found a light switch. A couple of fluorescent strips flickered into hesitant life. In the uncertain light, he made his way along the stalls, breathing through his mouth as the air grew more pungent. He saw a pale brown pick-handle lying near one corner.

That, at least, is true enough. Perhaps the poor man did see something, a wild animal seeking refuge from the cold. And, in this light, imagination did the rest.

Going nearer, Bullingdon took out his half-moon reading glasses, adjusted them on the bridge of his nose. He could not risk crouching down, as his knees were arthritic. He stopped instead, holding onto the nearest stall. He heard a cow shifting uneasily.

The floor was damp with condensation and half-covered with straw. And there was something else. A rough shape was just visible in the flickering electric glow. It looked like a tiny skeleton, no more than a foot long, with a disproportionately large skull. The side of the skull was badly dented.

Even as he watched, the brown, twisted bones seemed to shrink. A faint yellowish vapor rose from them, like a waft of discolored steam. Bullingdon heard a slight fizzing noise.

"Good Lord!"

Bullingdon drew himself upright, unsure whether to trust his own senses. Then he thought of the extra gargoyle he had glimpsed the previous morning. He gazed down as the remains of Larkin's 'imp' dissolved into nothingness, leaving only a dark stain on the concrete floor of the barn.

The sound of the ambulance drawing up outside shook him from a reverie. The priest hurried out to greet the paramedics, grateful for the chance to simply do his duty, to focus on the mundane and knowable.

***

"It could be a fake," said Zoffany. Then, seeing Frankie's face she added, "Sorry, but we were all thinking it."

"Sure, it could be," Frankie said. "But take it from me, faking something like that takes a lot of effort. I've checked the lighting, shadow, motion blur. If it is a fake it's up to professional standard. I'm ninety per cent certain that it's something real, running up that church roof."

They were sitting in Gould and Zoffany's apartment, which was a little larger than the one the Americans shared. Denny's iPad was linked to a wide-screen TV so that the image of the 'gargoyle' was huge.

"It's much smaller than any we've seen before," Gould objected. "Smaller than the ones hatched in the Queen's brood-chamber."

"True," Zoffany said, thoughtfully. "But they evolved, we know that. The type Ones we encountered at the first portal couldn't live long in this world. Type Twos, the ones in Machen and Hobbs Lane, had much more endurance. This could be, who knows? A Type Three?"

"Well, if they're getting smaller as well, that's a definite improvement," Gould grunted. "If we can kill them with a cricket bat, I'm all for it."

"Do we know where the picture was taken?" Zoffany asked.

"Yeah," Denny replied. "I got in touch with the jogger who snapped the picture. He was kind of pleased when I messaged him, I suppose because we're all minor celebrities."

Zoffany chuckled.

"My niece told me that I peaked at around one thousandth of a Kardashian," she said. "Then she spoiled it by saying she didn't mean any of the really famous ones."

"Unfortunately, the jogger doesn't want to go on the record, because he's afraid of being ridiculed," Frankie said. "So I guess we're not the right kind of celebrities."

"But he did give us some information," Denny went on. "I was surprised when I found out where this St. Wystan's church is. A little village called Broughton-on-the-Wold. Which is less than two miles from the house where this guy died."

She reached down and put a picture of John Scoresby on the screen. Then, seeing Gould and Zoffany looking puzzled, she explained the dead man's connection to Lanier.

"That would be the ultimate irony," Gould said. "The media types who trashed our reputations getting killed by the very creatures they claim we made up. Serves them right for calling me a crank."

Denny nodded. Nobody objected to the implication that the Interloper must have killed Scoresby. It was too much of a coincidence. They quickly moved on to what they should do.

"First, find out if the little bugger has been seen anywhere else," Gould pointed out. "I suspect that's one for your pals on the internet."

They agreed to put out an appeal for information about the Interloper. Denny knew this would attract ridicule, and that they would be bombarded with hoax sightings. But it would also get them more hits.

And we've got no choice, she thought. *There's no official routine for telling the authorities that creatures from another dimension are among us, again. We just have to spread the word, hope enough rational people take it seriously.*

"I'm guessing," Frankie said, "that second on the list is going down to this place – Broughton-something? And asking people if they've seen a little creature running about."

There was a brief silence, during which Denny flicked back to the image of the blurred figure on the roof.

"We always suspected that some of them survived," she said. "But is it possible that one of the survivors was able to reproduce? That there's a Queen in our dimension?"

They all looked at Zoffany, who shrugged helplessly.

"I never got the chance to examine a Queen closely," she pointed out. "But if the ordinary, sterile Interlopers could be modified to live here, why not the reproductive female? The question is, what would she look like?"

Denny thought of the huge, bloated body of the Queen she had encountered, and shuddered. It was hard to believe that such a creature could have entered the human dimension and gone unnoticed.

"No," she said firmly. "If there's a Queen, she can't be big and slow. Simply getting through a portal would be impossible. They weren't that wide. That means we're talking about something human-sized."

"Something human-sized last year, when the portals finally closed," Gould corrected. "She could be much bigger now."

Frankie gave an impatient groan.

"Too much speculation," she complained. "We need more facts."

The discussion went on for a while, but eventually it was decided that Frankie and Denny would go to Broughton-on-the-Wold. Gould, aided by Zoffany when she was not working, would try to collate data.

"If there are just a few rogue Lopers out there, it's no big deal," Denny said as she packed up her gear. "But if there's an actual colony, we're in serious trouble."

"Are we calling them 'Lopers' now?" asked Zoffany. "Was there a memo?"

"Might as well, thousands of people online have been doing it for months," Frankie said. "And some of those people aren't crazy."

"The ones who claim to have met Lopers are all pretty deranged, though," Denny put in. "That's part of the problem – the more credible the witness, the duller the sighting. Which is why Broughton-on-the-Whatsit seems worth a shot."

"Wold," put in Gould, helpfully.

"Ted," Frankie said, hand on hip. "Can I ask you a deep and meaningful question, one adult to another?"

Gould smiled uncertainly, glanced at Zoffany.

"Okay, what it is?"

"What the hell is a Wold?" asked Frankie sweetly.

Nightmare Resurrection

Chapter 3: The Lady of Mountfalcon

Tim Garstang looked back at the wake of the boat. The spreading vee of foam led his eyes up towards the Welsh coast and the village they had just left. Night was falling. He was on the last stage of a journey that had brought him from LanCorp's headquarters in London halfway across the country. The last couple of days had passed in a whirl of phone calls, emails, packing, and frantic attempts to find someone to take care of his tropical fish. He had not even been allowed to tell anyone where he was going. A confidentiality agreement saw to that. Instead he had been required to simply say he was away on a foreign assignment.

Why am I here again?

He had been summoned from his mundane job as a sub-editor on a Sunday lifestyle magazine to become some kind of assistant to the Big Boss. He still had no real idea why. Tim had no idea how Sir Charles Lanier, with his tens of thousands of employees, had become aware of him. At first, he had suspected the request to meet Sir Charles was a hoax perpetrated by a colleague. But the expression on his editor's face – astonishment mixed with poisonous envy – had quickly confirmed that it was a legitimate offer.

"You should be looking to the future, not the past," said Murphy.

"Oh, right, yeah!" said Tim, looking round at Lanier's head of security.

Murphy had been pleasant enough when he met Tim at the dock in the village, but there was something about the man he did not like. The man had no small-talk about politics, sports, the weather. He also had a very low blink-rate.

Still, Tim told himself, *people in his line of work are seldom charmers. He's probably ex-military, or maybe an ex-copper.*

"The island is very pleasant," Murphy said. "The house has been extensively refurbished."

"Great!" Tim replied.

And that's another thing, he thought. *The guy talks like a robot.*

Shrugging off the minor annoyance, he did as Murphy bade and looked at Holyhaven. The island had, Tim knew, been a monastery of some sort back in the Dark Ages. But for hundreds of years it had been private property. Lanier had bought it back in the Eighties and had a kind of mini-kingdom of about twenty staff. And for some reason, Tim was about to join the select company.

"So," he said tentatively. "What's it like? Working for the man himself?"

"Sir Charles is a remarkable man," Murphy said.

Tim waited, but the security chief apparently had nothing more to say. The security guard at the controls of the boat had not looked back once, and there was nobody else on board. Tim suddenly had a vision of himself in the middle of the channel, heading towards a mysterious island. He felt nervous, afraid of what might happen next, while having no real idea why.

"You see, I've never met him," he babbled. "I mean, I've seen him on the telly, of course. Last year, when he told that parliamentary committee to get stuffed, you know? But never, you know, in the flesh."

Murphy looked at him, unblinking. Then the taciturn man gave an odd kind of shrug, which was almost a wriggle. Tim smiled at the thought that Murphy might be wearing ill-fitting underwear. Then he looked ahead of the boat, and saw that they were turning in a wide arc towards a small jetty. Above, looking suitably dramatic on a tall crag, were the lights of Lanier's house. Tim recalled that it was called Mountfalcon. The name, he decided, suited it.

Looming up there like a hawk surveying its territory, waiting to strike.

"Impressive," he said.

"Yes," said Murphy, turning his back on Tim and making his way forward.

The boat slowed as the driver idled the motor. Murphy balanced on the bow, and threw a line to another uniformed man on the jetty. As they came alongside a ladder, the security chief leaped onto the wooden platform. He moved clumsily and nearly fell backwards, arms cartwheeling. The guard on the jetty grabbed him in time, pulled him to safety.

And nobody makes a joke about it, thought Tim. *Is Murphy such a bastard to work for? Or do all Lanier's staff get some kind of humor bypass?*

He followed Murphy ashore, struggling with his suitcases. After a moment of staring blankly at him, one of the security men took a case without a word.

"Thanks!" Tim said, but the man looked through him, walked away.

The security team set off up a steep path that zig-zagged up the cliffs. In his best suit, and carrying his other suitcase, Tim was soon sweating. The others seemed to be in better condition, but again they looked wrong in some way. Finally, Tim worked it out. The guards were wearing the usual black pants and heavy-duty boots, but their jackets seemed a couple of sizes too big. The men, Tim realized, all seemed to be slightly hunch-backed. He wondered if they were carrying some kind of equipment strapped between their shoulder blades. But what that might be baffled him.

Parachute? Jet pack?

They finally reached the top of the cliff and security lights flashed on. After being blinded for a moment, Tim got his first good look at the house. It was a big, sprawling edifice, showing signs of extensive rebuilding and modernization. There was a large satellite dish in one corner of a large front garden. A circular area off to one side was marked with odd symbols.

"Is that a helipad?" he asked.

Murphy did not answer, instead pressing on with his team. Tim picked up his suitcase and followed, panting. As he approached the house, he glanced up at the windows of the second floor. A dark-haired woman was looking down at him. The reflection of the floodlights on the window glass meant he could not make out her features.

"Is that Lady Lanier?" he asked.

Again, his question was ignored.

***

"Here's something odd," said Zoffany.

"As opposed to all the normal stuff we've been looking at?" asked Gould, sourly. "Whenever I feel optimistic about the future of our species, I just have to go online for ten minutes. Then I become convinced we'll be extinct before the end of the century. If not sooner. Much sooner."

The couple were lying in bed, surrounded by fragments of pizza, enjoying Zoffany's first day off in six months. But they were also trying to trawl fringe news sites, blogs, and other sources for weird events that happened around the time of the Hobbs Lane Incident. Not surprisingly, there were a lot of reports.

"Shut up and listen, you old cynic," Zoffany said, leaning over to show him the screen of her laptop. "The day after the portals collapsed, when we were still trying to make sense of the mess in London – something weird happened. Guess where?"

"Machen?" Gould hazarded. "The only other accessible portal."

"Not exactly Machen," she said. "But not that far away."

Gould read the report, frowned.

"Hang on," he said, "according to this the dead truck driver was found in North Wales – that's about a hundred miles from Machen."

"But read on," she urged.

Gould did, raised an eyebrow, then kissed Zoffany on the end of her nose.

"Brilliant!" he said. "The guy made an unscheduled stop in the middle of nowhere, not far from Machen. Gizmo in the cab says he stopped long enough to pick up a hitchhiker, company said he wasn't the kind of guy to do that."

"Precisely," Zoffany said excitedly. "Respectable family man, well-paid job with a large haulage firm – why risk that for a hitcher? Unless–"

"It wasn't a regular hitchhiker, but someone he literally had to pick up," Gould put in. "Someone he felt an overwhelming attraction for."

"And then he's found dead," Zoffany pointed out. "And the police initially assume a thirty-two-year-old man was in his seventies, or older."

"Why?" Gould asked, puzzled.

"Because he was so badly desiccated, totally worn out," she said eagerly. "Doesn't that remind you of anything?"

Gould struggled to recall anything from his terrifying, chaotic encounters with Interlopers that fit this particular case. After a few moments he shook his head, smiled.

"Go on," he invited, "dazzle me with your brilliance."

Zoffany grinned and clicked on another browser tab. To his surprise, Gould found himself watching and listening to Denny. It was one of the online interviews they had all recorded to get their message across after the Romola Foundation had collapsed. Zoffany fast-forwarded a little, reached the point where Denny was describing her encounter with the Interloper Queen.

"I kind of – shared her mind, her memories, in a way," Denny was saying. "I got a strong sense of how they reproduce, for instance. It's not pretty. The males are just used up in mating, and then discarded."

Zoffany stopped the video.

"Jesus Christ," breathed Gould. "You're saying this hitcher could have been our hypothetical Queen? And that she can mate with human males? That's very hard to believe."

"Why?" Zoffany countered. "We know all their research was designed to merge our biology with theirs, to some extent. The first phase was to give the standard Loper foot soldier the ability to survive in our world indefinitely. The second phase, we've agreed, would be a reproductive female entering our world."

"But to use human - well, you know," Gould blustered. "It's too weird!"

"Sperm, is the word you're groping for," Zoffany said. "And it's not weird. If you want human genes, why not take them from a healthy human specimen? Clearly their mating process wreaks havoc on a man's metabolism. It's totally amoral, but then nature always is. Survival comes before ethics."

Gould stared at her.

"Have you always been like this, but I never noticed until now?"

Zoffany reached up, touched his cheek.

"We both did some very questionable things when we were working for Benson," she reminded him. "One thing it taught me was that no matter how sick and twisted something seems, if it confers some kind of power, or profit, or other advantage, somebody will do it."

Gould kissed her again, this time on the mouth, and slowly.

"God, I always fancy you something rotten when you talk like a supervillain."

Laughing, she shoved him away.

"The point is that, if this poor guy was – sucked dry, so to speak, over eleven months ago, what does that imply about our Queen?"

Gould leaned back into his pillows, gazed at the ceiling.

"God, I don't know. Maybe she could store the trucker's seed away for years and produce thousands of eggs?"

"Maybe," Zoffany echoed. "But remember, we're talking a human hybrid, here. A mix of the two species. So maybe she gets pregnant, squirts out some little Lopers, then has to get pregnant again. Just like a regular woman."

Gould sat up suddenly, lifted the sheets and looked down.

"What's the matter?" she asked.

"Just making sure nothing has shrivelled up," he said, without looking up. "Because if you're right, no-one with external gonads is safe."

Zoffany chuckled, then punched him on the shoulder. He rubbed the spot, looking hurt.

"I rather think," she said, "that our hypothetical Queen would be after fresher gonads than those."

Seeing his hurt expression, she put her laptop aside and lunged at him.

"You know me," she said as she overcame his half-hearted attempts to defend himself. "I prefer my fruit a little riper!"

***

Despite his best effort to seem blasé, Tim was impressed by the luxurious interior of Mountfalcon House. As he followed Murphy and his silent retinue inside, he whistled up at the vast entrance hall.

"Wow! My whole apartment in Holborn would fit in here about four times!"

"Your room is on the upper floor, towards the rear," said Murphy, ignoring the remark. "Phelps here will help with your luggage. You can freshen up after your journey. There is a light meal, and some coffee."

"Thanks, that's very – hospitable," Tim said, trying to keep a trace of sarcasm out of his voice. "And when will I meet the boss man – Sir Charles?"

Murphy's eyes flickered for a moment.

Was it such a hard question? Tim thought. *This setup is more secretive than MI5.*

"You will be kept informed," said Murphy. "Sir Charles is currently unwell. He is old, as you know."

"Yeah, right," Tim mumbled as he followed Phelps up the staircase. "Probably having his afternoon nap."

When the monosyllabic Phelps had left him in his room, Tim threw himself backwards onto the king-sized bed. Then he took out his phone to contact his girlfriend. The message 'No Signal' popped up immediately.

"Oh, come on," he said to the ornately-decorated ceiling.

Then he smiled ruefully at his own naivety.

As if Lanier would allow anyone to just call out as and when they felt like it. He probably has a gizmo that suppresses phone signals.

"Oh well, I'll probably get a Skype connection in due course," he muttered, getting up again.

Tim sauntered over to the window, paused to admire the view of the mainland directly across the strait. Then he turned to a side table, where a plate of sandwiches and a pot of coffee had been left. He suddenly felt intensely hungry and began to wolf down the sandwiches. However, after a few mouthfuls, he detected an odd aftertaste.

Would they serve dodgy food in a place like this? Seems unlikely.

He poured himself some coffee, which tasted good, then did some unpacking. After he had put away his meager supply of clothing he finished off the coffee and wondered what to do next.

"Freshen up," he said, recalling Murphy's words. "Okay."

There was no en suite bathroom, but he reasoned that this was a home, not a hotel. He stepped out into the corridor and looked both ways. Every door was closed, but the one at the far end looked promising. Tim set off, taking his shaving kit. He was prone to five o'clock shadow, and it was well after six.

It was a bathroom, modern and resplendent in marble and chrome. Tim was about to close the door behind him and have a shower when he thought he heard a voice. It was too faint to make out any words, but it seemed to come from one of the other rooms in the corridor. He paused, listening, and the voice came again.

"Hello?" he called tentatively.

This time he did make out a clear phrase.

"Help me."

Tim's first thought was that Lanier himself had had some kind of accident, or maybe a stroke. He had a sudden, heroic vision of himself saving his boss's life on the first day of his new job. He dismissed the improbable idea at once.

But someone seems to be in trouble.

Tim stepped back out into the corridor, stumbled, almost fell before catching himself by putting a hand against the wall. The corridor seemed to tilt wildly for a moment.

I should have finished those sandwiches, he thought. *Getting light-headed.*

He walked carefully to the nearest door, stopped to listen. The voice came again, the plea for help more insistent, urgent. He knocked on a white-painted panel.

"Hello? Are you okay?" he said, dismayed to find himself slurring his words.

"Please help me!"

The voice was shrill, evidently that of an elderly person. Tim tried the door, and it opened. The room was much like his own. A lamp by the large bed showed that it was occupied by a shrunken, pale figure. Tim could not tell whether it was male or female. He hurried across the plush carpet to the bed, stumbling again.

"What is it, what's wrong?"

"Tim! They got you, too."

The face on the pillow was wrinkled, the lips cracked, the red eyes half-closed by hardened yellowish mucous. Tim felt slightly sick at the aroma of stale sweat rising from the bed. Then he belatedly understood what the stranger had said.

"Do I know you?" he blurted out. "Have we met before?"

Another wave of dizziness nearly felled him. He sat down on the bed, propped himself up with one hand.

"Tim, it's me! Nigel!"

Tim struggled to think of anyone called Nigel that he knew. There was only his old squash partner Nigel Rodgers, who had worked in the marketing department. But Nigel had been about thirty, whereas this man could not be younger than seventy.

What happened to Nigel? He struggled to remember. *Something about a transfer overseas?*

"It is, me, Tim," croaked the man. "For God's sake, try and get away before they–"

"Please come with us, Mister Garstang."

Strong hands lifted Tim from the bed and carried him backwards, feet dragging, out into the corridor and back to his room. He tried to struggle, but felt very weak and confused. Murphy followed, and Tim tried to demand answers from the security chief.

"You – drugged – me!" Tim managed to say. "Why?"

Murphy regarded him with his neutral, unblinking expression. When they reached Tim's room, the security guards laid him on his bed. The men who had carried Tim left without a word. Murphy, however, paused at the door to look back for a moment.

"You are more privileged than you know," he said. "Your descendants will rule the world."

They're all bloody mad, Tim thought, struggling to sit up. *Maybe Lanier's been captured by some kind of brainwashing cult? It sometimes happens to old rich guys.*

His limbs would not obey him. When he tried to lever himself upright, his arms felt like jelly. He gave up, reasoning that whatever they had drugged him with must wear off. Since he had not lost consciousness, it was probably weakening.

Okay, assume I can move again soon, what do I do? Fight my way past Murphy's goon squad? Steal a powerboat? I'm not James Bond.

He tried recall how big the island was, and whether it might offer cover for him to hide by night.

But then what?

The room was in near-darkness, with only a faint light from the open window. When the door opened, Tim struggled to turn his head, managed to swivel his gaze a few degrees. There was a figure in the doorway, framed by diffuse light from the hallway. The silhouette was tall, apparently clad in some sort of long robe. It stepped into the room, closed the door. The darkness of the night returned.

Tim tried to speak, but produced only a dry, inarticulate sound.

The newcomer walked forward. He heard the rustling of the voluminous robe, gentle padding of what might have been bare feet on the carpet. The figure moved slowly. As it got closer, he became aware of a strange odor, not like perfume, more like the musk of an animal. Tim began to feel oddly excited, felt his fear begin to evaporate.

The silent figure stopped by the bed, and he sensed more movement. The reading light clicked on, and for the first time he saw the stranger clearly.

Oh my God.

For a moment Tim saw the face of the most beautiful woman in the world. She was looking down at him with a faint smile on her full, sensuous lips. Her eyes were a clear hazel, slightly tilted, her skin pale and freckled. Her hair was a cascade of auburn waves. The incredible woman reached up with slender hands to open her robe. Tim moaned again, this time in astonishment. He felt like a boy again, with the same frantic excitement when he had finally understood why adults got so worked up about sex.

Sharon Hutton. It's her – that face.

The woman looked so very like his first crush, the girl in his English class who had been a few months older than Tim, and far out of his league. He had not thought about Sharon for years, had barely spoken to her, had only pined for her. He had fantasized obsessively about what she might do to him, or let him do. And now, years later, a woman who looked like a curvier and taller version of Sharon had suddenly appeared in his bedroom.

Unbelievable.

The word drifted into his mind like a cloud obscuring the sun. The woman's smile vanished, and she leaned over him. Confusion reigned in his mind for a moment, and then his ecstasy began to fade. He felt the weight of the woman on the bed, the creak of protesting springs as she clumsily straddled him. His mind, still clouded by the drug they had given him, wondered whether it had made him hallucinate.

But why a teenage crush? Of all things.

"Try to relax," she said, running cool fingers along his cheek. "It will soon be over."

Tim was startled by her voice. It was deep, manly even, nothing like Sharon's. Now as he looked up, he could see that, even in the poor light, the woman's face was broader that he had thought. Her eyes seemed darker, smaller. What had been a rich head of auburn hair thinned and darkened, flowed away from her face like living tendrils. Strangest of all, her nose was lengthening, blending with her mouth to produce a kind of muzzle. He still could not move, let alone struggle.

Oh my God!

Strong hands gripped him, tore at his clothes. He heard cloth ripping, then felt cool, moist flesh against his. The huge muzzle-face descended, and a slender tongue flicked out, caressed his lips, nose, eye sockets. The small, black eyes closed in what might have been pleasure.

Tim tried to scream. Again, all he produced was a weak moan.

Nightmare Resurrection

Chapter 4: Shells

"This is a Wold?" said Frankie, disappointed. "It looks just like any other bit of England."

"That's what Gould told you," Denny reminded her. "The word used to mean a forest. Then they cut their forests down so they could have a jolly splendid Industrial Revolution. So now it means a moor where trees used to be. Which is kind of sad."

"Maybe it looks nicer in summer," muttered Frankie. "Still, the light's not bad for filming."

Their rental car crested the brow of a low hill and they saw the village of Broughton nestling in a shallow depression ahead of them. St Wystan's church was conspicuous thanks to its tower. Over to the right, a large farmhouse was visible behind a wall. This, they decided, must be the Scoresby home.

Denny pulled over by the side of the road and they got out, Frankie bringing a light video camera. They shot some footage of the farm, but it seemed that the place was closed up. Frankie, looking through her viewfinder, noted that there was no police tape visible.

"Looks like they're not treating it as a suspicious death," Denny commented. "The guy is supposed to have had a heart condition."

A cutting wind blew off the moor, bringing with it a spattering of freezing rain. They got back into the car and were about to head down to the village when a small, blue Peugeot appeared behind them. The car slowed, the driver evidently unsure of what to do.

"My spider sense is tingling," Denny said. "This could be the help, right?"

Frankie nodded.

"Best not spook them," she told Denny. "You get out and turn on the charm, I'll film you from here. Give it that dramatic, hidden-camera feel."

The woman in the Peugeot parked just behind their rented Nissan and got out. Denny saw a short, olive-skinned woman of about thirty, dressed in neat, dark clothes.

Okay, Denny thought, *honesty is the best policy.*

"Hi!" she said brightly. "I'm Denny Purcell, and–"

The woman's dark eyes grew huge with surprise and she cut in.

"You are the monster lady! From TV, yes? I wanted to call you, but my man, he told me no, people will think you crazy! But now you are here, I tell you all. I tell you if you promise not to use my name. I don't want to lose this job."

"We won't use any video or sound without your permission," Denny assured her. "We promise to run everything past you. Give me your cell number now, in fact."

Five minutes later, Dolores, who described herself as a 'very huge fan' of Denny, let them into the Scoresby house and was making coffee. All the while the woman talked, words tumbling out as she gave a disjointed account of the death of her employer. Denny used a voice recorder, trying to keep it within range as the maid bustled about. Dolores, it became clear, had not been taken very seriously by the police. She was keen on setting the record straight.

"We can alter your voice," Denny assured her. "Or just transcribe your words, edit out anything that might identify you."

"Okay, that is fine! Mrs. Scorez-bee, she ask me to take care of house," Dolores explained. "So I come in every few days to check, see no burglary, yes? But oh, all those – what is word?"

Dolores mimed scratching her face with clawed fingers.

"Wounds?" Denny suggested, trying to keep up.

"Wounds!" Dolores agreed. "The police, they say he cut himself, because things were broken," Dolores said, and made a dismissive noise. "These detectives, they say nobody could have come into room because all was locked up before I got there."

The little woman leaned forward over the table, lowered her voice. Without having to check, Denny knew that Frankie was now filming in extreme close up.

"But there was somebody there," Dolores breathed. "Or something. Because I saw footprints in his blood!"

"Footprints?" Denny asked. "Like shoes, you mean?"

Dolores shook her head impatiently.

"You know what I mean!" she declared. "Little bare feet, small toes, like a child. They went out of the bedroom. I saw one police point to them, and a detective, he just do this–"

Dolores shrugged emphatically.

"Detective say, maybe rat go into room, and Mister Scorezbee, he panic and his heart stop, and rat maybe chew him a little after he is dead!"

Frankie could not suppress a cynical laugh at that.

"So," Denny said, "the police weren't interested in the footprints?"

"No, but when they took me out I notice this thing," Dolores said, in her low, confidential voice. "I see the footprints lead out into hall, then up the stairs."

They all looked up at the ceiling.

"Okay," Denny said, pushing back her chair. "It went upstairs. Let's investigate."

Dolores gestured them to wait and, going to a drawer, took out a huge carving knife.

"I guess we're not going to take any chances," Denny remarked. "Okay, Frankie, you should probably shoot this bit. Just in case there's … anything up there."

The attic trapdoor was open, the ladder was down.

"Did the police come up here?" Denny asked.

Dolores shrugged. "I don't think so."

Denny looked into the camera.

"There have been massive cuts to British police budgets in recent years," she said soberly. "It means that, even if somebody has actually died in unusual circumstances, they have a limited amount of time and are short of personnel. So, they tend to go for the simplest answer, close the case, and move on. John Scoresby was an old guy with a heart condition, so that makes it nice and simple. But maybe the real answer is something far stranger. We're about to find out. In the attic."

Right, she thought, *that's a hat-tip to proper journalism. We'll almost certainly not use it, given the Dolores situation, but at least we'll have footage.*

"Okay, who wants to go up first?"

Dolores shook her head, offered Denny the knife.

"I'll go," said Frankie, with a rueful smile.

She climbed the ladder until she had nearly reached the top, then turned on the camera's small spotlight. Denny felt her mouth grow dry as her friend climbed the last few rungs and paused to sweep the light around attic.

"See anything, Frankie?" she remembered to call up.

"Lot of junk," came the reply. "Hang on."

Frankie vanished into the attic, and Denny followed her, returning the knife to the nervous Dolores. The attic really was full of junk. At first, it seemed to Denny that they were wasting their time. Then Frankie shone her light on a large cardboard box lying on its side.

"Hey!" she said. "This looks familiar."

Denny, crouching to avoid hitting her head on the rafters, scurried over to look more closely. She froze, then reached out to pick up a small, asymmetrical object. It was a roughly triangular fragment, clearly from a larger piece. It felt leathery, slightly moist. She dropped it, took the box and turned it so Frankie could illuminate the interior.

The round, dark-colored object had burst open at the top. The interior was lined with silvery strands that looked like saliva. Denny put on her gloves and carefully extricated the shell. Triangular flaps of tissue around the hole showed that it had burst open from the inside.

"Well, that's kind of conclusive," she commented.

"Understatement of the year," Frankie responded. "Now we know."

"What is it?" shouted Dolores from below.

"Shall we tell her?" Frankie asked.

"Sure," said Denny. "She'll be thrilled."

***

"Jackpot!" exclaimed Zoffany, her voice tinny over the speaker of Denny's phone. "And that proves something vital."

"That there's a Queen out there?" asked Denny, moving her cell so that Zoffany got an all-round view.

They had taken the eggshell down to the kitchen and put it on the table. Dolores had refused to go near it and was in the living room, still clutching her knife. Zoffany and Gould were now trying to examine the shell remotely while Frankie circled, filming Denny filming the egg.

This is getting kind of meta, Denny thought. *But that's showbiz these days.*

"Yes, Denny, there almost certainly is a Queen," Zoffany replied, "unless the egg was brought over from the Phantom Dimension nearly a year ago. But consider something more basic – that discarded shell still exists. It hasn't disintegrated the way Interlopers normally do when they perish."

Denny paused, startled, and stared at the knobbly, reddish-brown container.

"I never thought of that," she admitted. "So this is the first Loper tissue that behaves like ... well, like life as we know it."

"Precisely!" Zoffany declared. "It might rot away, but it's not simply going to rapidly sublimate into basic organic compounds."

"You mean go all fizzy and turn into bubbly gunk?" Denny asked.

"That's what I said!" protested Zoffany. "Stop dumbing down the science, we've got a world to convince."

"Is there anything else?" Gould put in, sounding impatient. "Any sender's address on the box, for instance?"

Why didn't I think of that? Denny wondered. *Maybe because I'm getting too excited.*

She turned to the cardboard box lying next to the egg, examined it. She quickly ascertained that there was nothing other than Scoresby's address, and the logo of a private courier firm.

"The company might tell us," she suggested, hesitantly.

"I doubt it," Gould said. "Client confidentiality."

"Denny," cut in Zoffany, "please pack the shell back into the original packaging and bring them straight back? I can steal some lab time at the hospital for some basic tests ..."

There was a short pause, then Zoffany resumed.

"Okay, guys? Better edit that last bit out, because I want to keep my job – but I definitely can do some tissue analysis."

"Right, will do guys. Talk to you later," Denny said, smiling. "Dolores, we're putting it back in the box."

From the doorway, the help looked on dubiously as Denny lifted the eggshell gingerly and sealed it up with some tape.

"Did Mister Scoresby say where this had come from?" she asked Dolores as she finished packing sealing the package.

The woman shook her head emphatically.

"No, he just said he did not like it. That it was bad taste."

They packed the shell in the back of the SUV and set off for the village. Denny felt that they had achieved more than they could have expected, and knew that the scientists would be impatient.

"First solid evidence of Lopers," she said. "First thing nobody can claim is CGI or a chemical leakage or terrorists releasing hallucinogenic gas."

"Listen to yourself," Frankie said cynically. "People can convince themselves of anything. There are thousands of people who seriously believe the earth is flat. We're always going to be battling wild-eyed crazies on the one hand and narrow-minded skeptics on the other. And why aren't we heading back to London?"

"Don't you want to take a look at Saint Wystan's?" Denny asked. "Remember the phantom gargoyle?"

"Oh, right," said Frankie. "Well, at least I'll get some shots of a quaint old village church. Because they're so hard to find in England."

They pulled up by a pub opposite the church and got out. An elderly man in a clerical collar was crossing the churchyard, and vanished around the corner of the building.

"Okay," Denny said. "Let's take this slowly. I doubt this guy is a big fan of ours."

Frankie was at the gate, filming the gargoyles above the porch.

"You never know," she remarked. "He might be crazier than we are."

When they caught up, the clergyman was in a patch of overgrown grass. As Denny approached, she felt slightly uneasy about interrupting him. He seemed to be talking to himself.

No, she thought. *He's praying.*

The old man had a bunch of wild flowers in one hand. Denny stopped, watching.

"You get the feeling," whispered Frankie, "that this is a private moment?"

She lowered her camera as Denny nodded, and they turned and went back to the church to wait on the porch. When the priest appeared, he looked preoccupied, his pinkish features knotted in a frown. He caught sight of the two women, however, and his manner changed at once.

"Hello!" he said with a friendly smile, eyeing Frankie's camera. "Are you here to take some pictures of our church? You're very welcome, of course, but we do encourage a small donation to the parish fund. Roof repairs, you know! These old buildings are so hard to maintain."

Denny smiled back and introduced them.

"Actually, we're keen to talk to you about one of the features of the porch," she said, gesturing up. "Those gargoyles? This is going to sound strange, but somebody—"

She stopped, startled to see the old man's expression change again. Now he looked shocked and troubled.

"Oh dear, oh dear me," he said. "Oh that's another matter entirely. You had better come inside."

They followed him into the church.

"I guess we're gonna get some more tea," whispered Frankie.

"And a story," Denny replied quietly. "I get the feeling this will be a good one."

***

When they returned from the country, they met with the scientists again and reviewed the new material over pizza and beer. After enthusing over the eggshell, Zoffany had been even more excited by news about the 'imp' killed by the farmer.

"Its spur-of-the-moment decision to mimic a dead child was a mistake," she pointed out. "Perhaps because it was not fully developed, incapable of foreseeing how humans might react. At least, that's a working hypothesis, as we can only guess how a psychic species might develop, mentally."

"Makes sense," Denny concurred. "But it also raises the question, why send an infant to do an adult's job?"

"Perhaps because to the Lopers, with their hive mentality, an infant is small, easily overlooked, and expendable," Frankie suggested. "If it could make its way home, fine; if not, then no great loss."

The four fell silent at the thought.

Frankie spent more time in their world than I did, Denny thought. *She gets them at an instinctive level better than I ever will.*

Gould had not been pleased by the description of the small Loper's death, because of what happened immediately afterward.

"If they still decay and evaporate when you kill them," he pointed out, "that makes evidence just as hard to gather as before."

Zoffany looked thoughtful.

"Maybe that's part of their strategy."

"You're thinking what I'm thinking," Frankie said through a mouthful of pizza. "Dead Lopers disintegrating is a feature, not a bug."

Zoffany gestured at a yellow-and-white biohazard container, into which she had put the eggshell.

"That shell proves they can generate new tissue that can survive in our world," she said. "We don't know how the original Queen created this new breed of Loper. But it makes sense for her to try and stop us from getting genetic samples and so on. She did understand our methods quite well, didn't she?"

Denny remembered her intense psychic contact with the Queen in the Phantom Dimension. She shuddered.

"She saw us as bizarre, insanely violent creatures," she said. "We were the monsters to her because we routinely used our science to evil ends. Human nature was so vile that she could never trust us, never risk a compromise. So, yeah, keeping us as ignorant as possible – that makes sense."

"There is another question," Gould said, looking over at Zoffany. "How big is the new Queen, judging by the size of that egg?"

"And how many more could she produce?" put in Frankie.

Zoffany shrugged.

"I've no idea." Seeing their disappointment, she went on, "I mean, obviously human sized, and not what you'd call petite.

But we don't know what interesting new features this hybrid being has."

"When I was a girl," Frankie said, "I lived on my uncle's chicken farm. Now a chicken egg is pretty big in relation to its body, but it can still lay it. Would that be the kind of ratio we're talking about?"

"That's not unreasonable," Zoffany agreed. "So, that egg is twenty-nine centimeters by fourteen. Actually, it's about the same volume as a newborn human infant, but the egg's a lot wider than the head of a baby."

"So, we're talking about some freaky arrangement downstairs?" Denny asked. "I mean, the original Queen was more like an insect in the way she just squirted those eggs out."

Gould quickly put his hands over his ears as they went into more detail, prompting general laughter and a flurry of cushion throwing. Eventually they concluded that any Queen could resemble a human female.

"But only when fully clothed," Zoffany added.

"Finished talking alien gynecology?" Gould asked. "Good, right. Do you think this little bugger was drinking milk from a cow? We know practically nothing about what they eat."

"If we're talking human hybrids, why not milk?" Zoffany mused. "In fact, any simple food with fat, protein, some trace elements, would probably be enough for them. You're right, we don't know what they ate in their world, but they must be adapted to feed in ours."

Frankie seemed about to speak, but fell silent, looking pensive.

"You remember something about your time – over there?" Denny asked.

Frankie shrugged.

"I have some vague memory that the Lopers ate some kind of worm. You know, those pale white things we saw in that desert? I think they may have farmed them."

"Yeuch," said Gould. "So they were carnivores?"

Zoffany raised a finger, and Denny imagined her in a classroom correcting over-imaginative students.

"Remember, we're talking about a new kind of Interloper," she said. "Being adapted for our world would logically make them rather more human, and that means they would be omnivores. But there's so much we simply don't know."

"Let's adjourn," Denny suggested, stretching out her arms. "We've got a lot to think about, but the main thing is to get the story out there and see who it stirs up."

"Who, or what," Gould corrected glumly. "Meanwhile, if a large package arrives for me by private courier, I'll take it into the back alley and set fire to it."

***

It took them a couple of days to put the new video together. Dolores had to be protected, and the Reverend Bullingdon had not wanted to say anything on record. This meant suggesting and implying more than they could tell outright. But Denny had been so relieved to learn that the Interloper had been killed that she had not pressed the old priest on that point.

Eventually, the video was edited, with titles and credits added. Frankie uploaded it to their channel. The first abusive or downright crazy responses appeared in seconds, before anyone could have had time to actually watch the film. Then, after a few hours, more articulate reactions started to appear. Most were critical, dismissive, with a hint of impatience.

"Yes, we are still going on about this stuff," Denny muttered as she scrolled down the page. "We will continue to go on about this stuff."

Reading comments on anyone's video tended to annoy her. Reading the comments on her own feed often made her feel old and defeated. But there were a few that seemed positive. One, indeed, made her pause and wonder who was hiding behind the online handle.

'There must be more of those things out there. Who will be next?'

"Good point," she muttered, taking a mouthful of coffee.
"Yeah," said Frankie, over her shoulder. "But nobody can answer the other obvious question. Why Scoresby? Why not, I

don't know, a politician or a top general? Or one of the royal family, that would be wild!"

Denny nodded, thought back to earlier Interloper attacks on people in positions of power.

"They did try to mess with politics, to sabotage the Romola Foundation," she pointed out. "It kind of worked. But maybe they've figured out that the media is where most of the power lies nowadays."

"Took them long enough," Frankie smiled, sitting down beside Denny. "But I guess the whole concept of media is alien to a psychic species."

Denny thought about it, then smiled wanly.

"Guess so – no fake news in their world."

They began to discuss how difficult Interlopers might find commonplace human ideas and behaviors when Denny's laptop chimed loudly. A flashing logo appeared.

"Somebody wants to Skype," she said. "Let's see who it is."

The name made her pause.

"LanCorp45," she read. "Our friends in the tabloid press, one of their corporate accounts."

"If they want another goddam interview they can piss off," Frankie growled. "Last time they made us look like lying assholes."

"You never know," Denny said. "Scoresby's death might have made them think again."

The face that appeared was furrowed with age, the lips thin and cracked, a few wisps of white hair falling over the leathery forehead. Denny recognized the man instantly. Any journalist on the planet would have.

"Is this for real?" she asked, half seriously. "How do I know you're not an actor like that Borat guy?"

"This is not a hoax," said the old man, slowly. "I am Sir Charles Lanier. And I'd like to apologize to you, Miss Purcell, Miss Dupont, for less than flattering coverage of your work. I'm sorry."

"Is this just a general apology for being a very rich white guy who publishes tons of bigoted crap?" Frankie shot back, angrily. "Or are you going to be more specific?"

Lanier smiled, and Denny thought of a corpse coming to life.

"Let us cut to the chase, as you say Stateside. I have something to show you."

"Quick, start recording!" hissed Frankie. "It might be his wiener."

Denny had already begun to record the conversation. Loudly, she said, "That would be unprofessional, you know that."

Lanier nodded to someone off screen. A pair of hands placed an object on the desk in front of the tycoon. It was an eggshell, identical to the one they had found in Scoresby's attic. It, too, had been broken open from the inside.

Nightmare Resurrection

Chapter 5: Serious Proposals

"Bloody hell," whispered Frankie, in a fair imitation of Gould's accent.

"As you may be aware," said Lanier, "I value my privacy and have a very efficient security team. They periodically sweep the shores of my little island. They found this object, intact of course, nestled among some rocks, just above the tide line. It may have drifted ashore, or been deposited by a boat. They brought it to me, and I immediately thought of those pictures you shot. Of the brood chamber. The hideous mother-creature laying all those eggs."

"Those would be the pictures your newspapers called obvious fakes?" Frankie said, suddenly loud with indignation. "You must feel like a prize asshole now, Charlie."

Denny expected Lanier to react angrily to the insult, but instead he smiled sadly.

"Please, find it in your heart to indulge an old man, Miss Dupont," he said, mildly. "I grew up in a world where satellites were new and exciting. I remember the Moon landing. I have a clear impression of my father's expression when he told my mother that Kennedy had been shot. It does take me a while to get to grips with new ideas. Especially when they are, as we used to say, really far out."

"Okay, so you've seen the light, and that's great. But what happened to the Loper?" Denny demanded. "It's not still alive?"

Lanier shook his head.

"My people are not idiots, Miss Purcell," he said. "They kept it under observation. In a locked room, via closed-circuit TV. When it hatched, they did not enter the room, on my express orders. Instead, they pumped some exhaust fumes from our generator inside and killed it. And I think you know what happened then."

"No body to show the cops, or whoever," Frankie said. "That sucks."

"Quite," said the old man. "But the proof was more than sufficient for me. It changed my position on the entire issue."

"Good," said Frankie. "But what's that got to do with us?"

"I want to make amends, Miss Dupont," replied Lanier. "I want to meet you, hear what you have to say – unfiltered, face to face. And then I want us to form an alliance. What do you say?"

"What if we don't trust you?" Denny retorted. "You're not exactly renowned for your ethical behavior."

"I stand by my friends," Lanier said, his voice still gentle, only a slight hint of reproof. "Indeed, I discreetly told quite a lot of my friends – in business, politics, and so forth – to take precautions. At least three other eggs have been detected, and destroyed."

Denny began to ask a question, but Lanier lifted a liver-spotted hand.

"No, I can't give you details, not yet. Remember, trust is a two-way street. I need to be sure you won't simply rush off, in your impulsive fashion, and publish names. It will take time to turn this tanker around, to get the public to accept the threat from the Interlopers. You and I have seen the proof, but millions will be asked to take it on trust. We must plan carefully."

Denny and Frankie exchanged a glance, then Denny said, "Okay, we'll talk it over."

"Of course," said Lanier. "Take a day or so. And message me when you decide. I've already made travel arrangements for both of you. They are open-ended. Be my guests. I can promise you an interesting time."

The connection ended, leaving the two women silently pondering the offer.

"I don't trust him," said Frankie. "Sure, it looks like he's being straight with us, but he has a bad rep. We all know the kind of bigoted crap his newspapers promoted. In the Sixties it was outright racism, then when AIDS emerged he switched to gay-bashing, then–"

"What would we do if we turned him down?" Denny cut in. "We'd be back to square one, with no solid evidence and practically no resources."

Their discussion threatened to become heated, but eventually Frankie had to concede to Denny's main point. No matter how unpleasant they might find Lanier's approach to journalism, no matter what he had called them in the past, he was a powerful ally. The offer was one they could not afford to pass up.

Frankie then raised a second, crucial point.

"He didn't mention Ted and Harriet," she pointed out. "Does that mean the science guys aren't welcome?"

"Well," Denny mused, "Lanier is an old newspaper man, not a scientific researcher. It's only natural for him to focus on us. But we'll raise that with him when we actually meet. We won't let him break us up, not after all we've been through. And we'll keep them informed, obviously."

Later that day, after deciding on the wording with Frankie, Denny recorded a brief message for Lanier. As she clicked 'Send', she wondered if she was doing the right thing.

"Time will tell," she said to herself. "It always does."

***

There was a loud, electronic ping from the computer in the corner of the study. Sir Charles Lanier, who had been dozing in a shaft of November sunlight, jerked upright. A quivering hand moved to the controls of his electric wheelchair, turned it, and sent it out of the sun to the desk.

"I'll get it, darling," said Cassandra.

She strode quickly across the room and put her pale hand on the mouse. The screen came to life, a message flashed. Another click, and the face of Denny Purcell appeared. The journalist spoke quickly, face serious, her manner thoroughly professional.

"Sir Charles," she said, "we both have doubts about whether we could work for you, but we are prepared to hear you out – that's only reasonable. See you soon."

The message ended, and Cassandra closed the window. Then she bent down and ruffled her husband's thin hair.

"Such a clever boy!" she said. "You sounded so professional."

"Did I?" asked Lanier, smiling vaguely up at her. "I get confused, sometimes. And then things seem very clear. Why do you think that is, darling? Could it be the new treatment?"

Cassandra wagged a reproving finger in front of his face, gave a little pout of disapproval.

She is so beautiful, he thought. *I am the luckiest man in the world. If only I could remember things clearly all the time, but I keep making mistakes, getting confused–*

"The treatment is doing you a lot of good," she insisted gently. "Remember how it was when I first came here? How much pain you were in all the time?"

He nodded, gave a slight shudder. His arthritis had crippled his knees and elbows, resisting all conventional treatment. Then Cassandra had arrived, and with her came a wave of comfort and happiness. Yet, Lanier had noticed, his mind had become more clouded even as his happiness grew.

Why is that? Lanier's mind struggled to form a thought. *I was once so sharp, so quick to notice things, judge character, make decisions.*

"Let's just make sure it's all right," she said. "Now, lean forward for nurse! I'll take a look."

Lanier did as she asked and let his wife slip his dressing gown off his shoulders. He felt the cool fingers on his back, then a slight pressure, a tingle like a mild electric shock up his spine. The Helper nestled between his shoulder blades wriggled, and its simple ecstasy spread into Lanier's body.

"All right, Charles," she said, standing upright and covering his thin torso again. "The Helper seems to be doing very well. The blood vessels are still intact. The pain will be kept at bay. It is helping you."

Lanier smiled up at her, reached for her hand.

"I don't deserve you, darling."

"No, you don't," she said, holding his knobby fingers for a moment. "But here I am, anyway."

Lanier tried to grasp her thigh, but she stepped back, just out of reach, tutted at him.

"No time for any smoochies today, Charles," she said. "I must prepare for our guests."

Her face, normally so serene, suddenly contorted into a frown.

"Another one?" he asked, concerned. "You must not overdo it, my dear."

"I'll be fine," she said, patting him on the head before going quickly to the door. "Try to rest, darling."

Her voice was strained now. Concerned, Lanier rolled after her, his chair motor buzzing. But by the time he reached the doorway, she was already gone, heading down the hallway to her private bathroom.

Lanier returned to his place in the sun, looking out over the strait that separated Holyhaven from Wales. He shifted irritably in his chair, wishing that the treatment was less physically awkward. However, Cassandra always ensured that he had a couple of nice, fluffy pillows at each side of the Helper. And it was a small price to pay to avoid much worse discomfort.

Soon he was dozing again, past and present merging into a swirl of nebulous images, half memory, half fantasy. He recalled the first moment he had seen Cassandra as she walked, with total confidence, up the path from the cliff. He smiled as he recalled Murphy and Phelps scampering eagerly beside her. Then the meeting, and the weird sensation that she knew him already, and that he somehow knew her.

Never a superstitious man, Lanier still believed in destiny. He had been certain the moment he saw her that Cassandra Bradley was the woman who could bring joy to his later years. It was as if an unspoken understanding had sprung up between them in the blink of an eye.

Love at first sight, he had thought at the time. *I was so sure of myself, so confident she would say yes. And she did.*

Strangest of all, though, was the way she had changed over the months after their low-key, discreet nuptials. He had only half-noticed it at first, put it down to his poor eyesight. But eventually he had had to admit it to himself, and mention it to her. Cassandra's face had filled out, her body grown more matronly. Above all, her features now resembled the faded, black and white picture he kept on his desk.

"Darling," he had said. "It's really strange, but you seem to look more like my dear mother every day."

Cassandra had smiled, wagged a finger at him in mock rebuke.

"You must be imagining it, darling," she said. "But they do say a boy's best friend is his mother, don't they? Now, try and finish your oatmeal. It will keep you regular."

***

"Lanier? Jesus Christ!" said Gould loudly, then lowered her voice as heads turned in the crowded pub. "That old bastard? He's done more to damage this country than, well, any politician I can think of."

"I agree," said Denny, "but what can we do? He's offering us a platform, resources – hell, LanCorp has an amazing legal team. You know what libel laws are like in this country. Imagine if we could do less skulking around and more in-your-face reporting."

"But why now?" Gould asked. "What's changed?"

Denny had anticipated skepticism from the scientists, but their outright loathing for Lanier came as a surprise. It took her a minute to figure out that the man seemed to represent everything they detested about their own country. She suggested this, choosing her words carefully, keeping her tone mild.

"Too bloody right!" Gould grunted. "It's like one of those old medieval pictures of the man with an angel on one shoulder and a devil on the other. The difference is that the devil, in Britain's case, is a dirty old man called Charles Lanier."

Frankie, who had been even quieter than usual, looked interested by Gould's remark.

"Why dirty, as opposed to just mean old man?" she asked. "I mean, is there scuttlebutt on his private life?"

"Don't you remember?" Zoffany asked. "Back in the summer he married a woman young enough to be his granddaughter. She was his nurse. Even his own newspapers couldn't spin that one as a whirlwind romance, so they just killed the story. But it was all online, and of course in the foreign press."

"Oh, yuck," Frankie concurred. "So, he has a calculating, gold-digger wife? That's not unusual for a rich guy."

"Okay," said Denny, trying to keep the conversation on track, "we know he's not Gandhi. But if we join forces with him, will you guys be on board?"

The scientists exchanged a glance.

"My first instinct is to say no," Gould said. "But if everything is open and above board, maybe."

Zoffany nodded, shifted closer to Gould.

If those guys had met twenty years ago, Denny thought, *by now we'd have a whole family of super-boffins to tackle the Lopers.*

"Okay," Denny said, "we'll meet the dirty old man who happens to be immensely rich and powerful, see what he has to say."

They talked for another couple of hours, enjoying a convivial evening. Denny and Frankie left first, needing to get an early start the following morning. Gould and Zoffany, by now tactile and giggly, prompted some eye-rolling from Frankie as they walked out into the chill London air.

"Those two need to get a room," she said.

Denny was about to reply when Frankie stopped, turned around, and mouthed a few words at her.

"We're being watched."

Denny frowned, glanced around at the street. It was just after ten at night, and a thin rain was falling. A group of young women were crossing the road, talking loudly, clearly on a girls' night out. A young couple had just passed them, both silently absorbed in their phones.

"Car," said Frankie, taking Denny's arm and leading her up the road. "Dark saloon. Two people in it. Don't look round, what are you, twelve?"

"One beer too many," Denny admitted ruefully. "But are you sure they were watching us?"

"Couldn't see their faces," Frankie admitted. "But I'm almost sure they were parked there when we arrived. Who feeds a meter in this town for that long? Not unless they've got a damn good reason to stay put."

"Maybe Lanier?" Denny hazarded. "Or the cops?"

Franke shrugged.

"Could be MI5. Or maybe Lopers can drive, now. Or maybe I'm just paranoid."

Denny took out her phone and messaged Gould, then Zoffany. Even if Frankie were wrong, it could do no harm for everyone to be on alert.

***

"Probably nothing," said Gould, checking his phone. "You got it, too?"

Zoffany nodded, then put her cell away.

"Maybe Lanier's spying on them," she suggested. "He might be planning some kind of sting to make them look like frauds, or whatever."

Gould nodded sagely, finished his pint. The familiar bell rang, with the traditional cry of 'Last orders please'.

"I wouldn't trust that old bugger further than I could throw him," he said. "Want another?"

"No, back to work tomorrow," she pointed out. "Best not to turn up smelling of booze. It doesn't inspire confidence in the patients, let alone one's colleagues. And, remember, I want to analyze that shell in a sneaky way."

Zoffany got up, clumsily trying to put on her coat. Gould tried to help, and they both got tangled, and eventually fell back onto the bench, laughing.

"God, we are too old for this!" Gould said ruefully.

"Speak for yourself," Zoffany retorted. "When I was young I spent all my time studying. Right, let's try that again."

A minute later, they were outside. The cold air sobered them a little. Gould looked up and down the street curiously. A car was just pulling up outside the pub. It was, he realized, a dark saloon. The window rolled down and a hand reached out, holding up an ID of some kind.

"Doctors Gould and Zoffany?" said a businesslike voice. "Could we have a quick word?"

"Depends on who you are," Gould replied, stepping closer to the car. "I can't read that in this light, mate. Could be anything. Why not just piss off?"

"I've got a message from Lucy," said the stranger. "She misses you."

Gould felt a flash of rage. Zoffany clutched at his arm.

"I'm sorry," said the man in the car, holding out a card. "But it's a sincere offer. Think about it."

After a moment, Zoffany took the card while Gould continued to stare in drink-fuddled anger. The car eased itself into the evening traffic and was soon lost to sight. Zoffany led Gould back to the pub doorway, under a brighter light.

"It's a firm that supplies office equipment," she said, handing it to him. "How weird is that? Do we need any Post-It notes?"

"Maybe not so weird," he said, grimly. "If it's some kind of intelligence outfit, they must have a number of front organizations. Come on, we'll catch our death standing here. We can still catch the last train."

They walked in silence for a while.

"Maybe," Zoffany said tentatively, "they could let you see Lucy. You never know."

Gould shook his head.

"They know which buttons to push," he said. "That suggests they're manipulative bastards. I had enough of that at the foundation."

"Me, too," she said, quietly.

They walked on for a while. They had never talked in detail about the experiments Zoffany had conducted at the Romola Foundation. Gould had often tried to talk to her about their time working for the mysterious chairman, Benson. But she had always turned the conversation away.

She did no harm to Lucy, he thought. *But she might have done, in a situation where everyone was doing morally questionable things. She never faced that test – being ordered by Benson to experiment on a child.*

"You'd like me to give it a try?" he said finally, as they stepped onto the escalator.

"Talking to them wouldn't hurt, would it?" she asked, looking up at him with a pleading expression.

And now she wants to help make amends for the crimes she might have committed against a little girl she's never met. Not rational, of course, but very human.

"Depends on your definition of hurt," he breathed. Then, aloud, he went on, "I can give them a call, hear them out."

They arrived at the Tube platform just as a train was approaching. Gould looked at the round, black aperture, saw the flicker of light on the curved wall. A roaring sound grew and a growing breeze stirred Zoffany's hair. An old cliché sprang to mind.

The light at the end of the tunnel, he thought, *might well be an approaching train.*

***

Denny sat in the kitchen nursing a cup of coffee and checking their online footprint. It made for depressing reading. It seemed to her that people were tiring of Interloper stories, no matter how well-researched. Hundreds of other fads, images, and memes were constantly vying for the public's attention. Eventually she closed her laptop and sat back, thinking about Frankie's throwaway remark.

"Why couldn't they learn to drive?" she asked. "I mean, why not?"

"What?" Frankie looked up from her phone. "I was kind of joking. I think."

"But why not, if they're more human?" Denny persisted. "Before, they spent so little time in our world, they had to make it count. Attack, kidnap people, withdraw. Then they evolved, adapted, to survive here. They became harder to tell from actual humans. And now there's a hybrid strain. The boundaries are blurring."

Frankie shook her head.

"Maybe, but can I just point out that the Queen is sending out her eggs to try and kill people? She's not shooting her enemies with a Walther PPK. Also, she lays eggs. That's gotta influence anyone's perspective on life."

"PP-what?" Denny asked.

Frankie did her eye-roll again.

"James Bond, girl! Walther PPK with a short silencer was his gun..."

"Do I even know you?" Denny asked, laughing at Frankie's sudden enthusiasm.

"My grandpa loved those movies," Frankie went on. "When I was little, I thought Sean Connery was a typical British guy, or maybe Roger Moore at a pinch. Imagine my disappointment when I finally got here."

"Age inappropriate entertainment," Denny smiled. "No wonder you grew up all twisted and cynical."

"We must have a Bond fest sometime," Frankie said. "We can compare the classic Sixties movies to the new ones. Starting with Doctor No, of course. Gotta do it in chronological order. God, I can't believe it's so long since I saw those movies!"

At least she's found something good to cling to, Denny thought. *She's more like her old self when she's remembering this stuff.*

"Doctor No?" Denny asked. "Seriously? He was like, a really negative supervillain?"

"He was this mad scientist with metal hands. And he had a private island, with lots of guards and stuff," Frankie said, more soberly. "And when people went there he had various unpleasant means of killing them."

"I'm sure Lanier doesn't have a moat full of alligators, or whatever," Denny said, with mock reassurance. "But I guess we'll find out soon enough."

That night Denny slept uneasily, drifting in and out of strange dreams. She was in the Soul-Eater again, absorbed by the vast living mountain of protoplasm. Next to her, also encased in jelly-like tissue, was Frankie. She sensed other human captives, lying deeper inside the monster. Most had been partially consumed, but their brains and nervous systems still functioned. The Soul-Eater, essentially mindless itself, was an efficient user of the minds of others.

You won't get my brain, Denny thought. *I need it most days.*

She saw Frankie turning in the dark mucous, thrashing against the creature's tissue. Frankie's mouth was open in a cry of despair. Then she sensed Denny's presence, their minds linked via the Soul-Eater.

"I told you I'd come and get you," Denny said. "See? I got this talisman."

She reached for the talisman around her neck, the one thing that could force the Soul-Eater to vomit them up. But it wasn't there. The only substance that she knew could fatally harm beings from the Phantom Dimension, and she had lost it.

"No!" she moaned, battling against the semi-liquid tissue to search her disintegrating garments. "I had it with me, it was right there!"

"I thought you were going to save me!" Frankie cried. "I can't last much longer!"

The pressure of the Soul-Eater's colossal body increased, and gelatinous living matter flowed into Denny's mouth, choking her. Darkness enveloped her as she heard Frankie calling her name.

"Denny?"

She opened her eyes to see her friend standing over here, a piece of toast in one hand.

"You were thrashing about and moaning," Frankie explained. "Time to get up! Lanier's driver is going to be here soon."

Denny groaned, tumbled out of bed. Already the details of the dream were blurring, fading. But the essence of it was still with her.

"Nightmare?" Frankie asked, pouring her a cup of coffee.

"Soul-Eater nightmare," Denny confirmed. "I guess yours are even worse?"

Frankie shrugged, took a gulp of juice.

"I'll never be free of that thing," she said. "Sure, I was only part of it for a few hours, I know. But it was an eternity up here."

She tapped her temple.

"No wonder the poor bastards who were in there for years …"

Frankie trailed off, gazing down at her oatmeal. Denny recalled the bedraggled survivors who had made it through the portal after the rescue. Some had died soon after, their immune systems wrecked by weeks of interaction with the monstrous alien organism. All had been mentally ill, hopelessly confused and frightened by a world that had changed beyond recognition. A few weeks in the Phantom Dimension meant that years had passed on Earth.

Apart from Frankie and Denny, the escapees from the Phantom Dimension were all in psychiatric facilities. This had made it much easier to dismiss their claims. Lanier's publications had led the charge. One especially poisonous op-ed had suggested that the 'American hoaxers' should be confined for their own safety.

"I know," Denny said, walking round to put a reassuring hand on Frankie's shoulder. "I'm conflicted, too. But look at it this way. We put out the case to the people online. And some of them believed us, but it didn't change anything. Politicians don't want to know because it's too weird, so that leaves us with the media. Lanier is a big player, so–"

"I know," Frankie said, smiling up at her. "But if it turns out he does have a moat full of alligators, I will say 'I told you so.' Really loudly."

Nightmare Resurrection

Chapter 6: Code Nine

Shortly after first light, Gould met a man calling himself Comstock in a freezing cold, near-deserted park. They exchanged a few words, then Comstock led Gould to a seat. There he held up his phone, tapped the screen.

"See this as a kind of down payment," Comstock said quietly. "More to follow if you are willing to work with us."

"Hello Edward," said the girl in the video. "I'm really sorry I was naughty. I shouldn't have followed you into the woods. I just wanted to play."

Lucy was thin and pale. She was dressed in bright clothes that had a second-hand look. Gould wondered absently if nurses or visitors donated things for children with no family. Lucy began to prattle on about her friends in the home, the doctor who said she was very brave, the nurse who showed her penguins on the internet.

Or in this case, no family that officialdom recognizes. Legally she's a non-person, like all the rest.

"Does she know..." Gould struggled to frame a question, while trying to maintain control of himself. "Does she know how long she was away?"

Comstock nodded.

He's seen it before at least once, Gould reasoned. *And in his world, suppressing your feelings is vital.*

"I'm told that when they're small, they find stuff like that easier to believe," Comstock said. "World's still full of magic when you're, what, six?"

"Yes, she was six," Gould said in a monotone. "Two years younger than I was."

"The doctors," Comstock went on, "say she can't really remember everything that happened. She was abducted, there were monsters, she was scared. But she has nightmares, they say. She's on powerful medication, for a kid. Not my field, of course."

Comstock stopped the video.

"That clip will be sent to your Darkmail account," he said as Gould started to protest. "I just wanted to demonstrate that we were sincere. You can see Lucy again. And not just on a screen. See her regularly."

Gould was about to ask when he could see Lucy in person when something Comstock had said brought him up short.

"How did you know about the Darkmail account?" he asked. "I only ever used that for–"

"When you were communicating with the Romola Foundation," Comstock interrupted. "We've looked into that. Can you blame us? It was quite a security breach, to have a private contractor acting like that. A so-called charity studying the paranormal. Crazy situation. A couple of our top guys lost their pensions over that one."

Gould looked at Comstock, trying to weigh up the younger man. Comstock – he had given no first name and Gould had not asked – was between thirty and forty, wiry, a shade below average height. He had sandy hair, very blue eyes, sharp features. Dressed neatly in a business suit, he might have been a corporate accountant or a middle-ranking civil servant. The state agency Comstock worked for was not one of Britain's well-known Military Intelligence services. The man had refused to state who did employ him, only that it was not MI5 or MI6.

"So, what do I have to do?" Gould asked.

"Share information with us," the other man said. "Be prepared to join us if and when we move against them."

"You're going to attack the Interlopers?" Gould exclaimed. "An actual state-sponsored campaign?"

Comstock held up a slim hand.

"Firstly, don't use that word, we don't want to be heard saying it in public. Yes," he pressed on as Gould tried to interrupt, "we do accept that they are from some other world. My superiors were impressed by your work. And your tenacity."

"Okay, what do you call them?" Gould asked. "Alien monsters? Shapeshifting bastards?"

"Code Nine," Comstock replied, straight faced.

"What?" Gould asked, genuinely puzzled. "Why Nine?"

"I is the ninth letter of the alphabet," Comstock said.

"That's the best you could do?" Gould demanded. "It's a bit – well, dull."

"That's the point, it could mean anything," Comstock said, getting up. "Best not to sit in the same place too long, Gould. Might attract interest. Old habits."

They walked around the edge of the pond. A small flotilla of hopeful ducks shadowed them, leaving black wakes in the gray-green water.

"And what do I call you?" Gould asked. "I mean, your secret outfit?"

Comstock looked at him for a moment, then said, "Just call it the Task Force. And yes, it's very dull, before you say it. We were specially assembled for this specific problem. When we deal with it, we go back to our respective units."

Assuming you can deal with it, Gould thought. *Which is by no means settled.*

"Do you want to learn more?" asked Comstock. "If so, you'll meet Trent, the big boss. He seems to think highly of you already."

They reached the park gates. Beyond, Londoners were going about their lives.

Most of them never heard of Interlopers, thought Gould. *Those that have probably think they're no more likely than Bigfoot or flying saucers.*

"Okay," he said. "Let's see what your Mister Trent has to say."

Comstock nodded, his face still expressionless.

"Right, we go down here, the car's waiting."

As they set off, Gould asked, "If I do join you, do I get to know your first name?"

"Anything's possible," Comstock said. "But I doubt it."

***

Denny had expected Lanier's town car to take them to one of London's railroad stations. But instead, they headed for Stansted, the smallest of the capital's three airports. The driver, a talkative guy from Ghana, explained that they were going to 'fly to some place in Wales, then get a chopper to the island'.

"Like a Bond movie," Denny whispered to Frankie.

"Yeah, cool," Frankie said with a faint smile.

Any excitement Denny felt at flying in a charter plane and then a private helicopter was offset by apprehension. But she was determined to see Lanier as a potential ally.

And the fact that he looked like a frail old man is helping, she thought. *No matter how we try to factor out stuff like that, it still matters.*

"There it is!" cried Frankie, pointing. "Hey, can I film this?"

The pilot looked surprised.

"Why not?" he said. "It's been featured in lifestyle magazines, that sort of thing. Just make sure you get permission when you're inside the house."

The chopper landed about fifty yards from the huge, rambling mansion. Two men in dark uniforms were waiting on the edge of the pad. The older of the two introduced himself as Murphy, head of security. They took the guests' bags and led them to the house.

"Some place you got here," Denny said.

"Yes," Murphy replied. "The house is built on the remains of an old religious community. A lot of interesting archaeology has been done on the site."

"Great," she said. "I love these quaint old English houses."

"This is the Principality of Wales, not the Kingdom of England," Murphy replied in a dull monotone.

The security chief's stilted manner and tone of voice struck Denny as strange. He sounded like a man who was distracted by something. He reminded her of an elderly relative who had spent years living with chronic pain. The discomfort made it hard for them to talk naturally. Murphy also looked slightly stooped, as did his colleague. It seemed unlikely that a security guard employed by a billionaire would have any kind of health issue.

Still, she thought, *he's probably got a lot on his plate, what with the egg issue.*

"So, was it you who found the Interloper egg, Mister Murphy?" she asked.

For a moment, she thought he was not going to reply. Then he paused, half-turned, and looked at her. His unblinking gaze was unnerving. Denny stopped, suddenly less sure of herself.

"No," he said, "that was another man."

Murphy started walking again, with the women struggling to keep up with his long-legged stride. Denny looked down at Frankie, who made a face and mouthed the word 'creep'.

Oh yeah, Denny thought. *But I guess you'd expect Lanier to employ creeps, given his record.*

Murphy led them into the grand hall of Mountfalcon House, then without pausing, set off upstairs. Denny and Frankie tagged along, the latter filming all the while. They were shown to their rooms without any further conversation. Denny had given up trying to make small talk.

"After you have freshened up," said Murphy, "Mister Lanier will be waiting for you in his study. It is at the far end of the East Wing."

"And where are we?" Frankie asked.

"The West Wing," Murphy replied.

"Great! I always wanted to be in a hit show," Frankie shot back.

Murphy showed no sign of getting the joke.

"Tough crowd," Denny remarked under her breath as the security men went back along the corridor. "That British sense of humor not much in evidence."

"You want to freshen up, like the man said?" Frankie asked, looking around Denny's room.

"I guess," Denny replied. "But let's make it quick. I want to see the old guy and get it over with."

"Hey, look!" said Frankie, pointing at a side table. "They left some food. Well, sandwiches, anyhow. And real coffee, looks like."

She picked up a sandwich and took a bite.

"Hey!" said Denny, "that's mine."

"It's fun to share," Frankie retorted, then frowned. "You know, this is a typically lousy British sandwich. If I wasn't so hungry I probably wouldn't even finish it."

"Lousy or not, still my sandwich," Denny pointed out. "Go eat your own lunch!"

Frankie backed out of the room, filming her friend's mock-outrage.

"And stay out!" Denny shouted, laughing as she slammed the door.

***

Comstock's BMW drew up in a refurbished docklands district on the south side of the Thames, not far from the Globe Theater. As they got out, Gould could see the dome of Saint Paul's. The cathedral was just visible across the river, almost hidden among glass-fronted towers of financial institutions.

God and Mammon, Gould thought. *God seems to be losing.*

"High-rent area," he remarked. "You must have some financial clout."

"Not my area," Comstock said dismissively. Then, gesturing at a narrow alleyway, "We're just up here."

The gentrified neighborhood was busy with young people talking into their phones, and occasionally to one another. Comstock led Gould to a former warehouse. A man was up a ladder painting a new sign. Large letters proclaimed SAUNDERS' SURGICAL APPLIANCES. Gould gave Comstock a quizzical look.

"Discourages people, apparently," Comstock said, swiftly inputting numbers into a keypad, then swiping a card. "Dull and a bit embarrassing. Nobody's quite sure what it means, but they suspect it involves hernias."

Smiling at the man's deadpan delivery, Gould followed the agent inside, up a flight of stairs, and into a large, open-plan office. About a dozen men and women sat around in shirtsleeves, mostly working on PCs. They seemed very young and fresh-faced to Gould, who had a sudden flashback to the operations room at the Romola Foundation.

That seemed pretty efficient, too, he recalled. *Then shit hit the fan and it all fell apart.*

Comstock nodded to various people as he led Gould through the room to a glass-walled office at the far end. The door, Gould noticed, bore no name or title. He was ushered in, and greeted by a small, plump man in casual clothes.

"Mister Trent," Comstock said. "You were right."

"Welcome, Ted!" said the short man, scuttling around his desk, hand extended. "So good to finally meet you!"

"You're Trent?" Gould said, surprised. "I expected – well, someone more…"

Trent laughed, pumping Gould's hand with both of his.

"More like a spymaster, eh?" he said. "A bit sinister, cold, remote? Comstock has that covered, as you've seen. Besides, I believe in creating a friendly working environment. Now, please, take a seat!"

Trent swiftly launched into a detailed description of how much Gould would be paid if he 'came on board'.

"You found my Achilles' Heel," Gould put in. "But what would my actual work involve?"

"Science!" exclaimed Trent, flinging up his hands with such enthusiasm that Gould had to smile. "We need an actual scientist who has seen the Code Nines, crossed swords with them."

"To help us kill the buggers," Comstock added.

"Quite!" said Trent. "But first, we must understand them. For instance…"

The little man scurried to a small safe in the corner of his office and keyed in a combination. Gould watched with interest as Trent took out a small metal box and laid it on the desk.

"We hitched a ride on various commemorations of the First World War," Trent said, as he unlocked the box. "Asking people if they had any memorabilia from great-granddad, that kind of thing. Took us ages to find this, and buying it blew a big hole in our budget. It's a bit beyond our expertise, so perhaps you help us turn it into a weapon of some kind?"

Gould was baffled for a moment, then saw what Trent was lifting out of the box. It was a purplish stone suspended from a thick length of cord.

"A talisman from Machen!"

"Quite," Trent said, laying the stone on the desk. "A mysterious stone – magical, some might say, but of course we can't put that in an official report. But I understand it confers some protection to the wearer, being lethal to Code Nines?"

"Yes," Gould said. "Can I examine it?"

Trent nodded, and Gould picked up the stone, turning it over in his hand. It felt ordinary enough, but he knew the crystal had been formed under different natural laws.

From another universe, the scientist thought. *A substance that somehow alters probability to confer luck on the bearer. And kills Interlopers on contact.*

"Or does it?" he murmured to himself. "Or have they evolved in that respect, maybe?"

"I beg your pardon?" Trent asked, smiling quizzically.

"Nothing," Gould said, handing back the stone. "Speculation running amok. This is quite an achievement. You know how to get my attention. First the money, now this."

"Let me give you the tour!" said Trent, with his trademark enthusiasm. "No doubt you want to see what we're up to, meet the gang, that kind of thing. But first, I must ask – are you onboard? I do hope so!"

Gould looked from the little man's bright, enthusiastic face to Comstock standing impassively by the door.

"Yes," he said. "I'm on board."

This is the only game in town for me, he thought. *But at least there's nothing overtly sinister or incompetent about this lot.*

Gould followed Trent back into the main office while Comstock locked the talisman back in the safe.

***

"At last!"

Sir Charles Lanier advanced towards Frankie, a smile on his cadaverous features. His electric wheelchair buzzed quietly over the hardwood floor of the study. Denny tried to retain her composure, but she was startled by how old and ill the man looked.

He could be dead by New Year, she thought. *What would his job offer be worth then?*

"I'm so glad to see you both," said Lanier, looking up into the camera. "And please, film everything if you wish. I have no secrets from my friends."

The old man swiveled his chair around and headed over to his desk, where the remains of the Interloper egg lay. Lanier recapped the account he had given of the egg's discovery, its hatching, the death of the creature. Denny listened politely, nodding now and again, at the old man's long-winded manner. But she wondered when he would get to the real topic.

God, she thought, *it's warm in here. Old people like the heat. I'd better stay upright. If I sit down I might doze off.*

Denny swayed slightly and caught herself on the edge of the desk.

"But where are my manners?" Lanier exclaimed. "Please, ladies, sit down so we can talk more comfortably."

Denny had no choice but to sit, with Frankie next to her. She noticed that the camera drooped in Frankie's hands before swinging upright again.

Is she feeling the heat, too? God it is so warm.

Denny tried to concentrate on what Lanier was saying, but the old man seemed to be making little sense. He sounded like a radio station fading in and out, with a few clear words here and there.

"Alliance, yes, very important – threat of Interlopers – sensible arrangement – lucrative, generously remunerated – collaboration – excellent…"

God, he is making no sense, she thought. *Like he was wound up at the start and now his clockwork is running down.*

Then Lanier stopped talking and simply stared at them, head on one

side, with a look of good-humored puzzlement.

"Sir Charles?" Denny managed to say, her words slow and slurred. "Are you

okay?"

The old man gave no sign of understanding her. A thin trickle of drool oozed from the left-hand corner of his mouth. Then Denny heard the door open, over to her left. She could not move her head now. Out of the corner of her eyes she saw movement; a tall figure walking confidently into the room. She felt sure the newcomer was a woman – not just from the way she moved but also because she was wearing a long, scarlet robe or dress.

"Darling!" said Lanier, perking up. "Did I do well? Was it alright?"

"Yes, dear," said a husky, feminine voice. "You kept them talking just long enough."

I know that voice, Denny thought. *But from where?*

Her mind was so fuddled that she could not quite grasp what had happened. The realization that she had been drugged slowly surfaced from a sea of confused images, sounds, emotions. By the time she grasped what had happened, and tried to move, her limbs seemed to be weighted with lead.

"Take them through," said the woman. "It's almost time for emergence."

Two more figures entered her field of vision. They were clad in black, and as they stepped around in front of the journalists, Denny recognized Murphy and Phelps. She was hauled upright, then lifted off her feet and carried between the two men. She gave a vague moan of protest, tried to kick and struggle, but her body refused to obey her. She was carried along the hall toward an open door. Her own bedroom.

Denny felt herself begin to lose consciousness as the two men laid her on the floor. She heard them leave, then a few moments later return with Frankie. Denny felt hard, cold hands start to strip off her jacket, shirt, exposing her upper body. Then she was turned over onto her side. This allowed her to see Frankie, who was also half-naked, lying with her back to Denny.

One of the guards reached down and placed something close behind Frankie. Denny could see that it was a four-inch wide ball, black, glossy in texture. It was evidently an egg, but smaller than the Interloper eggs they had seen so far. Footsteps behind her told Denny that a similar egg had been placed behind her.

Whatever hatches will ... what? Kill us?

Even with her clouded thoughts, Denny could see no reason for such an elaborate form of murder. But she could think no further; just watch in despair as the black, glossy egg began to move. It oscillated from side to side, bulged, then split open. A pale gray liquid oozed densely onto the carpet. Then a creature like a six-inch slug emerged, its front end waving blindly. Its flesh, mottled gray-green, pulsed with life. It was semi-transparent, and Denny could just make out internal organs of some kind.

Oh God! Oh God no! Keep it away!

Again, Denny tried to shout, struggle, and again she failed to do more than moan faintly. The slug-thing showed no sign of having heard her. Instead, it wriggled out of its shell and paused, tip waving. It seemed to be blind. A wreath of thin filaments extended from one end and twitched in the air. Then the thing began to move, muscular waves travelling along the body. It was heading for Frankie. When it reached her, the filaments brushed against her flesh, making Denny feel sick with despair. Then the creature reared up, fastened itself to Frankie's back, and began to inch slowly towards her spine.

Denny tried to cry out in warning, but failed. Then she twitched, moaned. It was as much as she could do when she felt a tickling sensation in the small of her back. Then a cold, clammy presence attached itself to her, and began to climb up. It seemed to take forever to make its way to a point between her shoulder blades. Then she felt a stinging sensation. Finally, her confused mind worked out what the entity must be.

A symbiont. A thing that lives on my blood, taps into my nervous system.

Denny recalled the horrible, alien organisms that were fixed to humans by the Interlopers. She tried to recall the purpose of the repulsive organisms, but couldn't. All she could remember was that removing the symbionts tended to kill both the creature, and the host.

The sting faded slightly, became a more diffuse pain, a burning sensation that spread up and down her back. At the same time, Denny watched Frankie's symbiont settle in place and extend more filaments, penetrating the flesh to either side of the woman's spine. Frankie's flesh turned red, and she stirred slightly. The creature pulsed rhythmically, and Denny saw it darken. Sickened, she knew she was watching Frankie's blood passing through the symbiont.

Why? They can't take us into the Phantom Dimension, Denny thought. *It was destroyed, the portals are gone.*

Then she felt a new sensation, one that cut through both the pain and the fuzziness. It was like a rising chorus of voices, all babbling in her head. With it came a bewildering variety of images, moving perspectives that showed her Mountfalcon House and its surroundings. She recognized the path from the cliffs, Lanier's study, the bedroom. She saw herself and Frankie, lying helpless on the floor. She was looking down at her own body. The sensation was so startling she forgot her fear and pain for a moment.

I'm seeing through other eyes, hearing other thoughts.

Even as she became aware of the baffling, chaotic sensory input, it began to fade. In its place she felt an overwhelming calm, a new serenity that washed away her terror and suffering. At the same time, she remembered why the woman who had spoken to Lanier had sounded so familiar. It was not so much her voice as her manner that Denny recalled. She had encountered a similar being in her last foray into the Phantom Dimension.

'Yes,' said a strong, clear voice in her head. 'You are right. I am the Queen.'

Denny struggled to resist the surge of psychic energy that accompanied the thought. But her mind, already weakened, was quickly overwhelmed.

Yes, you are the Queen, she thought. *And so am I. We are all one.*

Nightmare Resurrection

Chapter 7: A Yellow Pin

"And this," said Trent, "is our incident map."

Gould examined the map, which looked surprisingly retro. A conventional paper chart of Britain and Ireland was dotted with pins of various colors. Most were yellow, a few were blue. A small number were red. He noted that the latter were clustered around London, the west of England, and a single one in Cheshire.

"The red is for portals?" he asked, before correcting himself. "No, there are too many. So, I deduce that they must be for the actual Interloper – sorry, I mean Code Nine activity?"

"Correct!" said Trent, looking pleased. "Yellow are for potential sightings, while blue indicates investigations that have drawn a blank."

Gould looked at the small man, then back at the map. There were only a handful of blue pins.

"You've got far more reports than an outfit this size could possibly investigate," he pointed out. "No way could you send even one person to check, what, dozens of possible sightings a week?"

"True," Trent admitted, "but we do prioritize. We don't list UFO sightings or anomalous big cats, for instance. We do list sightings of strange, humanoid creatures, especially if they seem to shun human contact. And we have other criteria."

Gould peered at the map more closely, frowned.

"What's this?" he asked, pointing at a yellow pin. It indicated a point on the far north-west tip of Wales. "Strange creatures?"

"Ah, not exactly," Trent replied. "Why do you ask?"

"Couple of friends of mine were headed up that way," Gould said. "Hard to tell on this scale, but that pin could be quite close to Holyhaven Island?"

Trent walked over to a young woman who, Gould saw, was scrolling through tabloid news reports online.

"Tania," Trent asked. "Do we have anything on a place called Holyhaven?"

The young woman quickly opened a database and checked it.

"No," she said, "but a few months back we had some odd reports coming out of a place called Maldwyn's Bay. That's opposite Holyhaven, I think – yes, the village faces the island across a strait. Why?"

"What happened?" Gould asked urgently. "I mean, why was this village flagged?"

Tania looked at Gould, then at Trent, who nodded, still smiling beatifically. She clicked on another link and a series of reports appeared.

"It seems," she said, skimming the paragraphs, "that a few people were worried when a kind of fortune-teller appeared in the village. Set herself up as a psychic. Foreign, some said. But then, after a few weeks, this woman seems to have vanished. So, no investigation warranted."

Gould stood up, looked at Trent.

"It's a hell of a coincidence, assuming it is one," he said. "What do you have on Sir Charles Lanier?"

***

Frankie writhed in pain. She could feel every twitch of the symbiont's filaments as they invaded her nervous system. The drug that had subdued her seemed to have almost worn off, but she still could not move. Now her body was not sedated but hijacked. What remained of her individual mind felt under siege, surrounded by alien thoughts.

The Queen – her mind – so strong.

She could not see Denny, but she could feel her friend's consciousness. Denny was flailing, trying to resist the Queen's power. But even as Frankie tried to reach out to her, Denny was submerged, assimilated, made one with the Queen's overwhelming psychic presence. Frankie felt rage and despair, and realized that she was still able to think independently.

No! You won't get me, you won't take my mind, I won't be taken again.

Frankie pushed back against the Queen's influence. It was the same trick, a stubborn mental resistance, that she had honed while trapped inside the Soul-Eater. She conjured up strong memories, a powerful but incoherent mass of feelings and images. Moments of childhood happiness mixed with flashes of pain and joy from her adolescence.

In addition, she threw in snatches of favorite songs, glimpses of secret desires, and random nonsense. Her grandmother's smile, the homely smell of baking, a first fumbling kiss in the back of a car, a cartoon she had loved, the exhilarating sting of cold water as she dived into a river. She fought furiously to be herself, with all her human flaws and contradictions.

I am me, I'm not part of your hive.

The pain grew more intense. But at the same time, she felt hesitation, a sense of doubt on the part of the Queen. The symbiont twitched, and Frankie felt its discomfort. She realized that, having been a captive of a being that was hostile to the Interlopers, she might have gained some kind of resistance to their strange powers.

No time for theorizing, she thought. *Let's get moving.*

She struggled onto her hands and knees and crawled slowly across the bedroom floor. The Queen's psychic attack was now like a migraine, distorting her vision, but Frankie could still see enough to make out her objective. It was the large, old-fashioned wardrobe a few feet away.

She reached it, managed to turn around so that she was sitting with her back to the sharp corner of the wardrobe. She could just make out the bedroom door. Murphy was coming through it. But he was moving stiffly, not too fast.

Maybe she's having trouble fighting me and controlling the rest, Frankie thought. *Let's give her more trouble.*

She shoved herself backwards with hands and feet. She felt pressure along her upper spine, a sickening squelch and then a popping noise as the wooden angle pierced the new-hatched symbiont. The pain from the dying organism shot along Frankie's nerves, a brief bolt of agony, and then she blacked out.

***

"It seems a little bizarre," mused Trent as Gould finished. "Your two journalist friends were contacted out of the blue?"

"As soon as they posted the story about the death of Scoresby, yes," Gould confirmed.

"What do you think, Comstock?" Trent asked. "You've been your usual self. Try talking for a change!"

"I think," said Comstock, looking at Gould, "that your associates may be in trouble. Or this may just be the way a rich, eccentric media baron behaves. Either way, it merits closer attention."

He's got a point, thought Gould. *And if we jumped at every self-proclaimed psychic who spooks a few provincials, we'd never get anywhere.*

"So, what are you going to do?" he asked Comstock. "I mean, you can't just turn up on that guy's private island? Or can you?"

Comstock began to speak, but Trent cut him off with a discreet wave of a plump hand.

"I think we may be getting ahead of ourselves, Ted," said the little man. "After all, you're not officially one of the team yet."

"I'm in," said Gould. "I'll sign any form you like. Just do anything you can to help them. If I'm right, you'll be helping yourselves, after all."

Trent raised an eyebrow.

"Really? How do you make that out, Ted?"

"Because if I'm right," said Gould, "there's a nest of your Code Nines on that island."

***

The blackout could only have lasted a few seconds. When Frankie came around she felt someone lifting her up. She opened her eyes to see a black uniform.

Murphy, or his pal.

The pain in her spine was still intense, but bearable. Sheer adrenaline, a desperate need to survive, sharpened her senses despite the discomfort. She looked up to see Murphy's face, still devoid of emotion, as he hoisted her to her feet. Behind

Murphy, she saw Denny, lying inertly. The symbiont on her spine was pulsing gently, dark with its host's blood. Denny stirred slightly, moaned, but her eyes stayed shut.

"Let – me – go," she gasped through her pain.

Murphy showed no sign of hearing her, let alone responding. He dragged her across the carpet towards the doorway. She guessed he was either taking her to be killed outright or, more likely, to be imprisoned somewhere.

Until another egg is ready, maybe? Either way, it's bad news.

Frankie reasoned that Murphy must have a symbiont, too. That would explain the slightly stooped appearance they had noticed when they landed, not to mention the man's cold-fish manner. Murphy's symbiont would be well-embedded by now, but still vulnerable.

My best bet, anyhow.

She stopped struggling and slumped, eyes closed, feigning unconsciousness. She felt Murphy hesitate, then stop to adjust his grip. As he loosened his hold on her, Frankie tried to reproduce her stunt with the wardrobe, shoving herself backwards to push the man off balance. It did not quite work. He reeled at the surprise move but did not fall onto his back. He did, however, reach out with one hand to stop himself falling. This allowed Frankie to break free and run into the corridor.

Another dark-clad figure was standing just a few feet away, between her and the staircase. It was Phelps, the second guard. He crouched, arms reaching out to prevent her dodging past. Instead, Frankie ran straight at him, head down, and butted him in the stomach. She heard a *whoof* of expelled air as Phelps doubled up.

Symbionts don't make 'em any tougher, she noted with satisfaction.

Phelps staggered back, fell onto his backside, but still snatched at her as she tried to leap over him. He caught her ankle and she stumbled, falling painfully on the wooden floor. She glimpsed Murphy approaching, Phelps getting up. She knew she could outrun them in normal circumstances, but the throbbing pain in her back was depleting her strength, as well as making it hard to think.

If I could make it to a boat, I'd have a chance.

Then she wondered if any boat would need a key to start it. If she headed for the jetty and could not get away, she would simply have trapped herself, with her back to the sea.

Gotta do something. Gotta help Denny!

Frankie dodged into her own room, a vague idea forming in her mind. She heard lumbering footsteps as the security guards ran in pursuit. Frankie's basic camera equipment included a microphone boom. It was essentially a lightweight, telescopic alloy tube. She grabbed it from the bed where she had left it and spun round in time to whack Murphy in the face with it. Blood sprayed from the man's mouth. His head jerked round and he stumbled sideways, against the door frame. Phelps collided with his superior, and the two men fell forward into the room, Phelps on top, arms flailing. Seeing her chance Frankie brought the boom down between Phelps' shoulder blades. There was a sickening, familiar popping sound.

"Gotcha!" Frankie gasped, as much in relief as in triumph.

Both men screamed. Both men writhed. She had raised her makeshift cudgel again, anticipating that Murphy would get up and resume the attack. But both security men seemed to be in a state of confusion.

Because they're all linked, she reasoned. *If one symbiont gets hurt, they all feel it.*

She brought the tube down onto Phelps' back again, got a satisfactory yell from both men. But then she heard another voice, higher, feminine, raised in a scream.

Denny!

Frankie vaulted over the two prone guards, and sprinted back up the corridor. She almost ran into Denny, who was standing in her bedroom doorway.

"Come on!" Frankie urged. "Grab some clothes, we can get out while–"

She paused, sensing something wrong. Denny was smiling, a fixed expression that made no sense in the situation.

"Yes," Denny said, stepping forward. "Let's go. We can give them the slip."

The voice was not quite right, either. It was too calm, rational, with none of the tension Frankie had heard so many times. She stepped back, away from Denny, held up the microphone boom.

"What is it, Frankie?" Denny asked, holding up her hands in a placatory gesture. "We're a team, right?"

"Oh God, Denny," she moaned in despair. "Turn around, turn around now!"

Denny instantly retreated, dancing backwards, dodging around the bed. Glancing back along the corridor, Frankie saw Murphy getting slowly to his feet. A thought occurred to her. She lashed out suddenly across the bed. The metal tube caught Denny on the cheek. It was not intended to be a severe blow.

But it will leave a mark, Frankie thought.

She turned and ran outside, striking out wildly at Murphy, giving him a glancing blow to the side of the head. She saw that Phelps was crawling along after his boss. He had vomited over himself, puke mixing with Murphy's blood on the floor.

"Help me!" she shouted at him, hoping he would realize what was happening.

Phelps gazed blankly at her, mouth open. He made an inarticulate noise, showed no hint of recognizing her. She wondered guiltily what kind of damage losing a symbiont might inflict.

I had no choice!

Frankie struck out at Murphy again, but this time he grabbed the tube and tried to wrestle it from her. She kicked at his groin, caught him right between the legs, and he let go instantly. She hit him again with the microphone boom and he went down, bleeding heavily from gashes to his head. Frankie ran past him and headed for the staircase.

"Miss Dupont!"

Lanier appeared, his chair rolling forward onto the landing, blocking her path. Frankie hesitated, club raised, but hesitant to strike at an old man who could not even walk.

"Miss Dupont," Lanier repeated. "Please don't prolong this unpleasantness. My wife is most distressed."

Beyond the old man, a woman in a long red robe stepped out of the study. The Queen was well over six feet tall, broad-shouldered, with a mass of auburn hair. Frankie got a brief glimpse of a wide mouth, a broad, flat nose, and large dark eyes under low brows. Then Frankie was shoving Lanier aside and bounding down the stairs.

"Come back, Frankie," called the Queen. "There's nowhere to go. Join us now, and save yourself much suffering."

"Screw you," gasped Frankie. She reached the hallway, skidded across the marble floor, almost crashed into the front door, wrenched it open, and then ran out into the icy air. November sunlight was playing on the gray waters of the strait, and a bitter wind blew into her face.

It was then that Frankie remembered she was still half-naked.

***

"Perhaps the sensible thing," Trent said mildly, "would be for you to give your friends a call?"

Gould felt a surge of impatience with the little man's unhurried attitude. But Trent was on his own turf and his suggestion did make sense.

"I don't think cell phones work on that island," Gould pointed out. "It would have to be Skype, or a landline call."

"Let's just use the phone in my office," Trent suggested. "If the two journalists are safe and well, one of them will be available to talk, one would think?"

"I'd prefer Skype," Gould said. "It would help to see as well as hear Denny, or Frankie. Just in case."

As Trent issued instructions to Tania, Comstock stepped closer to Gould, not looking at him.

"You think the Code Nines could imitate your friends well enough to fool you?" he asked quietly.

"Of course not!" Gould snorted. "I could tell a fake, even on screen. I know these people. We've been through a lot."

I wish I could really be sure, Gould thought. *Depends how good these new-breed Interlopers are.*

Comstock gave a slight nod.

"Way I heard it," he said, still looking at Trent and Tania, "one of them fooled a politician into thinking it was his mistress. That's pretty good undercover work in my book."

Gould said nothing to that.

"Oh, well done!" exclaimed Trent, stepping back from Tania's desk. "We seem to be getting through to them."

An unfamiliar face appeared on the screen.

"Who is this?" demanded the stranger. "And how did you get this number?"

Trent waved Gould forward as Tania vacated her chair.

"My name is Ted Gould," he said. "And I have an urgent message for Denny Purcell. Or Frankie Dupont, either will do."

The face on the screen remained expressionless. Gould saw that the man was wearing a black uniform, and assumed he was a security guard.

"Is there a problem?" Gould asked. "I understand they are guests of Mister Lanier?"

"That is correct," said the guard. "Please wait."

Then man stood up and went out of shot. Gould felt his mouth grow dry, became conscious of his heart pounding under his ribcage.

What if I can't tell?

Denny appeared, looking slightly flustered, dressed in her familiar gray business suit. She sat down and peered into the screen, then smiled.

"Ted!" she exclaimed. "What's happened? Is Harriet okay?"

Gould felt a surge of relief at the sound of her voice. Everything about Denny seemed normal. It occurred to him that he had to say something.

"Oh," he stumbled, "she's fine. I was just worried because – well, we hadn't heard from you. Is everything going well?"

Denny smiled, then gave an odd little shrug. It was not a natural gesture for her, so far as Gould could remember.

But she is probably quite nervous, he thought. *Big money at stake, career in the balance.*

"It's fine," she said. "I think Lanier is serious about helping us."

She paused, then smiled again.

"Hey, Ted," she went on, "where are you? That's not your apartment, right?"

Gould glanced up at Trent, who shook his head decisively.

"I'm – at an internet café," he said, trying to sound natural. "Terrible coffee, but fairly quiet. So everything's okay?"

Denny gave a thumbs-up gesture, looking awkward. Her smile vanished, replaced by an anxious, slightly pained look.

"Everything – is five-by-five," she said, and her voice was weaker this time. "Gotta go."

Before Gould could say anything, the connection was cut. He stared at the logo, then got up, feeling disoriented.

"That was her, right?" said Comstock. "Looked human to me."

Gould nodded.

"Oh yes, that was her all right. She seemed – a bit stressed out towards the end."

"But unharmed," Trent pointed out. "And not under obvious duress. I would need more than that to authorize a team raiding Lanier's retreat."

"Can we take another look?" Gould asked. "Just to be sure."

Tania slid back into her seat and replayed the call. The young woman laughed as Denny appeared, then looked up at Gould with a guilty expression.

"I'm sorry," said Tania, freezing the image. "I know she's your pal. But she looks like she put that jacket and blouse on in a hurry. All rucked up around the shoulders."

Trent rolled his eyes at Gould behind Tania's back.

"I don't think her fashion faux pas is the issue here," said the little man.

Tania sniffed.

"And she's wearing a ton of makeup," she added. "Really slathered it on. But it doesn't hide that mark. Did she have that before?"

Again, Tania froze the picture, then zoomed in on Denny's face. Now that his attention had been drawn to it, Gould could see that a patch of Denny's right cheek was discolored. He struggled to recall if she had had a bruise of some kind before she left.

"No," he said flatly. "No, I'm sure she didn't."

Gould looked at Trent, not trusting himself to say any more. He felt a terrible certainty that something was wrong, but as a scientist, he could see how flimsy the actual facts were.

"It's not much to go on," the little man said. "But in the circumstances, further investigations would seem to be warranted. Comstock, you're up."

For the first time since they had met, Gould saw Comstock's face break into a broad smile. It lasted all of two seconds.

***

Frankie ruled out heading for the jetty opposite the mainland. After just a few seconds outdoors, the cold was cutting deep into her bones. She ran around the house, keeping close under its walls, aware that watchers could be at any of the high windows.

She still carried the microphone boom, finding its weight increasingly burdensome. Despite years of toting cameras, her recent ordeals had weakened her, and she was gasping for breath.

She reasoned that such a large, rambling structure might have outhouses where she could hole up for a short while and think. As she rounded the back of Mountfalcon House, she saw that she had been right. An array of buildings had been tacked onto the mansion at various times, ranging from what looked like a greenhouse to a couple of nondescript sheds.

The nearest shed was locked, but she was so desperate for any shelter that she tried smashing the padlock with her makeshift club. The actual catch was so rusted that it simply fell off at the first blow. Frankie half-fell into the shed, slammed the door closed, then drove the metal tube into the dirt to try and jam the door shut. It was almost pitch black, with only a small, dirty window admitting a little light.

As her eyes became accustomed to the gloom, she made out the contents of the shed. It was full of junk, including an overturned quad-bike, various crates and cardboard boxes, and what looked like two large freezers. She started to search around for anything that might be useful, and found a small flashlight. She flicked it on, covering the glass, only to find it produced a weak, flickering light.

Batteries almost dead.

Frankie flicked the feeble, yellow beam around the shed. She had been right about the freezers. She paced around the small space, hoping to find something more effective than her club. But it became clear that there was nothing useful. There was, however, a few pieces of what looked like old clothing by the freezers.

Frankie squatted by the heap. It consisted of a surprising mixture of male garments – mostly suit jackets but with some more casual wear, plus pajamas and a silk dressing gown. She searched the pockets for phones, but there was nothing.

"Still, clean clothes," she muttered, putting on the smallest shirt, and then the warmest jacket. "Thank you, God."

She was about to return to the shed door when she noticed that the lid of the nearest freezer was slightly ajar. Frankie lifted the lid and pointed the flashlight inside. There were bodies in the freezer. Shriveled, gray-skinned bodies that looked mummified to Frankie's inexpert eye. She covered her mouth, feeling her gag reflex kick in, but managed not to throw up.

One thing about meeting a few monsters, she thought. *It toughens you up a tad.*

She leaned over the corpses. There were three, jumbled together as if they had just been thrown in. At first glance, they all looked like very old men, with wasted limbs, hollow cheeks, scalps almost devoid of hair. Then she noticed a couple of details that made her think again.

One man had a sleeve tattoo, the parchment-like flesh of his arm covered an elaborate, Maori-looking pattern. Another had a single gold earring. Frankie checked the nearest hand, flinching at the touch of cold skin. The hand was very well-manicured, for all its withered feel.

Disposal of the bodies, she thought. *Always tricky. Can't bury 'em on a small, rocky island. Can't just chuck 'em in the sea. So here they are in storage.*

She took a few shots from different angles, hoping that somebody would get to see the footage. Then she opened the next freezer. This, too, contained corpses, but their heads had been cracked open, the plates of the skull peeled back. Gagging, Frankie focused on the nearest skull. Zooming in, it was clear that the interior had been scooped out. A few ragged fragments of tissue were all that remained.

They eat brains, she thought. *Well, guess that makes them omnivores. Zoffany will be pleased.*

The flashlight died.

Chapter 8: Hunted

"You can't come," said Comstock bluntly. "You're not even officially on the team yet. Even if you were, you're not mission-trained."

"How many Interlopers have you actually met, face to face?" Gould countered. "Are you sure you could even recognize one? I can. They're not human, and you need to get that into your head. Your counter-terrorist methods are all very well, but real knowledge is priceless, and I have it. I got it the hard way."

The entire Task Force team was watching the standoff with interest. Gould's question prompted a sharp intake of breath from Tania.

None of them have actually been near one of their precious Code Nines, Gould thought. *That's my only card.*

Comstock shook his head.

"So far as I know, Doctor Gould," he said evenly, "you blundered into a difficult situation and made the best of it. As an amateur investigator. That's not the right way to handle things."

Gould bridled at the implication.

"I spent years of my life doing original scientific research into a threat your kind never even noticed! You were too busy waterboarding some peasant from the arse end of nowhere–"

"Gentlemen, gentlemen," Trent protested, stepping between the two men. "Ted is clearly concerned about his friends, and he is indeed a valuable asset precisely because he has had close encounters with Code Nines."

Comstock seemed about to protest, but Trent waved him to silence with a pudgy finger.

"I was about to add," said the little man, "that as our senior field officer, Comstock, Doctor Gould will of course come under your orders."

Gould was about to protest, then decided against it.

"That's fine by me," he said. "All I want to do is help."

"Splendid!" declared Trent. "Now, Tania? If you wouldn't mind organizing transportation. I'm sure I'm not the only one wondering how many places in Wales offer helicopters for hire."

***

"Frankie?"

The call was faint, but the voice sounded familiar.

Frankie moved closer to the door of the shed, pressed her ear against the rough wood. All she could hear was wind and the spatter of rain. It had been about ten minutes since she had taken refuge, though time was hard to tell.

Wish I had the sense to wear a watch like Denny.

"Frankie!"

The voice was low, urgent. And recognizably that of Denny's. For a moment, Frankie's spirits soared. Then she remembered the overwhelming force of the Queen's mind, how she had nearly succumbed.

She's one of them now, she thought. *I can't trust her. But I must try and save her.*

"Frankie, if you're in there – I got away. I did what you did, I managed to kill that thing. Or at least I hurt it, hurt it very badly. I don't think it's quite dead. I can still feel it inside me, feel its pain."

Doubt quickly arose, but still Frankie wondered if Denny might have somehow rebelled, despite appearances.

"Frankie, help me – I think they're coming."

What if she needs help and I do nothing? I'm guessing here, making so many assumptions.

Feeling sick with apprehension, she jerked the microphone boom out of the ground, letting the door swing inward. Outside she saw Denny standing in the rain, smiling tentatively at her.

"Get it off me," Denny pleaded. "It might recover."

Frankie started forward, hefting the alloy tube. Then she stopped, puzzled. Denny was fully dressed now. Yet Frankie had never seen the clothes before. In fact, they looked more like a children's outfit.

British kids dress like that, she thought. *Teenagers, young men in cheap sportswear.*

"What's the problem?" asked Denny. "Hurry!"

"Okay," Frankie said. "Turn around, I'll try to knock it off."

Denny turned as Frankie advanced. It was only then, as she got within a few feet, that something else struck her as odd. Denny seemed smaller, frailer than before. Frankie was a good two inches shorter than her friend was. Now they seemed to be about the same height. Suddenly she recalled the changeling children of Machen.

"What's the problem?" Denny said, turning around to face her. "Don't you want to help me?"

"Got the time?" Frankie asked. "Check your watch. The one you always wear."

What had looked very much like Denny hissed, fell into a crouch, and started forward, arms outstretched. Already its face was changing, the eyes retreating into deep sockets, mouth and nose fusing to an ugly snout. Frankie smiled grimly, and swung her club.

The tube caught the Interloper on the side of the head, sending it sprawling. There was no protest, none of the hurt reaction that Frankie would have expected from her friend. Instead, the small figure jumped back onto its feet with shocking speed, and before Frankie could raise her makeshift mace to strike again, it had bounded out of reach. At the same time, Frankie saw movement out of the corner of one eye.

The second Interloper had not bothered to assume human form. It bounded around the corner of the shed, and was too close and too quick for Frankie to take a swing at it. She decided to shove the end of the microphone boom into the creature's muzzle, feeling grim satisfaction at the sound of metal on inhuman teeth. The monster screamed in anger and pain, and staggered back, dark blood gushing from its mouth.

How many of them are there? Frankie wondered. *I can't hold off a small army.*

The first Interloper had tried to circle round behind her, but had come a little too close. Frankie lashed out swiftly and struck one of its clawed hands. There was a loud crack and the creature leaped away. Frankie retreated into the shed, hefting her club with both hands. The Interlopers seemed to hesitate, their heads to one side.

They're getting orders from the Queen.

"Come with us," said the first creature. "You will not be harmed."

Despite her fear, and the throbbing pain from her injured back, Frankie had to laugh.

"That is the lamest thing you could say in the circumstances," she pointed out.

"The Queen does not want you killed," said the second Interloper, its voice slurred by the damage to its mouthparts.

"You know why," added the first creature.

Figures, Frankie thought. *If I vanish, it's a little too suspicious. They want Denny and me as turncoats, to trash all the work we've done so far.*

"All we want is to survive," the first Interloper said, with a tone of pleading in its voice. "Our world is gone. All we want is a small part of yours. We are no threat to your kind."

Frankie recalled her abduction from the cellar of Malpas Abbey. She had been bundled through the portal, dragged by Interlopers across the unworldly deserts of the Phantom Dimension. Then she had been staked out on the ground in the path of the Soul-Eater, the colossal mountain of voracious protoplasm that had engulfed her.

"You're full of it," she retorted. "Nobody can trust you."

She expected some kind of reply, but it seemed the time for talk was over. The two creatures darted forward, one at each side, and Frankie retreated into the shed. They could not both come through the door at once. They were fast, but not fully-grown at just a shade over five feet tall.

But what if they get reinforcements?

Frankie slammed the door, leaned against it, catching her breath. One or both of the Interlopers slammed into the door, and she heard old hinges creak. It occurred to her that the whole structure was ramshackle, obviously neglected.

Good gust of wind might knock it down.

A desperate thought occurred to her, along with an illegal trick she had learned from an old boyfriend. She jammed the microphone boom into the ground again to wedge the door, then ran over to the old quad-bike. She heaved at it for a few seconds, rocking it so that eventually it fell upright. The movement produced an encouraging sloshing sound.

Only need a little fuel in the tank.

Frankie clambered into the quad-bike as the Interlopers began to batter more vigorously at the door. She imagined them being stirred into frantic activity by the Queen's all-pervading mind, impatient to recapture the one rogue human in her domain. A slit of light appeared as the old door began to give way.

Frankie worked hastily under the wheel of the vehicle, locating the wiring caps. Fortunately, it was the same setup as the motorbikes she had hot-wired a few times back in her teens. She managed to trigger the ignition, heard the motor turn over, then die. The door splintered, came off its hinges. Gray light spilled into the shed, and a small, agile figure scrambled past the broken door.

Frankie tried again and the motor roared to life. She twisted the throttle and the quad-bike surged forward just as the second attacker bounded inside. The vehicle zoomed around in a tight arc and hit the first Interloper with a sickening thud, bumping over the small body. The second one dodged out of the way as Frankie aimed the machine as best she could at the doorway, praying that the whole structure was as rotten as it seemed.

Frankie closed her eyes and put her head down as the quad-bike hit the door jambs on both sides, juddering but not coming to a stop. Frankie felt debris falling around her. Something hit her on the back, triggering intense agony from the wound where the symbiont had fastened itself. The pain made it hard to steer the bike, which slewed to one side, nearly hitting the glass-walled conservatory.

Frankie regained control just as the engine faltered and died. The machine quickly rolled to a halt. She jumped off, looking back at the gap she had smashed in the old storage shed. There was an expanse of shattered planking, but among it she could make out a smoking, twisted heap of gray-white flesh. The dead Interloper was decaying rapidly.

One down, at least.

Even as she exulted in killing one foe, the second appeared, nightmare visage pointed Frankie's way. With no weapon, Frankie felt a resurgence of panic. She looked in the quad-bike, saw a small toolbox, and picked it up. As she did so the lid came open. Wrenches, screwdrivers, and various nondescript plastic and metal objects spilled out. Cursing, Frankie went down on her knees, groping for the biggest wrench.

The Interloper, however, was not coming at her with its usual speed. Instead it was limping badly. As it emerged from the shadow of the wrecked shed, Frankie saw that one of its legs was badly twisted, and unable to bend at the knee. One arm hung limply by its side. The head, too, was injured, with dark blood streaming from a gash across the low forehead. But despite its injuries, it advanced toward her, reaching out with its one good arm.

Frankie swatted the clutching talons aside with the wrench, and raised the tool to strike the creature down. She hesitated, then forced herself to land the blow.

I put it out of its misery, she thought, as she stood over the second heap of smoking remains. *Like a wounded animal.*

Glancing around, she saw a dark-clad figure running toward her around the corner of the main house. Guessing it was Murphy, she set off in the opposite direction, hoping that he could not catch her. She wondered if the symbiont could be used to spur a human to make otherwise impossible efforts.

Suppose the Queen could force her slaves to battle on to the point of collapse, or even death?

It was not a happy thought. Frankie tried to keep fit, but she was tiring now. Each breath seemed to burn her lungs, and the pain in her upper spine was not easing up. She managed a slow jog around the conservatory, then saw two people heading her way. They were a middle-aged woman and an older man, both dressed in coveralls.

The cook, the caretaker, whoever, she thought. *All under control.*

She was still clutching the wrench, and for a moment contemplated fighting her way past the two strangers. But then she felt ashamed of her bloodthirsty impulse. Instead she went to the door of the conservatory, tried it, found it open.

Not much reason to lock doors on a private island.

Inside, the heat struck her like a physical blow. She paused, looking around the large, glass-enclosed structure. The windows were steamed up, offering her some cover. She leaned against a bench, breathing heavily. Then she took stock of her surroundings

Weird. Not what you'd expect in a rich guy's house.

The conservatory seemed to be as full of junk as the shed. Then Frankie saw that what she took to be a haphazard array of stuff was in fact quite orderly. A row of three bathtubs took up most of the over-heated space. In addition, there were several electric heaters, all going full blast.

Hot as the Phantom Dimension, she thought. *Though a lot more humid.*

She walked over to the nearest tub, moving cautiously, then looked inside. The bath was full of eggs. There were three of the large, reddish kind they had already seen. Then there were about a dozen smaller, darker eggs. As she watched, one of the large eggs began to bulge, and to roll around in the shallow water. A split appeared in the shell, and a small, black claw appeared.

Sudden rage took hold of Frankie. She raised the wrench and smashed it down onto the emerging creature. There was a splash of dark blood, a bestial squeal. Frankie kept hitting, smashing not only the emerging Interloper but all the other eggs, destroying every unhatched organism. As she killed, her mind was a whirl of fear, fury, and resentment. The feelings she had kept carefully at a distance since her abduction were free, and she was lusting for revenge.

They took me, they sacrificed me, they treated me like a goddam object.

Even as she smashed the eggs, a more rational part of Frankie's mind was trying to warn her that the Queen must surely be aware of what she was doing. She forced herself to stop when she had destroyed the contents of the first tub. As she stood upright, the outer door opened and Murphy rushed in, wielding a baton. He was followed by the two servants.

Frankie moved quickly to the next tub, held the wrench above the largest egg.

"Stop right there or I'll kill the rest!" she shouted.

Murphy hesitated, then advanced another couple of paces, raising his weapon. Frankie struck down viciously with the wrench and smashed a symbiont egg. The splatter of blood and tissue was a sickening sound.

"No!"

Frankie gawped in surprise. Not just Murphy, but all three of her pursuers had shouted out in dismay. Even more surprisingly, they had flinched as if in pain themselves. The old man seemed to be hit hardest, staggering, holding his hands to his head, almost falling to his knees.

They're all connected to the Queen, she thought. *And she can't switch it off. Hurt the eggs, hurt her. Hurt her–*

With a grim pleasure, she struck down again, this time aiming at an Interloper egg. She deliberately hit lightly, with just enough force to do damage, but not destroy. The shell cracked, oozed sticky mucous. The three enslaved humans all yelled, but showed no sign of attacking her.

The Queen's instincts are their instincts. And she can't decide.

"Get away from me!" she warned, holding up the wrench, which was now clotted with blood and tissue. "Get out of here! Now!"

Slowly the three retreated, Murphy last to go. They closed the outer door, which surprised Frankie for a moment. Then she reflected that letting the conservatory grow colder would be unacceptable to the Queen.

Even while I'm right here threatening her spawn, she has her procedures.

"That is correct, Frankie."

Frankie turned to see Lady Cassandra Lanier standing in the doorway to the main house. She almost dropped the wrench in surprise. The Interloper who had seduced the media tycoon was now at least six feet three, and heavily-built. The red robe she wore was, Frankie realized, some kind of blanket that the Queen had wrapped around herself.

"I'm still growing," said the Queen, stepping into the room. "In case you were wondering. Soon I will not be able to pass for human."

As the Queen stepped into the light, her face was revealed. Her features still showed the fading remnants of beauty. But now the face was distorted, the mouth a wide gash filled with razor-sharp teeth, the nose flattened, the eyes disproportionately small in deep sockets. A mass of oily black hair spilled over the Queen's shoulders.

"Surely Lanier has noticed?" Frankie gasped. "That his wife is something between a demon and a Disney witch? He can't be totally ga-ga."

Cassandra's mouth twitched in what might have been an attempt at a smile. She took another step forward. Looking at the creature's long, thick arms, Frankie estimated that she would soon be within grabbing distance. She raised the wrench, and did not bother to utter a warning.

"Yes," the Queen said, standing still again. "I can read your intentions. And I can still feel the pain, the fear, of my dying children."

"Don't play the grieving mom!" Frankie snarled. "They're just extensions of your own mind, tools that you use – like I use this wrench."

Cassandra's expression did not change. But for the first time since she had killed the symbiont, Frankie felt the mental energy of the Queen. It felt like soft fingers caressing her mind, then growing stronger, and starting to grasp at her individuality. Frankie wondered how close Cassandra would have to get before her psychic powers were irresistible.

"Don't try any ... any of your tricks!" she gasped, raising the wrench. "Keep back!"

The Queen shook her head.

"This is not a standoff," said the creature. "I will not let you destroy my offspring. If I have to, I will kill you. And I can."

"But if you do, it will raise too many questions," Frankie pointed out. "And I get the feeling that you're still kind of vulnerable, yes? Holed up on this island. And Scoresby – that was risky, drew our attention. You're still improvising, feeling your way in a new world."

The Queen remained silent, but stepped forward again, raising her hands. Frankie imagined those hands grabbing her, forcing her down while another symbiont was attached. She heard the conservatory's outer door open behind her. She dodged sideways between the bathtubs. At the same time, she tried to think of a way to cloud Cassandra's perception of her thoughts.

Those feet are huge, she thought. *You'll never get a pair of Jimmy Choos to fit those slabs of meat. Seriously enormous feet, girl.*

Frankie threw her wrench through the glass wall of the conservatory, smashing most of one pane. Then she crouched, pulled her man-sized jacket over her head, and took a dive. The remaining glass shattered around her. She felt a piercing pain in one leg, landed awkwardly on wet grass, then struggled to her feet. Her leg was badly cut, and she felt the warm gush of blood flowing down into her shoe.

I can't last much longer, she thought, and felt a sudden calm, a clarity of purpose. *I'd rather die than let them get me. Let Cassandra and her puppets explain that away. I'd rather die!*

She hurled the last thought out in a hot rage, and turned to run unsteadily away from Mountfalcon House. The island, she recalled from her arrival, was surrounded by cliffs.

'A terrible way to die. Slowly, in pain.'

The Queen's thought cut through her pain, and with it came a dizzying vision of a fall from the cliffs. Frankie shook her head, trying to banish the illusion. The Queen bombarded her with images. Frankie saw her broken body splayed on wet rocks, sea-foam turning red as waves broke over her.

Don't care. Death is better than life as a slave.

Frankie heard feet pounding behind her, guessed that Murphy was the fastest of the pursuers. She glanced back and saw the black-clad man running over the rain-sodden turf. Two other figures were far behind him. They were no threat. But Murphy was gaining, would stop her before she reached the cliff. She skidded to a near-halt on the damp grass and dodged to one side. Murphy almost lost his footing on the slippery surface, and as he passed close to her, Frankie punched him between the shoulder-blades. Murphy bellowed in pain, lashed out wildly, lost his balance and fell.

Frankie set off again, hoping she had bought enough time. Again, she felt the Queen's mental tendrils tugging at her mind, trying to undermine her will. But now the edge of the cliff was just a few dozen yards away. Gulls rose before her, riding on air currents, their white wings shifting. Across the strait, a shaft of sunlight penetrated the low cloud and lit up the shore.

Beautiful, she thought. *As a last glimpse of this world, it's hard to beat.*

She slowed and turned around. The pain in her leg had merged with the throbbing discomfort from the wound in her back. Murphy was on his feet again, but too far away to grab her. A bulky figure in red was standing in the conservatory doorway. She decided to fall backwards.

"Frankie!"

The voice was distant, but unmistakable. A small figure dressed in gray was waving at her from the house, running down towards the cliff. It was Denny, waving her arms frantically, shouting and sobbing.

"Get back!" Frankie shouted at her. "I've got to do this."

Denny gave no sign of having heard her. She kept on, and now she was close enough for Frankie to see how disheveled she was, her clothes in disarray, makeup smudged.

"Don't leave me!" Denny bawled. "I didn't abandon you! I saved you!"

Frankie hesitated.

"She's making you say that," she said, but half-heartedly. She could not be sure if it was Denny or Cassandra talking, or some combination of the two.

Does it matter?

Movement on the edge of her vision told her she had waited too long. Murphy had circled round and was charging in, close to the cliff edge, arms outstretched. Frankie tried to dodge but Murphy collided with her and they fell. Frankie felt the ground give way under them, and she was falling. A gull swooped close by her face, shrieking outrage. Murphy flailed his limbs in the air a few feet away. The rush of wind past her head grew louder, almost deafening, but she could still make out the growing sound of waves below.

Going down, she thought. *Sorry, Denny.*

Chapter 9: Survival

She's dead. Oh God, she's dead.

Denny knelt by the edge of the cliff, sobbing and howling, for what seemed like hours. Eventually she was lifted up gently by the housekeeper and caretaker, who led her slowly back to the house. There she was escorted upstairs to her room, undressed by the middle-aged woman, and laid gently on her side to rest.

'*I am sorry we could not save her.*'

Cassandra's voice was always in her head, but usually it consisted of persistent commands. This new thought seemed genuine in its compassion. It was still a cold, alien compassion, but with a slight tinge of humanity.

"She's still dead," Denny said into her pillow. "And it's your fault."

'*We must survive.*'

This time the message was more emphatic, harsher. With it came a strange image, just for a moment. It was a pattern, reminding Denny of a simple crossword. It was gone in an instant, and the mental pressure returned, clamping Denny's mind in a psychic vise. Then, once more, Cassandra's attitude seemed to soften.

'*Rest. Rest, and regain your strength. Let the Helper work free of your emotional turbulence.*'

Mention of the symbiont made Denny try to get up, but the overwhelming force of the Queen's mind held her still. Her muscles would not obey her, her limbs remained inert. She struggled, tried to fight off the psychic influence, but it was futile.

'*I have fewer subjects to focus on,*' Cassandra pointed out. '*Now that Murphy and the two young ones are dead. That means I can more easily control you. Do not struggle. Rest.*'

Denny felt herself start to drift into sleep, or unconsciousness. It was hard to tell. The pressure of Cassandra's will was forcing her to abandon thought; close her eyes, remain immobile.

I ... don't ... want ... to ... sleep!

She was too tired to resist, and sleep claimed her. Her dreams were chaotic, dark, violent. Over and over again, she saw the whirling sky and cliffs through the eyes of Murphy. Before he struck the rocks, he had glimpsed Frankie falling. Denny saw her friend surrounded by white birds, circling her like angels. Then came the moment of impact, the shattering extinction of Murphy's mind.

When she woke up it was dark. Denny reached out for the bedside light, and as she stretched her arm there was a twinge of pain from the symbiont. She had forgotten its presence, if only for a moment. With the reminder of her enslavement came a cascade of other memories, emotions, thoughts.

Denny walked into the bathroom, still naked, and studied herself in the mirror. She half-turned, trying to make out the entity that clung between her shoulder blades. She glimpsed a grayish bulge, and suppressed the urge to retch. A phrase swam into her mind, whether from her own memories or someone else's she could not be sure.

Hag-ridden. Witches, the night-hags, were supposed to ride their victims, clinging to their backs. But this is not some folk tale. No magic remedies for this.

She padded back into the bedroom, the carpet cold under her bare feet. She looked at her best suit lying neatly folded on a chair. Then she went to the wardrobe and took out a baggy tee-shirt, jeans, flat-heeled boots. It was only as she was selecting clean underwear that she realized she could not wear a bra with the creature nestling along her spine.

Maybe never again, she thought. *Getting a little saggy is the least of my worries, though.*

When she had dressed, she checked the time on her phone. It was nearly nine pm. The message NO CELL SERVICE reminded her that she was totally isolated, in a trap that she had walked into more or less willingly.

But where's my jailer?

Denny tried to find some trace of Cassandra's mind overseeing her thoughts, tracking through her senses. She detected no alien presence. This raised a question that had never occurred to her before.

Does she sleep? If she's part human, surely, she must? And if she's asleep, she can't retain conscious control of anyone – I guess?

It was such a simple idea. Denny cursed herself for not thinking of it. If the Queen slept, did her powers slacken, or fade completely? Again, she tried to detect any mental intrusion. She sensed nothing, felt no strange power at work.

"Okay, let's check out the area."

Denny got a small flashlight. Leaving her room, she tried to recall the layout of the house, but struggled, grew confused. Then she heard a faint moan from the direction of the staircase. There was a glass dome above the main hall, and it admitted enough light for her to see her way without the flashlight. As she approached the landing, she saw a thin sliver of light coming from a doorway. She tiptoed up to the door, listened for a moment. The moaning came again. It sounded like Lanier. She decided to risk going in.

"Oh God, it hurt so much! All that pain! And so much fear, so much hate. I never knew there could be so much hate in the world."

Lanier was slumped sideways in his wheelchair, looking colorless and exhausted. He seemed to be wearing some kind of hospital gown, the kind that fastened at the back. Her first thought was that he had had a heart attack. Denny had not given much thought to how much pain and stress had leaked through to him.

Judging from his current state, quite a lot.

She walked quickly over to Lanier, knelt down by him. His pulse was weak and his eyes seemed to be glazing over. One of the two large pillows that had been placed behind him had fallen onto the floor. She moved to pick it up, and saw the symbiont on his back. She recoiled in horror.

It was enormous, like a great pulsing slug. The repellent organism covered a third of the old man's back, running almost the whole length of his spine. The symbiont was a darker, richer green than the young creatures that had fastened themselves onto Denny and Frankie. From the plump body, dozens of dark filaments extended into Lanier's body, the strands clearly visible under thin skin.

"Jesus Christ," she breathed. "It must be taking so much blood."

"No," moaned Lanier, and she felt his frustration in her mind. "No, it is not harming me. It is keeping me alive. It is my Helper."

Denny replaced the pillow behind Lanier, moving carefully to avoid touching the symbiont. She wondered if Lanier had simply been deceived, or if there was an element of truth in his claim.

"I'm not the old fool you think, Denny," he croaked. "When Cassandra came, I knew, deep down, that she could not possibly feel any real desire for me, for this body, this face."

Denny felt ashamed. A man she had seen as a stereotype suddenly seemed very human. She realized that Lanier, too, was facing a terrible loss.

"I loved her," he said weakly. "I know you have a low opinion of me, but I was just so very lonely, and when she came, I fell in love."

She pulled up a small stool and sat holding Lanier's hand as he talked, sometimes rambling, but often speaking clearly and to the point. She had had plenty of experience building up a coherent story from disparate fragments of data. She quickly got a picture of how Cassandra had taken over the island, starting by psychically enchanting its owner.

Putty in his hands, Denny thought. *We often say it, but this time it was true. She could become his ideal woman, so she did.*

What Lanier called the Helper had been presented to him as a kind of exotic folk-remedy for the cancer that was eating away at his bones. Denny reasoned that, if he had not been old, ill, and smitten, he would have resisted such a bizarre idea. But infatuation had blinded him, and he had not recoiled from the grotesque idea. From then on, it had been simple for Cassandra to produce symbionts and attach them to various employees.

"Kind of like a twisted fairytale," she said, during a lull in Lanier's monologue. "But are you sure that this thing is keeping you alive? Really?"

Lanier nodded slowly.

"It was all explained to me," he said slowly. "But I have trouble remembering. If I could only–"

Denny squeezed his hand gently, then froze. She was receiving fragmentary memories that must have been Lanier's. She saw Cassandra, preternaturally beautiful, leaning over the old man. She saw the Queen writhing in a lukewarm bath, producing dark, leathery eggs. She saw the two Interlopers who had joined Cassandra, survivors of the Machen incursion. She witnessed Cassandra draining her human lovers, harvesting their genetic material. And then Denny saw the aftermath, as the three Interlopers feasted on the brains of the victims.

Denny jerked her hand away. She was so appalled by the final images that it took her a moment to grasp what had happened. Without any conscious intervention by Cassandra, Denny had shared memories with Lanier.

The fact that we both have symbionts, maybe that establishes a link on its own, if we're in physical contact?

Denny rejected speculation, and tried to focus on the facts. If she could focus Lanier's thoughts while the Queen slept, she might have an unexpected advantage.

"Where does she sleep?" she asked urgently, again clutching the old man's trembling hand. "Charles, can you tell me where she sleeps?"

Lanier's rheumy eyes gazed at her blankly. He gave no sign of having heard the question, let alone thinking of an answer. Denny clutched his fingers more tightly in both hands, closed her eyes, and tried to concentrate.

Come on, come on, gimme something.

"Where does Cassandra sleep?"

Denny's mind was caught up in a swirling maelstrom of thoughts. Her sense of self felt ragged, parts of her character drifting, falling, moving beyond her grasp. At the same time, she was aware of the minds of others. Not just Lanier, but the surviving staff, the elderly caretaker and the middle-aged woman who kept house. She also felt other presences, more distant but still part of the psychic network. These, she realized, were on the mainland. Cassandra had confederates in the village across the strait.

All very interesting, but where does she sleep?

Then Denny touched Cassandra's sleeping mind. It was dormant, or very nearly, but still frightening in its potential power. Denny reached out with her mind, clumsily trying to touch the Queen's mind without triggering a reaction. But she botched it, somehow. She felt the powerful alien consciousness stir slightly, then grip her own mind. She was bombarded by chaotic dreams. Violent images, cold and ruthless impulses, memories of monstrous acts, made Denny reel. She flinched away from the contact.

"Useless," she gasped. "Lanier, for God's sake, have you any idea where she sleeps? Is it in a locked room somewhere in the house?"

The old man stared at her for a moment, then shook his head. His mouth opened, but no words came, only a thin trickle of drool. She clutched at his hand, tried to probe his mind. Random thoughts, dull and confused, swirled at the edge of her perception. Then a recurring idea caught her attention. Lanier was trying to communicate.

Mountfalcon House was built on the site of a medieval monastery.

"Cellars," she said, surprised by the obviousness of the idea. "Cellars, catacombs, they must have had some underground spaces."

She stood up, releasing Lanier's hand, which fell limply back onto the old man's knees.

"Thanks, Charlie," she whispered. "Don't know if I'll see you again."

She looked around Lanier's study for something sharp or hefty enough to kill Cassandra in her sleep. There was nothing more dangerous than a crystal paperweight. But then she recalled the array of swords, axes and other medieval weapons fixed to the walls of the main hall.

If I can reach one without a ladder, I'll take it.

***

"Not easy, landing in the dark," Comstock shouted in Gould's headphones.

Even using the intercom, the racket from the engine and rotor blades almost drowned out his voice.

"You do surprise me," Gould replied, yelling. "I assume you've done it before?"

Comstock looked around from the controls of the helicopter.

"Couple of times," he shouted back. "Point is, it might be a tad bumpy. Brace yourself."

Gould looked down at the elaborate safety belts that held him into his seat.

Brace myself? How?

"He's messing with your head," put in Matheson, the most talkative of Comstock's team. "We'll be fine, he's got all sort of fancy night-landing gizmos."

The fourth man in the chopper, Collier, showed no sign of having heard the conversation. Collier was even more taciturn than Comstock. Gould had become garrulous during their journey from London partly as a reaction to long silences. Now, as they approached their destination, he could think of nothing to say.

"There it is," Matheson exclaimed, pointing.

There was a blur of light below them, and the aircraft circled it in a wide arc. The security lights of the house did not illuminate much. There was no sign of the helipad. But Gould saw that Comstock's helmet had what he hoped was a night-vision attachment.

"Okay," Comstock shouted. "I'll drop you guys as near the house as I can, then park this bus. Don't wait for me."

"You mean we're supposed to jump out?" Gould bellowed in dismay.

"All part of the fun, mate!" said Matheson, punching him playfully on the shoulder.

There is such a thing as too much enthusiasm, Gould thought.

***

The great house was a labyrinth of corridors, dead ends, and small rooms long since abandoned or filled with junk. As she explored the ground floor, Denny got the impression that, since Cassandra's takeover, everything had been devoted to her agenda.

Denny hefted a short sword that she had managed to remove from a display in the hall. The weapon had looked more fearsome on the wall, but she had deliberately chosen something small enough for her to wield. Now she was faced with the problem of finding her way underground. After repeatedly drawing a blank, she began to wonder if Lanier's clue had in fact been merely a random thought in the mind of a confused old man.

But if there's an entrance, it has to be big enough for Cassandra, and she's not small.

When she reached the kitchen, an idea from an old movie occurred to her. She recalled someone searching for a secret passage, detecting a movement of air. She found some matches and an old newspaper. She folded a couple of sheets of paper, set it alight, and held it up. The flame burned vertically. She dropped the blazing paper, stamped it out, and went into the corridor. She repeated the trick several times, feeling increasingly desperate.

But then the result she had hoped for came.

In a side passage just off the main hall, the flame flickered and smoked, almost went out. It led her along to a small door that she had already tried and found to be locked. Dropping her makeshift torch, she inserted the tip of the sword into a narrow gap between door and wall.

Let's see who breaks first.

***

Collier and Matheson easily outdistanced Gould as they sprinted for the house. Gould saw that the Task Force agents were trying to keep low, and take advantage of natural cover.

Why? We arrived in a helicopter, for God's sake. Interlopers aren't deaf or blind. I suppose that's the military mindset for you.

Gould resisted the urge to shout for them to wait, and was rewarded to find Matheson waiting on the threshold. The agent flicked on the flashlight attached to his carbine and grinned down at Gould as he ran panting up to the doorway.

"Here," he said, handing over a black plastic box. "Comstock says you shouldn't have a weapon, so just say I dropped it."

"Is this a taser?" Gould asked, turning the plastic box over in his hand.

"Yeah," Matheson replied, pointing at buttons. "This one turns it on, this one fires it. Shove it up against their body. Or their head, if you really don't like 'em."

Gould wanted to ask for more details but Matheson was already heading into Mountfalcon House. Inside they found Collier crouching by the staircase. The agents took out flashlights, as the house was in darkness. The flickering beams created moving shadows, and Gould clutched his taser more tightly.

"Right, we stick together from now on," Collier said. "Sweep the ground floor first. Gould, stay in the middle. You're less likely to get picked off there."

In the silent house, the clang of metal was loud, startling. The noise seemed to come from one of the two corridors that led out of the hallway, towards the back of the mansion.

"Okay," said Collier. "Now we know where to go."

"We're not waiting for Comstock?" Gould hissed, suddenly remembering the team leader.

"He's backup," Matheson said simply. "Also, he's waiting to guide in the bio-hazard gang."

This was news to Gould. He had a flashback to the wheels-within-wheels methods of the Romola Foundation, where nobody could ever be sure exactly what was going on. But before he could form a question, Collier had set off, and Matheson prodded him firmly in the ribs.

"Get going," Matheson hissed, "he hates sloppiness. And he's a got a gun."

"Message received," Gould mumbled to himself.

Bio-hazard gang, he thought. *Which implies they're going to try for live specimens.*

He remembered Trent's amiable, open features, his benevolent manner.

Sneaky little bugger. Wonder what else he forgot to mention?

***

The door yielded to the sword, and Denny paused a moment, waiting for a response to the noise. When she heard nothing, she pushed the door halfway open and shone her flashlight into the space beyond. She saw she had forced the entrance to a cellar, with steps leading down.

Been here before, she thought, recalling Malpas Abbey. *Maybe things have come full circle.*

With both hands full, she picked her way carefully down the stone stairway. The flashlight showed her a low-ceilinged room that had obviously been hacked out of the living rock centuries ago. At the far side of the cellar was a doorway,

The rough walls and ceiling were moist, and once a drop of cold water found the back of her neck. The drop found its way down to the symbiont, which twitched, sending a wave of alarm and confusion through Denny. She nearly fell, clutched at the wall, dropping her flashlight, which clattered down the steps and went out. The noise of the mishap echoed, seemed immensely loud.

Crap.

Denny waited a few heartbeats, waited for Cassandra's mind to focus on hers as the Queen came awake. But there was nothing, apart from a slight rustling sound. Denny thought of small animals moving in the dark.

Rats, maybe? Well, I've seen plenty of those. All those 'haunted houses'.

She groped her way down the stairs until she found her flashlight. After she had flicked the switch a few times, it came on. The blue-white radiance illuminated a pale, black-eyed face about three feet away.

Denny screamed, raised her sword, and lashed out clumsily. The blade was not quite long enough, and swung by the Interloper's face. The creature leaped back, clawed hands raised, then darted out of the light. Denny swung the beam around, trying to keep the pale figure in view. Then she saw another Interloper, and a third, all advancing rapidly from the doorway.

Sentries, she thought. *Of course, Cassandra wouldn't just sleep unguarded.*

She retreated upwards a couple of steps, waving the sword in what she hoped was a menacing manner. She noticed that the creatures trying to dodge out of the beam were all smaller than she was.

Immature. And with Cassandra asleep, maybe not too smart either? But how soon before she wakes up?

The nearest Interloper leaped up the steps, abandoning subtlety, charging straight at her. As she lunged at its face, Denny got a sudden flash of the creature's emotions, the way its killer instinct drove it to attack her. She saw herself through its eyes, all her features hideously distorted by its viewpoint. Her eyes were enormous, her skin dark and weirdly mottled, her nose a huge beak above a slit-like mouth.

Disoriented, Denny thrust at her assailant, hoping to do some damage. The Interloper seemed to hesitate, flailing its arms, deflecting the sword thrust. The steel point might have grazed the creature's shoulder, but now it went straight into its left eye socket. The Interloper screeched, clutched at the blade. Denny felt the agonizing pain of its wounds, felt it cutting its fingers as it pulled at the sharp steel.

We're getting each other's thoughts.

The other two Interlopers were closing in, but the narrowness of the staircase hindered them. One grabbed at its wounded comrade and pulled it off the sword, the blade coming free of the head with a sucking noise. The injured creature slumped sideways, fell to the cellar floor. Now Denny was seeing herself in stereo, and feeling the rage and disgust of the surviving guards. She tried to back up another step, misjudged the move, and fell on her ass. The nearest Interloper crouched, gathering itself for a leap.

"No!" she shouted, dropping her flashlight to hold up the sword with both hands, praying that the little monster would impale itself.

The leap never came. Instead, there was a deafening noise from somewhere above Denny. A small, dark hole appeared in the Interloper's low forehead, just above one eye. The creature jerked, stood upright, then fell backwards onto its comrade. A fusillade of shots followed, like claps of thunder, and both creatures tumbled down the steps. A welter of dark blood spread out on the cellar floor.

"Denny? Is that you?"

She looked around, dazzled by intense light. Dropping the sword, she shielded her eyes. The voice had seemed familiar.

"Ted?"

"That's Purcell, right?" said an unfamiliar British voice. "Give her a hand, Matheson, I'll cover you."

She felt strong hands lifting her, glimpsed a smiling stranger in camo gear, then saw Gould's worried face. Someone touched the symbiont as she was manhandled up the stairs. The creature reacted with a jolt of pain. She failed to suppress a scream.

"What is it? You wounded?" demanded the first man.

She shook her head.

"Worse than that," she gasped. "There's a – a creature, on my back. Ted's seen something like it before."

"A symbiont?" Gould sounded startled. "But they don't need them anymore."

Denny shook her head, tried to explain about the psychic link with the Queen. But before she could speak more than a few sentences, the vast, cool presence of Cassandra was suddenly in her mind again.

Chapter 10: Clash by Night

Comstock talked the second chopper down, then went to meet Trent, who disembarked wearing a full hazmat suit. He explained the situation, rounded up his second team, issued orders.

"Tania," he rounded off, turning to the one female member of the team, "make sure you're sweeping broadly with that thing, don't just point it ahead. These creatures are famous for ambushing people."

"Yes, sir," said the young woman, face invisible behind her filter mask. She held up a portable infrared scanner, then pointed it at Comstock. "I am just calibrating it now."

"Good, keep it up," Comstock said. "Okay team, no time for fancy stuff, we go in through the front door, back up the recon guys."

"Sir?" Tania held up the infrared device, a bulky tube with a pistol grip. It was linked to a tablet computer. "I'm getting something, it seems quite close."

Comstock frowned. Tania was pointing her scanner away from the house, towards the cliffs.

"It's very faint," she said, with an apologetic air. "But you said if I saw anything…"

"Could it be a bird?" he demanded.

"No, bigger than that. Size of a small adult, or a child."

"They could be behind us," Comstock snapped, swinging around and releasing the safety on his carbine. "Don't fire until you have a target."

"Remember," Trent added, "there are human beings here."

The only light came from the security lights of Mountfalcon House, about fifty yards away. It was too diffuse to make out anything on the cliff edge.

"Put some light over there," Comstock commanded.

A spotlight from the second chopper stabbed out, high overhead, then swept down in a wide arc over the wet grass.

"There it is!" someone shouted.

A pale face was caught in the light, vanished, then appeared again as the operator focused the beam. There was a crack of a shot, and the figure spun round, fell. It lay inert.

"I said no firing!" Comstock bellowed, running towards the fallen body.

He approached cautiously, keeping the prone figure covered, finger outside the trigger guard.

Unlike the moron who shot it. Just pray it's a Code Nine.

As he neared the small body it moved, raising itself up on one elbow. The pale face, dark-eyed under a mop of untidy black hair, peered up at Comstock.

"I guess you must be the good guys," said a woman's voice, weakly. "What with the guns and all."

American accent, Comstock thought. *Oh shit, it's the camerawoman.*

The woman slumped, face forward, into the grass. Comstock ran a little closer, reached out to check her pulse.

"Medic!" he yelled.

***

Denny struggled to speak as the Queen tried to take control of her. She sensed some alarm, but also a cold determination to fight, to survive.

And it not just Cassandra she sensed, but many more minds. These others were weaker, but just as alien, and just as hostile. She felt alarm, anger, and saw through a dozen pairs of eyes flickering lights at the far end of a tunnel. She felt herself bounding along, underground, determined to attack the intruders. Cassandra's children were going to defend their mother.

"There are lots more Lopers down here!" she croaked. "Queen's guards. They're coming."

"We can handle them," said Matheson.

"They see what I see, know what I know," she told him. "They outnumber you. Fall back, please!"

She saw hesitation in the big man's face. But the other stranger, who was clearly in charge, shook his head.

"We've got a good position here," he said, stepping aside from the cellar door. "We can hold them off while Gould takes you to the choppers."

"That a good idea, Denny," Gould said, putting an arm across her shoulder, then pulling back as she flinched.

"Close your eyes!"

Matheson's shout was followed by a metallic clink as he threw something onto the cellar floor. There was a bright flash, and a bang far louder than the earlier gunfire. Shock and pain from the Interlopers blended with Denny's own fear and confusion. She stumbled out of the cellar, leaning on Gould.

"They'll all die rather than let her be killed, or captured," she gasped. "And there's something else. Cassandra isn't afraid. Why is that?"

Gould shrugged, then flinched as a burst of shots rang out. Matheson and the other man were shouting at each other, spotting targets. There was a second flash and terrifying detonation from what Denny assumed was some sort of grenade. But in her mind's eye, she saw the Interlopers dodging, closing in on the staircase, even the badly wounded still moving, taking part in the attack until their minds blanked out.

"This symbiont," Gould said, half-carrying her along the passage to the entrance hall. "How long has it been attached?"

"Hours, just a few hours – I don't know, Ted, it's so hard to think," she mumbled.

"Zoffany worked it out, once," Gould explained, "the time factor. The longer it's attached, the more likely removal will kill the host."

Denny nodded, unable to speak. More pain, fear, rage washed over her.

"Do you want me to try and remove this one?" he asked urgently, stopping to look her in the face. "Improvise, cut it away?"

Denny was about to say 'No.' But then she thought of the way that pain was routed through the entire hive-mind of the Interlopers.

If it hurts me, it will distract them. Buy time, maybe.

Another burst of fire came from the cellar. There was more shouting amid the shots, and this time she detected a hint of panic.

"Okay," she said, forcing the words out, "let's...find...a knife. Kitchen."

"Wait," Gould said urgently, stepping around behind her. "I've got something here. It might do a cleaner job."

Denny felt him pull up her tee shirt.

"Oh God," he breathed. "They've evolved, all right. Okay, brace yourself."

***

"I'm out of bombs," said Collier.

"I can count," said Matheson, throwing his last stun grenade.

The metal cylinder bounced down the stairway, exploded in mid-air between two Interlopers. The creatures squealed, covering their eyes, blocking the way for three more attackers at the foot of the stairs. Between them the men shot three dead and maimed another. But the fifth got close enough to slash at Collier's face, gashing open his cheek, before Matheson finished it.

"Where's the cavalry?" Matheson gasped, reloading. "There are too many of the little sods."

"We're winning," said Collier grimly.

Matheson looked at the pale, slender bodies heaped on the cellar floor. It resembled the scene of a massacre, an atrocity he had witnessed and tried to forget. As the image of slaughtered children rose, unbidden, into his mind, one of the small bodies stirred, raised its head.

"Oh God," he breathed.

"Matty, shoot!" yelled Collier, as he removed an empty clip from his carbine.

Matheson stared, horrified, as a child's face gazed up at him. It was a little girl, one he had found quivering in terror under the corpses of her murdered relatives. He had tried to save her, but the girl's wounds had been too severe.

"For Christ's sake, man!" Collier bellowed, ramming in a fresh clip, and taking aim.

"No!" Matheson said, knocking the barrel of Collier's gun so that his shot missed.

The two men grappled as Collier tried to take aim again.

"It's a trick!" he shouted. "That's not a child, you know that!"

Matheson hesitated, confused, grappling with his memories. In that moment, a wave of Interlopers surged up the staircase. Matheson raised his gun, hit the first attacker in the face with the butt. Then the attackers were within reach. Matheson felt talons clawing for his eyes, heard Collier bellowing in anger and pain.

Suddenly, the attack stopped. The Interlopers stopped slashing and gouging at the men, and instead began to thrash around randomly. Some injured one another, a couple fell from the stairs onto the stone floor.

Like rats in a sack, Matheson thought.

"Come on," he said to Collier, who was clutching his throat, blood oozing between his fingers.

Matheson half-dragged his comrade out of the doorway and pulled it shut. As he did so, he saw Comstock leading the second team toward them.

"You took your bloody time," he complained.

"What happened?" Comstock demanded.

"Thought they had us, sir," Collier said. "Then they seemed to ... I dunno, go a bit haywire."

***

Denny leaned against the wall, clenching her teeth. She expected a searing pain, perhaps the sensation of being stabbed. Instead, the shock was more like a bludgeon smashing into her brain, crushing her sense of identity as her body jerked manically. The pain seemed unbearable, yet she did not black out. After what seemed an eternity of suffering all she could think of was the joy of oblivion that persisted in eluding her. And through it all, she felt the organism on her back shrinking, writhing, the tendrils it had embedded in her shriveling.

"That's it!" said Gould. "Did it work?"

"I ... maybe, I'm not sure," she admitted, struggling to her feet. "You could have just knocked it out."

The symbiont's pain was my pain. We were already one, at some level. But I don't want to believe that. I could be wrong. Need a second opinion, at least.

"It's still attached," he said dubiously. "But there's a medical team of some kind on the way. Maybe they can help."

Gould supported her as she staggered a few more paces, then they stopped at the sound of voices up ahead. Lights pierced the gloom in the corridor. More uniformed men appeared, and behind them people in what looked like spacesuits.

"Bit of help here!" Gould shouted.

Figures crowded around, Gould trying to explain, almost drowned out by more shots and detonations. The armed men rushed past them toward the cellar, leaving them to the white-suited, masked strangers.

"We found the other one," Denny heard, unable to identify the speaker. "She's alive, but in a bad way."

As they helped her out of the house, she struggled to extract some profound truth from the phrase. She knew it was there.

I'm the other one. Who's the first one?

"Frankie?" she asked. "Is Frankie alive?"

"Why?" Gould asked. "What happened? No, it's okay. Don't try to speak."

***

After she hit the water, Frankie was so badly winded that she thought she would drown. The freezing cold seemed to penetrate her bones in a few seconds as she thrashed her way back to the surface. She coughed out water, took in a lungful of air, and shook her hair out of her eyes.

A few yards away, Murphy was gazing at her. His face was upside down, his body contorted. He lay across a flat, black rock. As a wave surged over him, Frankie saw the foam turn pink with blood. She began to swim towards the rocks, aiming to pass Murphy. The cold was painful, now, and she was gasping for breath. It took her three tries to heave herself out of the sea. Her wet clothes seemed to weigh a ton.

She lay on a slab of sea-worn granite, spluttering, starting to shiver. Waves broke over her, and she suddenly wondered if the tide was coming in. If so, the rocks around her would soon be submerged. She rolled over onto her side, looked up. The cliff seemed unclimbable.

Even if I was in perfect condition, she thought, *I could never do it.*

A big wave hit her, and its backwash almost dragged her into the sea again. She got to her hands and knees and crawled towards the base of the cliff, wondering if she could clamber a few feet up.

If I can get above the tideline, I might have a chance.

Frankie tried not to think about the cold, which was intense enough to make her teeth chatter. She knew that vigorous exercise would at least generate some body heat, and tried to move faster. But the treacherous rocks, uneven and slick with weed, made progress difficult. It took her several minutes to get to the cliff base, climb a few feet higher, where she was no longer getting splashed every few seconds.

Now what?

The base of the cliff was a jumble of boulders, some of which were rough, sharp-edged. She forced herself to pick a way, still on all fours, as high as she could. She saw lights moving on the opposite shore.

Headlights, maybe half a mile away. Might as well be on the moon. No way to signal.

Then she looked along the waterline, both ways. To her left, which she thought must be north, the rocks petered out towards a small headland. There was no way she could get past it without swimming. To her right the rocks seemed to continue, a sprinkling of black dots against the gray, turbulent waters. Frankie recalled seeing a jetty of some kind in that direction.

Okay, got to go that way.

The intense cold did not let up, but it never quite became unbearable. As time passed, Frankie forgot everything except the rocks immediately ahead of her, the looming cliff to her right, the noisy, restless sea to the left. The symbionts, Denny's enslavement, the chase and the fighting, might have happened to someone else. The November night fell swiftly, slowing her progress still further. But eventually she rounded a small promontory and stopped to stare. A small red light was shining in the gloom ahead of her.

End of a jetty.

Frankie found herself in a small cove with a shallow beach. As her steps crunched on shingle, she wondered what to do next. She could make out a couple of boats tied up at the jetty. She climbed up onto the wooden platform and examined possible means of escape. One boat was small, with an outboard motor. The other was a sleek pleasure cruiser, almost a yacht.

Clothes. Warmth.

Frankie, still shivering, almost fell into the cruiser, stumbled around in the dark looking for the cabin entrance. Once inside she switched on a light, reasoning that it would not be visible from the house. Then she found the shower, set the dial to Hot, and finally dispelled the piercing cold that had tormented her.

After toweling herself dry, Frankie went in search of a change of clothes. She found some waterproof boating gear. She hunted for food but found nothing more than a candy bar, which she devoured in a couple of seconds. She also found a First Aid kit, took some painkillers, and put a dressing on her wounded leg. Then she started to examine the interior of the boat more carefully, wondering if there was anything that might help her.

She considered trying the radio to call for help, but soon gave up. She found a sharp knife in the galley. She searched drawers, hoping for some vital piece of data that might give her an edge. But there was nothing other than a folder of what looked like financial documents. Among them, she recognized Treasury Bonds, and their British equivalents.

A ton of cash, she thought, and this led to another idea. *I wonder how much of Lanier's money Cassandra has moved, siphoned off, whatever?*

Frankie shrugged off such speculation, focused on ways to help Denny. She could try to actually use the boat to cross the strait.

What then? What would the police say if I called and told them they had to raid Lanier's private island? So, I've got to go back.

The throbbing from her back had become more noticeable now that she had warmed up. Her leg wound was painful too. Tiredness vied with discomfort, and she had to resist the temptation to lie down in a bunk. Instead, she searched for food again. As she rummaged in the cabin, she became aware of a droning noise.

Could be an aircraft.

She went up on deck and paused, looking up at the cliff. She was about to start the long slog up the winding path when she heard a droning noise, somewhere out to sea. Peering upward, she saw a flashing light approaching.

A chopper.

She began to jump up and down, waving her arms, then stopped, crouched behind the cabin door, cursing herself. The most likely scenario was that Lanier had ordered his personal helicopter, perhaps to take Denny to another location. If Frankie did not try something now, she might not have a chance.

If they think I'm dead, she reasoned, *at least I've got the element of surprise.*

She stepped ashore, took a deep breath, and set off for the bottom of the cliff path.

***

"Let me talk to her," Denny pleaded. "Please, I've got to see her."

"Trent?" said Gould. "What harm can it do?"

Denny studied the short man who was apparently in charge. He seemed an unlikely leader of a military-style covert operation.

Not that it's been all that covert, she thought. *Anyone on the mainland must have seen the choppers land, and probably heard some shooting.*

Trent seemed to hesitate, then his smooth, plump features broke into a smile.

"Of course!" he said, warmly. "You are the reason we're here, after all. You and your brave friend."

The newcomers had already set up a tent. Inside, Frankie was being given an injection by a man in combat fatigues, and wearing a red-cross armband. The medic began to protest when Denny and Gould entered, but he fell silent at the mention of 'Trent's orders'.

Denny ran over to the stretcher Frankie lay on, grabbed her, kissed her on the forehead. Frankie laughed, playfully tried to shove her friend away. Denny looked at Frankie's arm, which was elaborately bandaged and dressed.

"They really shot you?" she said, aghast.

Frankie made a dismissive gesture, followed it with a raspy noise.

"Yeah, but some great medication is kicking in," she replied, "so I don't give a damn. I forgive them, yeah, that's it."

Denny laughed, then winced as the unaccustomed movement caused a spasm of pain from the symbiont. Frankie looked concerned, her jokiness evaporating in an instant.

"They can't take that thing off?" she asked, with a glance at the medic.

Denny shook her head.

"Gould zapped it with a taser," she explained. "It was ... not good. If they try to cut it away here–"

She glanced up at the medic, who remained stony faced.

"You still in touch with the Queen?" Frankie asked quietly.

Denny paused to think. She had not received any mental impulses from Cassandra since the jolt from the taser. But she was convinced that the creature nestling her shoulder blades was not dead. An occasional tingling up her spine, vague bursts of sensation, suggested that it was attempting to do something. But, Denny explained, it was definitely not channeling Cassandra's will.

"I think maybe it got lobotomized?" she added. "Or blinded, or something. It's impaired, anyhow."

"For now," Frankie said. "So, that means you can't find her?"

"Maybe not, but I guess I can give it a try."

Denny closed her eyes, tried to take deep, slow breaths. She saw nothing but darkness, and felt a mixture of frustration and relief. She wanted to help track down the Queen, but also to be free of Cassandra's influence. She was about to give up when she glimpsed a light in the darkness. It was a faint red pinpoint of light. It winked out as soon as she saw it.

"A red light," she sighed, opening her eyes. "Electric light, I think. Does that make sense?"

"Not to me," Gould admitted. "Unless she's looking at the helicopters, they've got red lights. But there's no way she could hijack one, surely?"

There was a pause, then Frankie sat bolt upright, suddenly seeming more focused.

"The boat," she exclaimed, and explained about the red light at the end of the dock. "Tell that Trent guy to get to down to the cove."

"There's no way," protested Gould. "Cassandra would have to pass the entire Task Force."

"No!" exclaimed Denny. "No, she wouldn't!"

The odd crossword pattern she had glimpsed in Cassandra's mind suddenly made sense. It was a map of the island, but not of the surface.

"There are tunnels right underneath us," she said. "Built all those centuries ago by monks, right? If there's only one place where you could get to a boat, it would make sense for the tunnels to reach it."

Gould was already shoving his way out of the tent, calling for Trent. The young medic hesitated, then left as well.

"They'll be too late," Denny said. "She was already on the dock."

A few minutes later, Gould returned with the news that Denny was right. The luxury cruiser Frankie had investigated was heading up the Welsh coast, fast. It was likely to reach landfall long before the nearest Coast Guard vessel could get to it.

"They can't, like, drop a bomb on it?" Frankie asked, speaking slowly. "Action movie. Kaboom!"

"Too late to call in the actual military," said a voice from the entrance. "And it would raise awkward questions with our political masters."

Trent was holding up the flap, still smiling benevolently despite what seemed to Denny like a massive failure.

"Guess you already have some explaining to do," Frankie said, cheerfully. "Lanier is gonna sue your ass."

Trent's smile faded.

"Ah, well," he said. "The situation with Sir Charles is...problematic. Good to see you both looking so well!"

Before Denny could ask about Lanier, the plump little man ducked out, letting the tent flap fall behind him.

"How so?" Denny asked Gould. "What's problematic?"

"The problem is, he's dead," said Gould. "The symbiont seems to have detached itself, and died. And Lanier expired with it."

Denny felt a sudden chill.

"You mean, Cassandra sent some kind of self-destruct order to it?"

Gould shrugged, not meeting her gaze.

"Maybe, or perhaps all the stress he's been through affected both him and his so-called Helper. The other enslaved humans Frankie mentioned seem to have gone with Cassandra, so we can't examine them."

"But this little monster on my back," Denny said, "could kill me with no warning. Maybe. And taking it off could kill me."

Gould reached out and laid his hand on hers.

"Hey," he went on, "we know quite a bit about these things, and Zoffany has experience of removing them, so if I can persuade Trent to let her–"

Denny jerked her hand back, eyes wide. She felt a wave of pain run up her spine, a nerve-tingling sensation. When Gould had been speaking, another Gould had seemed to speak in her head. It was a warm, human voice, nothing like the cold, imperious feel of Cassandra's thoughts.

I've got to keep her morale up, even if there's not much hope. Maybe Harriet could pull off a miracle.

"What you're saying is not what you really think, Ted," she said. "I can tell."

Gould looked puzzled, glancing between the two women. Frankie, too, seemed confused.

"When you touched my hand," Denny went on. "I touched your mind, somehow. I could read your thoughts."

Gould stood up, took a pace back, his face pale.

"But that's an Interloper ability," he whispered in horror. "How could you – I mean, we've never seen anything like this before."

"I doubt it's going to be much use," Denny said, trying to sound neutral. "But I noticed it with Lanier, earlier. I assumed it was the symbiont. Maybe it was something else."

"What's happening?" Frankie asked, her words slightly slurred, eyelids drooping. "You turning into a Loper, Denny?"

I don't know, she thought. *Maybe I am.*

Nightmare Resurrection

Chapter 11: Aftermath and Departure

"You're sure nobody else knows?" Denny asked.

Frankie shook her head.

"You, me, Ted, and Harriet," she said. Then, with a puckish expression, she added, "Sounds like a comedy show from the Seventies."

Denny had to smile. Frankie had recovered from her wounds, though she would apparently have a permanent stiff shoulder. Denny, by contrast, was still sleeping on her side and wearing baggy sweatshirts.

At this moment, the two were in a special infirmary unit under the Task Force's HQ. It had been hastily equipped under Zoffany's supervision after the doctor had been taken on as an expert consultant. Or, as Frankie had put it, she was 'the only doctor who knows how to carve up a Loper'.

Zoffany was currently examining Denny's symbiont. Occasionally Denny felt a twinge of discomfort. But the doctor, to her credit, seemed to have a light touch. In a mirror, which she had insisted upon, Denny watched as the woman probed the pulsing, slug-like creature with gloved fingers.

"The problem," Zoffany mused, "is that the little bugger seems designed to get its nerve endings into your spine as soon as possible. So even after a few minutes, it was probably too late to simply cut it away."

Denny made a noncommittal noise. It was no surprise to learn that Interloper enslavement was meant to be for keeps.

"But," Zoffany went on, "Ted's rather cavalier decision to zap it raises interesting questions. Unlike the first symbionts I encountered, this one has a fairly complex, if small, brain. And it's apparently suffered brain damage, meaning it can't function correctly anymore."

"Its hard drive is corrupted," Frankie put in, looking smug. "That's a trendy analogy, thought you needed one."

"Thank you, this old lady is suitably grateful," said Zoffany, with exaggerated politeness. "But the last time my laptop had a problem, it did not fix itself. Whereas this creature, it is slowly regenerating."

Denny raised herself up on one elbow and looked around at Zoffany.

"You mean Cassandra will be able to control me again?"

Zoffany raised her hands in a guarded gesture.

"It might not fully recover," she said. "Some of the growth I've observed could be just scar tissue—"

Denny reached out and took Zoffany's hand, resisting the doctor's attempt to pull away. Then, after a couple of seconds, she released the doctor's fingers.

"No need for that," said Zoffany, eyes downcast.

"You're sure it's regenerating," Denny said evenly. "But you're not sure if it will be a hundred percent. Fine. You could just say it, without any fancy jargon."

Zoffany stood up and, still not meeting Denny's eye, gathered up her medical instruments.

"What you call fancy jargon," she said, "is how human beings are, how we behave."

Zoffany walked over to the door, opened it, and then looked back at Denny.

"You're getting into the habit of using your power as a lie detector," she pointed out. "I don't blame you. But maybe we need some ambiguity, some uncertainty between us – just so we remain human."

After the door closed, Denny looked down at her hands.

"She's right," she admitted. "It's not human to touch someone else's mind. Not directly, anyway."

Gould nodded.

"All our art, culture, music, religion – the things they don't have, because they never had to invent them."

They fell silent. Denny found herself, not for the first time, listening for the thoughts of the other people in the room. But she heard nothing.

"So, what do I do?" she asked.

Frankie got up from her chair and sat on the bed next to Denny.

"Keep fighting," she said. "Keep searching for Cassandra. Keep doing what we do."

"Yes," Gould chimed in. "At least the Task Force are on the case."

Frankie grimaced and rubbed her shoulder.

"Yeah, right."

Gould reddened slightly.

"Okay, they're on a learning curve. But they're keen. And they can bring in more expertise, find new ways to deal with that thing."

Denny looked up at him.

"And if nobody can get this thing off without killing me, and I become unreliable, start to respond to the Queen's instructions, or simply act as her eyes and ears – what then?"

"Well, it might not come to that," Gould mumbled.

"If it does, I don't want to end up like Lanier," Denny said emphatically. "Classed as a victim of some – what was it? – terrorist attack, unknown militants. That's getting old."

"They'll keep using that one so long as people believe it," Frankie pointed out. "And Lanier was widely hated, you know that."

Without thinking, Denny reached out for Frankie's hand. Frankie flinched, began to pull her hand away, then stopped. They looked at each other for a long moment.

"See?" Denny said. "Already I'm like a leper to my friends. What happens when Trent and his oh-so-efficient outfit discover I'm a potential liability?"

"But – but I don't see what other options you have!" Gould spluttered. "You can hardly walk into a regular hospital and say 'I seem to have an alien life form on my back'."

"True," Denny said. "I'll have to deal with this my own way."

She stood up, crouched down carefully to avoid stressing the symbiont, and opened her bedside locker.

"I want to get dressed now," she said, without looking up. "Bit of privacy, please."

After the others left, she put on one of the loose sweatshirts Frankie had bought her, and a pair of old denims. She pulled on socks, a pair of old runners, and tied back her hair in a ponytail. In the bathroom mirror, she studied herself.

Like a regular professional woman on her day off, she thought. *On her way to the gym, maybe. Or the supermarket.*

She closed her eyes, focused again on a strange void in her mind that was not quite empty. In it, thoughts and memories sometimes formed, flickered into life, then died away. These impressions were as ephemeral as shooting stars, and as hard to see clearly.

Are you there? Am I imagining you?

She felt nothing but the cool, conditioned air on her skin. If Cassandra was able to touch her mind, she felt no hint of it. It was always when she was thinking of something else, half-asleep, or dreaming, that she felt sure the Interloper Queen was watching her.

Or I'm going crazy because I've got a monster on my back.

She opened her eyes, turned and craned her neck. She kept expecting to see a huge bulge under her clothes, making her look like Quasimodo. But, as before, the symbiont was well-hidden.

I don't need to stay here. I can go anywhere I like.

Denny went back into her bedroom and began to pack. When Frankie returned, she was ready to leave.

***

"You've got nothing? Seriously?" demanded Gould. "All these resources and you can't find her?"

Everyone in the Task Force office was intent upon their screens, but Gould had no doubt they were listening to his latest spat with Trent.

"Ted," said the little man, "it's not that simple. Much of our time and effort has been devoted to building our cover story over the Mountfalcon incident."

"You found the boat!" Gould protested. "How far could they have gone?"

Trent shrugged, his smile intact.

"We think the Code Nines are still in the UK," he said. "That's something."

Gould was about to demand more answers when Trent held up a small, plump hand.

"Now, Ted, I know you're new," he said, mildly reproving. "But this sort of thing should be dealt with at the daily team meeting. Shall we go through?"

Trent indicated his office. Gould snorted and followed his new boss. Zoffany and Comstock were already waiting for the meeting to begin. As Trent went through his usual amiable small-talk, Zoffany interrupted. Denny, she explained, wanted to leave. As if on cue, Comstock's radio crackled to life.

"She's being detained at the main entrance," he explained. "She seems very determined, sir."

Trent looked concerned for the first time that morning. He got up and set off to 'reason with our young friend', as he put it. Gould, following, could not help feeling amused by the site of the Task Force leader scuttling along.

He moves fast for a guy with little legs, he thought. *He's about Denny's height in fact. If it comes to fisticuffs, my money is on her.*

"She shouldn't leave, Ted," Zoffany said urgently. "Nobody knows what long-term effect that creature could have on her health. In an emergency, anything might happen."

"Maybe that's what she's afraid of."

Denny was remonstrating with two security guards. Frankie was there, obviously taking her friend's side. Hearing Trent calling her, she turned and looked at the little man with frustration, weariness.

"Tell your goons to let me out," she said. "Last I heard, I wasn't a criminal."

"No, Ms. Purcell," Trent said, holding up his hands in a placatory gesture. "And this is not a prison. You are of course free to leave–"

Denny glanced at the guards, opened her mouth to speak.

"But," Trent went on, "consider the risks of going out into a world that knows nothing of your – let us call it your unique conditions. As Doctor Zoffany has pointed out, anything could happen."

Denny shook her head, and Gould could tell she was not impressed by Trent's mild-mannered show of reasonableness. She picked up the bag that had been lying by her feet and slung it carefully over one shoulder.

"Let me out, Trent," she said. "Or get your heavies to forcibly put me in a locked room. Your choice."

Trent seemed unwilling to make the choice, instead stepping forward, hands fluttering.

"Can't we just talk about this?" he asked. "Give me five minutes of your time–"

Denny, clearly angry now, put up a hand as if to stop Trent. One of the little man's hands brushed hers. Denny's mouth fell open, her eyes widened, and she turned pale. She seemed to stagger, recover her balance.

Trent, seemingly startled by this response, stepped back a pace.

"What is it?" Frankie asked, taking her friend by the elbow. "You feel faint?"

Denny shook her head. She never took her eyes off Trent as she replied to Frankie.

"No, I'm fine, just frustrated. I need to go. Now."

Gould expected Trent to continue his attempts to change Denny's mind. But instead, the little man was looking oddly inert, his face expressionless, hands by his sides. For a second, Gould wondered if Trent was the one about to faint. But then Trent's face resumed its familiar, jovial expression.

"Of course, she must go if she insists," he said, speaking more quickly than usual. "What was I thinking?"

The guards immediately stepped back. One ran an ID card through a reader and the door clicked open. The traffic noise, a distant siren, the voices of passersby, all filled the corridor. Denny rushed out of the door without saying anything, vanished into the alleyway. Frankie, with a glance back at Gould, followed her.

"This is very reckless," moaned Zoffany. "It's not just metabolic harm, she could develop some kind of psychosis thanks to–"

Gould, anticipating what she was about to say, stepped heavily on his girlfriend's foot. She yelped, looked up at him.

"Sorry, darling," he said. "We're all a bit stressed, aren't we? Perhaps we'd better get back to our meeting."

Trent looked from Gould to Zoffany and back.

"Yes," he said brightly. "When in doubt, have a good old chinwag."

***

"You're going back to the flat, right? Right?" Frankie said, half-jogging to keep up with her friend's rapid stride.

"Yeah, for now," Denny replied. "Thought I might get out of London, maybe hole up somewhere."

"You're not going back to the States?" Frankie asked. "No, stupid question."

She could hardly sit in a cramped airline seat for eight hours.

"No," Denny said, still not looking at Frankie, "maybe take a train somewhere. Get myself lost."

Despite a steady, chill drizzle, the streets were crowded. Frankie almost collided with a couple of teenage girls as she tried to get around in front of Denny.

"Goddam it, stop for a minute!" she shouted. "I want to talk."

Denny stopped, looked down at her.

"I need to get away," she said. "I won't let them treat me as a lab rat. Now, can we try and get a cab? That's always fun."

Denny started walking again, more slowly this time.

"I might have stayed close by," she went on. "But now I know – I can't."

"Why?" Frankie asked. "What changed? And what are you going to do, for Christ's sake?"

"Can't talk freely in public," Denny said. "Wait till we're alone."

***

The meeting began with Gould outlining his research into what he dubbed 'talismanic crystals'. It was a short outline, as he admitted he had made little progress. He ended with a plea for better facilities, and better qualified assistants.

"We'll see what we can do," Trent said, beaming benevolently. "Now, Harriet – I take it your conclusions on the symbionts did not exactly fill Ms. Purcell with joy?"

Understatement of the century, thought Gould as Zoffany, looking flustered and unhappy, outlined her conclusions.

"So," said Trent, "we are not making a great deal of progress on the science front, and we have lost our one and only specimen of a symbiont."

"In much the same way that your crack squad lost Cassandra," Gould pointed out, annoyed on Zoffany's behalf.

"Quite," Trent said, turning to Comstock. "Any progress on that front?"

The security chief gave a brief shake of the head.

"So much of Lanier's money was transferred into cash or other hard-to-trace forms that the Code Nines could be lying low anywhere. But they can't remain hidden for long. Not in a country this size, with such a large population."

"Of course," Trent said, his manner still upbeat. "And what do you think their next move will be?"

Comstock paused, tilted his head to one side.

"Cassandra almost succeeded with Lanier – rich, influential, but vulnerable. I would expect her to try something similar, perhaps with a politician, general, senior civil servant. That kind of target."

"I agree," said Trent. "It is at the top of the social pyramid that we will find the Code Nines. We will focus our attention on the commanding heights of finance, government, and so forth."

"Great," grumbled Gould. "The people with the most influence, who are most likely to get this outfit disbanded if we mistakenly kick their front doors in."

Comstock looked mildly annoyed at that, but clearly thought better of responding.

"Good point, Ted!" Trent said. "Which means we will have to be careful to kick in the right doors, hmm?"

***

"Okay, so you don't trust them," Frankie said, watching Denny fill a bag. "Me neither. But what makes you think going off alone will help? Don't you need someone to watch your – I mean, offer some support?"

Denny paused in her folding of clothes to sigh.

"The phrase 'watch your back' is not off-limits," she said. "But the way you feel now, tiptoeing around me, not sure you want to actually let my skin touch yours? That's not how I want it to be. We'd drive each other crazy. We need some time apart."

Denny resumed packing while Frankie paced, then sat down and ran a hand through her short hair.

"Denny," she said. "What will you live on? What will you do for money, have you thought of that?"

"I've got some money saved," Denny replied. "Enough for a month or two, maybe."

"And then what?"

Denny closed the bag, swung it off the bed and placed it by the door. She turned to face Frankie.

"Then I'll think of something," she said. "Maybe I'll change my mind, come back. Maybe I won't."

Frankie got up, started to move towards Denny, then stopped. Denny nodded.

"And there it is again," she said sadly. "Out there, among the uptight British, I'll be getting a lot less of other people's feelings shoved into my head."

"Is that all?" Frankie demanded. "Because I get the feeling there's something else."

Denny turned her back and opened the closet, sorting out more clothes.

"I can't take everything," she muttered. "But I can't decide what to leave behind. Always the way, huh?"

"What happened with Trent?"

Denny did not seem to have heard the question, continued whisking clothes along the closet rail.

"I said–"

"I heard you!" Denny snapped, looking over her shoulder. "You were there, you saw what happened."

Frankie walked up behind Denny, who turned to face her.

"You got a flash of what he was thinking," Frankie said. "Care to share?"

Denny shook her head.

"You won't tell me?" Frankie asked. "Or you got nothing?"

Denny took a step closer, and stopped. She raised a hand, turned it over as if it was a strange, new appendage.

"I touched him for less than a second," she said, wonderingly. "And, at first I thought there was nothing. That it didn't work. But then I realized I was sensing something. Like nothing I've ever experienced before."

Denny reached out suddenly, took Frankie by the wrists.

"I need to know you believe me," she explained. "When I touched Trent I didn't sense anything human. Instead, it was like a void. Huge and dark and cold, like I imagine the space between the stars must be."

Frankie tried to pull free, but Denny had gripped her too tightly.

"I thought Trent was nothing, a nobody, an absence of being," Denny went on, staring intently into Frankie's eyes. "But then I realized that void, that total darkness, was alive somehow. It sensed me. It knew I was aware of it. And it started to reach out–"

With a frantic effort, Frankie pulled herself free, stepped back.

"You're saying Trent is a Loper? Is that it? Because that makes precious little sense."

Denny shook her head sadly.

"That's not it. He's not a Loper. The point is that he may not be human either. I didn't sense any mind at all. I ... I don't know, maybe this damn thing misfired, somehow. Maybe some people are immune to telepathy or whatever power it is, like some can't be hypnotized. But I would wager everything I have that Trent is not a normal man. There's something wrong there. And I want to get away from it."

"And from me," Frankie said quietly. "And what about Cassandra? Are you just giving up, bugging out? Maybe letting them win?"

Denny paused, then resumed taking clothes out of the closet, throwing them onto the bed.

"Remember how I got this thing on my back?" she asked. "I believed a guy who offered to help me beat the Lopers. Just bear that in mind if you pitch in with the Task Force. That's all I'm saying."

"Not quite," said Frankie. "You're also saying goodbye."

Epilogue: The Bottom of the Pyramid

Jack Munby brushed a cockroach from his desk with distaste, sighed and reached down to open a drawer. Inside was a bottle of cheap Scotch he had been given for Christmas by a well-meaning relative. January was five days old, and the bottle was nearly empty.

This place is going down, he thought, looking around his dismal office. *Going down in flames, financially speaking.*

Moment of Truth was a charity supposedly devoted to helping the poor and marginalized. It took its name from its founders' belief that, if young people could be confronted with the reality of their situation, they could be shocked into turning their lives around.

Trouble is, nobody's going to turn Moment of Truth around.

Munby found it bitterly ironic that he was now facing just the kind of poverty he had spent so long fighting. Small charities always scrabbled for funding, and lately all the usual sources of money had dried up. Times were hard.

"Too hard," he said bitterly.

A knock startled him. His door was half open, and standing just inside was a middle-aged woman with graying hair.

"Sorry!" he exclaimed, spilling the whiskey as he sat upright. "I didn't hear – I mean, can I help you?"

"I hope so," said the woman, walking in. She showed no sign of noticing as Munby shoved the bottle back in the drawer, along with the half-empty glass.

"Please take a seat!" he said, indicating a chair whose stuffing had just begun to escape. "Sorry for the mess, I was trying to sort out some paperwork, Miss ...?"

He waited for the woman to volunteer her name. She sat, smiled thinly.

"Jones," she said. "Fiona Jones. I represent a private benefactor who is very interested in your work here, Mister Munby."

Munby blinked, stared at the stranger. A few scenes from feel-good Christmas movies played in his head. He dismissed the idea of a guardian angel, albeit reluctantly. Fiona Jones seemed an unlikely savior, anyway. The woman was stooped, as if suffering from arthritis or some other illness of ageing. Yet she seemed about forty-five or fifty.

Perhaps this benefactor makes a point of employing disabled people, he thought.

"I'm pleasantly surprised," he said. "Moment of Truth is – well, I'm not giving away any secrets when I say we might have to close down soon."

Ms. Jones nodded sympathetically.

"My employer understands perfectly," she said, enunciating her words rather stiffly. "She is very keen to meet you and establish a lifeline for your splendid charity."

I wonder if she's in pain, Munby thought. *Poor woman. She does not look well.*

"Wonderful!" he exclaimed, feeling elated, but also a little cautious. "I'd be happy to talk to your – erm, what is the lady's name?"

"She is a very wealthy philanthropist," Jones said, still speaking with difficulty. "But wishes to remain in the background. However, if you are willing to come and meet with her, she will explain what she has in mind?"

"Of course!"

Munby jumped up, grabbing his jacket.

"No time like the present, eh? Is the lady staying in a hotel?"

Jones shook her head.

"She has purchased a business premises on the outskirts of town," she explained. "She has an office there."

Munby frowned, thinking back over the last few weeks. He had not heard of any new companies setting up in the area. All the news had been of business closures, job losses, a bleak economic outlook. The town of Fordham was dying on its feet. It was hard to believe anyone would put money into the place.

Still, if she's a bit secretive, it might not have been picked up by our local rag.

A few minutes later, Munby was driving out of central Fordham towards the old industrial areas, where derelict factories were in various stages of decay. Jones directed him to a site where refrigerators had been manufactured until a few years ago.

"This place?" Munby said. "Is it safe?"

"It is quite safe," the woman replied.

Jones got out and unlocked the graffiti-covered gates, and locked them behind them when Munby steered his ageing Ford inside. He got out and followed her to a side door, where she had to undo another padlock.

"From the outside, you'd never guess anyone had bought the place," he said, more to make conversation than anything else.

"Inside it is different," Jones said, closing the door behind them.

The doorway to a short passageway. Munby felt a sudden, humid heat and undid his jacket. Jones led him through another door, and they were inside the factory. He looked up to see the stained and broken panels of the glass roof, then around at the debris of a failed industry. Again, there was no sign of revitalization.

"Do many people work here?" he asked. "Or is it a skeleton staff?"

"The office is up there," Jones said, gesturing to a rusted iron stairway. "I will show you the way."

As they clanked up the rackety stairs, Munby began to feel dubious about the whole venture. He wondered if this was some kind of elaborate scam. Then it occurred to him that nobody knew where he was. He took out his phone, wondered if he should send a text to his part-time assistant. Then he decided against it.

No need to bother her, she's probably out with her kids.

Just as he thought of children, he saw small, pale figures running along the gantry above him. Munby could not make out if their gender but got the impression of long, dark hair. He glimpsed a pale face, tiny black button eyes. Then they were gone.

"Are there children here?" he asked. "Surely it's not safe, will all this junk?"

"She will explain," Jones said. "Here. She is waiting."

Jones stood to one side of the door of a small office, where presumably the plant supervisor had once overlooked the factory floor. The windows had been whitewashed over and the interior was dark. Munby stepped forward, hesitated in the doorway. An unusual smell washed over him, musky and intense.

"Hello?" he said. "Is there a problem with the light?"

"She has a condition that makes her sensitive to light," Jones said in her stilted way. "Please, go inside."

From the dark office came a sound like a moan. There was a peculiar squelch, and the musky smell grew stronger. Then someone spoke.

"Come inside, Jack. I've been waiting for you."

Munby felt sudden fear, a sense that everything he had assumed was wrong. Instinct told him to turn and flee. But as he spun around, he saw that Jones was no longer alone. On either side of the woman, pale, naked figures were advancing.

Oh God, they're not children. Not human children, anyhow.

He recoiled, tripped, fell heavily inside the office. The pale creatures bounded forward, stopped to crouch on the threshold, peering at him.

"Don't be afraid," said the deep, resonant voice behind him. "We will not harm you."

Munby felt himself lifted by hands that seemed preternaturally strong. The pale creatures scampered into the room. He began to struggle, but the creatures gripped his arms, pinned them to his sides. He felt their sharp talons through his shirtsleeves. Terror made him start to cry out and kick violently.

"Don't struggle," warned the voice. "It will be easier."

The unseen speaker lifted him off his feet and turned him round in mid-air, as easily as an adult might move a small, fractious child. In the gloom, Munby could just make that he was gripped by huge, fleshy arms. Then he was dragged over the uncarpeted floor into the darkness in the corner of the room.

"Now," said the voice, "let us give you a Helper, and then we can begin."

Some twenty minutes later, Munby awoke to a new life. The pain, previously intense, was fading now that he had stopped resisting. Now the plan, so vital to the survival of the hive, was becoming clear in his head.

Yes, he said, as the Queen probed his mind for contacts, opinions, details. *Yes, it will work. This town has hundreds of lost children. Few will notice when the process begins.*

Beside him, in the dark, he felt the Queen's vast body give a shudder as she expelled another egg. Her complacent thought filled Munby's mind.

Few humans will notice. And none will care.

* * *

Nightmare Spawn
Nightmare Series Book 5

Nightmare Spawn

Prologue: Moment of Truth

"Where's the soup kitchen gone, Rusty?"

Keith looked up in puzzlement at the facade of the Methodist Hall. The building was locked, for the first time since Keith had started sleeping rough. Soup with the Methodists was one of his weekly routines. But lately things had been going awry.

"First the Quakers went, now this."

He looked down at his dog, Rusty, who peered back up at him from beneath a fringe of shaggy brown-and-white hair.

"They were always nice, the Methodists," Keith said forlornly. "Always gave you a bit of toast, didn't they? Even a bone sometimes. And those little cakes they had."

Rusty gave a happy bark at the mention of food, then whined a little. The dog was expecting to go inside. For the second time, Keith reached up and rattled the door handle. It was still locked. He shuffled awkwardly in his oversize shoes, felt the damp newspaper lining yield with a squelch.

Stupid, he thought. *I look stupid doing that. An idiot.*

Keith glanced around, but there were few people passing. Those that did look at him quickly glanced away. He was used to that. Not looking at homeless people was, he had long since worked out, a way of pretending that they were not there at all.

But I am here, and I'm hungry. And so's Rusty.

It was cold, damp, and light was fading fast. He suspected it was February, though he was not sure. Certainly, it had been a long while since he got Christmas dinners from the various charities. At the thought of turkey, cranberry sauce, roast potatoes, Keith's stomach rumbled. Rusty whined again, gave a sharp bark that told Keith somebody was coming.

"They closed then?"

Keith looked round to see Karen pushing her lopsided shopping cart toward them, rattling along the uneven pavement. The trolley was full of odd items, ranging from empty cereal packets to a broken doll. Karen was much more confident than Keith. He recalled someone calling her 'articulate'. And she was built like a truck. But he figured it really meant she was better at talking than most people who lived on the streets.

"Yes," he said. "No soup."

Karen frowned up at the meeting hall.

"No notice on the door," she said slowly. "You'd think there'd be a notice. If they'd changed the day."

Keith, who could not read, had never thought about notices. He felt a sudden surge of hope. Karen was clever enough to sort things out for him and Rusty. She could be aggressive, even violent sometimes. Keith knew this was because of problems in her head, but could never remember the hard words for them. But most off the time, Karen was honest and kind, and among the street people in the town of Fordham, she was respected.

"Reckon we'll have to find somewhere else for Thursday nights," Karen said, sounding unhappy. "You'd think the buggers would have let us know."

Just then, the door that Keith had rattled twice was unlocked, and a woman looked out. She was smallish, gray-haired, and slightly stooped. To Keith she looked a bit like a street person; she was wearing a jacket that seemed too big for her. For a rough sleeper, that was normal, because you always wore lots of layers in winter. For a normal person, someone with a home, it seemed a little odd.

"Good evening!" said the woman. "I'm so sorry to keep you waiting. Do come in!"

Keith had never seen the woman before, and was never prone to trust strangers. But along with her appearance, a waft of flavor had drifted out the door and into the cold street.

Rusty barked again.

"Yes," he said, smiling down at his friend. "Soup. Smells like chicken."

"Oy, Keith! Give us a hand!" Karen said, already trying to work her trolley full of junk up the three steps to the doorway.

Keith sprang into action, taking one end of the basket and lifting it up to the doorway. The gray-haired woman looked dubiously at them for a moment, then stepped aside. Between them, Keith and Karen manhandled the cart inside. Keith found himself staring down at the broken doll. He was never sure if it was the same doll every time, could never remember. This one had part of its face smashed in, an eye missing. It was wearing a stained blue dress, the bright color just making the damage seem all the sadder.

"You leave her alone," Karen warned, moving a checked tea towel up around the doll's neck, like a blanket. "She's in a different world to you."

Keith backed away at once, almost stumbled as Rusty suddenly jerked at the leash, barking frantically. The dog had taken a dislike to the gray-haired woman, who stepped back, holding up her hands.

"It's all right," Keith said, smiling. "He just gets a bit funny sometimes."

"Never mind that," Karen put in. Then, to Rusty, "Shut up that racket, you!"

The dog curled his tail between his legs and retreated behind Keith.

"Right," Karen said, "where's the usual lot? The minister, the black chap, the girl with the big teeth? I know them, I don't know you."

"You can call me Fiona," said the woman. "Fiona Jones."

Karen snorted, gestured at the long tables set out in the middle of the hall. There was nobody sitting at them. Normally, Keith recalled, there would be at least a dozen other rough sleepers getting a hot meal.

"Well, Fiona Jones," she said, "what's going on?"

Fiona Jones made her calming gesture again.

"The local Methodist church, like several others, have handed over this particular facility to us."

Karen put her big, meaty hands on her hips.

"Us? And who's this 'Us'?"

The gray-haired woman pointed up and past them, at the wall above the entrance. Keith turned and saw a big banner, white with bright red letters. As usual, the letters seemed to jump about, blur, shift. Words never behaved themselves when Keith looked at them.

"Moment of Truth?" Karen exclaimed, turning away from the banner. "You took over from the Quakers, and that Hindu lot."

Fiona Jones gave a peculiar shrug, as if someone had just prodded her in the back.

"We are very busy in Fordham, yes," she said quickly. "But please, would you like to help yourself to soup, bread? It's all laid out."

Keith felt his stomach churn with hunger again. He looked at where Fiona Jones was pointing, saw a large metal urn, trays, bowls, spoons, slices of bread. He shuffled towards it, and Karen followed a moment later. Rusty had recovered his confidence and, tail wagging, looked up eagerly at Keith. Keith, in turn, looked furtively at Fiona Jones.

"By all means give your little doggie a bowl, too," she said.

This was more generous than the Methodists had been. But somehow, Keith felt it was not right, another thing that had changed since last week. Still, Rusty seemed to enjoy the soup, and while Keith ladled out another bowl for him, the woman did not object. As he put the bowl on the floor, he noticed that the whole area around the table with the food was covered with a plastic sheet.

In case people spill the soup, he thought. *People can be messy. And Rusty doesn't have manners.*

"Come on, short-arse, get your own soup," said Karen. "There's a queue, you know."

Keith felt a slight flash of anger at the jibe about his height. It was not his fault that he was small, any more than he could not help understand writing. But he knew better than to argue with Karen.

After he had got his first helping, he carried the tray carefully to the table and ate it quickly, mopping up the last of the soup with bread. He looked questioningly at Fiona Jones, who nodded.

"Of course, you can have seconds, thirds – we've got plenty!"

"Enough for a dozen people," grunted Karen, sitting opposite Keith. "So how come there's nobody else tucking in? All the homeless gone to Pizza Express or something?"

Fiona Jones smiled down at Karen, and again gave her odd shrug. Keith wondered if she was ill. He could not really blame Rusty for not liking her.

Nightmare Spawn

"We, at Moment of Truth, have been very successful at helping the homeless, along with other less fortunate members of the community," said the gray-haired woman. "Quite a few of the people you know now live at one of our special homes. We provide a bed, washing facilities, fresh clothes. Now if either of you would like–"

Karen interrupted, voice echoing loudly in the hall.

"You can stuff all that," she declared. "I don't go inside, don't hold with indoors. I'm all right on my own."

"Nobody can force you to join us, of course," Fiona Jones said smoothly. "We seek willing converts only."

Karen snorted, clattered her spoon into the empty bowl, then got up and stumped back to the table with the soup container. Keith wanted to ask about the new charity, but was afraid of Karen's scolding. The hall was not especially warm, but felt good.

It would be nice to be indoors, at least until the winter's gone.

A rattling noise made him look down to where Rusty was licking the last of his soup, shoving the bowl around the floorboards. He could not go anywhere without his only real friend. Keith looked up at Fiona Jones, and tried to ask a question about Rusty. But the words, always hard to find, were not there at all.

"Are you all right, young man?" the gray-haired woman asked.

Keith tried to speak again, but now everything he could see was misbehaving, shifting around crazily like words on paper. He tried to stand up, but failed and slumped back onto the bench. There was a crash of crockery breaking from the direction of the soup urn. Keith tried to turn around to see if Karen was all right, but instead he slumped forward. Head resting on the table, he watched Fiona Jones walk to the back of the hall and open a door.

The creatures that emerged were small, the biggest of them only about Keith's size. Their skin was unnaturally pale, and their faces looked half-finished, tiny black eyes above blunt muzzles. Their mouths were wide and black, and full of teeth. Keith tried to count the creatures, but they moved quickly out of his sight. He heard frantic barking, snarling, and then a yelping that made his heart go far too fast. Again, he tried to move, but failed. There were tearing sounds, slobbering noises.

Something sharp touched the back of his head. More sharp things moved slowly through his scalp. Then his hair was grabbed, his face lifted up. He looked at one of the nightmare beings, saw its little, deep-set eyes glinting. He sensed its hunger, smelled a sour scent, and heard its quick, panting breaths. The mouth opened, revealing a circle of needle-like teeth.

Monsters! The monsters have come for me.

"Yes," said the monster in a high, mocking voice. "We have."

The face changed. The tiny black eyes expanded, bulging out, while the muzzle shrank back until something like a human face was there. A nose appeared, nostrils forming, while lips appeared around the new-made mouth. Keith thought the creature looked like a kind of cartoon, a face simpler than a real person. But then it became more lifelike. And familiar.

No, no it can't be me!

He saw his own face looking back at him. It wasn't like looking in a mirror, because the other Keith had no stubble, no dark half-moons under his eyes, no smudges of dirt on his skin. Fear vied with outrage as Keith struggled to move his leaden limbs, make his numb lips speak.

You're not me!

"No!" agreed the other Keith. "I'm better in every way. And I'll be a useful member of society."

The imposter stood up and stepped back, still holding Keith's head up by his hair. Three of the other creatures were clustered around a mound of dark clothing on the floor. A moment later, Keith realized it was Karen, and that most of her head was gone. The three little monsters looked up, muzzles bloody, fragments of gray stuff falling from their mouths. They made hissing noises and started to move towards him.

"Keep it on the sheet, remember," he heard Fiona Jones say. "Keep the blood and brains on the sheet."

The interloper gripped him by the collar of his coat, pulled him roughly off the bench, then dragged him across the floor.

As he reached the blood-covered sheet, he saw a nondescript lump of bloody fur lying nearby. It was brown and white, splashed with red. For a moment, Keith forgot his terror and emitted a low moan of anguish. Then he felt sharp teeth cutting into his scalp, felt his skull splintering, and there was no room for anything but terror and pain.

Nightmare Spawn

Chapter 1: Rustbelt

Denny woke up to sunlight streaming through her apartment window. The sun, she thought, seemed high above the London skyline.

Did I sleep late?

She rolled over, checked the clock radio by her bed. It was after nine, late for her. She stretched luxuriously, and lay sprawled on her back for a few delicious moments. Then she threw back the covers and got out of bed. She shoved her feet into bright green Kermit slippers, which had been a joke Christmas gift from Frankie.

Something's wrong.

Denny paused, frowning. She listened. There was the familiar roar of London's rush-hour traffic, a sound double-glazing could only muffle but never exclude. The bedroom seemed normal enough, with yesterday's clothes flung casually over a chair.

Sorry Mom, she thought, standing up and pulling on an old sweatshirt, slightly newer sweatpants. *Still not tidy.*

The sounds of breakfast filtered through from the nearby kitchen. Denny smiled, thinking of toast and coffee, wondering if Frankie had been out for doughnuts. She caught sight of herself in the mirror above the dresser, paused, tidied her hair a little, stuck out her tongue.

"Sleepyhead. Nothing's wrong, you're just a ditz."

In the kitchen, Frankie had already laid out toast, coffee, juice. She smiled up at Denny, mimed clapping.

"At last!" Frankie exclaimed. "The Sleeping Beauty has awoken."

"Your mock applause is greatly appreciated," Denny said, slumping into a chair. She surveyed the breakfast table. "Now, where's that amazing Scottish marmalade?"

Frankie did not reply. Denny looked up.

"Fancy marmalade?" she asked again. "We didn't finish it, did we?"

Frankie remained silent. Denny stopped buttering her toast, smiled uncertainly.

"Cat got your tongue?"

Frankie smiled back. But it was not her usual shy, lopsided smile. It was too wide. Frankie's face was changing, too, growing paler, her nose flattening, eyes shrinking as they retreated into deepening sockets. Denny sat frozen in horror as the Interloper revealed itself, rising from its chair, gathering itself to leap across the kitchen table.

"Gonna get your tongue," rasped the creature. "And all the rest."

Denny raised her knife to ward off the attack, but her hand moved far too slowly. The vicious maw of the Interloper was closer, closer, as the creature hurled itself toward her, black-taloned claws reaching for her face.

"Hello? Are you in there?"

Denny jerked awake, fragments of the nightmare already drifting away, leaving only a sense of bleakness, loneliness. She was lying on her side in a rented room, her bed a pull-down, her body covered with an old tartan rug.

A tentative knock at the door. Again, a feminine voice spoke.

"Hello? Are you in there?"

"Just a minute!" Denny called, dismayed by the croak of her voice.

Lousy cold, she thought. *Goddam dismal British winter. Lasts forever.*

She levered herself upright, careful not to move too quickly, anticipating the spasm of pain from Jabba. She had given the damaged symbiont a nickname that seemed apt for a fat slug. Satisfied that the creature was happy with her slow, cautious movements, she got up and padded across the threadbare carpet to the door.

Let's see the latest client, she thought, wincing in the light of the naked bulb in the hallway.

"Erm, are you the – the psychic lady? The American?"

American. I'm in a town where that has novelty value.

Denny Purcell looked up at the young woman. Her latest client was typical of the people who came to see her. They tended to be female, somewhere between thirty and fifty, with a careworn expression. This one, Denny estimated, was near the younger end of that range. The client was also taller than average, and overweight, bordering on obese. As the woman ran a hand through purple-streaked hair, a ring glinted.

Married, engaged, divorced, whatever, Denny thought. *It's usually man trouble. Let's see.*

"I'm Denny," she said, extending her hand. "And you are?"

"Trisha," said the woman, looking at Denny's hand dubiously.

Come on, come on, Denny said, beaming fixedly at the woman. *I can't do it unless…*

"Nice to meet you Trisha," she said.

After another heartbeat, Trisha took the proffered hand. Denny clasped the woman's plump fingers, gave a perfunctory shake, and withdrew her hand. The wave of impressions she received in the moment was more powerful than usual. Not by any means overwhelming, but strong. Denny steadied herself against the doorframe, then withdrew a couple of paces, gesturing Trisha inside. She could not trust herself to speak. She got a few facts, such as Trisha's age, her job, her difficult background. But, as with most people, emotions were dominant, mere reason driven to the margins by turbulent feelings.

Oh God, a bad one. Worse than she knows, maybe. So much of this is buried, half-acknowledged. So much self-deception.

"Come in," she said, flicking on the light. "Sorry about the mess."

Trisha looked around dubiously, but after hesitating, she did as Denny asked and sat down on a shabby armchair. Denny pulled up a small stool and sat opposite the woman, just a couple of feet away.

"I've never done this before," said Trisha. "But my friend Sushila said you were really good when she asked you about – you know."

Denny nodded.

Sushila just needed to be told what she already knew, that an intelligent, professional woman can find herself a husband without endless interference from her family. But this is a bit more complicated. Telling Trisha what she already knows could lead to a meltdown.

"First, a warning," she said. "I can offer insights into your life, like the decisions you might make, or how you got here. I can give advice. But I'm not a miracle worker. If you want your life to change for the better, it's up to you."

Trisha nodded.

"It's about – I've sort of started this relationship, with a new guy? And I really like him, but–"

Denny raised her hand, gently waving the woman to silence.

"Wayne is not a nice man," she said. "Your friends don't like him, neither does your mother. But it's more than that, isn't it?"

Trisha's eyes widened as Denny went on, revealing everything she had gleaned from the brief moment of contact.

"He nearly hit you. Not quite, but nearly, after he'd been drinking. Sure, he apologized, he said he was sorry. But he likes controlling you, doesn't he? He's started telling you what not to wear. He's jealous when you talk to other men. And the way he looks at Chelsey bothers you, doesn't it?"

"He's never done anything to her!" exclaimed Trisha.

"Did I say he had?" Denny asked gently. "But you worry that he might. She's thirteen going on thirty, and she likes acting out, and you argue a lot. And he takes her side, doesn't he? He flatters her a little, jokes around? And you wonder what he does when you're not there."

Trisha's bottom lip was quivering.

"You've got a dirty mind, you have!" she whimpered, but she could not look Denny in the eye.

"Deep down, you know the guy's poison!" Denny said, reaching out to take Trisha's damp, flabby hands between hers. "You don't believe you deserve to be loved by a good man. You think all you can get is garbage like Wayne. Believe in yourself, girl!"

Denny heard her words twice, once in her head, and again in the other woman's. Trisha was afraid, confused, and so desperate for love that she struggled to acknowledge a threat to her own daughter. She saw Denny as a stranger, pretty but oddly stooped for a young woman. Someone passing judgment on her, making her out to be stupid. A hectoring man-hater, not a helpful adviser.

She doesn't want to hear some stranger telling her what she already knows. A very human response.

Trisha pulled her hand away, tears streaming down her cheeks. Denny leaned back on the stool, exhaling. The stress of contact was always severe. The people who came to her were usually unhappy, frightened. Denny did her best to make them feel better if she could. But sometimes she could not reel off comforting lies.

"I've got to go," mumbled Trisha, getting up, not meeting Denny's eyes. "I – I don't think – I don't believe – I reckon you're just making it up!"

The plump woman clumped to the door and struggled briefly with the loose knob before opening it. Denny decided not to call after her. But Trisha stopped in the hallway, head down, back to Denny. Then she half-turned and threw a couple of banknotes onto the floor. Denny stood up, the crouched carefully to pick up the cash.

Twenty pounds. Well, it's enough for a pizza and a beer.

She closed the door, shutting out the sound of Trisha's heavy footsteps on the stairs. It had not been a good week. After a few lucrative clients, things had tailed off. Word-of-mouth business was always problematic. Denny had stayed briefly in three towns since leaving London, making a little money with her psychic act to top up her meagre savings. She had the conviction that remaining too long in the same place would invite trouble.

Could be this particular seam is mined out, she thought. *Or maybe my act needs work.*

The symbiont twitched and sent a mild shaft of pain through her spine. The creature, though damaged, was still vigorous at times. It usually reacted strongly if Denny had had psychic contact with a client. If there had been intense emotion involved – which was normal – it seemed to dislike it.

"Sorry, Jabba," Denny muttered. "I know you didn't ask for this gig."

Her initial revulsion at the alien creature had been replaced by a weary acceptance that bordered, at times, on affection.

Jabba was at least a living being that shared her life, not to mention her blood supply and nervous system.

All things considered, I'd have preferred a hamster.

She had just gotten comfortable when there was a loud rapping at the door.

"Who is it?" she called peevishly.

"Your rent's overdue."

No it isn't, you creep, she thought. *But you won't let me rest until I pay, will you?*

Desmond the landlord was a bloated, unshaven fifty-something with a shaved head and a neck tattoo that was now unreadable thanks to folds of colorless flesh. He always stank of beer, sweat, and cheap cologne. As she handed over a few crumpled notes, Denny's hand brushed hers, and she got a familiar flash of his mind. He was peering down at her breasts, despite her loose sweatshirt. He was also imagining what he would like to do to her. And what he would like her to do for him.

Denny snatched her hand back as if she had been scalded.

"Nervous little lady, aren't you?" the man leered, shuffling forward a little so that his belly was across the threshold. "No need to be scared of anything. I'm just downstairs, remember."

"How could I forget, Desmond?" she said sweetly. Then, on a sudden impulse, she added, "I feel so safe knowing you're around."

Denny reached up and briefly pinched his cheek, seeing his eyes widen in surprise. In the brief span of contact, she forced herself to delve deeper into his mind for something to use against him. She skimmed over the surface of a vast swamp of degrading images, murky secrets, and squalid impulses. What passed for Desmond's mind was a near-random agglomeration of greed, ignorance, and animalistic impulses. But one stood out, one dark impulse that she could use against him to devastating effect.

"Hey!" she said brightly. "I'm a huge fan of Barry Manilow. How about you?"

The confusion on the landlord's face as he stepped back in alarm was worth the renewed protests from Jabba. She slammed the door, smiling to herself.

Psychic ninja attack, she thought. *But that settles it, I can't stay here any longer,* she thought. *I'd better move on.*

Denny took out her phone and looked at a map of central England. She frowned at a dozen half-familiar place names, towns and cities she had sometimes heard on the news when she had lived in London. She needed a place with a large population, so she could rely on word of mouth to bring in some more clients. This ruled out most English towns. She finally settled on a place called Fordham. The data she found was not exactly cheerful,

It can't be any worse than here, she thought. *Might even be nice. You can never tell.*

As she made a train reservation, she caught herself humming 'Bermuda Triangle'.

***

Kat pounded her way down the alley, boots raising echoes from the crumbling brick walls. This was the bad side of town. Not that Fordham had a good side, so far as Kat knew. The only good areas were the suburbs, well away from Kat's home turf. But the alley she was in was smack in the middle of a part of town where police raids were as familiar as the dismal weather.

She reached two dumpsters behind a pub. Kat flung herself up against the wall between them and listened. She heard no footsteps, no shouts, nothing to indicate she was being pursued. That did not prove that she was free. There was only so much a fourteen-year-old girl could do to survive on the streets without being detained. And trying to find refuge with any adult brought its own perils.

Might not have a choice, though, Kat thought. *Might even have to tell the cops.*

Going to the police would have been unthinkable only a few days earlier. To Kat, and her kind, a dark blue uniform was never something to run towards. But she had had to revise her views on a lot of things in the last few weeks. Her grandma, the one person in her life who had truly cared about her, often talked about 'the lesser of two evils'. To Kat, as she slumped down the wall, sobbing at the stitch in her side, the cops seemed a lot less evil than what she was fleeing.

But if they don't believe me, she thought. *What then? They'll just send me back to that place. And then ...*

The clatter of cans, a rustle of paper, the hollow scraping of cardboard. Someone or something was moving nearby. Kat stiffened, heart racing. She tried to suppress her sobs, her breathless gasping. Another movement, this sound a little closer. A fast-food carton shifted.

Too small, she thought, with intense relief. *Not one of them.*

Confirming her hunch, a whiskered, beady-eyed face appeared from under the carton. The rat was so small, especially by Fordham standards, that Kat judged it was not fully grown. Simply seeing a normal living thing made her feel more secure, almost happy.

"You a misunderstood teenager, then?" she whispered. "On your own?"

The rat regarded her for a moment, whiskers twitching, then scuttled back into the heap of garbage.

At least you've got a home, she thought.

At first, it was just the Weirdoes, and Kat was not too worried. But then the Replacements came and things got serious. It got so bad that she had had to escape. But she could not simply leave town. She had someone else to worry about.

Knowle House was the latest of the homes Kat had been put into. Her chaotic early life had led to spells in foster care, a failed adoption, and too much time spent with what social workers called 'disruptive influences'. Those influences had included her mother, her mother's boyfriends, and the drugs they were into.

When she was eight, Kat had been taken into care, a term that later amused her in a grim kind of way. By the time she had reached her teens, she had had enough of being ordered around. The only thing that stopped her quitting the whole system and going it alone was Tommy.

Tommy was her little brother. He had what the social workers called learning difficulties. Most kids called Tommy stupid, at least until Kat set them straight. Then they only dared say it when she was not around. But Tommy was still bullied. A kid with his problems was never selected for adoption. The social workers had long since stopped trying to place him with a family. When Tommy was upset, he broke things, screamed, and made a mess. But he was always Kat's little brother, and the love she felt for him was the most ferocious, powerful thing in her world.

No matter how much she hated the system that bound them, she could not leave it while he was still in its clutches. Kat was not considered adoption material either, because she was sullen, sometimes violent, never a nice girl. She made sure she stayed with Tommy, even though she could have stopped acting up, and maybe even impressed some wannabe parents. After a while, as with Tommy, they gave up on Kat.

It was just after Christmas that Kat noticed the way the staff were becoming Weirdoes. At first, it was hard to tell. The people who ran the care homes were always tired, irritable, or just indifferent. But suddenly, over the course of a couple of weeks, Kat spotted a change in the way things were done at Knowle.

Firstly, the staff seemed to work harder. They actually cared about rules. They tried to make sure everyone actually went to school. They checked the older kids' rooms for cigarettes, for alcohol, for weed, and for knives.

Sure, Kat thought at the time. *They're supposed to do searches. But they hardly ever bothered before. Not unless somebody got stabbed or set their room on fire.*

Kat realized that the staff was becoming weird when Lassiter, the chief care assistant, found a small packet of marijuana behind the skirting board under Kat's bed. Lassiter was a massive, gray-haired woman who had, in the past, pinned Kat down and hurt her severely just to stop a fight. The fight had been about Tommy, as usual. Lassiter's bulk had cracked one of Kat's ribs, but she had known better than to tell the doctors the truth at the clinic.

When the weed was found a few weeks after that incident, Kat had waited for some kind of punishment to be doled out. Lassiter, while very lazy, could be clever and vindictive. But instead, the big woman had simply confiscated the tiny packet and told Kat her 'violation of the rules would be recorded in her file'. Kat had stared at the closed door for a full minute after Lassiter left. It was then that she seriously wondered if something was happening to the staff.

As the days passed, things got weirder. It was not just Lassiter who displayed a radical change of personality, but also a few other staff members. They seemed to stoop, slightly, even a couple of ex-military types. They all grew quiet, subdued, adhering strictly to the rules, but never losing their tempers with youngsters who broke them. This in turn produced uncertainty, as some of the other staff carried on being sloppy and brutal by turns. There were rows, disputes, and eventually most of the non-Weirdoes were replaced.

On one occasion, Kat was prowling around the kitchen area, hoping to steal some cheesecake for Tommy. It was after lights out, and she should have been in her room. She heard someone coming and hid. She was small enough to squeeze herself into the cupboard under the sink. She saw the light come on through a chink in the door. Then she heard Fordyce, one of the more unpleasant staff members, arguing with someone else. She recognized Lassiter's voice, and then heard a scuffle. It sounded like two or maybe three people struggling.

There was a tearing sound, a crash, then Fordyce started yelling. Though she loathed the man, Kat still felt a chill as he cried out in terror. She had never heard a man sound so scared.

"Get that thing off me! Get it off me! No!"

Another crash, the sound of crockery breaking, then an ominous silence. Kat listened intently, but all she heard was heavy breathing. Then Lassiter spoke, sounding slightly breathless, but unemotional.

"This all needs to be cleaned up."

"Yes," came Fordyce's voice in reply. "I'll do it."

For a minute, Kat heard fragments of crockery being thrown in the bin, then the light was switched off. She waited a long time before emerging from the cupboard, and crept back to her room empty-handed, Tommy's cheesecake forgotten.

Things became even weirder at the Knowle House when Kat saw a notorious young troublemaker kick a male staff member right in the groin. The Zombie doubled up, gasping, to the general amusement of the kids. But the fierce retaliation everyone expected did not happen. Something else did, though. The kid in question, a stocky twelve-year-old called Jay, was taken away for 'anger management therapy'. Nobody was told where.

A week later, Jay returned. The members of Jay's gang were waiting for him, and the other kids were hanging around in the foyer. Everyone, Kat included, expected to see Jay come swaggering back into Knowle. But the figure that walked back into the building had no swagger.

At first, Kat thought Jay had been drugged. Medication was sometimes prescribed for the more troublesome kids. But Jay did not look drugged. He just seemed different, as he walked straight past his old crew, nodded politely to the staff, and went straight to his room. He started going to school regularly, surprising teachers, some of whom had never seen him.

Inevitably, some of the other boys saw Jay's good behavior as weakness. Eventually a couple of them stopped him outside the first-floor bathroom, refused to let him pass. Normally such a situation would have led to violence, but Jay simply folded his arms, smiled faintly. Kat and a couple of other kids looked on as the bullies moved in, starting to shove Jay.

"Pussy!" sneered one. "What they do to you, mate, cut your balls off?"

What happened next was over in a split-second. Jay moved at tremendous speed, grabbing his first tormentor by the throat and shoving him against a wall. Then Jay shoved his face close to the other boy's ear and whispered something. A moment after that, Jay was walking away, as if nothing had happened.

"What did he say?" Kat asked the boy who was still rubbing his throat.

He looked furtive, embarrassed, angry.

"Nothing!" he said.

But after that, nobody tried to bully Jay again. And after a few weeks, he was put up for fostering. Jay, once considered likely to go straight to juvenile jail from Knowle House, would soon have a family home.

Jay was the first of several boys and girls who were taken for 'therapy', often for the most trivial offence. As the process continued, the kids grew quieter, and became a lot better behaved. But barely a day passed without some infringement of the ever-increasing house regulations that were posted on the notice board. Soon, even talking loudly or clattering your cutlery in the dining hall could be enough.

Kat was clever enough to control herself, trying to figure out what was going on. But Tommy was not. She had to watch him like a hawk, try to head off any trouble. It was exhausting, and stressed her out.

"You've got to watch out," she pleaded. "Don't give them a reason."

They were standing outside in the freezing cold in early February. As siblings, Kat and Tommy were allowed some together time, but they could not talk indoors without being overheard. They had gone for a walk in the so-called garden, a bleak concrete expanse garnished with a few dead saplings.

"Don't tell me what to do!" Tommy snarled.

It was his usual reaction to any kind of order or request. Kat felt her own anger rising, and forced herself to keep her voice level.

"You saw what happened to Jay," she said. "You know something weird is going on."

"Jay was a pussy," Tommy replied, but sounded less certain now.

"You know that's not true!" she hissed. "Don't pretend to be stupid. You know something is off!"

Tommy muttered something, looking down at his shoes.

"What was that?" she demanded.

"They're all Replacements," the boy said. "Jay's not really Jay. None of them are the kids they're supposed to be. They're Replacements. You're stupid if you can't tell."

Kat stared down at her brother.

"That's bollocks!" she exclaimed, then glanced around, knowing how far a voice could carry.

Tommy's mouth firmed into a familiar, obstinate line.

"It's not bollocks, it's dead obvious," he yelled. Ignoring her frantic attempts to shush him, he went on, "They're not really the same, they just *look* the same!"

After a couple of minutes, she had calmed him down enough to reason with him.

"They can't be different people," she said patiently, as they walked around the garden for the hundredth time. "That makes no sense. And anyway, where are the real kids, if those aren't them?"

Tommy shrugged, kicked a piece of gravel.

"I dunno. Probably dead. Probably all dead and burned up or buried or dissolved in acid."

Kat was confused.

"That's barmy," she declared. "They can't just – I mean they couldn't …"

She faltered. The world seemed to tilt on its axis as she struggled, and failed, to fight off a horrifying idea.

Suppose the kids nobody wanted are being replaced by kids grown-ups would like. Now he's said it, it makes sense. In a crazy way.

Kat felt sick in her stomach at the thought. She looked down at her brother, with his long record of making trouble.

"Can we go in now?" Tommy whined. "I'm bloody freezing!"

"Don't swear, you know the rules," she said automatically. "Yeah, it's cold."

As they went back inside Knowle House, Kat looked at a group of other kids standing outside the kitchen. These were trusted residents, deemed well-behaved enough to have access to cutlery, cleaning products, and the like. All the boys and girls that had been sent off to therapy were allowed special privileges. The group looked at the siblings without speaking.

"Take a picture," Kat muttered. "It'll last longer."

As she walked away, she felt an odd, crawling sensation on the back of her skull. It felt like cold fingers touching her mind.

Imagination, she told herself. *Don't let them creep you out, Kat.*

The next day things got worse.

It happened at breakfast. Two girls who had been to therapy were behind Kat in the line. When the queue moved forward, one of them pushed Kat so that she barged into Tiffany, another girl who had been away for treatment.

"Hey!" Tiffany exclaimed, squaring up to Kat, "you watch who you're shoving!"

"Sorry," said Kat sullenly.

She wanted to turn around and punch the girl who had pushed her, but she was keenly aware of being watched by the staff.

"You just watch it, fatso!" Tiffany hissed. "Or I'll make you sorry you crossed me."

This time Kat said nothing, but felt herself reddening. Her rising anger was dangerous, and she suppressed it. She was puzzled.

If Tiffany's had therapy, how come she's acting out?

Another shove in the small of her back caught her off balance and Kat grabbed at Tiffany to stop herself from falling. Tiffany screamed in alarm, grabbed Kat, and began grappling with her. Furious, Kat forgot her self-control and soon the two girls were screaming, kicking, biting.

Two burly attendants dragged them apart. Tiffany, after all her provocation, was suddenly blank-faced. When she was freed, she simply walked away as if nothing had happened.

"Hey!" Kat objected. "She started it, it was her fault!"

"Not true," said a familiar voice. "You were always a troublemaker."

Kat found herself staring up at Lassiter. The big woman looked down at Kat, arms folded, face as devoid of emotion as Tiffany's.

"I'm the victim here," Kat protested. "You're talking bollocks."

"Pack a bag tonight," said Lassiter. "You're slated for anger management therapy this afternoon."

Kat felt sick in her stomach.

"What have I done?" she demanded, forgetting to keep her voice down. "I've done nothing wrong!"

Lassiter gestured to the attendants. Kicking and screaming, Kat was dragged back to her room, locked in, told once more to pack a bag for a stay at 'the unit'. Cursing at the top of her voice, Kat kicked the door until it splintered.

"Final warning," said Lassiter, still speaking in her emotionless, Zombie voice. "We'll use the restraints if we have to."

Kat stopped kicking and screaming. She had seen a couple of kids held down and tied at the wrists and ankles. Like that, she would be no good to herself, or Tommy.

I need to get out, she thought. *I need to get away, save myself, then come back and save him. Maybe get help.*

She looked around the room. The window was barred. She thought of smashing the glass, squeezing through. But even if she could get her skinny frame between the bars, her room was on the third floor. Climbing down, or somehow going sideways to escape through another room, seemed impossible.

There must be some way ...

She remembered an incident at a foster home when she was much younger, a mistake that somebody else had made, a fact that she had learned. Kat had filed the information away for an emergency. She grabbed a can of cheap deodorant from her bedside and aimed it up at the smoke detector in the middle of the ceiling.

Let's see if it works.

The jet of white vapor sprayed onto the plastic cylinder, and for a moment, she thought it would not work. Then the fire alarm went off, followed a couple of seconds later by shouts, the banging of doors, running footsteps. She heard the Weirdoes giving orders in their usual robotic way, showing no sign of panic. But Kat was banking on the normal kids creating just enough confusion for her to slip out.

The assembly point outside the building was in the garden. The corridor was crowded, and Kat found and stayed in the biggest clump of older kids. Luck was on her side. As they emerged onto the driveway of Knowle House, a delivery van was coming through the gates, one of the staff waving it on.

I won't get another chance, she thought, and ran for it.

She had only gone a few paces when a strong hand grabbed her by one arm and swung her round. Kat realized she had misjudged her move. Lassiter had grabbed her, and other staff members were closing in. Instinct kicked in and Kat slumped, letting her body go limp so that Lassiter would support her weight. The big woman shifted her balance. Kat head-butted her in the stomach, driving her back against the front of the van.

The effect was far more drastic than Kat had expected. Lassiter screamed, let her go, and collapsed. Kat stood gawping for a moment. The woman had simply not hit the vehicle that hard. Then Kat saw something even stranger. The other Weirdoes were writhing in pain, as if they had been hurt, too.

Don't waste time thinking about it!

Seconds later, she was out of the gates. She was almost hit by a car as she dodged through the morning traffic, but that worked in her favor, too. The first time she glanced back she saw a couple of pursuers, care attendants in blue overalls. The second time, she saw nobody, but did not dare stop. When she got to the alley, she was almost sure she was safe, for now.

***

As the train approached Fordham Station, Denny felt Jabba tingling, shifting slightly. She had reserved a seat in the quiet coach, despite the extra cost, and brought a cushion to lean against. It was now second nature for Denny to keep the symbiont happy, even if it meant contorting herself into unnatural shapes. She had pins and needles from sitting scrunched up in a corner, so at first the creature's odd behavior did not register.

What's up, sluggy boy? Denny thought. *You never got excited about a new town before. What's special about this one?*

There was nothing special about Fordham, so far as she could see. As the train rattled and screeched through the suburbs she saw graffiti-covered concrete, old factory buildings, and a typical mid-size soccer stadium that had seen better days. Towards the center of the city, she noted the usual concentration of Victorian churches and other old buildings amid high-rise blocks from the Sixties.

Just another badly-planned urban sprawl, she thought. *Ah well, let's make the best of it.*

Denny decided to find somewhere a little classier to stay this time. She zeroed in on an area with a lot of B&B's, talked to their owners, skimmed their thoughts. After striking out with the first two, she chose a cheerful, elderly lady who had just the right attitude.

"So, what brings you to Fordham?" asked the landlady, Mrs. Brackett.

"Partly business, partly pleasure," Denny replied, smiling. "I don't know if you believe in such things, but – I have a gift. I use it to help people. If I can."

As Denny had expected, the landlady became her first client, and promised to put the word out.

***

Kat had no idea how much time had passed while she sat between the dumpsters. The February day had grown darker, the drizzling rain grown heavier. As a result, she was damp, cold, miserable. She was also hungry. The gnawing need for food was starting to drive away her anxiety, even make her doubt whether she understood what was happening at Knowle or not.

No, she told herself. It's wrong, it's weird. It needs sorting out.

She got slowly to her feet, kicked away a sheet of paper. Then she paused, reached down, and smoothed out the sodden paper against the side of a dumpster. It was the front page of the Fordham Gazette. The headline read RECORD FALL IN HOMELESS NUMBERS. Kat had never bothered much with news, but remembered her grandma telling her the 'local rag' had won some kind of award.

Investigative journalism. That's what she called it.

She began to scrabble among the garbage around her feet, trying to find some way of contacting the newspaper. Eventually she found a ketchup-stained page with contact details. The address of the newspaper building was in the town center. She would have to walk busy streets, with many eyes watching.

Nightmare Spawn

For Tommy, she thought. *Never mind me. Gotta save the boy.*

Kat emerged carefully from her hiding place, hood of her jacket pulled right up to conceal her face. She set off at a brisk pace, and soon she was feeling warmer, if not more confident.

***

Denny rested after giving the landlady her psychic reading. It had not been difficult to tell the old lady what she wanted to hear. In fact, Denny felt relieved at touching a less troubled, more pleasant mind. Flora Brackett had her share of worries and hang-ups, but compared to most of Denny's clients, she was living the dream.

Living the dream, Denny thought, as her eyelids grew heavy. *Not the nightmare.*

On her back, Jabba pulsed slightly, a boneless sack of muscle and organs. Denny lay under a duvet in a room scented with lavender, decorated with paintings of quaint rural scenes. She wondered, as sleep slowly claimed her, what Mrs. Brackett would think if she knew she had just checked in two new guests, one of them far from human. Denny recalled the NO PETS sign above the desk, smiled.

Her sleep was uneasy, beset by confused dreams. She saw robed and hooded figures in a vast room, a space as vast as a cathedral but far uglier, darker. She felt a presence that she knew all too well, a mind more powerful than any human.

No, no, I won't go.

Denny's point of view floated through the huge, gloomy space, above the people gathered below. Tall windows and a glass ceiling allowed some light into the building, but the panes were dirty, and many had been boarded over. At one end of the building, there were no windows, and the darkness was intense. Denny felt herself drawn into the darkness, where something stirred. It sensed her, reached out, grasped her mind and ran cold tendrils through her brain. Each mind, she had learned, had a unique quality. This one was the first she had encountered after the symbiont had been forced onto her.

Cassandra.

Denny snapped awake, levered herself upright on one elbow. The symbiont was throbbing, sending waves of discomfort through her nerves.

No way could I have come to the one place where she's holed up. Not just by random chance.

Denny recalled the way she had settled on Fordham, the fact she had rejected four or five other, similar towns.

"If it was random."

She got up, went into the bathroom, pulled her sweatshirt over her head. Turning, she craned her neck to look at the gray-green organism nestling between her shoulder blades.

"Hey Jabba," she murmured. "You trying to go home to mamma?"

She picked up a small mirror, and with practiced efficiency, held it up to get a clearer view of her bare back. The symbiont did not seem to have changed in appearance. It was still a mottled, gray-green tube with a lighter-colored patch at the upper end. Ted Gould had tasered it in what he assumed was its head. The result, according to Doctor Zoffany, had been to cut the entity off from its parent, the Queen. Denny had wondered if it would simply die in time, but it seemed as vigorous as before.

But there is something different ...

She adjusted the mirror, trying to see if the symbiont's shape had changed, or if it had sprouted some new tendrils. All she could see where the dark strands just under her skin where the creature's nerves and blood vessels hooked into her body. Then a thought struck her.

"You losing weight, Jabba?"

It seemed that the creature was slightly smaller, or at least thinner and maybe a shade shorter too. Denny had not taken any pictures in case they were discovered, nor had she made any measurements.

Am I convincing myself it's shrinking, hoping it will simply shrivel up, drop off, fade away?

She took a deep breath, laid the mirror down, and pulled on her sweatshirt. The idea that the symbiont might be slowly dying brought her no joy. It merely added another element of uncertainty to her plight.

Nightmare Spawn

What if it dies?
What if I die with it?

Nightmare Spawn

Chapter 2: Mind Games

Denny was suspicious of the caller from the start. There was something a little too articulate, a little too pat, about this would-be client. But she had never turned anyone down if they asked for help. She had cleared it with Mrs. Brackett to use her sitting room for what Denny termed 'readings'. The landlady had been so helpful that, despite the grimness of Fordham, Denny felt she might stay for a month or maybe longer.

"Okay, Lucy," she said to the woman on the phone. "I'll see you tomorrow, around ten pm."

"How much will it cost?" asked Lucy. "I mean, will it cost me a lot?"

Not unreasonable questions, Denny thought. *But again, she's a bit too keen to get information. Could this be some kind of sting?*

Denny had encountered hostility from others claiming to be psychics, mediums, fortune tellers and the like. An outsider taking trade away from locals was bound to make waves. But Lucy did not sound hostile, so much as inquisitive. In fact, Lucy reminded Denny of her younger self.

Well, we'll soon find out.

"I don't have a fixed charge," she explained. "You can make a gift as large or small as you like. And if you feel I've not helped you, don't feel obliged to pay. Some people don't."

Lucy seemed about to ask another question, but then her voice became muffled.

Covering the mouthpiece, Denny thought. *Office phone.*

"Okay," said the client. "I've got to go now, but I'll see you tomorrow!"

"Looking forward to it," Denny said, but the call was cut off before she reached the end of the sentence.

"Okay, Lucy," she sighed. "We'll see just what you really want in due course."

***

"This is – look, Kat, I can't just print accusations of malpractice," said the reporter. "I know you're upset, but you have to tell me something. I need details."

Kat sat nursing a can of soda in the tiny newspaper office. She had expected to find the headquarters of the Fordham Gazette to be big, bright, and busy. Instead, it seemed half-dead. Just one reporter was on duty, and she seemed skeptical. Laura Bell was a tall, red-haired woman with freckles and a friendly manner. But she talked to Kat like other grown-ups.

All pretend-friendly, Kat thought. *Humoring me. Trying not to upset the bad girl.*

"I'm not good with words," Kat said, suddenly feeling much younger and shyer. "Something bad is happening. At Knowle. And I'm worried about my brother."

"But according to you," Laura said slowly, "no child at the home has been seriously hurt, and nobody has actually disappeared."

"They're – they're messing with kids' minds!" Kat insisted. "They take them away for this – this treatment, and when they come back, they're different."

Kat had not dared talk about Weirdoes or Replacements, knowing it would make her sound crazy. Laura nodded thoughtfully.

"Now that is interesting," she admitted. "Where are they taken? Somewhere nearby?"

Kat shrugged. "I dunno! They don't tell us anything, they just tell us what to do."

"Is this something to do with Moment of Truth?" Laura asked.

Kat stared, baffled. "I've never heard of it. What is it?"

Laura shrugged, made a note on a small pad.

"It's a local charity," she said. "It works with the poor, drug addicts, victims of domestic violence, troubled kids. It's taking over all the children's homes, homeless shelters, seems to have a ton of money from somewhere. My editor is interested in finding out just how it got rich. But you never heard of it?"

Kat shook her head. She was starting to feel frustrated with Laura's questions, angry at her own inability to find the right words.

"Does it matter who's doing it?" she demanded. "I just want you to stop them doing it to Tommy. And me."

"I can ask questions," the journalist said, getting up from behind her desk. "Maybe I can wangle a visit to this home. But you understand, if a crime's been committed, it's a police matter?"

"No police!" Kat insisted.

"That's a reflex action, Kat," Laura said. "I understand it, but if we do find any evidence of wrongdoing, who do you think will get involved?"

Kat felt herself growing hot, anger rising with her confusion.

"I thought – the government, or something?" she blurted.

Laura smiled, and Kat realized she had made a fool of herself.

"I don't think this is one for MI5," the reporter said carefully. "Seriously, if you want something done, sooner or later the cops will be involved. Now come on – I'll buy you a burger or something. You look half-starved."

***

"Gary says he needs some time to himself," said the girl, sniffling into a tissue. "We had a flat together, but now he's moved out."

Note to self, thought Denny. *Buy more Kleenex.*

"Sometimes people do need a little time apart, Angela," she pointed out. "Maybe this is just a bump in the road? You have had fights before."

"But we were engaged," the girl whined, leaving streaks of make-up on the tissue.

Their brief skin-to-skin contact on meeting had told Denny the basic story. A young woman in what she thought was a serious relationship had been heartbroken when her beau's ardor had cooled. It was a story as old as love itself, being told in the suitable old-fashioned surroundings of Mrs. Brackett's sitting room.

She seems kinda needy, Denny thought. *Maybe he had cold feet, felt smothered, or just decided he didn't want to be tied down.*

Denny was preparing to sum up her client's problem in more tactful words, when she felt the symbiont stir again. Jabba had not settled down since their arrival. In fact, since her strange dream of Cassandra, the creature had been wriggling as much as it could. She had resorted to painkillers to reduce the discomfort from nerve-spasms, but was cautious about dosage. She did not know how any drugs might affect the creature.

"Angela," she said, trying to keep her voice normal despite the pain. "Sometimes men say things they don't mean. Or maybe you heard things Gary didn't really say. Let me try to find out more."

Denny held out her hands, smiling invitingly. Angela reached out across the little table, and Denny held the girl's fingers lightly. At first, she received the familiar mish-mash of feelings, memories, ideas. She could never go too deep into someone's mind. The maimed symbiont was not able to haul out information that was buried, locked away, or repressed. All she got was information just below the surface, if that. But there was still something odd about Angela's memories of her supposed fiancé.

She's misremembering it, Denny thought. *He would recall things differently.*

However, the close relationship that had existed between the two young people seemed real enough. Denny felt a twinge of regret as she surveyed Angela's memories of holidays, parties, dinner dates, quiet nights in. Then she felt herself start to redden at vivid, if somewhat chaotic, recollections of very energetic sex.

Well, that was a healthy relationship in one respect, she thought, keeping her smile fixed. *What next?*

As she riffled through Angela's memories, trying to screen out a ton of irrelevant material, she came to a point when her boyfriend had suddenly become remote. And it was abrupt. And it coincided with something else, which Denny felt might be connected somehow. She released Angela's hands, leaned back, and exhaled.

"Before he called off the engagement," she began, pushing the box of Kleenex toward Angela. "He seemed really stressed about work, yes?"

The girl nodded, still tearful, her nose very red now.

"He said the new management were messing staff around, trying to pressure them," Angela sniffled. "Gary said he might quit. That was just before he dumped me!"

Denny patted her client's hand, stealing a few more memories. She glimpsed tall gates, a Victorian-style house, a handful of sullen-looking children of various ages. Gary in a blue coverall with a name tag. FORDYCE.

"He worked with kids?" she asked. "Some kind of care home?"

Angela's eyes widened. She nodded dumbly.

"I can see him meeting you outside the gates," Denny explained, following her policy of telling the truth, or at least some of it. "And he still works there?"

"Yes," Angela sniffed. "It's Knowle House. He seems to spend more time there than ever. He never gets back to me. It's like he finds me repulsive."

Denny uttered some platitudes, well-rehearsed phrases to try and ease the pain. She put in a few references to happy memories from Angela's childhood, a therapeutic trick she had evolved over the months. It seemed to work, at least in part. The next time she patted the girl's hand Denny sensed less misery, more confidence, a greater self-respect

Angela had arrived feeling fat, ugly, and generally hopeless, Denny thought. *At least she'll leave less miserable.*

There was a knock at the door, then a genteel English voice.

"Are you ready for some tea, dear?" asked Mrs. Brackett.

"Are we?" Denny asked Angela. "She makes these great homemade cookies. Here, dry your eyes."

***

Kat was halfway through her cheeseburger when she noticed the Weirdo.

The journalist, Laura Bell, had kept her word. She had bought Kat a meal, promised not to report her to the police, and even offered to pay for Kat to stay in a cheap hotel for one night.

"My editor will be bloody annoyed," Laura added. "It will blow a big hole in my expense account."

"Thanks," mumbled Kat through a mouthful of food.

She glanced around the restaurant, which was nearly full. Couples were laughing, talking, families were bickering, a solitary man was staring straight at her. Kat normally stared back, defiantly, if anyone did that. This time she looked away, not wanting to attract attention. But a moment later, she glanced back. The man was looking at her again. More discreetly, this time, but looking nonetheless. He had a blank, humorless expression. And he seemed slightly hunched over his salad.

"Kat?"

Laura wore an expression Kat knew well. A grown-up was being patient with her, despite provocation.

"Sorry, what?"

"I said," Laura went on, "that allegations of abuse in these homes are nothing new, but we need something more. You say kids are taken away somewhere and brought back, changed somehow?"

Kat nodded, forcing herself not to look back at the man in the suit.

"It's like ... like their minds are different. They're not the same people."

Laura paused, a folded bit of pizza halfway to her mouth.

"Are they given drugs?"

Kat shrugged.

"I mean, are they prescribed drugs when they come back?"

"Don't think so," Kat admitted. "It's this therapy thing, that's what changes them."

Again, she wondered if she dared talk about the Weirdoes, the Replacements. Maybe Laura, working for the press, would be more likely to believe strange stuff.

"Where do they take them?" Laura asked, leaning forward.

"I dunno!" Kat insisted.

Laura began to ask another question, then stopped, peered past Kat. Other diners were looking, too, and conversation had died down. Kat twisted around in her seat to see two uniformed police entering the pizzeria.

"You told them!" she shouted accusingly at Laura.

Kat jumped up, ignoring the journalist's protestations. The teenager ran along the back wall of the restaurant, hoping to escape via the kitchen. She slammed into the double doors, flinging them wide. She glimpsed a waitress reeling back, flying dishes, heard a crash. She saw surprised faces, smelled food, felt a wave of heat.

"Get her!" shouted a male voice.

A man in chef's clothing grabbed at Kat, but she dodged under his arms and was through the door into the alleyway. To her left was a blank wall, to the right a heap of trash, and beyond it the street. She ran, heart pounding, boots ringing on stained cobblestones. But even as she felt hope rising in her, a white police car screeched to a halt across the mouth of the alley. Again, she tried to dodge the adults, but this time they were too fast, too clever. She felt her arms being twisted up her back, saw the hood of the car coming up to meet her face.

"Hey!"

Kat heard Laura shouting, then more voices.

"If you know what's good for you, Ms. Bell, you'll walk away from this."

"You can't treat a minor like that!" Laura shouted. "And why does it take so many of you to detain one fourteen-year-old girl? You haven't even cautioned her."

Laura was making such a fuss that Kat felt sorry she had accused the reporter of calling the cops. As she was dragged around the car, she saw the journalist's shocked face over the shoulder of a policeman. The cop seemed slightly stooped. As her hands were cuffed, Kat realized, with a terrible resignation, that she had put her trust in the grown-up world, the normal world. And it had not saved her, not protected her little brother, but done the opposite. Part of her had always known this would happen.

"Tommy!" she shouted.

"Don't worry," said one of the police officers flanking her.

The man looked at her with expressionless eyes.
"You'll be seeing him soon enough."

**

"What do you mean, not a story?"

Laura glared at her editor, who looked stolidly back at her across his cluttered desk.

"I'm sorry," he said, "but this is the word from up high. According to the cops, they're investigating some kind of abuse at Knowle House. They don't want us stepping all over their investigation."

"Whatever happened to press freedom?" Laura demanded, jumping up.

"Nothing," replied the editor. "We just never had that much. If we break this story and it leads to guilty people getting off scot free, we'll be the villains. Not the abusers."

The editor stood up, rounded the desk, put a meaty arm around Laura's shoulders. She shook off the unwanted contact, and began pacing and gesturing in annoyance.

"So I'm supposed to just forget about the cops crashing into the middle of an interview with a witness? Why can't I speak to the girl? Where did they take her?"

The editor shrugged irritably.

"For God's sake, she's already assaulted at least one staff member and caused all sorts of damage," he said, voice hardening. "We all know these troubled kids can make all sorts of claims. And you have plenty of other stories to work on. There's illicit chemical dumping, the plans for the new road tunnel, and this American psychic. Are you on top of that?"

Laura snorted.

"Yeah, give the girl reporter the trivial stuff," she said. "And yes, I have fixed up an appointment with yet another fake psychic. Why do you keep sending me to sniff them out? Every town has them."

The editor looked out over the town. The February afternoon was grim, the sky a solid sheet of low cloud. Rain spattered the window pane.

"These so-called psychics can be dangerous," he said. "Taking advantage of vulnerable people. You hear about old ladies giving their life savings to some medium."

Laura frowned, puzzled at the contrast between the man's words and the lack of real passion in his voice. Lately she had noticed him become less energetic, more cautious.

"Okay," she said wearily. "I'll lay off the children's home story for now. And I'll expose the fake psychic, like a good little reporter."

The editor did not reply. Laura went to the door, then paused, grasping the handle.

"Are you okay?" she asked. "You still going to the gym?"

"No," the man said. "No time for that."

Laura made a noncommittal sound and left the office, closing the door behind her. She went to her cluttered desk and sat down, wondering if her editor was ill.

Maybe he's just depressed, she thought. *He certainly looks like he's got the weight of the world on his shoulders.*

***

They hauled Kat out of the car and dragged her along, boots scraping the tarmac. She did not recognize the area; they had driven her out of town. She had expected to go to the police station or Knowle House. This was somehow worse. The big building in front of her looked like some kind of factory, with an assortment of vehicles lined up outside. She caught a glimpse of a newly-painted sign above the big, double doors at one end.

Moment of Truth.

The cops did not take her to the front. Instead, they manhandled her around the side, opened a side door, and dragged her inside. She kicked out and cursed, but knew she had little chance of escape. Already she began to feel despair welling up, a sense of fatalism that she had experienced many times before.

"You sure this is the right place?"

Kat felt one pair of hands on her slacken slightly, and looked up. A young police constable was gazing up at the huge factory space. Above them, rows of windows admitted the dull winter daylight.

"Just get it over with," snapped the other officer.

Kat sensed hesitation in the first cop, and took her chance. She twisted around, using her captors for leverage, and kicked the second cop in the gut. He doubled over, wheezing, and let go. As she had hoped, the first cop hesitated again, and she broke free. Knowing there was another policeman just outside in the car, she decided to make a break through the building. She raced out of the short corridor into the main part of the factory.

"Don't just stand there, you idiot!" she heard the second cop wheezing. "Get her!"

Kat race across the concrete floor, heavy footsteps behind her. She tried to get a mental map of her surroundings and find a likely exit. Much of the old factory floor had been portioned off into smaller units, like cubicles in an office but devoid of windows. This created a maze that Kat raced through, hoping she would not hit a blind alley. Inevitably, she did, and as she retraced her steps she heard the cops, still cursing, just around the corner.

In desperation, she tried the nearest door, which opened. She threw herself inside the cubicle, slammed the door, and set her back against it. The cops had split up, judging by the way they were bellowing at each other. She heard footsteps pass by, stop, then continue.

"Anything?" came a shout.

"Nah," said the man just outside the door. "She could be anywhere."

The footsteps moved away. Kat remembered to breathe again, forced herself to do it as quietly as possible. She took stock of her surroundings properly for the first time. She seemed to be in a kind of bedroom with a couple of bunk beds. At first, she thought neither was occupied. All she could see were heaps of bedclothes. But then the mound of blankets on the lower bunk moved, and she heard a faint noise that might have been a human voice. The mound was small, too small for an adult to be underneath the cheap, washed-out blankets.

None of my business, she thought. *I should try and get away.*

She could not bring herself to open the door, or look away. Instead she moved stealthily across the cubicle, knelt by the bottom bunk. Again, the occupant moved slightly, and now she heard a whimper. Kat reached out, lifted a corner of the blanket. A pale hand appeared, clutched at hers. She flinched and almost cried out. A small, round face appeared, big dark eyes staring.

"Have you come to take me away?"

The child's voice was quiet, but not quiet enough for Kat.

"Shhh!" she urged, then whispered. "Are you okay?"

"I'm very tired," said the child, still holding onto her hand. "And I have nightmares."

"That's very sad," she said quickly. "But can you please keep it down? If I get out of here, I'll get help, I promise."

"Don't you want to hear about my nightmares?" the child asked.

"Not now!" hissed Kat.

She tried to pull her hand away, but the little fingers gripped her so tightly she felt she would have to pry them off her. The child's huge, dark eyes reminded her of Tommy's.

"Look," she whispered urgently, "I've got to get away so I can help my little brother. He's just like you …"

She paused and stared at the face in front of her. It was not easy to make out in the shadow of the upper bunk. But the child did seem to look like Tommy. A few moments earlier she had not even been sure of the child's gender, now it was clearly a boy.

"Don't worry," said the child. "Tommy will be fine."

Kat jerked her hand back, feeling nails raking her skin. She stood up and backed away a couple of paces, colliding with the door. The sound seemed to echo.

"It's all right," said the child, throwing back his blanket. "I'll be Tommy if you like."

Beneath it the body was not quite right. Like the face, it was an attempt at being human that almost worked. Pale, smooth, and sexless, the child stood up and gazed at Kat, who felt her mind starting to lose its grip on this new, impossible reality.

"What are you?" she breathed.

"I'll be Tommy when I get close enough to him," said the creature, as if explaining a simple thing to a dull-witted person. "But I'm getting a lot of him from you. Thanks!"

Tommy was right about everything, she thought. *Replacements are real.*

"Of course, we are," said a new voice. "And we're very good."

The second figure, swinging itself down from the top bunk, did not have purple streaks in its hair, but in other respects, it was very like Kat. The green eyes she thought were too close together, the snub nose she did not like, the thighs she felt self-conscious about – all reproduced with cruel accuracy.

"Don't think like that," said the false Kat. "I can improve, over time. I just need another moment to get most of your memories. Then we can eat your brain."

"It's our favorite treat," added the false Tommy, with a horrifyingly familiar grin. "Does us good. Nourishing."

Kat groped behind her for the door, not knowing where she could run to, determined to flee nonetheless. The false Kat moved quickly, winding its arms around her, pressing its impossible face against hers, running its rough tongue over her face. She felt cold fingers scrabbling through her mind, memories starting to churn and scatter. Fragments of herself were somehow drifting away, carried by some dark current towards the monstrous being that held her.

"No!" she screamed, struggling to break free.

But now both of the creatures were holding her, dragging her over to the bunks and forcing her onto the worn mattress. Her double's mouth started to change, bulge out into a kind of tube containing a ring of needle-sharp teeth. Kat screamed, kicked, but this time her assailants were far too strong and agile.

Tommy.

He was her last thought.

***

"Is that Laura?"

The voice on the phone was familiar, but it took the reporter a moment to place it.

"Kat? Is that you?"

"Yeah, they're letting me call from Knowle House."

Laura looked at the roughed-out story on the screen in front of her. She had described the police raid on the eatery as 'shocking', their treatment of Kat 'disturbing to several bystanders'. She had larded the piece with quotes from people, mostly young, who had characterized the officers as brutal, thuggish, 'Gestapo'. But the tone of the young woman's voice suggested the piece would need a major rewrite.

"So the cops took you back to the home?" she asked. "Are you all right?"

"Yeah, I'm fine," Kat replied. "I was just freaked out by the whole anger management thing. But it's no big deal."

This is bullshit, Laura thought. *They're making her say this, somehow.*

"Is anybody with you, Kat?" she asked.

"Yeah," came the reply. "Ms. Lassiter is here, but she's cool."

That's it, Laura decided. *No way would she describe any grown-up as 'cool', let alone a member of staff.*

"Well," she said, picking her words carefully, "I'm glad you're feeling more positive about things. How's Tommy?"

The pause seemed a little too long.

"He's fine," said the girl. "Just acting up, like a typical kid. Like me, he was in a bad place, confused about stuff. But he'll be okay."

"Can we meet up again?" asked Laura. "Just for a brief chat?"

If she's being coerced, they won't let her talk to me in person.

"Yeah, no problem," Kat said. "Maybe after school tomorrow? I'll text you the time and place – they've let me have a phone, now! Okay, gotta go!"

The call ended.

Laura contemplated her story for a full minute, then deleted it all.

***

Is this my nightly ritual, now?

Denny stood in front of the bathroom mirror again, compact mirror tilted in her hand. The creature that shared her blood pulsed gently, apparently content. She tried to convince herself that it had not shrunk in the hours since she had last checked. She failed.

Could Zoffany take it off?

She thought of the doctor, a woman whose ethics had been flexible enough to work for Benson and his shady outfit. Denny had never asked exactly what Zoffany had done in the laboratories of the Romola Foundation.

And now Harriet's working for Trent.

The mere thought of the leader of the Task Force sent a shudder through Denny. At the same instant the symbiont quivered, gray-green flesh heaving. She shied away from the memory of the void, the utter lack of anything human, that she had felt when she had brushed against Trent. The plump, ever-amiable little man was not what he seemed. What he was, she had no idea.

Could be a malfunction, old Jabba getting it wrong.

It was the only comforting explanation. Frankie had suggested it during one of their infrequent phone chats. Denny did not believe it.

I can't go back. I can't trust them. But if I go on – what will happen?

Denny regarded herself in the mirror for a few moments, then went to bed. As usual, she propped her back up with a pillow so that she would not roll over onto the symbiont. She imagined waking up to find the creature dead, lying shriveled and blackened, and feeling her own life ebbing away. A line

from an old book or maybe a movie came to her, as tiredness closed her eyes.
　　Something will turn up.

Nightmare Spawn

Chapter 3: An Evolving Situation

Frankie Dupont swiped her biometric card, typed in her six-digit code, and watched the heavy door swing inward. The guard nodded to her, but still checked her ID. She walked down the corridor, came to another security checkpoint, and showed her card again.

"Just another lovely morning at the Ministry of Truth," she remarked.

The guard frowned down at her, clearly puzzled.

"Hey, the guy was British," she said. "You should know that stuff."

She walked over to the elevator, went through another swipe-and-code routine, and went down to the basement. Another security check admitted her to the lab, where Gould and Zoffany were already deep in lively conversation. When Frankie came in, they stopped.

"Hello!" said Gould, a little too cheerfully.

Sounds like bad news, Frankie thought. *He never sounds that happy if things are going okay.*

"Hi," she replied, perching on the end of a bench. "How are things in the realms of paranormal science?"

"Great," Zoffany said, but her expression suggested otherwise.

"Really? Because it looks like all your hamsters died overnight," Frankie commented. "What gives?"

The scientists exchanged a look Frankie knew all too well. In the three months, since they had joined the Task Force, she had felt increasingly marginalized, and surplus to requirements. Without Denny, she felt cast adrift inside a secretive bureaucracy that spoon-fed her information. She was convinced that Gould and Zoffany were making strides in their research, but that they were unwilling to share. It was frustrating, and now she felt her annoyance starting to boil over.

"Look," she said, glancing up at the security camera in the corner of the ceiling. "I know you can't always talk freely. But Denny's gone, and I haven't uploaded a damn thing to our channel since she went. I'm not a reporter. I'm just some random camera guy who stumbled into all this. And I don't appreciate being kept out of the loop by Trent and his goons, or by people I thought were my friends."

Gould reddened slightly, while Zoffany looked down at her shoes. Then Gould ran a hand through what remained of his hair and sighed.

"You're right, of course," he said. "We've become paranoid. We can let you know – well, something, here and now. And later, we can maybe talk about other matters."

Zoffany clutched at his arm, then looked pleadingly at Frankie.

"Maybe we can meet up at the pub later?" she said.

I'm guessing she means a noisy London pub, Frankie thought, *where nobody can overhear us.*

"Fine!" she said. "Keep it simple, I got a D in biology."

"Okay," said Zoffany. "Since Trent is going to see this soon, we might as well let you know. We think that the Lopers are evolving in a Lamarckian fashion."

The doctor paused, looking at Frankie expectantly.

"Am I supposed to know what that means?" she asked.

"Not really," put in Gould. "It's a rather obscure reference. Jean-Baptiste Lamarck was a French naturalist, quite the famous thinker in his day. His day being around the year 1800."

It was Frankie's turn to sigh.

"Okay, but what's a very dead French guy got to do with this?"

She gestured at the computer screen, on which digital images of molecules were rotating, merging, splitting apart.

"Lamarck came up with a theory of evolution," Zoffany explained, "the first one, in fact, decades before Darwin. But he was wrong. So wrong that Lamarckism became a by-word for bad ideas."

Gould was nodding eagerly.

"The giraffe's neck," he put in, "and the blacksmith's arms."

Frankie stared at him.

"Are you talking in private code now, or are you just high?"

Zoffany waved the spluttering Gould to silence and continued.

"Lamarck argued that the giraffe has a long neck because once, short-necked animals –like antelopes or deer – stretched up to reach leaves higher up the tree. This led to their offspring having longer necks, and they stretched a little bit higher, and so on. Eventually, you've got giraffes."

"Oh, I get it," Frankie cut in, pleased with herself. "So this Lamarck also argued that it applied to people, because the village blacksmith's son would have big, strong arms, too?"

"Precisely," said Zoffany, with the air of a teacher complementing a not-very-bright student. "And it's nonsense, of course. Other scientists mocked Lamarck, rejected his ideas, and the whole concept of evolution by any means was discredited. So much so that when Darwin put forward his theory of natural selection, he avoided the 'E' word. It was taboo for a long time."

Frankie jumped off the bench and went over to the computer, pointing at the gyrating cartoon molecules.

"I'm guessing there's a point to this lecture?"

Zoffany reached for the computer mouse and clicked on a file. Frankie wrinkled her nose at a film of a blob of wriggling protoplasm.

"I'm guessing that's a sample of one of the symbionts? Cute little fellas. Not."

Zoffany nodded, and grew more animated as she expounded her theory.

"These things may be the product of a kind of Lamarckian evolution. The Interlopers might be able to will new kinds of organism into existence. Well, the Queen, at least. It would explain where these mind-control symbionts come from in the first place."

Frankie peered at the writhing entity. The Task Force had recovered a few eggs from Holyhaven Island after Cassandra and her retinue had fled. From them, symbionts had been hatched.

"So Cassandra Lanier – or whatever she is now – can produce new life-forms? Whole new species?"

"Sub-species," corrected Zoffany. "Genetically all the Lopers seem very similar. But then, so are people, chimps, tamarinds. An octopus has a lot of DNA in common with a snail, but it's a genius in comparison. It's all down to slight variations in genetic coding."

Frankie tried to grasp the concept, struggled, then gave up.

"Is this a roundabout way of saying the Queen can literally squirt out some new little monster, whenever she feels like it?"

Zoffany made a helpless gesture.

"It's a lot more complex than that," the doctor said, "but yes, she can cook up a new genetic structure, albeit one based on what's gone before."

"Great. Does that mean everything we think we know about them may be wrong by now? Or will be soon?"

"I think," Gould offered, "it's fair to say that, the sooner we track them down, the better. Or they might have evolved way beyond anything we can realistically deal with."

"But what about Denny?" Frankie asked, impatience driving out any intellectual curiosity she might have felt. "What do we know about the way these things affect their hosts, long term?"

Zoffany looked away. Gould looked uncomfortable.

"We've got to tell her, darling," he said awkwardly. "She's entitled to know."

"Not here," Zoffany replied, keeping her voice low. "Let's meet up at the pub tonight."

***

Mrs. Brackett showed the day's first client into the parlor, then left with promises of tea and home-made shortbread in due course. As soon as Denny saw the young woman, she guessed she was a reporter. The brief handshake confirmed it. Denny wrestled with apprehension, knowing that the inevitable was about to happen.

"Lucy, isn't it?" she asked, gesturing her guest to a chintz-covered armchair.

"Yes, that's right!" said the tall, red-headed woman brightly. "I'm a bit nervous!"

"No need," Denny said, sitting opposite the woman. "Now, what can I do for you?"

Nightmare Spawn

Laura put her purse onto the small table between them. It was open, and Denny guessed there was a recorder of some kind inside. Possibly just a phone.

"I'm having some trouble with my boyfriend," said the reporter. "And this friend of mine said you could help, because you gave her such brilliant advice."

Denny shifted in her seat, leaning on the well-stuffed arm of the chair. She felt the symbiont shifting, perhaps sensing her unease and her rising annoyance.

"Craig, you mean?" she asked. "I thought that was over, Laura. He said you were married to the job, right?"

Denny had the satisfaction of seeing the woman's mouth fall open, her eyes widen, before the reporter recovered.

"Okay," she said, smiling ruefully, "you got me. But my pic is on the Gazette's website, and a lot of other places. How did you tumble my disguise?"

"I'm psychic," said Denny. "But I don't expect you to believe that."

Laura shook her head, her manner polite but firm.

"You're a reporter, too," the Englishwoman pointed out. "Or at least, you were. Basic research is not hard for you. What does surprise me is that somebody with your profile decided to pass yourself off as a psychic, of all things."

"Suppose I convinced you?" Denny went on. "Give me your hands."

"You're going to read my palm?"

Denny sat waiting, her own hands outstretched. After a moment, Laura Bell reached out and laid her fingertips lightly on Denny's palms. Denny, closing her eyes, breathed deeply.

A strong mind, she thought, as she skimmed Laura's thoughts, *more orderly than mine. But troubled by something recent, something that does not add up ...*

She withdrew from contact, opening her eyes. Laura was staring at her, puzzled, obviously skeptical.

"This girl, Kat," Denny said. "You're going to see her later? Can I come, too?"

Again, Laura looked comically surprised, but as before she quickly recovered. They began to discuss how Denny might have known about Kat. As Denny revealed more about the

Knowle House story, the peripheral details such as the meals Laura ordered in the pizzeria, she could see her visitor's confusion grow.

"Come on," Denny said eventually. "Do you really think I know all this because I Googled you?"

Laura slumped back into her chair, then suddenly sat upright again. She reached into her purse and took out a small digital recorder, turned it off. It took her a couple of attempts as her hands were shaking.

"Maybe this should be off the record," she said sheepishly. "I'll wipe what I have so far. And, sorry. I did think I was dealing with a fake."

Denny waved the apology away.

"Okay, I guess some of the stuff I've been involved in is hard to credit. If I were you, I'd have been suspicious."

She stood up, went over to the door, listened. Then she took a chair and shoved it under the doorknob.

"Just in case Mrs. Brackett arrives with the tea and cookies," she explained. "She may get the wrong idea."

"About what?" Laura asked.

Denny walked over to the window, drew the curtains, then took a deep breath.

"Just look, don't say anything," she said, as she lifted her sweatshirt to reveal her bare back. "Just look, satisfy yourself it's real. But please don't touch. He doesn't like it."

Half a minute later, the curtains were open again and Laura Bell was pale, trembling. Denny patted her on the back of the hand. Laura flinched, drew away.

"Sorry," she said quietly. "But I've never seen anything like that – that thing. It's a bit disturbing."

Denny removed the chair from under the doorknob.

"You might be seeing a lot more of them, if I'm right about this town."

***

The team meeting took place in Trent's newly-enlarged office. As she went in, Frankie noticed that, for the first time, there was a title on the door. It read TASK FORCE

COMMANDER. She had to smile at the thought of Trent, short and plump, as a leader of a quasi-military force.

"Welcome one and all!" said commander, waving at a side-table. "Help yourselves to coffee, tea, some nice biscuits. I promise not to keep you too long."

Every time she met Trent, she wondered if Denny had been mistaken in her judgment. She had looked for signs of something sinister, duplicitous, in her erstwhile boss. Instead she saw a typical bureaucrat, albeit one who seemed determined to be jolly and positive at all times.

"Coffee?" said Comstock, the taciturn head of security.

"No thanks," she said, smiling politely. "Just one more thing that keeps me awake at night."

Comstock had been attentive to Frankie since the incident on Holyhaven Island, but had never quite got to the point of asking for a date. She was not interested, but at the same time felt vaguely flattered by his maybe-admiration.

But I still don't trust you, fella, she thought, as she took her seat next to Gould.

"Shall we get started?" Trent said brightly. "Perhaps Ted could give us an update on our mysterious crystals?"

Gould began to explain that the talismans from Machen had been difficult to analyze, having 'properties at odds with normal physical laws'. But he revealed that, thanks to tests on Interloper eggs, it was possible to use the strange crystals to make a kind of detector.

"You mean we can scan an area for Lopers?" Frankie asked. "If so, cool."

"Yes," Trent murmured, "it is indeed *cool*. But how close would we have to get to Code Nine to spot it?"

"A few meters at most," Gould conceded. "But we would need to test it in field conditions."

"Not much chance of that," said Comstock, sourly.

This prompted a pause as they all pondered the central problem facing the Task Force. They had located no Interlopers at all since Cassandra's escape.

"Be not downhearted!" exclaimed Trent. "We expected them to lay low for a while. Sooner or later, they will tip their hand, or claw. Such beings can't remain invisible for long."

"Yes," said Gould. "But maybe we're looking for signs in the wrong places?"

This prompted a heated discussion over what tactics the enemy might adopt. Trent's line was that, as the Interlopers had tried to influence politics and the media in the past, they would try to seize 'the high ground' in future. Frankie had accepted this logic at first. She had spent thousands of hours monitoring global media, searching for any strange stories that might indicate Loper activity. But now, with every day that passed, she wondered if they were looking in all the wrong places.

"Frankie?" Trent said. "You're very quiet. Do you have anything to contribute?"

She looked around at the team.

"What's their game plan?" she asked. "What do they want?"

She heard Comstock sigh and looked over at him.

"Sure, we could just talk about seek and destroy stuff," she said. "But maybe we need to work out what the Lopers are trying to do. Why escape into our world just to become hunted fugitives? There must be more to it than that."

"Not necessarily," Comstock riposted. "Their world was dying, collapsing. They had to escape, and they somehow created a new breed that could survive more easily here. From then on they might well have had to play it by ear."

"I don't buy it," Frankie said, stubbornly. "They're not dumb. They learned a lot about us, our world, our strengths and weaknesses. Maybe they've got a detailed plan and all we've done is set it back a few months?"

This prompted another discussion, during which Trent continued to play his role of benevolent leader. Eventually the commander ruled – in his polite, amiable fashion – that they should all carry on exactly as before.

Well, Frankie thought, as the meeting broke up, *now I know why the British Empire went down the tubes.*

It was only later, as she waded through the internet's endless supply of weird material, that Frankie began to wonder. It occurred to her that if Trent was not what he seemed to be, he might want to divert the Task Force away from the Interlopers. It was when she tried to guess why, her imagination failed.

***

Laura was glad she had not brought her car. The school gates were the focus of a traffic jam that extended all the way down the street. Dozens of students were being collected by parents, while others set off on foot. There was also a queue of kids at a bus stop. The reporter passed by on the other side of the street, checking to see if Kat was there.

The teenagers in the line seemed normal enough. Laura was still trying to process the things Denny had told her. The shock of seeing the repulsive creature on the American's back had made it difficult for her to think clearly. She shuddered again at the thought of the symbiont.

At least some of what she told me must be true, she thought. *But these creatures that can take on human form are hard to believe.*

"Hey!"

Laura almost collided with Kat, who was smiling up at her. The girl still had purple streaks in her hair, but otherwise looked neater and happier than the person who had sought Laura's help.

"Hello again," the journalist replied. "You look a lot happier today. How come?"

Kat glanced around, then took Laura's arm and started to walk her back up the road.

"I don't want the others to hear this, but – before I came to see you I'd taken something. This pill a boy at the home sold to me. It sent me a bit barmy for a few hours. The cops were cool about it, said it was his fault. So, they didn't charge me. He's been sent to a young offenders' center, though. It wasn't the first time, apparently."

Laura nodded.

"Yeah, that's their policy, I understand," she said. "Hey, can we go up here? There's a little park."

Kat looked dubious for a moment.

"I don't want to miss the bus," she said. "Will this take long? I've already told you what happened."

"I can get you home in a cab, if needs be," Laura reassured her. "I just want to sit and talk for a while."

The park was almost deserted. Laura guided Kat over to a seat by a small clump of leafless trees. She glanced around and saw a small figure in a black coat heading toward them. Laura made a quick estimate of the time she needed to fill.

"Look, Kat," she said, "you said you were really worried about Tommy. Why was that?"

Kat shrugged dismissively.

"I told you, I was paranoid, bonkers," the girl insisted. "All that stuff, it was just crazy. Sorry, I've got to go."

The teenager stood up, but Laura reached out and grabbed her coat sleeve.

"Wait just one minute, please," she said. "I made time for you. What's the name of the boy who gave you the drugs?"

"Let go of me," Kat said in a low, urgent voice. "I've got to go."

"There's someone I want you to meet," Laura urged, glancing over her shoulder. "Here she is now. Tell her what you told me."

"No!" shouted Kat, yanking her arm free. "I've got to go."

Denny was just a few yards away, but even as she started to run forward, Kat fled, putting on a startling turn of speed. Laura watched as Denny tried and failed to catch the girl, who vanished through the park gates.

"Guess I'm not as fit as I used to be," Denny said ruefully as Laura caught up with her.

"You – you didn't sense anything?" Laura asked.

Denny shook her head.

"No," she said. "But didn't you sense something kind of obvious? The fact that she saw harmless little me, and ran?"

***

The pub was not crowded, but just noisy enough with televised soccer to make other people's conversations hard to overhear. Frankie picked a corner alcove. As soon as they were settled, Zoffany took out her phone and pulled up some images.

"Again with the poor mice," Frankie remarked. "What have you science types got against them?"

"Ideal test subjects," Gould said. "Similar metabolism to humans, but a lot faster. And they're easier to handle."

Frankie leaned over to peer at the screen.

"So what did you learn from these poor little guys?"

Zoffany tapped the screen.

"These mice were infected with tissue from symbionts. As you can see, the amorphous mass of protoplasm tried to form itself into the familiar, slug-like entity we've seen."

Frankie took Zoffany's phone and examined the image on the screen. The white mice looked cute, innocent, not especially worried by the gray, lumpy sausages of alien tissue along their spines. Frankie scrolled through, saw the mice apparently remaining healthy while the symbionts gradually shrank.

"Hey, are those things dying?" asked Frankie, handing the phone back. "Isn't that a good result?"

Zoffany did not answer, instead swiping onward to a picture of a white mouse seen from above. The rodent had a thin line of pink down its spine, where hair had yet to grow back. But there was no sign of the symbiont.

"So – it shrank and shrank until it fell off?" Frankie hazarded. "Or you removed it, right?"

Zoffany closed the photo app and put the phone down by her wine.

"No, Frankie," she said. "I couldn't remove it, because there was nothing left to remove."

Frustration welled up, and Frankie turned to Gould.

"You know what happened," she said bluntly. "Spill the beans. What's so terrible about a mouse with no symbiont?"

"They merged," said Gould, his voice low. "The symbiont did not shrink. It merged with the host until the cells of one organism became indistinguishable from those of the other."

Frankie stared at Gould, then at Zoffany. She struggled to process what she had just heard. She thought of the creature nestling between Denny's shoulder blades, imagined it gradually blending its alien body with hers.

"What would a human being become, if it merged with them?"

Zoffany took a gulp of wine and put her glass down before answering.

"Best guess is, a person would be the perfect Interloper slave. Their whole neural setup would be geared to the hive-mind, controlled by the Queen."

"And this is happening to Denny, now?" Frankie said, struggling to keep her voice down.

"We don't know," Zoffany admitted. "But it seems likely."

Frankie looked around the pub. At a quiz machine, a group of students were arguing about history. A party of young women in elaborate costumes was laughing uproariously. A young couple was sitting silently opposite each other, absorbed in their phones.

All so goddam normal. All totally oblivious to what's out there.

"You can tell her, can't you?" Gould said. "We know you keep in touch."

"Well done, Sherlock," Frankie replied. "Yeah, we've stayed in touch. But don't think this will make her come back to London. She really – she just doesn't trust Trent."

Gould looked skeptical. Frankie had often toyed with telling him everything about Denny's decision to leave. But she did not wholly trust Zoffany, and the two scientists were an item.

"I wish you'd told me this sooner," she said, and finished her drink. "I gotta make a call."

***

For the first time in weeks, Denny spent some time simply talking to another human being. Laura Bell had suggested they discuss 'this weird situation' in a town center pub frequented by younger professionals. Denny had been reluctant, at first. She felt that people would spot her odd, hunched profile, and stare.

"It's not that conspicuous," Laura had reassured her. "We're all wearing baggy winter clothes, after all."

Nightmare Spawn

After more urging, Denny had agreed to a coffee, reasoning that Laura was the nearest thing she had to an ally. She felt an instinctive liking for a fellow reporter. While the Englishwoman was nothing like Denny physically, she reminded her of her younger self, struggling to make an impact in a very lowly job. However, Laura also had the stubbornness and ambition of a stereotype young reporter. Denny wondered how willing the younger woman would be to take her advice.

"I think you're still too self-conscious," Laura said, putting two cups of coffee down on their table. "You could take your coat off."

Yeah, and people can see Jabba wriggle under my shirt, Denny thought.

"I'm fine," she said, smiling up at Laura. "It's not exactly warm in here."

"Skimping on heating, probably," Laura replied. "A lot of local businesses are struggling. This whole town has taken a beating, economically speaking."

Denny nodded and glanced around. There were a few prosperous-looking young people in suits enjoying lunches. But there were also one or two shabby-looking drinkers nursing pints of dark British beer.

"I don't like to judge solely on appearances," she said. "But I'd formed the same impression of Fordham. In the States we'd call it a rustbelt town."

Laura nodded in turn.

"That's the right term for it," she agreed. "There was a car factory, other major plants producing refrigerators, agricultural machinery, you name it. Lot of well-paid jobs, so young people had a chance at a decent life. But the companies shut down, one by one, until there were virtually no big employers apart from ones paying minimum wage. There's the university, some retail. It's hard to keep council services running at even a basic level. So when Moment of Truth found a ton of cash, it really made a difference."

"And nobody knows where the money came from?" Denny asked. "Nobody asked?"

"We asked, loud and often," Laura insisted, sounding defensive. "But we were told that a generous private benefactor had turned the charity around. And their results spoke for themselves. Fewer people sleeping on the streets, which was obvious enough. And more money for troubled kids, help for the elderly. The mayor was delighted, as you can imagine. He was presiding over a declining city. Well, he still is, to be honest – but things would be a damn sight worse without Moment of Truth."

"It's a hell of a contrast with London," Denny remarked.

"The London factor," Laura groaned. "We get sick of talking about it in the Gazette. Most of the nation's wealth, the media, and political power, is concentrated in one city. Not healthy. Everyone else is left fighting over the scraps from the rich man's table."

Denny felt a twinge in her back, glanced around. She caught one of the solitary drinkers staring at her. The man, gray-haired but not especially old, looked down into his glass. Nobody else seemed to be paying any attention to her.

"You're still quite jumpy," Laura commented. "We can leave if you like."

"No," Denny said at once. "At least this is a public place. Lopers are good at getting you when you're alone, isolated."

Laura was silent for a moment. Then she asked, "Can you hear my thoughts at this moment? Because I am still a tad skeptical about everything you've told me. I mean, this whole saga of portals, beings that can take on human form. It's all a bit ... well, it's an alien invasion story, in a way. B-movie stuff. With a few twists, sure. And you're someone who made her name presenting a cable show about haunted houses."

"How skeptical are you, really?" Denny shot back, irked by the way Laura was belittling her career. "At a gut level, I mean? And no, I can't hear your thoughts unless we're touching."

"Well," Laura said carefully. "I've seen mind-reading acts that were almost as good as yours."

Denny reached across the small table, but Laura pulled her hand back. It was probably an instinctive reaction, but Denny still felt vindicated. And slightly hurt.

"See?" she said. "You react to me the way people used to react to lepers. You believe in my psychic powers at a gut level, despite your skepticism. You've seen Jabba, and you can't explain what he is. But you're struggling to accept some other stuff."

"Sorry," Laura replied, looking slightly ashamed. "But I'm just trying to process a ton of new information. I mean, I've seen some of your work online, but to be honest, I thought you were just—"

"Attention seekers? Hoaxers? Most mainstream journalists thought that," Denny admitted. "But now you know things aren't so clear cut. So, what do you want to do about it?"

"Get the story," said Laura instantly. "Always, get the story."

"That's what I was afraid of," Denny said quietly. "Maybe it's a good instinct. It's how I used to think when I was young, fresh, new to the game. But if the Lopers are here, even in small numbers, they're too dangerous to tackle in conventional ways. You can't hope to expose them like they were – I don't know, a corrupt politician, a businessman avoiding paying his taxes."

"So what do you advise?" Laura countered. "Should we tell the police? They didn't believe you before, did they?"

"No, and in a relatively small city like Fordham they might have been infiltrated anyway," Denny said. "The Lopers have influenced doctors, politicians – powerful members of the community. They understand networking and string-pulling, that's for sure."

"So what do we do?" Laura demanded. "Because all my instincts say, expose this scandal, put it out there, maybe win a few awards."

The discussion went back and forth, with Denny unable to fully convince Laura that the Interlopers were real. But she also realized that the reporter had convinced herself that a great opportunity had been placed in her lap. Laura Bell had her own theory about what was happening.

"Isn't it possible," she said, "that these parasite creatures, symbionts, are being used to manipulate kids like Kat?"

Denny shook her head emphatically.

"Everything that girl told you suggests they're being replaced by Lopers. It would make sense. We know Cassandra was producing offspring in Wales. They've experimented with replacing children before. I guess they're using controlled adults to work the whole care system."

"Seriously?" Laura countered. "Think about it. They replace the kids with their own, alien, kind. Then what? Those kids might be adopted or fostered. What would happen if a foster parent discovered the truth? It all seems very risky for the Interlopers, doesn't it?"

Denny pondered the question. She struggled to form a clear picture of the scale of the infestation in Fordham. It was certainly far bigger and more elaborate than the situation on Lanier's island.

"There might be dozens of Interlopers," she said, "with Cassandra in control of dozens more human beings. The human slaves, or whatever you want to call them, could act as adoptive parents, or foster the young creatures."

"You think it would be that easy?" Laura said. "Sure, maybe they could manage to fool some people in one or two cases, but what you're suggesting involves lot of people who can't all be enslaved. Some of them would spot oddities. Kids have accidents, apart from anything else. They cut themselves, fall down. They get vaccinated, have other medical procedures. They get older, they go to school, college. How big would this conspiracy have to be to prevent word getting out?"

"Maybe that's what you need to look into," Denny suggested. "Find out just how many people are involved in this Moment of Truth sect. But please, do it carefully. And don't break cover, don't try to publish anything, without letting me know."

"What are you going to do?" demanded Laura, sounding slightly petulant. "Apart from give me orders, of course?"

"Get in touch with some people in London who may be able to help," Denny said carefully. She gave a brief, sketchy outline of the Task Force without giving any names or solid details.

"So they might be able to help?" asked Laura, sounding dubious.

Denny shrugged.

"Even though I don't trust the guy in charge," she said, "if I'm right, and Cassandra is in Fordham, the Task Force need to know."

She thought about meeting Trent again and shuddered.

No way am I going near him again. If I help them, it'll be on my terms.

Laura was regarding her with curiosity and some concern. Again, Denny wondered how reliable a confederate the British reporter would be.

"Hey," Denny said brightly. "Shall we get something to eat? I see they have fish and chips."

***

That evening in her rented room, Denny spent half an hour staring at her phone, wondering how best to call for help. One thought kept recurring to her. If Trent were something inhuman, something evil, he might simply not want the Task Force to wipe out the Interlopers, or at least not wholly succeed. Calling them in could, therefore, make things worse. It might endanger her friends to no good purpose.

But I've got precious little to bring to this fight, she thought. *If this city is turning into a Loper nest, I'm way out of my depth.*

She reached for the phone, then jumped as its ringtone blared out. She saw Frankie's name, and felt relief. For the first time in weeks she had something to share. Their old partnership could be revived, albeit at a distance.

"Hey!" she said, snatching up the phone. "Have I got news for you!"

"Can I go first?" Frankie asked, her voice strained. "Just got some bad news for you, from the science guys."

Forty minutes later, Denny ended the call, not wanting to hear Frankie's voice any longer. She could not bear to hear so much fear, pain, and confusion in someone she cared about. She put her phone down and walked into the bathroom. Everything she did, it seemed as if she were doing it for the first time. The world had changed during a simple phone call.

How long will the evening ritual endure? How long before it is me, and I am it?

In the angled mirror, the symbiont heaved slowly, waves of motion passing up its glistening body. She tried to convince herself it had not shrunk, was not shorter and slightly less protuberant. That it was not sinking into her flesh, slowly blending its tissues and nerves with hers.

I used to fool myself I'd lost weight, too, she thought. *When I was fifteen and kinda chubby.*

"Looks like we're either going to be torn apart very soon, Jabba," she said, matter-of-factly, "or we'll be together until the bitter end."

Nightmare Spawn

Chapter 4: Under the Surface

"What do you mean, you can't be sure?" Frankie demanded. "Denny's pretty damn sure, and she knows more about this whole subject than you!"

Trent made placatory noises, but persisted with his argument.

"I lead a relatively small organization dealing with a big problem," he pointed out. "And you come to me with a rather alarming report. But no actual, physical evidence."

Frankie started to protest again, but stopped when Gould put his hand on her arm. The meeting was not going according to plan. She had expected Trent to be delighted at reports of Interloper activity, or 'Code Nine' as he insisted they call it. Instead, the leader of the Task Force seemed unwilling to credit Denny's story.

Makes me think she's right about him, Frankie thought. *Or at least he's got some weird agenda.*

Comstock, the security chief, spoke for the first time since Frankie had insisted that 'friggin' Lopers are taking over some crummy English town'. He had raised an eyebrow at that. Now he raised a hand and got the nod from Trent.

"It's worth checking out, sir," he said. "Obviously we can't send a full tactical squad, but I would be happy to go along with Frankie here. And maybe Doctor Gould, as another person Ms. Purcell knows might reassure her."

"Quite so!" Trent said, eternally upbeat. "Excellent notion, Comstock. And if it turns out that there is something serious going on, we'll have a tac team up there pronto."

"But," Comstock went on, "we have to consider other possibilities. Doctor Zoffany's report on the symbionts has raised an interesting possibility."

Zoffany looked puzzled.

"What are you referring to?" she asked. "All I've really accomplished is show that blending of human and Interloper tissue is possible."

"In rodents," added Frankie.

Comstock nodded curtly.

"And that means Ms. Purcell could be under Code Nine control right now. She might be conveying a totally bogus account of activity in Fordham to lure us into the open, make us divert resources hundreds of miles away from the real threat. It's a classic tactic. Get your enemy to send his forces on a pointless expedition. Or into a trap."

Seeing Frankie's expression, Comstock moderated his tone, sounded slightly more compassionate than his usual clipped delivery.

"It's hard when it's your friend," he said. "But she could literally be living in a fantasy world, everything she sees and hears fed to her. And, completely sincere, she passes it on to her closest friend. Providing your enemy with bogus data is as old as warfare."

"That's total BS," Frankie began, but Trent was already nodding energetically.

"I think that is a remarkably astute observation, Comstock," he said. "What a splendid team I have! And yes, I know, Ms. Dupont – you don't believe your friend could be compromised in this way. Let us hope for the best, but plan for the worst."

Trent looked at Zoffany.

"While I don't like to send one of my top brains away, I feel that, as you also know, Ms. Purcell, you should go and examine her. See how far the process you identified has become."

Seething, Frankie kept her opinions to herself for the rest of the meeting. She could see some advantage in having Gould and Zoffany with her, but did not trust Comstock. Apart from a general aversion to military types, the Englishman was obviously loyal to Trent.

Later, as she went through preparations for what was being called 'the operation', she faced another unpleasant truth. Part of her had found Comstock's argument horribly convincing. She had not spoken to Denny face to face in months. Frankie went back over their conversations, wondering if much of what she had been told had been untrue.

But she seems the same, Frankie thought. *Could she be under Cassandra's control, and still seem like the person I know?*

***

Does Cassandra know I'm here?
The thought had been with Denny since her encounter in the park. She was nearly certain that Kat had been replaced by an Interloper, and that she had been recognized. She had given much thought to what she might do. One thought had recurred to her, despite attempts to suppress it. It involved herself, Cassandra, and the symbiont. It concerned her future. And it would be thoroughly unacceptable to the Task Force, probably to Frankie as well. Considered rationally, what she wanted to do was insane.

But it might be my only chance.
After breakfast, Denny spent the morning seeing clients, but her heart was not into it. She delivered formulaic advice, found it hard to put on an act of any kind. Eventually she cancelled her noon reading and told Mrs. Brackett she was going out for some air. It was a half-truth. She really wanted to be among the locals in the heart of town.

"Are you wrapped up properly, dear?" the landlady asked, looking worried. "You do give so much of yourself to others. Remember to take care of your own health."

"Thanks!" Denny said, genuinely touched by the old lady's solicitude. "I'll be fine. If it rains I'll go indoors, get a coffee or something."

Mrs. Brackett stood at the door, watching her until she turned the corner of the street. It suddenly occurred to Denny that, with the exception of Laura Bell, the landlady was her only friend in Fordham. And she sensed that the reporter was not wholly reliable, in part due to her ambition.

Never mind that, she told herself. *Think about it later. In the meantime, let's see if I'm right. Let's find out how deeply they're rooted in here.*

The morning was crisp and bright, very cold, but not icy. In the brick and concrete heart of the city, buildings were ugly, and people looked pinched and miserable. The post-Christmas slump in spirits was evident on every other face. Ted Gould had once told Denny that 'in this bloody country, winter is always at least a month too long'.

Too true, she thought bleakly. *It wears people out. The darkness, cold, damp.*

She reminded herself that she was not there to ponder the morale of the citizens. She was dangling herself as bait, waiting for signs of detection. She remembered the gray-haired man in the pub who had stared at her. She pretended to look in shop windows, study house prices, holiday bargains, sad arrays of clothing, while secretly looking out for watchers.

After a while, Denny started to feel peeved. While she was devoid of make-up and swaddled in layers of winter clothing, she had hoped to spot at least one man checking her out. Feeling the cold of the February air seeping into her bones, she entered a small shopping mall. People were closer together inside. In the past, she had avoided close-packed groups such as crowds, queues, surging commuters at stations. But now she wondered if she might try to brush against someone, touch flesh to flesh, and confirm her suspicions.

Not easy to accidentally touch a Brit in winter, though, she thought, noting how well-wrapped most people were. Then she saw a shop assistant helping an old lady with some pastries. Denny smiled to herself. *Of course! Now all I have to do is buy something I don't need. Maybe a whole bunch of somethings.*

With her limited funds, she decided to start in a shop selling greeting cards and cheap gifts. It was only then that she noticed all the heart-shaped stuff around her. Valentine's Day was nearly here. Trying not to look sour-faced, she plucked a few cards at random. At the checkout, she smiled and made a point of sounding very American as she fumbled with 'all this confusing British money', which she had been using for well over a year.

"Oh, what part of America are you from?" said the girl, and before Denny could answer, she went on to talk about how much she loved Florida. Denny handed over some notes and coins, touching the girl's hand. She got a wave of jumbled

Disneyworld memories, glimpses of fantasy characters and plates heaped high with junk food, nothing more.

"Thanks!" Denny said brightly, taking her unwanted packet of glittery sentiment.

Okay, I can't just buy stuff all day. But I'm here, under a lot of eyes. I'm making myself conspicuous. If Cassandra's spies are everywhere, I've been seen.

Denny sat in a coffee shop for a while, treating herself to a slice of cake. She managed to brush against a server's skin, and again felt nothing. A few people looked at her, but none seemed to pay her an unnatural amount of attention. She smiled to herself and thought of an old saying.

I can't get arrested in this town.

Denny tried to think herself into the mind of the Interloper Queen. They had been in contact for several hours before Gould had damaged the symbiont's rudimentary brain, cutting the link. But being under Cassandra's control had not provided Denny with much of an insight into her opponent's thinking. The Interlopers' overwhelming desire for survival was clear enough. Everything else remained murky.

Denny got up to go, and as she did so, she bumped into a gray-haired woman, who dropped her purse. She apologized, picked up the purse, and handed it over. The brief contact between their fingers was enough to show Denny that the woman had a symbiont. She felt a brief cascade of sensations, flashes of many perceptions, all vibrating like cocooned flies on a psychic web. And at the heart of the web was a cool, inhuman mind she knew.

"She would like to see you again," said the woman, who Denny knew now was called Fiona Jones. "You can come with me."

Jones tried to grasp Denny's hand. She pulled away, almost colliding with another passerby. The older woman shook her head, and walked off without speaking again. Denny watched her go, wondering how many other people around her were in Cassandra's network. She found herself suspecting everyone who was slightly stooped, then reminded herself that half the people she could see were seniors.

Still, she thought, *at least I know for sure, now. They're here.*

Denny walked out of the mall and into the chill air, heading back towards her B&B. She thought about Jones's offer. Her thoughts turned to ridding herself of the symbiont, and she felt the creature's unease, its restless movements pulling at her violated flesh. She thought back to the moment on Lanier's island when she and Frankie had been drugged and the creatures had hatched, fastening themselves to the women's bodies. Frankie had been stronger, braver, and had escaped enslavement. Denny had endured a messier fate, leaving her caught between the world of human and Interloper.

But at least when I was linked to the rest, I got a pretty clear picture of how their system works.

Cassandra, she felt, could restore her humanity, if she chose. The power of the Interloper Queen over her subjects was virtually limitless. Removing a symbiont was possible, Denny was sure. But she was still struggling to think of a plausible way to make the near-miracle happen.

I can choose human science with Zoffany, and take my chances. It may already be too late for her to deal with Jabba. Or I can risk it all and go to the real expert, who could simply kill me. Or ensure I become a loyal little slave forever.

She arrived at the bed and breakfast, put her key in the door. As she turned it, she racked her brains for ways to make Cassandra co-operate, at least long enough to free her. She walked into the bright hallway just as Mrs. Brackett appeared from the kitchen, carrying a tray of homemade cookies.

"Hello dear!" said the landlady. "Chocolate chip?"

"You talked me into it," Denny replied.

What I really need, she thought, *is a bargaining chip.*

***

"Why brains?" asked Frankie.

The Fordham team were meeting at the lab, checking out some of the equipment that might come in useful. Frankie had become impatient with Comstock's apparently endless lecture on correct procedures, non-lethal weapons, the need to for regular check-ins, and a lot more.

"What?" Comstock asked, looking slightly flustered.

Frankie, always happy to ruffle the security chief's composure, repeated the question.

"I mean," she went on, "the old-school Lopers didn't eat human brains, so far as I know. Hell, they could have eaten mine when they snatched me. But I found a lot of corpses with empty skulls at Mountfalcon House. Harriet? You solved that one? Because it's been bugging me, and yet it never seems to come up at meetings."

Zoffany looked more uncomfortable than Comstock did.

"It never comes up because I'm simply not sure what it signifies," she admitted. "Of course, brains are a source of nutrition in themselves. It's dense tissue, about a third of the body's blood supply fuels the brain. But why they eat cerebral tissue and not other human organs is a bit of a mystery."

"Maybe they just like the taste," put in Gould, with a grimace.

"That could be it," Zoffany agreed. "We eat some animal body parts but not others. We're disgusted by the thought of eating brains, but not so long ago there were tribes that practiced headhunting so they could get what they regarded as a delicacy."

Comstock gave a little snort.

"I know a bit about those tribes," he said. "I met some of them on active service, talked to a really old guy whose granddad had been a headhunter. They might have liked brain casserole, or whatever, but that wasn't their main motive. They believed that eating an opponent's brain meant you acquired his virtues – courage, strength, that sort of thing."

Frankie felt her stomach heave slightly.

"So, Lopers might be literally taking some human qualities by eating gray matter?" she asked. "But they don't need to do that to read people's thoughts. So what else is there?"

Zoffany shrugged.

"It could be a way of maintaining themselves in our world," she hazarded. "Or part of it, anyhow. Just as we need certain trace elements in our diet, perhaps Interlopers need to regularly absorb something essentially human to mimic us. Problem is, I have no Interlopers – sorry, Comstock, no Code Nines – to experiment on. Depriving them of brain matter for a while would be interesting. How often do they need to eat?

The group fell silent as each person contemplated that idea. Finally, Gould broke the silence.

"If there were thousands of Code Nines," he said. "They'll need an awful lot of brains. Even if they rationed themselves to just one at birthdays and Christmas."

"All the more reason to deal with them quickly," Comstock said. "So, can we get back to this detector, Doctor Gould?"

Gould started to describe how his research into the Machen talisman had led him to produce 'a potentially useful gadget'. After a minute, Frankie put her hand up, smiling sweetly.

"How do we know it will actually detect a Loper?" she asked, pointing to a box that looked something like a Geiger counter. "If we don't have one to test it on?"

"It works on tissue samples from symbionts," Zoffany said, always quick to defend Gould. "On the basis of lab tests, it should work in the field."

"Good to know," Comstock said in his usual deadpan away. "I'd hate to shoot an actual human being in the head by mistake. The paperwork is a nightmare."

***

Laura had just put her bag and lunchtime sandwich down on her desk when she heard her editor calling from his office.

"What is it, Mike?"

"Come in for a minute, please. There's something I need to share with you."

The man sat hunched over at his desk, looking shrunken and pale. His skin, normally ruddy, looked gray in the diffused winter light. Laura paused in the doorway, shocked to see him looking so unwell.

"God, Mike, should you be at work? Is it the flu? Should I call Monica?"

The editor waved away her concern, motioned her to sit. As she did so, he burst into a fit of coughing, covering his mouth with a tissue. When he had recovered, he looked over at her, his expression unreadable.

"I wasn't entirely honest with you," he said finally. "About the girl from Knowle House?"

Laura started to speak, wanting to give him some background on what had happened since. But Mike raised a hand.

"Please, let me talk. The reason I wasn't keen for you to talk to her, is – well, for a few weeks now I've been going to these meetings. I suppose you could say I've joined Moment of Truth. It was really something Monica wanted to do, you know she does a lot of charity work."

"Why didn't you mention it before now?" she asked quietly. "I thought we were friends."

"I was told to keep it to myself," he croaked, before breaking into more coughing. Again, he took a few moments to recover. Laura felt alarm growing. Her formerly healthy, if workaholic, boss seemed to have become a wreck in a matter of hours.

Or was he getting worse for days and I was just too wrapped up in my work to see it?

"And there's something – something not quite right, something I can't seem to ..."

Laura stood up in alarm as her editor struggled to form words. She feared he was having some kind of seizure. A dribble of saliva appeared at the corner of his mouth and trickled onto his stubbled chin. She strode around his desk, loosened his tie, and tried to push him back into his chair. But he gave a half-strangled yell and shoved her away.

"I'm alright, really!" he insisted. "It's just one of those viruses that go around, it's that time of the year."

The editor sat up straight, apparently forcing himself to adopt his usual business-like posture. He waved Laura to a chair and waited while she sat. Then he gave a smile that looked forced.

"I should see the doc, you're right," he conceded. "It's just so hard to get an appointment that fits around my schedule. You know how it is?"

Laura nodded uncertainly.

"About Moment of Truth?" she reminded him.

"Oh, yes," he said. "I know you've done a few reports on its activities, but there's an aspect to it that you probably don't know. And it's frankly disturbing."

He leaned forward confidentially.

"They've started going in for these weird rituals," he explained. "At the old factory they took over, there's a kind of – temple, I suppose. A place of worship, anyway. And it's distinctly un-Christian. In fact, it's not like any faith I've ever heard of. It's a bit too big for me to handle alone, I think. I need your help."

Laura was elated.

"I've been talking to a rather unusual source about this," she said quickly. "I'd really like to get at the truth, and if you already have an entrée to this cult–"

"I can get you in," Mike confirmed. "If you want to see what goes on."

Laura thought about what Denny had told her. She remained skeptical about many of the American's claims, and there was also a touch of professional rivalry. If she could get to a big story, blow the lid off a conspiracy, it would do her career a lot of good.

"It might be risky," the editor added, dabbing his mouth with a tissue. "We could contact the authorities in London – Scotland Yard, perhaps. But without any real evidence, they would be within their rights to treat us as cranks. Whereas if we could get some hidden-camera footage, it would at least prove something odd is going on."

Laura agreed, already wondering how best to go about filming the ritual.

"How many people attend these rituals?" she asked. "And when is the next one scheduled for?"

***

Comstock got into the elevator, inserted his key, and pushed the button for the sub-basement. He did not know how long he would be away in Fordham and wanted to check that all was secure. He had decided to start with the so-called panic room, which most of the civilian operatives did not know existed.

The brief journey from the ground floor ended and the doors rumbled open. A uniformed guard nodded and checked Comstock's ID carefully. The man knew better than to just wave his boss through.

"Boss is down there, chief," the guard added. "Went in about ten minutes ago."

Comstock paused, then nodded, walked along a short corridor, and stood before a heavy door that reminded him of a bank vault.

EMERGENCY CONTROL CENTER

He had no idea why Trent would have decided to check out the underground chamber, but it did not change Comstock's plans. He swiped his card again, entered his code, and the door clicked open. The lights, as expected, were already on. Comstock walked in, saw a familiar row of desks and terminals. The 'panic room' in fact consisted of a set of linked rooms, with a self-contained system that could – in theory – let personnel survive a major disaster. Comstock was always skeptical about untested claims but felt that a refuge of some sort of made sense, given the Task Force's role.

Okay, let's check it out. See where the boss is.

He made his way along one wall of the room, stepping around various boxes of dried food and canned goods. He made a mental note to get someone to store the provisions properly, then hesitated at the inner door. Comstock, for the first time since childhood, felt an odd sense of trepidation. Hairs stood up on the back of his neck. It was an unwelcome sensation, and it took him a few moments to recognize it.

Fear of the unknown. Bloody ridiculous.

He grabbed the handle and yanked the door open. The inner room was a sleeping area with bunks, more randomly-dumped boxes, plus TV screens and a home entertainment system. A door led to a washroom. But Comstock only glanced at these, as his attention was caught by what looked like a strange optical illusion.

What the hell is that?

About two feet above the floor between two rows of bunks, the air was curved. Comstock seemed to be looking through a huge lens about three feet wide. It seemed to shimmer, reminding him of warm air rising above a radiator. He took a step toward it, reached out a hand, then pulled it back.

Don't stick your fingers into something if you don't know what it is.

He took out a notebook, tore off a scrap of paper, and held it above the weird, transparent bubble. When he dropped it, the paper fluttered into the shimmering sphere, and vanished. He took out a pen and threw it at the anomaly. The pen flickered out of existence. Comstock took out his phone and filmed the flickering globe for a few moments. He tore off some more paper, dropped it into the sphere, and it vanished. He stopped recording and saved the video to the cloud.

If it destroys things, it's dangerous. If it somehow moves them somewhere else, it could be even more dangerous.

"Portal," he said aloud, surprised at taking so long to realize the obvious. "It's a bloody portal."

***

"Don't do it!" Denny warned. "I can't believe you're contemplating this at all. Wait for my – wait for the team from London to arrive. At least promise me you'll do that."

Laura shook her head firmly. She had come to meet her erstwhile ally, explaining that she wanted to keep Denny in the loop. But she was obdurate about getting the story herself. Now they were sitting in a coffee shop, trying not to raise their voices.

"Wait for London to sort it out?" she asked. "Wait for them to come in, clear things up, and leave us ignorant provincials in the dark?"

Denny gawped. Despite living in England for nearly two years, she had never really grasped the resentment people outside London felt for the 'elite' in the capital. Seeing Laura's stubborn expression, she decided to change tack.

"Laura," she pleaded, "a dead reporter can't file the story. You go into their lair, they will read your mind. Know your intentions. And deal with you."

Laura titled her strong chin up a little, a gesture Denny had started to become familiar with. She wondered if anything she could say would get through to the Englishwoman.

"I've been thinking about all this," she said. "Yes, I've seen some evidence of – let's call it the paranormal. But that thing on your back could be some kind of parasite I've never seen before. And, like I said, your mind-reading trick could be just that. I don't have to accept everything you tell me. There's a story here and I'm determined to get it."

She's suspicious of claims made without supporting evidence, Denny thought, frustrated. *It's not a bad rule to follow if you're a reporter. But in this case, it might be fatal.*

"Okay," she said. "Do what you like. But please, keep me in the loop? I'm not your enemy, here, Laura."

"I know," said Laura, getting up to go. "But we don't really know each other, do we?"

"I know you," Denny said quietly. "That's a fact."

Laura said nothing more, and simply left. Denny looked at the closing door, the sound of the quaint bell echoing around the half-empty room. She wondered if she would see Laura again.

And if I do, will she be a free woman, or another one of Cassandra's minions?

Her phone chimed. It was the latest in a steady stream of text messages from Frankie, updates on the Task Force's activities. Denny frowned at the words 'Still stuck in friggin' London!', then had to smile. Frankie's perennial impatience was clearly not a good fit when it came to bureaucrats and security types.

'Is Trent coming?' she texted back.

If he does, I will have to steer clear of him, arrange to meet Frankie separately.

'No,' came the reply, 'me, G, Z, and C. If C ever gets his act together.'

That's one less thing to worry about, Denny thought.

She was preparing for her next client when an idea came to her. It was simple, and might actually work. She turned the notion over in her mind, pondered whether it would be the key to ridding herself of the damaged symbiont. The creature, sensitive to her state of mind, throbbed uneasily. Even its damaged brain might be aware that Denny could, for the first time, see a clear path to freedom. Clear, but very hazardous.

"Sorry, Jabba," she murmured. "Like they always say in these situations, it's not you, it's me."

***

The portals all vanished, Comstock thought. *That's what Gould and the other scientists said. That's what we all assumed. But now they're back. Or at least one of them is.*

Comstock's military training kicked in and he moved slowly away, backing out of the room, preparing to report the anomaly, possible intruders. It would be wise to keep the information from all but high-level personnel. He was heading for the entrance when a voice stopped him in his tracks.

"Comstock?"

The security chief did not jump. But he spun around, adopting a fighting stance, his breathing suddenly quick and shallow. Standing in the doorway to the inner room was Trent. The Task Force commander was in his shirtsleeves, tie a little crooked. His belly bulged out over his pants waistband.

"Is there a problem?" the little man asked. "You look a trifle disconcerted, old chap."

"Sir," Comstock said, stepping aside from the doorway. "There's something – I don't know what it is, but it's unnatural. Perhaps Code Nine related."

Comstock suddenly felt foolish. His boss had obviously just been in the room.

How could he not have seen it? I must have imagined it.

Trent went up to the inner doorway and stopped on the threshold to look up at his subordinate.

"Not one of them, surely?" he whispered. "An Interloper?"

Comstock's surprise and confusion gave way to mild annoyance. He shook his head and gestured into the room.

"No, sir, not a creature – more of a phenomenon, something I've never seen before."

Trent walked back into the inner room and went out of sight. Comstock heard the little man, sounding quizzical.

"Well, if there's something odd in there, I can't see it. Care to point it out?"

Comstock stood in the doorway, staring at the very ordinary rows of bunks, the scattered boxes.

"I'm sorry, sir," he said. "I thought … Well, whatever it was, it seems to be gone now."

"Best to make sure," Trent said, pointing at the area where the sphere had floated. "Check it out more closely."

Comstock was already inside the room when he realized what Trent had said.

"How did you know where it was?" he demanded. "I didn't tell you it was between those two rows. What's going on, sir?"

Trent was his usual smiling self as he approached on small feet, hands outstretched. Momentarily off balance, Comstock retreated, then paused and raised a hand in warning. Then he stared, open-mouthed. There was more than one Trent.

That's impossible.

Without any warning, three, then four, then five of the short, smiling men were closing in on him.

"What is this?" Comstock stammered, reeling back, fighting against a rising sense of panic. He groped for his holstered pistol, almost dropped it. "Who are you? Interlopers?"

One Trent shook his head, another waved an admonitory finger. The Trent in the middle, which Comstock thought might be the original.

"We are all Trent, there is really only one of us. We were Benson a while ago. We might be someone else soon."

"Humans are easy to forge," added the Trent on the far right. "We enjoy it, but it's hardly a challenge."

Comstock had managed to draw his gun, and he pointed it at the nearest Trent. The small figure raised his hands in an exaggerated gesture of surrender. The other four moved a pace forward. Comstock shifted his aim to the left, then the right. He thumbed off the safety catch, sure that the move would be clear at such short range.

"You can't harm us with that crude weapon," said the second Trent from the left, as the others shook their heads. "If you try—"

The implicit threat was cut off by the dull, heavy thud of the pistol. Despite his confusion, Comstock's aim was good. A small hole appeared in the forehead of the middle Trent of the five. A spatter of blood on the wall behind the row of Trents showed that the bullet had gone right through the little man's head.

"Oh dear," said the Trent who had been shot. "You've gone and done it. Very unprofessional, shooting your boss. I hope you're not expecting a bonus next Christmas."

Comstock stared as the bullet hole closed up. At the same time, another Trent took the gun gently from his hand, and two others gripped him firmly by the arms. He felt himself forced backwards. Suddenly he was falling, the mundane room and the weird assailants vanishing.

And then he was in another world.

Nightmare Spawn

Chapter 5: The Cult

According to Mike, the next meeting of Moment of Truth would take place on Saturday evening, two days away. Laura decided to inform Denny about it, but leave it until the last minute so that the American could not muscle in on her story. In the meantime, she prepared for the encounter as best she could. She decided to use a more effective hidden camera than simply turning on her phone and leaving it in her bag.

"What would you recommend?" she asked her editor. "I mean, our choice is limited. Which gadget gets the best sound quality? Video might not matter so much in the circumstances."

"Use that one," Mike said, pointing to a compact black box. "It's the most reliable."

It was the day after Mike had revealed his link to Moment of Truth. His health seemed to have recovered overnight, and he was even enthusiastic about exposing the cult. He explained in some detail, complete with diagrams, what the venue of the meetings was like. He also set out a rough outline of the way services were conducted.

"I'm still not clear," Laura said, "who actually runs things? I mean, you said it was un-Christian, so what is it like? Are we talking about devil worship or something? Because that would make a great story? Or is it just hippie stuff, chanting and meditation? Because that's quite dull."

At that point, Mike seemed puzzled, as if struggling to remember.

"Who runs it?" he said quietly. "Jack Munby is the director of the charity, of course. Always has been. Very nice bloke."

"I know," Laura said, slightly impatient now. "But does Munby run the meetings, rituals, whatever? Or is it someone else?"

Mike looked at her, seeming to struggle to find words.

"Munby welcomes us all," he said. "Then she appears. And everything feels different."

Laura perched on the edge of Mike's desk and laid a hand gently on his shoulder. She felt protective of her boss, their roles suddenly reversed as she saw a child-like confusion in his heavy, pale features.

"Who's she, Mike?" she asked gently. "You can tell me."

The editor peered at her for a long moment, then smiled, shook his head.

"Oh, you'll see what it's like on the night," he said. "Nothing I tell you can prepare you for – for how odd it is. How peculiar."

"Okay."

Laura stood up, hesitating before returning to her desk.

"You are feeling better?" she asked. "You just seem a little – vague at times."

"Oh, don't worry about me," Mike said. "You get on with the background stuff. I'll be fine – always full of energy when I'm actually running down a scoop."

***

The Task Force Team arrived in Fordham by train, then got a hire car at the station. Comstock drove them to a large, private residence, set back from the road, and screened by trees.

"So who owns this place?" Frankie asked, looking around the spacious entrance hall. "Her Majesty, the Queen?"

"The correct term is the Crown," Gould corrected her. "As I understand it, these discreet properties are all over the place. Special Branch, MI5 and the like, need secure little places to stash a captured spy overnight, or hide a defector. That kind of thing."

"That so, Comstock?" Frankie asked.

The security chief stared at her blankly for a moment, as if not recognizing her.

He's been a little off since yesterday, she thought. *Wonder if he's coming down with something.*

"Gould's right," Comstock said. "It's a secure property – alarms, cameras, the lot. And the ground floor windows are barred, as you see."

"Great," Zoffany said sourly, putting down her bags. "Like a Victorian asylum."

"We having something to eat after the journey?" Frankie asked.

Again, Comstock was slow to respond.

"Kitchen must be through the back," Zoffany said, finally. "Let's see what's in the freezer."

After they had eaten, they sat around the kitchen table, roughing out plans based on Denny's messages. The question arose as to whether they should work closely with her. A split developed between Comstock and Zoffany, on the one hand, and Frankie on the other. Gould tried to mediate, uneasily.

"All I'm saying," Frankie insisted, "is that I should be the one to work with her, simply because she has some trust issues."

"I would rather," Comstock said, "have her close at hand. People who go off on maverick crusades tend to get themselves, and other people, in trouble."

The argument petered out with everyone accepting that Denny would decide for herself, and that Frankie would try to win her over.

"What about this Moment of Truth meeting?" Gould asked. "Might it be significant?"

"No way could we get in as potential recruits," Frankie pointed out. "We're all known to them. Same reason Denny can't try to sneak in."

"There are other ways to get into a building than through the front door," Comstock said. "I'll check the place out. And we'll be able to track this Laura Bell woman."

From one of his numerous buttoned pockets he produced a small tablet computer.

"With this I can hack into cell phones. At the very least we'll know her location."

"Same goes for Denny, I take it?" Gould asked. "And of course, the rest of us?"

Comstock nodded and put the device away.

"Now, Ted, how about your Code Nine detector? We could take it out on the streets for a trial run."

As the scientists began to discuss technical issues with the detector, Frankie raised a hand.

"Can I take a rain check on this? I've got to see an old friend."

***

"Oh God."

Denny pulled her sweatshirt back down to conceal the symbiont. Frankie struggled to find words.

"That thing is getting smaller," she said finally. "I'm sure it's shrunk. And anyway, you'd expect it to grow, right?"

Denny resumed her seat in her chintzy armchair. They were in Mrs. Brackett's parlor, with Frankie posing as a client for now. The customary tray bearing a pot of tea, china cups, and a plate of homemade cookies sat on a small table between them. The horror of what clung to Denny, contrasted with the setting, only made it seem more nightmarish to Frankie.

"You said something about a cure?" Frankie hazarded. "I'm guessing this doesn't involve Zoffany and her medics?"

Denny shook her head firmly.

"Nope, I was hoping to get Jabba taken off by a real expert."

It took Frankie a moment to realize what her friend was implying. She felt a sinking sensation, disbelief, and then wondered if Denny was still wholly sane.

If she's gone a little crazy, Frankie thought, *who could blame her?*

"When we agreed to film at Malpas Abbey, I never thought we'd end up like this," she said. "And now that I've said that, I feel kind of stupid. But still, if I'd known."

"We couldn't have known," Denny said wearily. "We didn't really believe in ghosts, back then. And we were right not to. Turns out there was something far worse out there, hiding in the dark."

"From what you've told me," Frankie said, "they might not need to hide for much longer. You really think they're placing young Lopers with controlled parents? Because that's way more ambitious than anything they've tried before."

Denny turned her head to look out at the street through the lace curtains.

"This world is their home, now," she said quietly. "Or at least, they need it to be. I don't know what the end game is, I never got any sense of their strategy. But Cassandra clearly has a lot of offspring. If they successfully infiltrate society, spread out, then they'll be like a virus. We'll need a magic bullet to stop them."

Frankie stared down at the plate of untouched cookies.

"And you're planning to try and cut a deal with her?" she asked. "How could that ever work? What do you have to offer?"

Denny looked at her friend.

"I can't tell you," she said. "Because if I did, it might put you in danger."

"That's a load of BS!" Frankie exclaimed, jumping up. "We've been through hell together. The Phantom Dimension was as near to hell as you can get and come back alive. But now you can't trust me? Now you keep secrets?"

There was an uncomfortable silence. Eventually Denny leaned forward, picked up a cookie, dipped it into her teacup. After she had taken a bite, she adjusted the cushion behind her back.

"I want to get rid of this thing, sure," she said. "And maybe my judgment isn't perfect. But I know there's something not right about Trent. Don't ask me what, just accept it. So long as you work with the Task Force, anything else I tell you might put you at risk. You see that, don't you?"

Frankie said nothing and got up.

"If you need any help, you know how to get in touch," she said. "This Moment of Truth thing – looks like Comstock is planning to run surveillance on it. So, if you want to avoid him, and us, probably best keep away."

***

Gould, Zoffany, and Comstock paused in their trial run of the Code Nine Detector. They had made a couple of sweeps along the leafy, quiet streets around their base of operations. The device, disguised inside a digital camera case, had not flickered. They had passed dozens of homes, and been passed by cars and a couple of buses. It was a bleak, drizzly afternoon, and pedestrians were rare. Gould had scanned a couple from the other side of the street, again with negative results.

"Maybe," Comstock suggested, "it's a range issue? If you have to get within a couple of meters, it would be impossible to hide your identity from a Code Nine, right? They read minds at close range?"

Zoffany nodded unhappily while Gould tinkered with the settings on the makeshift gadget.

"Or," Comstock went on, "perhaps that talisman-crystal is faulty in some way? Do they run out of juice after a hundred years?"

"The basic physical properties of matter," said Gould, "do not change over time like that. Or at least, they shouldn't. It could be that there simply aren't that many Interlopers – sorry, Code Nines – around."

Zoffany, recognizing Gould's lecturing tone, tried to change the subject.

"Maybe we should go to a more crowded area," she suggested. "Somewhere with shops, or maybe back to the rail station?"

The men agreed to her suggestion, and set off towards the center of town. They were about to cross a road when Comstock reached out an arm to stop Gould stepping off the curb. A bus roared by. At its windows, Zoffany saw two decks of faces, at least half of them peering into their phones. A few, however, were looking out, and stared at her as they swept by.

"Oh my God," said Gould, holding up the detector. "The bloody thing just went crazy. Who was on that bus?"

"It was a school bus," she said.

***

Saturday night came, and Laura accompanied Mike and his wife Monica to the old industrial district on the outskirts of Fordham. As they left the heart of the city, she gazed with distaste on great drifts of garbage in vacant lots and around closed stores, empty warehouses. She thought of rats, and shuddered. It came as a relief when they reached the newly-refurbished headquarters of Moment of Truth.

Nightmare Spawn

A dozen cars were already parked outside the factory when they pulled up. Prosperous-looking individuals and couples were heading inside. The general air was one of anticipation, with a slight hint of nervousness. Laura thought of an award ceremony, or some other high-toned social gathering.

Mike and Monica nodded to acquaintances and exchanged everyday gossip, as they filed in. Laura found herself in a large ante-room. Here, she had been told, they were expected to don ceremonial garb. This, according to Mike, symbolized the rejection of their worldly, everyday selves. As she put on a gray hooded robe, Laura wondered if it might also serve to conceal the identities of some of the members.

Whatever the purpose, she thought, *it makes life more difficult for this humble reporter.*

She had fixed a small microphone to her skin just underneath her collar line. Fortunately, Mike had been right when he told her that only coats and jackets needed to be removed before robing. She even found a moment when, back turned to the rest, she fixed the tiny camera just over one ear, half-hidden by her hair.

With the hood up, it should be undetectable.

She had just finished adjusting the camera when an inner door opened and people began filing slowly into the main part of the building. Laura had lost sight of Mike and Monica, and did not dare call out for them. She let the small crowd carry her through the doorway, reasoning that Mike would not be far away.

Inside the factory, Laura stopped, gazing upward. Spotlights hanging from the high ceiling illuminated a kind of low stage in the middle of the vast space. Behind it, she could just make out what seemed to be partitioned cubicles. Far above them was a kind of metal gantry, with steps leading up to what had obviously been compact offices for management.

But it was the stage that drew the eye. There were around fifty people gathered around the raised dais, which was backed by a dark-red curtain. It reminded Laura of a small theater, and she inevitably found herself wondering what might be behind the curtain.

Not the Great Oz, presumably.

She glanced around the crowd again, hoping that the camera was getting some usable shots. Laura frowned, started counting heads. It seemed as if the number of people had grown considerably since they had filed in. She looked around at the entrance. The door was shut. She wondered if people might have come in some other way.

Seems to be more women and kids than I'd expected, she thought. *At least, most of these people seem to be on the small side.*

There was a slight stir of anticipation as someone appeared from the shadows and climbed up onto the low platform.

"Welcome!" said the man on the dais. "Welcome, friends, to this communion. I am proud to say that our little charity has become a little larger recently."

There was a ripple of amusement. Laura felt herself relax slightly. The weak attempt at levity was typical of regular church services. She recognized the speaker as Jack Munby, the charity boss, who had always seemed reasonable and good-natured.

Maybe Moment of Truth is exactly what it purports to be, she though. *Or maybe it's just good at disguising its dark side. We shall see.*

Munby launched into a fairly standard speech about the charity's good work, its ongoing achievements, and how vital it was to build a better world 'for the children'. So far, so conventional. If the congregation had not been wearing hooded robes, Laura might have been among Quakers. But she sensed, as Munby reached the end of his litany of platitudes, that something more unusual was coming.

"And now," Munby said, "let us give thanks to the one who has made this all possible. The one who is the source of all our spiritual strength. The one who will transform our city, our nation, and eventually our world."

No explicit reference to God, Laura noted. *Just the reference to some higher power.*

Without any preamble, the people around her launched into what she took at first to be prayer, but which she soon realized was more of a chant. She struggled to pick out the first few words, but caught most of what followed.

To bring peace to all the nations
To unite the warring tribes
To end all wars, abominations,
Make earth fruitful, hopeful, wise

From the darkness set us free
Fair exchange and covenant
Bring our world sweet unity
Fair exchange and covenant

Laura puzzled over the meaning of 'fair exchange'. Then Kat's story came back to her, with renewed force. She felt a sudden chill, a disorienting fear that Denny Purcell had been right all along.

No, she thought. *I can't believe children are sacrificial victims of some unimaginable cult. Nothing that's happened here supports that crazy notion.*

Laura began to feel an odd sensation, a tingling that ran through her limbs. It made the hairs on the back of her neck stand on end, sent her heart racing, and her breathing became more rapid. The chant rose, became more urgent, but somehow, she could no longer make out the words. Her mind was fuddled, and she started to feel hot.

They can't heat up such a huge space in February, she thought. *But it seems warm in here.*

"I see we have some new faces here!"

Laura realized that the chanting had ended, and that Munby was smiling down at her from the lectern. The serried ranks of worshippers parted, moving with silent precision, as if in a well-rehearsed maneuver. Laura felt the people around her ushering her forward. She tried to resist, then decided that she did not want to make a fuss and draw even more attention. At least two others were being led up to the dais, which reassured her slightly. However, she could not think of a way to conceal the camera taped above her ear. If the hood was lowered and she was seen up close, in a good light, she would be exposed.

I'm screwed, unless Mike can help me.

"Don't worry," said the person on her left. "It'll be fine. We've all met her."

Laura looked round to see Mike's face under the gray hood. Monica was on the other side, eyes bright, smiling cherubically.

"I had to pretend there was a problem," Mike explained, as they approached a short flight of steps onto the platform. "You would hardly have come if I'd simply told you it was wonderful, now would you?"

Laura began to struggle, but the combination of the couple holding her arms and the odd sensation of heat soon left her exhausted, passive. She stumbled, was lifted onto the first step, and Munby bent down to help her onto the stage.

"No!" she pleaded, trying to sound confident, authoritative. "Please, you can't do this. You won't get away with it."

"Nothing to be scared of, people!" Munby said cheerfully. "Once you meet her, all will be made clear."

He stepped back a couple of paces and pulled back the curtain a few feet. Mike and Monica bundled Laura through into a darkened room. The curtain fell back into place and Laura was released.

"Welcome!"

The voice came from somewhere immediately in front of her. Stray radiance from the spotlights above just allowed Laura to make out a large, ill-defined shape.

"Come closer, let me see you, Laura."

The voice was strong and deep, but still clearly feminine.

"I can't see you," she said. "Can you turn up the light at little?"

A faint glow appeared, brightened, to reveal an imposing figure. The pale-skinned woman lying on the huge, well-padded couch was astoundingly beautiful. Laura felt a sense of sudden well-being, as if she had walked into a patch of sunlight in a dark forest. The factory, with its stained walls and high, grimy windows, seemed to recede to a vast distance. They were in a small room, plainly furnished.

"Is that better?" the majestic woman asked.

Laura nodded, took a pace forward. Then she recalled what Denny had told her, and hesitated.

"Are you – Cassandra?" she asked, hesitantly.

Nightmare Spawn

The woman laughed, a deep, throaty sound.

"I go by many names," she said. "I am what I am. Call me Cassandra if you like. Come closer. Sit by me."

***

"The detector is going wild again," Gould muttered. "It's a prototype, so it might simply be unreliable."

The Task Force team were parked about a hundred yards along the road from the old washing machine factory. Gould had registered Code Nine emissions from every vehicle that passed them. Now that the Moment of Truth ceremony had begun, the device was producing erratic readings, some spiking to maximum

"If it's not unreliable, what do all those red bars signify?" Zoffany asked.

"Maybe some kind of energy emission," Gould hazarded. "No matter how their paranormal powers work, they must release energy. They can't be totally immune to basic physical laws."

"You love saying that," said Frankie, half-joking. "But they're psychic monsters from another dimension, so pardon me if I'm a tad skeptical."

"Fair point," replied Gould, squinting at the detector's small screen in the dark. "But the fact remains, something is happening in there."

There was a brief pause while they waited for Comstock to say something. The security chief was in the driver's seat, staring into the night at the glow of Fordham's street lights.

"Comstock? What do we do?" Frankie asked finally.

"One round discharged," said Comstock, apparently talking to himself. "But I never fired it. All live rounds must be accounted for."

Frankie looked at Zoffany, who shrugged.

"Comstock!" rapped Gould, looking up from the detector. "What?"

Comstock looked round, betraying slight annoyance at being caught apparently daydreaming. Then he took out his pistol, checked the clip, holstered it again under his jacket.

"Okay, this is dangerous work, but we have to assess how many there are and, if possible, what they're up to. I'd prefer you all stayed here, but Gould knows how to work that gadget, so I'm willing to let him come."

"So generous," said Frankie. "But what makes you think I'm going to sit around doing nothing?"

She hefted a video camera.

"This thing has night-vision, plus infra-red," she explained. "Your little spy mission might benefit from actual pictures of the bad guys, right?"

"All right," Comstock began, "the two of you can accompany me so long as you do as you're told."

The team climbed out of the rental car. Comstock pointed at Zoffany, who was fastening her winter coat.

"What are you doing, doctor? You're not a trained field operative."

"I'm buggered if you're going to leave me sitting in the dark by myself," Zoffany protested. "Plus, don't you Special Forces types usually go into action with a medic?"

Comstock sighed.

"All right, let's make it an episode of Scooby Doo," he said. "But if there's trouble, don't try to be heroes – simply run back for the vehicle."

"Don't you mean the Mystery Machine?" asked Frankie, as they set off down the road.

***

Cassandra gestured languidly at a stool by the couch. Laura felt that she had no choice, although there was no way the tall woman could miss the miniature camera. She walked over to the stool and sat down. It was only then that she realized just how large Cassandra was. Laura, at five eight, had never felt dwarfed by another human being. Cassandra, she guessed, could be up to seven feet tall. It was hard to judge accurately, because most of the woman's body was draped in rich, brightly-colored layers of what seemed to be silk.

Saris, Laura thought. *Layers and layers of saris or stuff very like them.*

"You came to find the truth," Cassandra said. "But you don't need your cameras and microphones for that. Let me help you."

The big woman held out a large, white hand, and smiled broadly. Laura felt another wave of benevolence wash over her, an all-embracing contentment that recalled all the good, comforting things of childhood. She reached out and put her hand in Cassandra's.

At the moment of contact, Laura's sense of well-being multiplied. She closed her eyes, enjoying utter happiness. All ambition, all doubt, all anxiety was submerged in a warm ocean of joy. But even as the wonderful feeling made her entire body tingle with pleasure, she felt something dark and strange in her mind.

No. This is all a trick.

Laura opened her eyes, pulled her hand away. The glow of contentment faded, and she felt her personality start to assert itself. Cassandra was no longer smiling.

"You have a strong will," the big woman said. "Some do have the capacity to resist me, for a while. But it does help if you join us willingly. It makes the process painless, even pleasant."

Laura stood up, backed away. As she did so, Cassandra's body heaved, and the woman emitted a slight groan. There was an unpleasant, squelching noise from beneath the rich draperies. A patch of wetness appeared, darkening the red and gold patterned material.

"Oh God," Laura exclaimed.

"The young ones must find their place in this world," Cassandra said, her voice no longer warm. "Some humans are needed to make this possible. You are useful. That is all."

Laura turned to run. The two other robed individuals who had been ushered to the stage were still standing just inside the curtain. They reached up and lowered their hoods simultaneously. Laura gasped as she recognized the taller of the two.

"Kat! You're here?"

The other person was a child, a frail-looking boy who looked about eight or nine.

"Is this Tommy? Your brother?"

The youngsters did not reply. Instead, they both crouched, arms swinging low, as if playing some childish game. But their faces were deadly serious. Laura backed away, circling Cassandra's couch, as the two small figures advanced. As they circled around to the left and right, Laura noticed something else, something that seemed impossible.

Their faces, she thought in horror. *How can their faces be changing?*

Kat's features were blurring, seeming to melt, then reforming into a nightmarish visage. It was that of a huge rat. Laura saw with rising terror that Tommy, too, was changing. She was flanked by rat children, beady eyes bright with cleverness and hate, vicious chisel-teeth protruding from below their pointed snouts. They advanced in a crouching scuttle, occasionally falling onto all fours. From the baggy sleeves of the gray robes, dark claws protruded.

Laura heard a scream and realized that it was her voice. She hurled herself at the curtain, trying to avoid the monstrous entity that had been Kat. Laura became entangled in the heavy velvet cloth, thrashing wildly to try and get through. A claw raked down her back, while a chittering sound from behind her suggested inhuman amusement. Finally, the curtain gave way, the rail above crashing down, striking Laura on the head. She disentangled herself from the curtain and ran across the stage, leaped into the congregation, stumbled and fell, got up gasping from a bruised and twisted ankle.

"Help me!" she shouted into the serene faces of the onlookers, but they simply moved aside to let her run through the small crowd. Glancing back, she saw the rat-creatures scuttling after her. Sobbing in fear, she ran for the entrance door, wrenching it open. The outer door was just a few feet away. But even as her hopes arose, she was struck squarely in the back and knocked down onto the concrete floor. Winded, she struggled weakly as the larger rat-child shoved its evil face into hers.

"Oh God no, no!" she whimpered.

"No room for anything but fear," hissed the creature. "Fear purifies. Shall I bite off your nose, Laura? Shall we eat out your eyes, my brother and I? When you were a little girl you were so scared of that, weren't you? When your brother told you about that horror movie?"

Laura begged and pleaded for her life, abject and hopeless. She kept pleading when someone picked her up and led her back inside, up onto the stage.

"You'll be fine, dear," said Monica. "It was just a little demonstration, to show you can't go back to your old life. This is the Moment of Truth, after all."

"I'm sorry I had to deceive you a little," said Mike. "But you wouldn't have come if I had simply said it was wonderful."

Laura felt busy hands removing her robe, her jacket, then her shirt. But even as she tried to fight them off, her eyes were fixed on the small, dark ovoid that Cassandra was nursing in her large, shapely hands. As the cultists urged her gently forward to the stool by the couch, the egg began to jerk and crack open. They forced her down onto the stool, her back to Cassandra, and she waited. Moist living tissue touched her back, and she shuddered.

"There we go!" said Monica cheerfully. "Little chap's getting settled in."

There was a moment of pain, a stinging sensation up Laura's spine. Then she felt a new presence in her mind, a growing influence that casually observed all her emotions, memories, hopes, fears.

"No!" she shouted, struggling to break free of her captors. "Get out of my head!"

A vastly powerful mind toyed with hers, easily suppressing her will. She felt herself flooded with light, Cassandra's thoughts replacing her own. She saw the passive subordinate minds of the controlled humans. Then she became aware of sharper, more feral thoughts and realized she was sharing the sensations of Interlopers.

Laura stood up, was handed her clothes, and began to dress herself. Deep within her captive brain, a young, ambitious journalist struggled to survive. But the overwhelming sensation she felt now was a numbing bliss.

"Are you alright now, Laura?" asked Mike.

She looked at her editor, then smiled.

"I'm fine," she said, buttoning her shirt. "Never better."

Laura walked over to Kat and Tommy, who now looked like children again. She felt sentences begin to form, Cassandra's desires being filtered through Laura's enslaved mind.

"Of course, I lead a busy life," she said, rehearsing for the interview she would have to go through with social services. "But I really feel I would be a good foster parent. And I'd like to do what I can to help these kids, give something back to society."

The youngsters smiled up at her. Laura felt a surge of maternal feelings.

Nightmare Spawn

Chapter 6: Contact with the Enemy

"Nice of them to leave the gates open," Zoffany remarked.

"Quiet!" hissed Comstock, gesturing for them to follow him.

The area around the factory was illuminated by halogen floods that cast a harsh light on the bleak surroundings. Comstock had briefed them on various possible entrances to the building, and was equipped with tools for picking locks or simply breaking in. But as they dashed from one patch of shadow to the next, Frankie wondered if they were biting off more than they could chew.

"This is it," Comstock said, stopping by a door with a pane of frosted glass in its upper section. "Check it with your heat camera."

Frankie did as she was told, switching to infrared. There was no sign of warmth from the interior, no moving shapes, human or otherwise. Interlopers, she knew, were warm-blooded. But that simply meant that they could not be told apart from humans by heat sensors.

"Nothing," she said. "It's cold in there."

Comstock was already working at the lock, and the door swung open with a muffled click. The security chief drew his gun and darted inside. Frankie followed, finding herself in what looked like a large factory kitchen, complete with ovens, sinks, and cupboards.

"Gould?" Frankie asked. "That gizmo doing anything?"

"Still going up to eleven at intervals," the scientist replied. "Far stronger response than I got from that school bus."

"So it's a Loper convention," Frankie said. "Hear that, Comstock? We've done enough. You can report back to Trent and ask him to send in the cavalry."

"We don't know enough about numbers and capabilities," Comstock said, in his usual clipped monotone.

"Oh, come on!" she protested. "Gould's detector is off the scale, and you want to go poke the hornet's nest?"

Frankie saw the flicker of a torch, the blue beam playing around the handle of an inner door before being switched off.

"Anybody on the other side of that door?" Comstock whispered.

"Yes," said Frankie instantly. "An unknown number of Code Nines, let's get out of here!"

The door handle rattled, and Comstock moved until he was flat against the wall. If the door opened, Frankie saw, the security chief would be behind it. Gould took out a shock baton and moved to stand opposite Comstock. Frankie joined Zoffany behind a row of cabinets.

What one knows, they all know, Frankie thought, as the door opened. *So, yeah, let's attack one.*

The door opened slowly, and a small figure entered. It was framed in harsh light, and Frankie could not make out its features. Gould raised his baton as Comstock emerged from behind the door, gun pointed up, finger over the trigger-guard. There was a sharp click and the lights came on. A gray-haired woman was standing in the doorway. Frankie recognized Fiona Jones from their briefing on the Moment of Truth charity.

Jones opened her mouth to speak, but Gould was already bringing the baton down onto her back. There was a crackling noise as the weapon touched the woman between the shoulder blades, and she dropped to the floor.

"Okay, let's get her out of here!" urged Comstock.

The two men lifted the woman and half-dragged her to the outer door. Jones was writhing, and starting to lash out with hands and feet.

"Make it quick, Harriet!" hissed Gould.

Zoffany moved in quickly. Comstock's torch flashed again, showing the struggling woman's neck. Frankie saw a needle glint and realized that Zoffany was injecting something into Fiona Jones' neck.

"What the hell is this?"

"Plan B," said Gould breathlessly. "Sorry we couldn't keep you in the loop. Orders."

Frankie stood watching, confused, as the others carried the now inert body outside. She heard running feet, shadows beyond the inner door. She hurried to follow the others while keeping her camera pointing into the building.

"You couldn't just tell me about this?" she said furiously as she caught up with Gould.

"Comstock was under orders from Trent," gasped Gould, who was obviously bearing most of Jones' weight. "Too close to Denny."

"Who can't be trusted," Frankie put in. "Great. So now we're running like the Keystone cops."

They had reached the gate before the first pursuers appeared. A group of people, hard to make out clearly in the harsh floodlights, emerged from the factory. Comstock fired his pistol over their heads, and the small crowd seemed to hesitate. Then, moving fast through the milling adults, small figures appeared. Two, three, then four figures with pale faces bounded after the Task Force team.

"Lopers," Frankie said flatly. "They'll catch us."

Comstock fired again, this time aiming low. One off the Interlopers leaped into the air, fell, got up again. When it continued the chase, it was limping. More shots had the same effect, not stopping the creatures but slowing them down. One Interloper raced to the fence and clambered up, clearly aiming to cut off the fleeing group. Comstock shot that one as it reached the top of the fence and sent it flailing back into the factory car park.

"Start the car," Comstock said to Frankie, tossing her his keys.

She needed no further encouragement and ran for their SUV, unlocking the vehicle with the key fob. A rapid series of shots rang out, and Frankie wondered how many bullets Comstock had left.

This is insane, she thought. *Why do this?*

She dragged open the driver's door, tossed her camera onto the back seat, and started the engine. Someone screamed. She checked the rear-view mirror and saw a confused melee, small figures leaping, clutching, lashing out with claws. Zoffany was on her knees, with Gould hitting at small assailants with his baton. Comstock put his pistol at the head of a stunned Loper and fired. A splatter of fluid and tissue shot out the opposite side of the creature's head. The other three Lopers made a screeching noise and hurled themselves at Comstock, who went down under the pale bodies.

"Leave him!"

It was Gould's voice, grabbing Zoffany and dragging her to her feet. Frankie slammed the big Honda into reverse and drove diagonally past the two scientists. Gould had enough presence of mind to open the door and shove Zoffany inside. A cry of pain cut through Frankie. She realized it was Comstock.

"Just go!" shouted Gould. "Drive!"

Frankie hesitated for a moment. In the wing mirror, she saw pale forms standing up, peering at the car. On the ground between the creatures lay a black-clad body, unmoving, its face turned away.

"For God's sake, get going!"

She reversed into the nearest Loper, sending it spinning into its fellows, then changed messily to first gear and drove off. The nightmare creatures, the small crowd gathering behind them, faded in the mirror, vanished as she rounded a bend and passed behind the dark bulk of a ramshackle warehouse.

"Is Zoffany okay?" she asked.

"I'll be all right," the woman said. "I was slashed across the face but it's not too deep."

"What the hell were you thinking?" Frankie demanded, anger finally replacing terror.

"Remember back at Holyhaven Island, in the old cellar under the house?" Gould gasped.

"I wasn't there," Frankie reminded him. "I'd jumped off a cliff before you guys arrived."

"Sorry," he said. "Getting things mixed up. Point is, when I tasered the symbiont on Denny's back, the shock went right through the entire hive-mind. A couple of agents in the cellar were almost overwhelmed by Lopers. But when I zapped the symbiont they lost all co-ordination, for a minute or so. Comstock thought that would buy us enough time to get away."

"Kidnapping a controlled human?" she said, anger mixing with incredulity. "You really thought you could do that?"

"It was the perfect opportunity," said Zoffany. "All the humans here tonight must be controlled. We could not risk grabbing someone on the street, or invading a person's home.

You wanted me to find out how to save Denny? This was our best bet, getting a live subject."

"By any measure it was a hell of a gamble," Frankie observed. "And it didn't pay off. What you gonna tell Trent? The guy who was supposed to assess the threat got killed by it?"

"Comstock could have saved himself," wailed Zoffany. "He sacrificed himself."

She's cracking up, Frankie thought. *Comstock was right about one thing, Zoffany is not ideal for this action stuff.*

"Okay, he died a hero," she said. "So what do we do? I assume reporting this to the cops is out of the question?"

Gould said nothing, and Frankie did not labor the point. She glanced back and saw Gould rummaging inside a First Aid kit. Zoffany was holding a blood-soaked dressing to her face.

"Okay," Frankie sighed. "We'll get back to base, then call London for new orders. God, what a mess."

"When we were talking about this," Gould said. "Comstock said something, an old military quote. 'No plan of battle survives contact with the enemy'."

Well, his plan certainly didn't survive, Frankie thought. *And neither did he.*

***

Comstock lost consciousness, regained it to feel himself being dragged across a rough, wet surface. It took him a moment to grasp that he was outside the factory, being taken inside. He tried to get to his feet, but the creatures holding his arms were moving fast. He had just about regained his footing when they reached a flight of steps. His knees struck the steps, the blow adding to the pain from his wounds.

Inside he squinted up at intense spotlights and tried to calculate the odds of escape.

Not good, he thought. *But at least the others got away. Trent will send help, but it won't get here in time.*

His silent captors dragged him forward, up to a kind of low platform, then lifted him onto it. He was struck for the first time by silence. He had been in many conflicts, and even when the shooting stopped, the shouting tended to go on. But here, nobody spoke. All he heard was rough breathing from the Code Nines, three or possible four of them, as they hurled him across the wooden floor.

"Who are you?"

Comstock looked up to see a reclining woman. She was strikingly tall, with a mane of reddish hair, pale skin, and a large heart-shaped face. He had no doubt that this was the Queen, the one called Cassandra. He had no intention of giving any information.

But if she's psychic, she'll find it out anyway. Never had training to deal with that.

"That is true," said the woman, smiling. "I can find out a great deal. Come closer."

Comstock was wounded, slashed by vicious little claws. He felt warm blood pooling under his jacket, sticking one pants leg to his skin. His head throbbed, suggesting a concussion. He was not inclined to crawl over to the woman on the couch.

"I'm fine right here," he croaked. "Might take a nap."

Cassandra gave no signal, but he felt small, wiry hands grasp him under the arms and half-drag, half fling him forwards. Cassandra reached down with one of her pale, flawless arms, and put a hand on his head. He flinched, tried to pull away, but one of the Interlopers grasped him viciously by the back on the neck. A science-fiction novel Comstock had read as a boy came back to him, a trick a character in a world of telepathic police had used to blank his own mind.

"Mary had a little lamb," he began, "its fleece was white as snow, and everywhere that Mary went—"

"Clever, but limited," Cassandra said.

Again, she gave no command, but Comstock yelled in agony as one of his captors jabbed its claws into his leg wound. He tried to begin the nursery rhyme again, only to feel more claws piercing what felt like a bad puncture under his ribs on the left side.

"We can do this all night," Cassandra said mildly. "Or you can let me in. But excuse me for a moment, I must perform my primary function."

With her other arm, she made a sweeping, easy movement that removed the bright draperies from her torso. Comstock stared in disbelief. Then he threw up, a gush of vomit surging past his lips, splashing over the knees of his black combats and onto the chipped concrete.

Cassandra's body passed for human from the waist up. Her arms, breasts, were those of a woman, albeit an oversized one. But she had no navel, no belly as such, and what had been her legs seemed to have fused together. The effect was almost like that of a mermaid, but there was nothing charming or quaint about her appearance. Her huge lower body was semi-transparent. Where legs should have been was a tube of pulsing, rippling tissue that reminded Comstock of a maggot.

Inside the creature's torso, Comstock saw organs working. Even his basic knowledge of anatomy told him that Cassandra's internal plumbing was alien, bizarre. He saw a corrugated tube of tissue, inside it a string of black globules. Below it was a dark ovoid. A sphincter-like aperture opened halfway down what had once been Cassandra's thighs. A reddish-brown egg, slick with greenish-white mucous, was pushed out, to be scooped up by one of the enslaved humans.

"Now," said Cassandra, "you have my undivided attention, Philip. Oh, very few people use your first name? Only your mother and your sister. Such a solitary life. No real friends, only comrades. But I'm sure there is much of interest, nonetheless."

Her fingers began to grip his head more tightly, and he sensed that there was still immense strength in reserve. Despite the pain from his injuries, he could now feel the monstrous being's psychic influence, the cool tendrils of her mind touching his memories. And, as fragments of his identity swirled, he felt Cassandra's interest growing. She was hungry for knowledge.

"So this is your Task Force?" she murmured. "Small, but ambitious. And who is in charge?"

Memories of Trent bubbled up, the avuncular little man smiling, gesturing, patting Comstock on the back, talking incessantly. At first, he sensed Cassandra's contempt, the creature's amusement at the thought of such a feeble human pitting his talents against her. But then her emotions changed, turned darker, more turbulent.

"Something is wrong, here," she said sharply. "What are you trying to hide?"

Comstock screamed as a burning shaft of pain seemed to pierce his skull. Cassandra's power ripped through his mind, shattering all coherent thought. He was dragged back to the day before the team set out for Fordham, to a routine security check, to a strange incident in the sub-basement bunker.

He saw the portal, the sphere of shimmering distortion, floating between the mundane rows of bunks. With that memory, all the others were released, and suddenly he understood why the clip of his pistol had been one bullet short. Then Cassandra's thoughts swamped his again, a mixture of confusion, anger, hope, fear.

"You do not know anything else," she said, finally.

Comstock felt her disappointment, and then flickers of ideas passing swiftly through her alien mind. He saw a symbiont attached to his spine, then the picture faded, Cassandra recognizing that he could be no use to her as an agent. There was a moment of mental quiet, and he sensed her vast body heaving again. He heard a glutinous sound.

He squeezed his eyes shut and tried not to retch.

"Hey!"

The shout came from somewhere behind Comstock, and echoed in the vast space of the old factory. He wondered vaguely why an Interloper would need to shout, or use their voice at all.

"Hey! I'm talking to you!"

The voice was familiar, and Comstock tried to turn his head. He failed. Cassandra's grip was too tight.

"You wanna let him go?"

Through his pain, revulsion, and fear, he recognized the voice.

Denny Purcell. What the hell is she doing here?

***

The Interlopers formed a half-circle around Denny, screening Cassandra, but not advancing to attack. Behind her was another group, controlled humans, looking puzzled. Again, they showed no sign of interfering as she walked toward the platform.

I was right about this stuff – I'm kind of like them, but different, Denny thought. *I'm human, and I have a symbiont. But because Jabba's not all there, I'm not properly linked to the group. They're confused, because they can never attack one of their own kind.*

"Cassandra," she shouted, still trying to keep the huge creature's attention. "I'm a lot more valuable to you than Comstock. I've got information you need. Believe me, it's not just humans you need to worry about."

Cassandra showed no sign of releasing the man. Instead she smiled, and spoke mildly.

"Come closer, Denny," she said. "Close enough for me to feel your thoughts."

"I'm fine where I am," Denny responded at once. "Old-fashioned, human-style talking is good enough for me."

Cassandra's smile faded. She looked down at Comstock, then back at Denny.

"Why did you come here? You must know you can never leave. The creature you call a symbiont must be replaced. Then you will truly be one of us, blended with the greater community."

Denny felt a surge of panic, along with anger. Cassandra chuckled and nodded.

"Ah, I felt your emotions then," said the Interloper Queen. "You fear me. But you also resent me for what I did to you."

Denny gave a slow hand clap.

"Bravo, your mind-reading talents are extraordinary," she said. "Sure, I hate you. You're an evil bitch from another dimension. But like I said, I have some info you need, and I want to cut a deal."

Cassandra did not reply in words, instead staring at her enemy. Denny felt an unpleasant sensation, cold fingers in her mind. A few flashes of alien thoughts appeared, hostile and cunning. She took a step back, but not before she had glimpsed something grotesque, horrific. Denny gasped at the loathing she felt at second hand, Cassandra's emotion almost swamping her.

The brief vision she had was of a weird, humanoid creature, its skin mottled in shades of ruddy brown, its eyes enormous. The freakish entity had straw-colored clumps of hair sprouting from its head. Its face was an expanse of pulpy flesh, discolored and with huge pores. There was a tiny snub nose, a weirdly wide mouth with odd, squarish teeth.

Oh God, that's me, Denny thought. *That monster is me.*

She had briefly seen herself as Cassandra and the other Interlopers perceived humans. With the vision came a sense of nausea and disgust at having to survive in a world of humans.

"Now you know a little more about us," Cassandra said, her tone almost casual. "Did you really think we would see ourselves as monsters? Perspective is something your species seems to lack in so many areas."

"Right back atcha," said Denny, feeling shaken. "Okay, we're never going to be besties. And I'm sorry your world collapsed, and all that. But let's stick to the point. There's another threat out there, to you and maybe to us. Something even more alien than you."

"Trent."

Cassandra spit out the name, and then lifted Comstock by the scruff of his neck, so that he was dangling in front her like a puppet. Denny gawped in surprise and confusion. Cassandra turned Comstock around, and shook him slightly.

"This one," she explained, "has had contact with a being that is not human. You, too, I sense, encountered this Trent-creature, felt its strangeness."

Denny gulped, nodded, tried to regain her composure.

This is actually a good thing, she thought. *I don't need to persuade her Trent is a threat.*

"So you know about Trent, good," Denny said. "I'm guessing that his existence was a big surprise to you, just like it is to me?"

Cassandra lowered Comstock to the ground, keeping a firm grip on him with one huge hand. The black-clad agent looked at Denny, blood trickling from one of his nostrils. Denny wondered how much mental and physical damage had already been inflicted on the man.

"Yes," Cassandra admitted. "This man's mind has been altered in a way that we – we have yet to master."

Oh, Denny thought. *This is a touchy subject. She doesn't want to admit someone else has better mojo.*

"I have access to Trent," Denny said, deciding to go for broke. "I have friends, allies. Between us we can find out more, share the data. I'll co-operate if you help me control this symbiont, even if you can't remove it. And you release him."

Denny pointed at Comstock, then stared. The man was mouthing silent words. It was clear, after a couple of seconds, what they were.

Don't trust her! Run! Run!

"No," said Cassandra simply. "You do not dictate terms to me. And as for this one–"

The Queen shifted her grip and put both hands on the side of Comstock's head. Denny started forward, shouting a protest, but half a dozen Interlopers moved to block her path. Comstock gave a pitiable cry of agony as the Queen's fingers tore into his flesh.

"No!" Denny yelled, and tried to push through the Interlopers. But the first contact between her flesh and theirs unleashed a further wave of nausea, disgust, and hatred. Again, she saw herself as the creatures saw her. She was hideous, an abomination that had no right to exist.

Even humans with symbionts are repulsive to them, she thought.

Denny reeled back from the cordon just as Comstock gave a last, weak groan. Then there was a sickening cracking noise, followed by several more. Blood streamed from the holes in the man's face and skull, gushed from mouth and nostrils. Cassandra shoved her fingers into the shattered mess of bone and tissue and scooped out a handful of Comstock's brain.

"You bitch!" Denny cried, furious at her impotence.

"We do what we must," Cassandra said, her tone cool, contemptuous. "Our sole purpose is to survive."

The Queen lifted the mess of bloody gray matter from Comstock's wrecked skull and offered it to a nearby Interloper. The small monster plunged its muzzle into the tissue, slurped and sucked at it, licked the Queen's hand clean.

"My children need to be nourished," Cassandra explained, as she plunged her hand into Comstock's ruined skull. "As do I, Denny."

The Queen gulped down part of what had once been Comstock, then cast the almost headless body aside. A couple of smaller Interlopers moved in to finish off the brain tissue. Denny felt her stomach heave, nausea vying with rage at Cassandra, at the casual destruction of a life.

"You humans are such hypocrites," sneered Cassandra, running a black tongue over her full lips. "I can sense your emotions, but even if I could not, it would be easy to guess what they were."

The bloated creature paused, frowning, and Denny saw an orifice open in the semi-transparent body. An egg, covered in pale green mucous, gradually emerged. An Interloper took hold of it gently and carried it away into the shadows. Denny wondered how many Interlopers had been spawned in the factory, how many of them were already in place impersonating dead humans.

"In the time it took for me to kill and consume that man," Cassandra went on, licking blood and tissue from her fingers, "your own species killed far more of its own kind. You killed them in acts of deliberate violence, or by neglect through preventable accidents, curable disease, needless starvation. To us, killing our own kind is the ultimate atrocity. To us, you are collectively insane, naturally vicious, and you are actively in the process of destroying your planet's ecosystem. And you ask me for some kind of truce?"

"Yeah," Denny said. "Weird, huh? But it's my best shot. And maybe it's yours, too. I want this thing off my back. Can you do that?"

Cassandra's huge body heaved, and through the skin of the colossal torso Denny saw round, dark objects moving. She knew they were future Interlopers and symbionts, each egg a potential enslavement, a likely death. Another peristaltic wave contorted the Queen's bulk. A glutinous sound heralded the emergence of another Interloper.

"My function is to create life," Cassandra sighed, clearly relieved after her exertion. "I do not destroy it. The symbiont is part of you forever. If your scientists try to destroy it, you will both die."

Denny felt numb, but still determined to win through somehow. After the egg had been taken away, Denny framed a careful offer to Cassandra. The first phase was, arguably, the most dangerous. But it had to be done.

The Interloper Queen contemplated Denny for a few seconds before agreeing. She did nothing else, but clearly a mental command had been issued. One of the nearby Interlopers moved closer to Denny, extended one of its pale claws. Gingerly, Denny reached out to touch the creature.

The jolt of revulsion as minds touched almost made her let go. Denny forced herself to hang on. She tried to focus on the incident that had led her, after so many weeks, to this derelict building. Closing her eyes, she recalled the encounter at the entrance to the Task Force building.

As the memory surfaced, she felt Cassandra's cold, predatory mind close in and capture the moment. Suddenly Denny was in the hallway again. In front of her was a plump little Englishman in shirtsleeves. Trent's clean-shaven face and bald head glistened in the fluorescents that lit the corridor. The image was so precise that she could see a tiny mole just under his right eye.

Trent was protesting, asking Denny to stay. His plump hands fluttered as he pleaded with her. Denny raised her own hand to wave him away, and they made contact. Cassandra froze the moment, halted Denny's mental time, imprisoned her in a moment of utter horror. Again, Denny felt the black, cold nothingness where Trent's mind should be.

A void as cold as the space between the stars.

Denny could not tell if the thought was hers or Cassandra's. She tried to scream, to struggle, but she was held captive in a blank nothingness. The only presence she sensed was that of Cassandra's, as the creature carefully examined the memory, tried to make sense of it. The next wave of thought clearly came from the Interloper Queen.

'Comstock's mind was merely modified by this strange being. But, thanks to the wounded symbiont, your mind made contact, of a sort.'

Denny felt her mind beginning to fall apart, a swirling dark chaos reaching out from the Trent-void. She knew that fragments of her would fall into this maelstrom. She tried to beg Cassandra to free her, release her mind from this terrifying moment. But Cassandra ignored her pleas, and continued to replay the moment. Denny screamed inside, a silent howl of despair.

***

Back in the kitchen of the Task Force's safe house, Frankie treated Zoffany's wounds. The scientist's face had three parallel slashes across one cheek. They were deep enough, Frankie thought, to leave scarring. Frankie cleaned the wounds then tried to dress them as best she could. Their small First Aid kit seemed inadequate.

"You should be seeing a doctor," she told Zoffany, as she finished the job, frowning at her clumsy handiwork. "I mean, see a doctor apart from yourself."

Zoffany smiled, then winced in pain.

"Explanations might be difficult," she said. "The best I can do is get back to London and be treated in the clinic at headquarters."

Frankie nodded dubiously, wondering if even excellent medics could save the woman's appearance. Gould was pacing back and forth, trying to decide what to do next.

"Call Trent," she said, not for the first time. "Let them know what's happened."

Gould nodded distractedly.

"I just don't understand it," he said, stopping to peer out of the window into the darkness. "Why did Comstock do something so stupid?"

"We may never know," observed Zoffany, examining her face in a compact mirror. "The poor guy's probably dead."

"Or he's got a little friend attached to his spine," Frankie put in. "Though I can't see how he would be an asset to them. No, chances are…"

She did not finish the sentence.

Nightmare Spawn

"Frankie's right," said Zoffany. "You have to inform the Task Force so they can send a tactical unit. It's obvious that Cassandra's base of operations is in Fordham. But if Trent acts quickly, we at least have a chance."

Gould put a hand on Zoffany's shoulder, and she reached up to grasp his fingers and smiled.

"You're right, of course," he said. "I will call headquarters. I just – I don't know. Something about this doesn't seem right."

He stepped out into the hall, and Frankie heard Gould speaking into his cell phone. She noticed how carefully the Englishman chose his words, stressing that the 'Code Nine situation was at the old factory, and that Comstock was 'missing, presumed dead'. The call was over quickly.

"Their tac team was standing by," said Gould, leaning against the refrigerator and running a hand over his forehead. "According to our glorious leader, they'll be in action before dawn."

Frankie checked the time on her phone. It was nearly nine pm.

A few hours, she thought. *Only a few hours have passed. Seems like a week.*

"What do we do in the meantime?" she asked. "While we're waiting for the cavalry to arrive, I mean?"

The three looked at each other. Eventually Zoffany spoke, "Watch reruns of Friends? It's always on somewhere."

That broke the ice and the three broke into nervous laughter for a few moments. Then Gould said something that made Frankie smile, as it was the most British thing she had heard for days.

"I'll put the kettle on. I could murder a cuppa."

It was while the scientist was filling the kettle that Frankie heard the clank of metal from somewhere outside. It took her a second to grasp that it might be the garden gate. She jumped up, gestured the others to silence, and managed to mime turning off the faucet. Gould obliged, and in the sudden silence, they all waited.

The doorbell chimed.

"Nobody knows we're here," Zoffany hissed.

Gould strode across the kitchen and turned off the light.

"Won't do us much good if it's Lopers," he admitted, "but if they're ringing the bell, we can assume they're posing as human. Maybe even as police. So let's wait them out. See if they go away."

The doorbell rang again, and then came the loud rap of the knocker.

"Persistent bugger," Gould remarked.

"Maybe it's Mormon missionaries?" Frankie suggested.

Nobody laughed.

"Again," Gould pointed out, "that would be a good disguise for Lopers. So, let's be prepared."

He stooped down to the bag lying under the table, took out his cattle prod. Then he moved into the hallway. Frankie followed, Zoffany bringing up the rear. The front door of the house had a frosted glass panel set in its upper half. The harsh radiance of a streetlamp outlined someone standing on the step. The figure was apparently a woman of about average height. Frankie felt sudden relief, followed by delight.

"It's Denny!" she said, her voice louder than she had intended.

"We can't be sure," Gould warned. "If they captured Comstock, they know where we are."

This had not occurred to Frankie, and she felt a twinge of shame at being so foolish. But she still wanted to believe that her friend was outside, willing to co-operate with the Task Force despite her reservations. The caller knocked again, rang the doorbell several times.

"Whoever it is, they're not going away," Zoffany observed.

Gould took a breath, stepped forward, and opened the door. Denny stood there, unsmiling, looking up at the Englishman. Frankie noted again that her friend seemed stooped, shrunken. Even someone who knew nothing about the symbiont could have guessed that Denny was a woman with a terrible burden of some kind.

"Don't just stand there," Frankie said, "come on in."

"Okay," said Denny. "But I brought someone with me. Don't over-react, Ted. We've got a few things to talk over."

A second person stepped into view, a tall young woman with a face that might have been attractive had it not been for her blank expression. Gould moved back, raising the electric prod.

Can it be a Loper? Frankie wondered, looking around to see if more shadowy figures were moving nearby. *Would Cassandra just send one?*

"This is Laura Bell, ace reporter with the Fordham Gazette," said Denny. "Well, the body is officially the property of a local reporter called Laura Bell. Unofficially, say hello to Cassandra."

Nightmare Spawn

Chapter 7: Broken Covenant

Laura Bell sat, stripped to the waist, apparently unconcerned to be the object of everyone's attention. She was tied to a kitchen chair with a length of washing line Gould had found in a cupboard. Zoffany was examining the symbiont on the woman's back. It was larger than Denny's and undamaged.

"Since it's newly attached," said the scientist, "it's only just begun to merge with her central nervous system. In theory, I could remove it with a basic procedure. Treat it like a growth, a benign tumor."

"That is not permitted," said Laura. "Do not interfere with this body."

The woman spoke in a bland monotone, betraying no emotion. Frankie thought of androids in sci-fi movies. But the goosebumps on Laura's skin, the dark semicircles under her eyes, a dozen other trivial details, proved that she was all too human.

Human, and a slave to a monster, Frankie thought. *How can we be a party to this on any level? We should be trying to save her. Save all the innocents.*

She tried to shake off the conviction that they were collaborators in a terrible atrocity. She recalled Denny's insistence that Trent was a threat.

"If anybody was to look in the window," Gould remarked, "they'd assume we were making a cheap porn movie."

He got up and closed the Venetian blind, then went to stand behind Zoffany. Both scientists were fascinated by the opportunity to examine a controlled human. But Cassandra, speaking through Laura, had made it clear that Laura Bell was not a bargaining chip. Her fate, it seemed, was sealed. But Denny could be freed. That was, at least, what Cassandra had said. Whether she would fulfill her side of the bargain seemed doubtful, to say the least.

"This feels wrong on so many levels," added Zoffany, filming the symbiont with her phone. "But it's a golden opportunity."

"We are here to talk," Laura Bell said flatly. "Information must be exchanged. Then Denny will be freed from her damaged symbiont."

The reporter turned to face Denny.

"Hurry up, or I will withdraw this human and attack with my full force."

"You heard the lady," Denny said. "We've got to come through with the goods. Each one of us has to be – examined. Just as we're examining Laura."

"Fair exchange and covenant," said Laura.

The three looked at her in surprise.

"Isn't that the chant the people of Machen used to summon the Lopers," asked Gould, "back in 1914?"

Laura Bell looked at him.

"Over a century of your time ago, of course. A short spell in our history. Fair exchange and covenant. Give us what we need, we will not harm you."

"For now," Frankie put in.

Laura Bell looked at Frankie, and for the first time her face contorted into a lopsided smile. Frankie wondered if Cassandra could not handle finer motor functions in her slaves, if this kind of remote control was difficult for the Queen.

"You killed a symbiont," the enslaved woman said. "And then slaughtered several of the young. That has not been forgotten. One day you might be our captive again. Choose your words carefully."

Frankie felt a chill and moved away, putting the kitchen table between herself and Laura. She thought of demonic possession, horror movies in which evil spirits spoke through the mouths of innocents. This felt far worse. Not only was it real, but Cassandra was not a spirit. No incantation could stop her or banish her to some other realm.

"What exactly do you want us to do, Denny?" asked Zoffany.

The doctor sounded quiet, reasonable, but Frankie noticed that she had reflexively put a hand to the crude dressing on her wounds. Zoffany, the least combative of the team, had suffered the most.

Apart from Comstock. Denny told us he died. I could tell there was a lot more to it from her expression.

"A moment of contact," Denny explained. "If each of you holds hands with – with Laura, here, Cassandra can find out if anyone's mind has been tampered with."

Frankie was determined not to go first, but Gould stepped up.

"Get it over with," he said roughly, holding out his hand.

Laura reached up mechanically and grasped Gould's fingers in hers. At first nothing happened. Then Gould's eyes rolled up in his head and he staggered back, collided with a chair, and sat down heavily.

"Oh God," he moaned, putting his hands over his eyes. "Jesus Christ!"

"What was it?" Zoffany asked, kneeling beside him. "What did she do?"

"Benson!" exclaimed Gould, looking wildly around at the others. "I saw him. Saw them. After the Romola Foundation was attacked, London was in turmoil. We were going to evacuate the building. I went up to the conference room, on the top floor. And it was empty. I came back and told everyone that it was empty."

He stared at Zoffany, then at Denny.

"Except that it wasn't. It was full. Benson was there, and he was – multiform. So many faces, bodies, all the same."

"I think I speak for all of us when I say this is confusing as hell," Frankie said. "Are we saying Benson and Trent are from the Phantom Dimension, too?"

Gould shook his head.

"I doubt it," he argued. "If they were, wouldn't Cassandra know about them? She seems as surprised as we are by all this."

"They are not from our world," Laura said in her robotic voice.

"Could they in fact be natives of our world?" Zoffany suggested, hesitantly. "Creatures that have always existed alongside us, but unknown? They could live among us in secret, thanks to this power they have over human minds."

Gould shrugged, looking confused and unhappy.

He likes to solve problems rationally, Denny thought. *Suddenly discovering that his own mind is part of a problem can't be easy.*

"They are not from your world," Laura repeated, causing the others to stare at the young woman. "But they may have visited ours in the remote past. We have a legend of such beings that existed before the portals. A human term for them might be 'nomads'. They are thought to have no home. Instead, they travel always."

"What are they?" Denny demanded.

The bound woman looked up at Denny and shook her head.

"The concept is hard to grasp," she said finally. "They exist in many places at one time, one being occupying many worlds, one mind in many bodies. They are not as us. Or you."

"Holy crap," declared Frankie. "Scarier monsters have a mythical story about even scarier monsters with superpowers. That's reassuring."

Laura Bell extended a hand towards Zoffany.

"We are not finished," said Cassandra via her slave. "You too must be tested."

"No!" said Denny, surprising Frankie. "You got the information you wanted, more than enough. You've already had access to the mind of our chief scientist. You've absorbed a ton of data on security from Comstock. You don't get to scan Zoffany's medical knowledge as well."

Damn, Frankie thought, I never thought of that. *Of course, Cassandra would rummage around in Gould's mind, find out as much as she could about the Task Force.*

Laura Bell's inert expression did not change. When she spoke, it was in the familiar monotone, showing no sign of anger.

"Very well, release this body. Let the woman Laura Bell return to me, or I will send my spawn to retrieve her."

"What about Denny's symbiont?" demanded Frankie. "You said it would be removed."

"It will be," said Laura's voice. "When this body is returned safely. Not before."

"I think we just got scammed," Frankie said.

"So, what should we do?" Gould asked.

Nobody moved, as the rest of the team looked to Denny for a lead. Instead of speaking, she went to the kitchen drawers, found a knife, and cut Laura's bonds. The woman stood up, put her shirt back on, then donned her winter coat. The group watched as Laura Bell walked out without another word. With the slam of the front door, the discussion began.

***

The Task Force team arrived at just before two in the morning. It consisted of six men and one woman led by Matheson, the acting head of security. His first question for Gould was not a surprise.

"Comstock's dead? You're sure?"

Gould glanced over at Denny.

"I didn't see him die, but Ms. Purcell did. There's no doubt about it. Cassandra killed him."

And ate the poor bastard's brains like an oyster, Denny thought, *but no need to overshare.*

"Why did he go in at all?" asked Collier, Matheson's deputy. "It's not like him to take that kind of risk."

Frankie looked away, as did Gould and Zoffany. During the long wait for the Task Force agents to arrive, they had discussed the botched raid on the factory. Gould had suggested that Trent might have influenced Comstock's judgment, forcing the security chief to try and capture a symbiont. They agreed that Trent's ultimate goal was a mystery, but his alien nature would make him indifferent to the safety of human tools.

"Whatever the reason," Gould said carefully, "he gave his life to let us civilians escape. He was a hero."

Matheson nodded, clearly unhappy, but satisfied.

"That was the chief," said Collier. "Knew no fear."

There was a murmur of agreement from the rest of the agents. Looking around the living room, Frankie felt a stirring of confidence. The tactical team seemed competent, focused, and were well-equipped with carbines, stun grenades, flash bombs, and night-vision gear. The latter was particularly important, given the Interlopers' preference for darkness.

Rather than wait for daylight, the paramilitary unit was going in as soon as possible.

"The local police have been informed?" asked Zoffany. "Because otherwise they'll be out to the factory when the first shots are heard."

Matheson nodded, a mite irritably.

"We can't keep them out of it," he said, "but our clearance means they have to stay well back. They'll cordon off all the roads near the factory."

"Are you clear on the risk to human beings?" asked Denny. "Controlled humans will probably be in the area. They will attack if Cassandra feels threatened. Are you willing to kill actual people?"

The room fell silent. Matheson took a breath before answering.

"We'll only shoot human beings if it's absolutely necessary," he said. "But from what I hear, once you've got one of those things on your back …"

Matheson trailed off and looked down at his weapon.

"It's okay," said Denny. "No offense taken. And you could be right, but in the meantime, you can see me as an asset."

"How so?" asked Matheson.

"I can sense Cassandra's presence at close range, for a start. Remember, she knows what Comstock knew. Don't argue, just take it as fact. That means she knows about your team – your weapons, tactics. She might have simply decided to leave, set a nice trap for you, or maybe a bit of both."

There was obvious dismay among the agents at Denny's blunt assessment. Collier frowned, pointing a gloved finger at Denny.

"Look, Ms. Purcell," he said. "Our orders are to make sure all you civvies are safely on your way back to London. Are you saying you want to go into that place with us?"

For a moment, Denny wanted to retort that she had already been into 'that place' and emerged alive. But the carefully edited version of events they had given the agents did not include that detail. It would be reported back to Trent.

"The others need to get away from here, I agree," she said. "But as you just pointed out so subtly, I'm not a normal person anymore. And the powers I have might help. Cassandra is expecting you, but not me."

Well, that's sort of half-true, Denny thought. *She can't be sure I'll be there.*

Matheson looked skeptical, but then sighed in resignation.

"Okay," he said. "It goes against the grain to let a civilian take part, but this is hardly a regular mission. We've got some spare camo gear that might fit you."

Twenty minutes later, the tactical team was on its way to the factory, while Gould, Zoffany, and Frankie were leaving Fordham in the opposite direction.

***

"What's that bloody idiot behind us think he's doing?" grumbled Gould. "If you're going to ride my arse, you could at least pull my hair!"

Frankie, half-snoozing in the back seat, sat up and twisted around to see what was annoying Gould. A large vehicle of some kind was close behind them, its lights blazing directly into the rear window of their rental car. They had opted to drive to the nearest airport and get a Task Force charter plane rather than wait for the first London train. Frankie was glad to leave Fordham behind her, though anxious about Denny.

"You'd think the motorway would be deserted so long after rush hour," Zoffany observed.

But here's some guy crowding us, Frankie thought. *Might just be some random idiot. That's the most likely explanation.*

"Just ignore the jerk," she offered.

"He's not leaving adequate stopping distance," Gould complained. "And in this wet weather, that's a recipe for disaster."

Zoffany was peering over her shoulder, now, her pale face anxious.

"Could it be them?" the doctor asked. "Could they have followed us?"

"I doubt it," Frankie said, reassuringly. "They don't even know where we are."

Zoffany looked at her, eyes wide.

"Cassandra was at the safe house," she said. "And saw this car parked outside. Some of them could have been watching. Lopers, humans, maybe both."

The vehicle behind them swerved out, started to overtake. Now that it was not shining its lights straight into her eyes, Frankie could see that it was an unmarked white van. A pale face, dark-eyed, peered in at them for the few seconds it took for the van to pass them.

Could be Lopers, she thought. *Or just pale Brits in the winter time.*

The white van pulled ahead a little. Then the brake lights flared red and Frankie saw the vehicle grow suddenly huge. Cursing, Gould jerked the wheel over and their car began to skid on the wet tarmac. They struck the van, and the shock hurled Frankie forward. Despite her seatbelt, she hit her head on the back of Zoffany's seat. The pain blinded her for a moment. There was another crash, louder this time, and a wrenching noise. When Frankie looked out of the side window, she saw fragments of the crash barrier flying up, past their vehicle. There was a brief sensation of weightlessness, then a third crash, followed by silence.

Frankie struggled to disengage herself from the tangled belt. The rental car was titled over at almost ninety degrees. When she found the catch she fell sideways and was knocked breathless against a door. Zoffany was moaning in pain, while Gould was trying to climb up and out of the driver's door.

"Frankie," he said sharply. "In the back, the shock-stick."

Frankie gawped at him for a moment in puzzlement, then remembered the electric baton. It was their only weapon, and it was in a bag on the back seat. Frankie groped around and realized that she was lying on the bag. She tried to right herself while feeling for the baton. After what seemed to be ages, her fingers found the distinctive black, rigid tube. She dragged it out just as Gould managed to climb out and then open the passenger door above her.

"Can you see them?" she asked as she handed the baton to him.

"Yes," he said tersely. "At least three. Small."

Lopers, she thought. *Cassandra's young. Makes sense she'd want to eliminate us. A golden opportunity.*

Gould reached down and helped Frankie climb out. The clumsy process drew her attention to a lot of fresh bruises. Zoffany, meanwhile, was peering around, gripping the steering column to stay upright. The dressing on her face had been dislodged. In the dim glow from the nearby motorway lights, Frankie could see the still-raw wounds on Zoffany's face, as well as the older woman's terror.

Frankie half-fell out of the car onto damp grass and got painfully to her feet. Gould gestured with the stunner, and she made out three dark-clad figures with pale faces under hoods. They were spread out, moving toward the crashed car from the highway. Frankie was painfully aware that she had no weapon, and she looked around to see if there was a rock or a tree branch. She saw a length of warped metal, probably part of the barrier they had crashed through. Picking it up, she cut her hand, cursed, and pulled down the sleeves of her hoodie so she could wrap the sharp edge.

"Frankie, take this while I try to get Harriet out," Gould said, offering her the baton.

"Never used one before," she protested. "And she's safer inside! We can't outrun them, Ted!"

Gould stared for a moment, then turned back to face the advancing creatures.

"Lock yourself in, Harriet!" he shouted. "We'll try to lead them away."

Frankie could not see Zoffany clearly, but there was movement in the car. She hoped the scientist had locked the doors, and that the Interlopers would not take the time to break into it. She looked around, her eyes adjusting to the murk. There were some buildings beyond a row of trees a few dozen yards away.

Houses, or maybe a farm. If we had our backs to the wall, we'd have more chance of surviving.

Without having to speak, Frankie and Gould started backing off quickly toward the buildings. The three small figures heading down the slope from the highway kept coming, but not especially fast. One paused at the car, seeming to sniff at it and run its claws over the windows. But then it rejoined its fellows, and they spread out as they stalked the two humans.

They know we've got no guns, Frankie thought. *The advantage is with them in close combat, even if they're small.*

The Interloper in the center started to run, advancing straight at Gould. The other two attackers had spread out, moving more cautiously, to approach from either side. Frankie reasoned that if Gould could disable one with his baton and she could smash a second creature's head straightaway, they might have a chance. But the longer the fight took, the greater the monsters' advantage would be. The humans would tire faster, and the claws and teeth of the Interlopers were at least as deadly as Frankie's crude cudgel.

***

"Okay," said Matheson. "Radio check, sound off."

Each member of the tac team gave their name, ending with Denny. She felt odd snapping out 'Purcell', hearing her voice through the tiny earpiece. But at least Matheson had included her fully. He had made a point of 'outlining their plans'.

If you can call them plans, she thought grimly. *There are a lot of gray areas, literally and figuratively.*

Although Matheson and Collier maintained a confident front, it was obvious that they had expected to be working under Comstock's orders. Without him, they were clearly trying to stick to his methods. Denny had tried to persuade them to let her reconnoitre first. But her insistence that the Interlopers could not harm her had been met with skepticism. She had had to point out, quite brutally, that few, if any, military types had survived encounters with Interlopers.

After some debate, a compromise had been reached. Denny, Matheson, and two squaddies would enter via the side door. They would try and determine the strength of the enemy. The rest, under Collier, would cover the main entrance and await the call to attack. Denny hoped that Cassandra was still on her platform. Matheson's improvised plan was to take out the Queen first, then try to mop up actual Interlopers. If controlled humans got in the way, then it was tough luck – in his opinion.

Denny's group found the side entrance shut but unlocked. Night-vision gear revealed no heat sources, and the squad moved inside. Denny's apprehension grew as they moved towards the inner door. She carried no weapon, just a powerful flashlight, reasoning that she could at least dazzle Interlopers and make them easier targets. Matheson gestured her forward, flung open the door, and the agents went through.

The first Loper dropped onto Matheson from above. Two others attacked from either side. By the time the squad realized what was happening, the creatures were within slashing distance. In a confused melee, one Interloper was shot in the face and collapsed, limbs flailing spasmodically. The others bounded away into the shadows, having inflicted deep wounds on Matheson and two other men.

"You should get out of here," Denny said tersely.

Before Matheson could reply she rushed after the Interlopers, trying to reach out with her mind, hoping to catch a hint of Cassandra's presence. Now that the human force was revealed she expected a major attack, but she felt she had a tactical ace to play. All she needed to do was find a controlled human.

If there aren't any around, I'm in trouble.

She had tried to explain her idea to Matheson and Collier, but the military types had seemed unconvinced. As she entered the main factory area, she saw that some of the spotlights, fixed his above, were still shining down. In the distance, figures moved in the patches of radiance, but it was impossible to tell if they were human.

A shot echoed around the high walls, then a burst of automatic fire, followed by more single shots. Denny could not be sure, but it seemed the firing was coming from two sides. She guessed that Collier's group had started to fight its way in. She hoped they were inflicting more damage than they were taking. But yells of pain or maybe rage, sounding very human, suggested otherwise.

Come on, where are you, hapless slaves?

Denny, wielding her heavy torch like a club, dodged around a partition and ran full tilt into someone coming the other way. There was no skin-to-skin contact, so she could not read the individual. But when she flicked on the flashlight, she recognized Jack Munby, the figurehead leader of Moment of Truth. He looked very different from the amiable character she had researched online.

"We must protect her from violence!" stammered Munby, eyes wide. "Outsiders are attacking!"

"Cassandra can look after herself, Jack," Denny replied. "It's our species I'm worried about."

Munby made to grab her, then frowned in puzzlement. Denny's maimed symbiont was still sowing confusion. She turned, pointed back the way she had come.

"Look!" she said urgently. "They're not far behind me!"

Munby lumbered forward, arms outstretched. Denny, sickened, felt certain that he was so in thrall to Cassandra that he would take on heavily armed men with nothing but his bare hands.

As he passed her, she brought the torch down hard between Munby's shoulders, aiming at the spot where she hoped the symbiont's rudimentary brain would be. As the blow landed, Munby arched his back, emitting a loud screech of pain. She forced herself to strike again and again as the hapless man writhed on the cold concrete floor.

***

The middle Interloper launched the attack, arms swinging low. Gould lunged at the creature, but Frankie resisted the temptation to shift her position. She was proven right when the Interloper to her left made its move, bounding forward at shocking speed. She flailed at it with the steel support and struck a glancing blow.

The same sharp edge that had cut her hand now laid open a gash along the creature's arm, and it emitted a piercing shriek. Frankie tried to land another blow but the diminutive monster leaped back out of range, then circled around, feinting with its claws. She heard a muffled yell from behind her, and glanced back to see that the two remaining Interlopers were attacking Gould. He was at bay, his back against the wall of a shed or barn. His superior height and reach made him less vulnerable than Frankie, but he was outnumbered two to one.

The scientist's stun baton made contact with one assailant, making it leap away. But in the couple of seconds that Gould had fixed his attention on one attacker, the other had leaped up at him and fastened its thin legs around his waist. Frankie saw vicious claws reaching for the man's eyes as he tried frantically to jab at his assailant with the baton. Gould threw himself forward, landing heavily on top of the juvenile Interloper. The creature lost its grip, temporarily stunned.

Frankie's Interloper tried to exploit her momentary distraction, and lunged forward again. She had expected the move and this time swung her heavy cudgel more effectively, bringing it up under the creature's vicious muzzle. She felt grim satisfaction at the crunch as metal struck flesh and bone. The Interloper was lifted off its feet, fell backwards, and lay still.

Maybe not dead, she thought as she spun around, *but out of the game.*

Gould was now trying to hold one Interloper at arm's length while zapping the second. Frankie took a swing at the first creature, but missed as it dodged, then came at her. The impact of the small body was still sufficient to knock her down, and she lost her grip on her makeshift weapon. Frankie gripped the pale creature by its throat, hoping it was sufficiently like a human to be choked.

The long muzzle, its mouth over-full of nightmare teeth, extended toward her face.

***

Basic design flaw, Denny told herself. *Symbiont damage scrambles the whole telepathic system.*

More gunfire sounded, with a flurry of shots. The sounds of battle got closer, and she saw flashes in the darkness. Then Matheson, his face bloody from a gash across his forehead, appeared.

"What the hell are you doing?" he asked.

Denny could not reply. She brought the flashlight down onto Munby's back one more time, then dropped it. Tears of anger and shame were coursing down her face. Munby had stopped moving. She hoped the shock had not killed him.

Matheson, after gazing in bafflement at the scene, rushed on, followed by two of his team. Denny followed. As they approached the stage, she saw that Cassandra was still lying on her well-padded couch, surrounded by small Interlopers. As Denny watched, one of the guards leaped into the air as a shot rang out. Soon, all of the creatures were dead.

"We got her!" shouted Collier, clambering onto the stage, his gun levelled at Cassandra. Then, voice dripping with revulsion, he added, "My God, what a freak."

The tactical squad were all on the stage, now, and Denny pushed through them to approach the Queen. Cassandra was looking at the armed humans surrounding her with no sign of fear. If anything, her expression was one of puzzlement. Then she saw Denny and nodded.

"You were right," she said. "We had to contrive the symbionts too quickly. Everything was done in haste. Their vulnerability is a weakness. But the mistake can be rectified. In future, they will blend with the host's body far more quickly."

"Will you free me from this creature on my back?" Denny demanded, desperation overcoming her reason.

Cassandra did not even bother to reply. Instead, she turned her large eyes on Matheson. The squad leader looked uncertain and raised his carbine. Then Denny saw him smile. Glancing at the other agents, she saw confusion on their faces. A powerful wave of telepathic influence washed over her.

We're close enough for her to reach into people's minds, and send emotions back.

"Guys, everyone move back a little," she urged. "Matheson? A little retreat here?"

There was no sign that anyone had heard. Instead Matheson shuffled forward a couple of paces and dropped to his knees, gun forgotten. The other agents now all had the same vacuous expression on their faces. Now Denny could see the illusion that was being projected. Cassandra was once again the beautiful young woman who had seduced Sir Charles Lanier.

More than that, she was a goddess, perfect in every way, utterly desirable to all men.

And quite a few women, Denny realized.

The false Cassandra was reaching out to Matheson. Pale, slender fingers caressed his cheek. The man was slack-jawed, worshipping an ideal compounded of a dozen fantasies. Denny tore her gaze away from the scene and realized that she could still think, and move.

Need some way to break the spell!

The nearest agent had a couple of cylindrical objects clipped to his belt. One was black, the other had a blue stripe. As she grabbed, Denny hoped she was right in choosing the striped grenade. She pulled out the pin and hurled if over Cassandra's head. Then Denny closed her eyes, covered her ears.

For a second, she wondered if the thing was a dud, or worse, something useless like smoke. Then there was a tremendous bang and a flash, the intense light visible even through closed lids. A flurry of gasps, swearing, and barked orders told her that the distraction had succeeded. When she opened her eyes, she saw Matheson hurl himself away from Cassandra, who lay motionless, huge hands clutching thin air.

"Jesus Christ," Matheson said, getting to his feet. "We owe you one, Denny. Several, in fact."

"How do we get this – this thing back to HQ?" asked Collier, stepping back off the stage.

The squad leader shrugged and waved his team a little further back.

"We can get a bio-hazard team out here by chopper," Matheson said. "Call Trent, explain the situation."

Collier left to obey the order while Matheson stepped forward to stand by Denny. He gestured at Cassandra's bloated body with his carbine.

"This is the only one that can breed, right? So if we've got her, the threat's effectively over, bar some mopping up."

"Seems like it," Denny agreed, reluctantly.

Hard to believe Cassandra would just lie there, knowing her enemies were closing in. Is there something we don't know?

"Okay, fellas," Matheson said, turning to his team. "Let's stay alert, there could be more of those things around. If they attack, we'll have to shoot the Little Mermaid, here. I'm sure they wouldn't want that."

Matheson had raised his voice, needlessly. Denny did not bother to explain to him that any surviving Interlopers already knew exactly what the situation was. If harming a symbiont hurt all the creatures, harming Cassandra would be even more disastrous.

No, that's not the problem, she thought. *There's something we're missing. This was just too easy.*

"I need to do something," she told Matheson. "Please cover me."

She removed one of the black gloves the female member of the squad had loaned her, and walked up to Cassandra's couch. As she came within reach of the massive being, Denny tensed up, remembering the crunch of Comstock's skull caving in. But Cassandra showed no sign of attacking, instead simply watching Denny as she moved around to stand behind the Queen's back.

"Be careful," Cassandra said quietly, her voice thicker than before. "You have never truly known one of us. Only pale shadows, hints of what we are."

Denny frowned, wondering at the glutinous sound of the Queen's voice. But she had more important things to consider. She needed to know just how large the hive was, and how far its conspiracy reached.

She reached out tentatively and touched the huge, pale shoulder, laying her fingertips on the smooth flesh. At the moment of contact, Cassandra's mind filled Denny's consciousness. She was flooded with emotions that were alien and frightening. Once more she experienced at first hand the Interlopers' primary impulse, to survive at all costs.

It was hard to probe beyond that raw, remorseless urge. But Denny tried, struggling against the power of Cassandra's mind. Behind the ruthless need to survive was a cluster of other desires, needs, hopes. Among them was a kind of strange, intense love for her offspring, a loathing for humanity, and a chaotic vision of a new, hybrid race that would dominate the world.

But they in turn shielded something else, a universal truth more basic than any mere thought or emotion. A profound darkness blossomed at the center of Cassandra's alien mind, and spread rapidly. It grew to become a freezing whirlwind that almost caught Denny and touched her mind with its icy chill. She saw Cassandra's mind start to fragment, the creature's whole panoply of memories, instincts, thoughts shattering, fading to nothing.

"She's dying!" Denny shouted, staggering back and clutching her temples. "Oh God, she's killing herself somehow, she won't live long enough for any scientists to study her."

"Sometimes ... I can ... slay my own kind," Cassandra gasped, purplish blood dribbling from her nostrils. "My ... my own life. My sacrifice. Your science will not know me. The Trent-being will not gloat over his prize."

A gout of blood gushed from the once-beautiful mouth. Ripples ran over the flawless skin, which in a matter of seconds became venous, blotched. Then the vast, bloated abdomen burst open, a torrent of bloody mucous spilling across the low stage. Amid the foul liquid were eggs, not yet fully formed. Some of the eggs broke open, their contents mixing with the sticky fluids. The stench was overpowering. One of the agents threw up. All retreated from the stage.

"Tell the chopper to hurry!" shouted Matheson into his mic.

***

Frankie twisted her head to one side and closed her eyes, anticipating the closing of razor-sharp teeth on her face. But the pain did not come. Instead, she felt the Interloper start to writhe, arching its back. Looking up again she saw that the tiny, deep set eyes were blank. She flung the small creature off, and saw Gould staggering to his feet by the car. It took only a few moments for them to deal with the helpless creatures. Frankie killed them without hesitation, feeling nothing but disgust as she smashed in their heads.

"Well, that could have been a lot worse," remarked Gould, watching the last Interloper body start to bubble and disintegrate. "All things considered."

"One day, I'll get this whole British understatement thing," Frankie replied. "Okay, let's get back–"

She was interrupted by a woman's scream. Looking back toward the road she could just make out movement. Two adult-sized figures were dragging a third up the slope, toward the white van parked on the highway.

"Harriet!"

Gould was already running, putting on an amazing turn of speed for a man in his fifties. Frankie still managed to overtake him, but by the time she had reached the crashed car, Zoffany was being bundled into the back of the van. Gasping, her lungs burning with exertion, she scrambled up the slope, almost reaching the vehicle as it started up. Frankie collided with the van's rear doors, and heard a plaintive cry from inside. Then the van was racing away, swerving back into the middle of the road, while Frankie bent over, totally winded.

Gould staggered up onto the road, useless baton waving as if in some bizarre relay race. Frankie shook her head and forced herself to stand up.

"Sorry ... sorry," she gasped. "But I got the license plate. I got the number."

Which might be worth nothing, she thought. *But we have to hope.*

Frankie became aware of blue flashing lights. A police car was pulling up next to the hole in the fence their rental car had made. She struggled to think of a plausible explanation for what had just happened, and gave up.

"Oh, crap," she sighed. "The fuzz. Do we have a story – one that any reasonable adult might believe?"

"We'll use our security clearance," Gould said, his voice shaky "I'll tell them – something. Tell them that some bad guys ran us off the road, abducted Harriet. Something like that. We've got to do something!"

After the cops had checked their IDs, a tow-truck appeared and got their car back on the highway. As soon as they were under way again, Frankie called Denny. They both had a lot to say to one another.

Nightmare Spawn

Chapter 8: The Queen is Dead

It was nearly dawn by the time the helicopter landed and the bio-hazard team entered the factory. There was very little for the experts to examine. All that remained of the dead interlopers were drying puddles of putrefaction. Where Cassandra had lain, black stains disfigured the massive divan. A few eggshells survived, and were duly collected.

At the same time, the local police had arrived and cordoned off the factory district. Collier explained to Denny that suspected terrorism was the cover story. As the area was non-residential, it would be easy to keep things quiet for as long as needed.

"You mean, digging up bodies?" Denny asked. "Including the replaced kids?"

"Yeah, mostly that," Collier said, cheerfully. "Not my job, glad to say."

"I think we'll call that a qualified success," Matheson said, as paramedics finished treating his injuries. "Pity Comstock wasn't around to share it."

"No news on the kidnappers' van?" she asked.

Matheson shook his head, his eyes following Denny as she paced back and forth. She wondered if he was offended by her abrupt change of subject, then decided she did not care.

"The van was registered as owned by that fake charity, Moment of Truth," he said. "The cops will find it dumped somewhere. Changing cars is standard for abduction."

Denny felt Jabba writhe and spasm, his response to her frustration and anger. She had not anticipated that leading Laura Bell to the safe house would end in this. But it was clear, with the benefit of hindsight, that Cassandra had identified the scientists as prime targets. Kidnapping one of them made sense, a way of finding out just how much the Task Force knew about Interloper abilities and weaknesses.

"I know what you're thinking," Matheson said.

"Don't tell me," she snapped, "you're psychic, too."

"No," Matheson said evenly. "But it's obvious enough. Why hang onto Doctor Zoffany if the Queen is dead? I mean, way you experts tell it, this Cassandra monstrosity was their hive mind, supreme commander, repository of ancient wisdom – basically the whole kit and caboodle. Right?"

Denny nodded reluctantly.

"That's true. There's got to be a Queen to produce more Lopers, and generally keep the hive focused on survival."

"So what happens to the little buggers when the Queen dies?" Matheson persisted. "Are they like wasps? Come the end of summer they just fly around at random, die eventually, but they can be a right bloody nuisance."

Denny sat down on the edge of the stage next to Matheson. Despite her mistrust of the Task Force, she respected the courage of its agents. And Matheson showed no signs of being two-faced.

I can half trust him, she said.

"So far as I know," she said, choosing her words carefully, "there's never been a time when they didn't have a Queen. I've encountered two. The first was in the Phantom Dimension, just before it collapsed. She was even stranger than Cassandra."

Matheson looked at her with what she realized was respect, and some amazement.

"I'd heard that," he admitted. "Wasn't sure if I believed it. You get a lot of BS in these team briefings."

Denny laughed and made a mental note to avoid being charmed by Matheson.

Loneliness can be a hell of a handicap, she thought.

"I hear you," she told him, smiling. "But in this case, it's true. The original Queen was very different from Cassandra, but they were both badass types."

Matheson nodded, then winced, fingering the fresh dressing on the side of his throat.

"That's why I don't understand how easily Cassandra went down," he said. "Surely, they could have gotten her away in time, if she'd told them to move her?"

It was Denny's turn to nod. She had one obvious answer to the question, but it was so disturbing that she did not want to voice it. Not until the scientists and technicians had checked over the entire factory complex. She gestured at the white-suited operatives moving back and forth, collecting samples of egg casings and fragments of tissue.

"They might have the answer," she told him. "We can learn a lot from what they find. And from what they don't."

***

During their flight back to London, Frankie and Gould agreed that neither one of them must be alone with Trent. Frankie was impressed by the way that Gould managed to focus on the Trent issue at all, given his concern over Zoffany. But, as the scientist pointed out, if there was nothing you could do about one problem, you should try and address another.

"And anyway," he added, "you were rescued from another world, and we can be fairly sure Harriet is still in this one."

When they arrived back at headquarters on the south bank of the Thames, they were given medicals and then shown into Trent's office for debriefing, along with the newly-returned Matheson. Trent was his usual effusive self, full of concern for their well-being, proclaiming his satisfaction with 'a job well done'.

Looking at the plump little man behind the large desk, Frankie found it hard to believe that Trent was anything but a senior British bureaucrat. The man's bald head, cherubic features, and slightly askew tie were so banal. As they took their seats, he offered them tea and biscuits, as usual.

"Or coffee?" he asked. "Or juice, perhaps? Vitamin C, very important, what with all those winter germs around."

The debriefing began with Matheson giving his detailed account of the raid on the factory. When it came to Denny's involvement, Trent frowned slightly and raised a pudgy hand to interrupt.

"I appreciate that you were the acting commander on the scene, Matheson," he said mildly. "But I note that Ms. Purcell has not come back with you. From this I conclude she was and remains a loose cannon, essentially a civilian outside this organization?"

Matheson looked uncomfortable as he grunted in agreement.

"I did try to persuade her, boss, but she refused – she doesn't really trust us, I think. But at the time I felt her help would be valuable, and it was."

"Don't feel that I'm criticizing, old chap!" Trent went on, folding his hands over his pot belly. "I'm merely disappointed that someone with her valuable knowledge – and abilities – should be so unwilling to work with us. Do go on, please, I interrupted your flow."

After Matheson had finished, Gould gave a brief description of Zoffany's abduction. He omitted any reference to Denny or Laura Bell. As a result, Trent and Matheson began to speculate about how the Interlopers discovered the location of the safe house.

"Cassandra captured Comstock, which means she would have known everything he knew," Frankie put in quickly. "They could have easily spied on the house, watched us leave."

"Indeed," Trent said. "Telepathic creatures – I quite forgot how hard it is to keep secrets from such strange entities."

Frankie met Trent's eye and wondered, for a fleeting moment, if he was mocking her. The little man smiled and turned his attention to Gould.

"Now," he said, "finding Doctor Zoffany is of course our number one priority. With Cassandra eliminated, the Code Nine threat is vastly diminished. The remaining creatures are still dangerous, of course, but without the ability to reproduce, their days are numbered. Yes?"

"So far as we know, yes," said Gould. "Obviously the controlled humans are a problem, but most of them seem to have vanished. Only a couple were captured at the site – Munby and a woman called Jones. They must have been ordered to disappear before the fighting began."

Matheson shifted uncomfortably in his seat.

"You have something to add?" Trent asked.

Matheson took out a tablet computer and flicked it on.

"If you'll excuse me, sir," he began, "there is a preliminary report on the organic remains found in the factory."

Trent waved the device away as Matheson made to hand it to him.

"We're all friends here," he said, "just give us a quick precis, old chap!"

Matheson looked pleadingly at Gould, who accepted the tablet. After a few moments, the scientist paled, scrolled on a page, then handed the gadget back to Matheson.

"They found three types of eggshell," Gould said, his voice hollow, despairing. "The smallest indicate hatchings of symbionts, dozens of them."

"We already knew that," put in Trent, needlessly.

"They also found many larger shells that show a great number of Interlopers were hatched."

"Again, no surprise!" exclaimed Trent. "Please, cut to the chase – or is the fashionable phrase 'land the plane'?"

Gould, still gray-faced with shock, seemed shrunken to Frankie, as if his large frame had suddenly collapsed in the comfortless office chair.

"They found fragments of unusually large eggshells," the scientist said. "About fifty percent bigger than the Interloper eggs."

Frankie felt a chill run up her spine, the points where the symbiont had penetrated her flesh tingling in horror.

"Queens," she whispered.

"At least two, judging by the shell remains," Gould confirmed. "Possibly three. No real way to tell when they were produced. "

"Or where their former contents are now," Matheson added.

"I see," Trent said ruminatively. "This does change things. If there are other queens, might kidnapping Doctor Zoffany be part of some wider plan?"

Gould stared at the Task Force chief, clearly startled by the suggestion. For a moment Frankie wondered if the scientist might blurt out something that would arouse Trent's suspicions. But Gould seemed to recover himself and simply shook his head.

"Too soon to tell," Frankie put in. "But we're still focused on getting her back, right? Right?"

"Of course, my dear Ms. Dupont!"

Trent jumped up and came around the desk toward them. Frankie almost knocked over her own chair as she retreated behind Matheson. Trent looked startled and paused, then gave a slightly embarrassed laugh.

"We're still very jumpy, I see," he said. "Well, that's not surprising! Please, all of you, go and get some rest. We'll resume this meeting later in the day. And in the meantime, I will be in touch with the various agencies involved in searching for Doctor Zoffany. Rest assured, she will be found."

Yeah, thought Frankie, as she left the office. *But in what condition?*

***

Collier called Matheson down to the panic room two days after they had returned from Fordham. Both men were still nursing minor wounds, and consequently on light duties. This gave them a few hours of slack time. Collier, who hated kicking his heels, took it on himself to inspect the whole. Matheson, who had a mountain of paperwork to deal with in his new role, was not best pleased when his deputy insisted he 'come and check something out'.

"So, what's this about?" Matheson demanded. "One tin of beans short in the stockpile? Drumhead court martial for that."

Collier did not offer a humorous comeback.

"Take a look at this, chief," he said, leading Matheson through the main room and into the sleeping area.

"Look at what?"

Matheson peered at the patch of wall his subordinate was pointing at. So far as he could see, it was the same unpleasant green color as the rest of the bunker's walls. The emergency control center had not been designed to its aesthetic appeal.

"I can't see anything," Matheson said bluntly.

"It's been repainted," Collier said. "You can see it's a bit paler. There's even a slight smell of paint, can't you smell it?"

Matheson sniffed dutifully. He knew better than to dismiss the younger man's sudden obsessions. In the past, Collier's eye for detail had saved lives, including Matheson's. But this time he could detect no smell of paint, and did not see how some fresh paintwork was an issue.

"Okay, so somebody maybe damaged the wall, moving bunks around or whatever. So what?"

Collier shook his head.

"No work's been done down here for weeks," he said. "Only inspections, no refurbishment. Also, feel the wall."

Sighing, Matheson did as he was asked, running his fingers over the plaster. There was a slight bump, a very small uneven patch, in the area Collier indicated. Again, he saw not significance in it.

"For Christ's sake, Ben," he said. "There's a bump in some plasterwork that was carried out by government contractors. Color me stunned."

Collier smiled for the first time.

"I only started looking for bumps when I found this," he said, reaching into the breast pocket of his uniform.

Even before he took hold of the small metal cylinder, Matheson knew what it was. A cartridge case from one of the standard pistols issued to Task Force agents.

"One of ours," Collier said, with a hint of smugness. "I dropped my pen when I was checking the inventory, bent down to pick it up, found that under the bunk. Somebody fired off a round in here. So, unless it went into a person or a bunk, it hit the wall."

Matheson nodded sagely, turning the expended cartridge over between fingers and thumb. Any agent who accidentally fired his sidearm had to report it. All ammunition was thoroughly accounted for. Regular checks were carried out. Yet, at some point recently, a pistol had been fired inside Task Force headquarters, and no report had been filed.

"Are we on the same page?" Collier asked. "Only Comstock could have gotten away with firing off a round and not filing a report. Nobody else."

But why would he fire his pistol in here? Matheson wondered, glancing around at the cramped, barrack-like room. *Was he going barmy? Maybe that's why he took stupid risks up in Fordham?*

"Who the hell was he firing at?" he mused.

"Who, or what," said Collier, quietly.

Matheson pocketed the metal cylinder, then led Collier out into the main part of the control room. He nodded at the surveillance camera on the wall and made a 'Keep quiet' gesture. Collier made no visible response, but Matheson could see his comrade's mind working.

If the security camera footage has been tampered with, we'll know we're in real trouble.

***

"Oh, are you cold, dear?" asked Dora Brackett, solicitous as always. "I could turn up the central heating. It's been a very harsh winter, I think."

They were sitting in the warm parlor of the pleasant old lady's bed and breakfast. Denny smiled over at Mrs. Brackett and shook her head.

"These aren't to keep me warm," she said, holding up her gloved hands. "They're to keep me from picking up thoughts and feelings. If I accidentally brush against someone, you know?"

Enlightenment dawned on Mrs. Brackett's kindly face.

"Oh, of course, dear," she said. "How silly of me not to realize. And what a pity that your destiny calls you elsewhere! I'm sure there's a lot of good work still to be done here."

The old lady picked up the china teapot and poured a stream of golden liquid into one delicate cup, then another. As she took a sip of tea, Denny wondered whether her next temporary home would be half so pleasant. She would have liked to stay with Mrs. Brackett, but Fordham held nothing else for her.

After making conversation and eating some biscuits, Denny made her excuses and went up to her room to pack. First, though, she performed her daily ritual. The angled mirror showed her that the pulsing, slug-like organism had shrunk markedly in the last couple of days.

"You're losing weight, Jabba," she murmured. "You should write a diet book."

She wondered if adrenaline, perhaps coupled with proximity to Cassandra, explained her body's rapid absorption of the alien tissue. Whatever the reason, the symbiont would soon be gone. It was already clear that surgical removal would be pointless, with most of the creature already in her system.

"On the plus side, Jabba," she said, "greater choice of stylish tops. On the downside, spending the rest of my life as a grotesque hybrid who can't touch people."

Before leaving, Matheson had told Denny about the eggshells that probably belonged to newborn Interloper females. For a moment Denny had fantasized about somehow capturing one of the immature queens and forcing her to remove her symbiont. But she could see no realistic way of achieving this, even if removal were possible.

"No," she sighed. "I'll just have to try and find out more – about the Lopers, Trent, the whole shebang. It's what a good reporter would do."

After she had packed, Denny called a cab to the station. The train to London would take about three hours. On the way, she hoped she could come up with a plan.

***

Frankie, Gould, and Denny met up three days after the raid on the factory. They had tacitly agreed that Denny would not return to the Task Force, but would work with them unofficially. They discussed the possibility that Trent would know about their sharing information. But, as Frankie said, the alternative was not to co-operate at all, and that was unthinkable.

Denny found Gould surprisingly upbeat, considering that the kidnappers' trail had gone cold. Nobody mentioned the obvious possibility, that Zoffany had been enslaved. Instead, Gould seemed keen on talking about something more abstruse. Denny surmised that, as he could not do anything practical to help find Zoffany, he was throwing himself into other work.

"Interlopers – were they really native to the Phantom Dimension? Let me show you something."

Gould took out a small plastic box and removed an SD card.

"I recovered some fragmentary data from the Romola Foundation," he explained, holding up the card. "And this is part of it. I didn't bother checking it until now, because I thought it would tell us nothing useful."

"Why?" asked Denny. "What is it?"

"Bodycam footage from one of the mercenaries who went through the portal at Machen," Gould said.

"But we all know what happened to them," Frankie protested. "They got their asses handed to them, big time."

"True," Gould said, smiling at Frankie's colorful language. "But it's how they were defeated that raises a fascinating question."

He inserted the SD card into a slot at the side of his tablet and opened a file. They all craned to see shaky footage of a group of men, all clad in Special Forces gear and wielding military-type weapons. There was a brief glimpse of a snowy landscape, a forest of leafless trees, then the unmistakable swirl of distortion that revealed a portal.

"I still think that's an Einstein-Rosen bridge," Gould said. "Though how it could remain stable without the presence of negative energy–"

"Please be gentle with us non-scientists Ted," said Denny, in a gentle voice. "You know the rules. No quantum physics in the pub."

Gould fell silent, and they watched as the point of view shifted. The bodycam was attached to the first man through the portal. There was a blast of distortion as the camera struggled to make sense of the gap between dimensions. Then the point of view shifted to the nightmarish world of the Phantom Dimension, with its weird, pale sky and grim desert landscape.

The nameless operative was standing on a rough stone platform, in the middle of what looked like a primitive city of mud-brick buildings. The camera swung round as the leader turned, and they watched other mercenaries come through the portal one by one. Then the group formed up and set off through the narrow lanes between the red-brown buildings.

"So far, so meh," Frankie remarked. "What's so fascinating, Ted?"

"You've already seen it," said Gould, looking a little smug.

Denny and Frankie peered at the screen again.

"I got nothing," Denny admitted. "I can't even see any Lopers yet."

"Oh, Jesus, Ted," Frankie sighed, "just tell us before we punch you."

Gould stopped the video, rewound a few seconds, and paused it. On the small screen was a vista of the city, a chaotic mass of single-story buildings.

"Okay, it's Lopertown, so what?" Frankie demanded.

"An Interloper city, you think?" Gould asked. "Doesn't that strike you as incongruous?"

"No, why should it?" asked Denny. "They're intelligent creatures, even if they are repulsive, so of course they–"

She stopped, truth dawning.

"Now you get it," said Gould, smiling.

"I don't get it," grumbled Frankie.

"What do Lopers need a city for?" Denny asked, turning to her friend. "They're not people. People live in houses, because they have families. Lopers have a hive, one collective like ants or termites. Remember the original Queen lived in a glorified burrow, all underground chambers and tunnels?"

"Quite so," Gould said. "They occupied the city and used it, but such a species would never have built such a community."

Frankie looked baffled for a moment, then the penny dropped.

"Ah, I get it," she said. "But if the Lopers didn't build the city, who did?"

"Good question!" exclaimed Gould. "Somebody else, clearly. A more human-like species wiped out at some point, perhaps by the Interlopers themselves."

"Or by whatever Trent is," Denny said. "Hope you guys are still following the basic rule – never be alone with him?"

***

Matheson hesitated outside Trent's office. He had compiled a short, enigmatic report on what might have happened in the emergency command center sometime the previous week. The problem was that, as he and Collier had anticipated, there was no security camera footage for the time in question.

And that would be bad in itself, he thought. *But the spent cartridge is a major concern.*

The door in front of him opened and Trent's cherubic face looked up. Matheson smiled thinly at his superior.

"You wanted to see me?" Trent asked. "I've just got a few minutes. Come in, old chap!"

Matheson entered, and Trent shut the door behind him. The Task Force leader then closed the blinds, shutting them off from the gaze of staff in the main office.

"Something tells me," Trent said, perching on the edge of his desk, "that you don't want anyone to lip-read our conversation. And believe me, some of those folks out there could do it!"

Matheson smiled as he sat down and took out the spent cartridge case. Trent frowned as his head of security held up the hollow metal cylinder.

"I'm no soldier," Trent said, "but I know what that is. Why is it pertinent? You must have fired off a lot of rounds lately."

"Yes, sir," said Matheson. "But this particular shot was fired inside this complex. In the panic room. The only conclusion I can reach is that we have a Code Nine inside the Task Force. Maybe more than one. Though how this happened I can't imagine, given the routine blood tests and so on."

Trent's thin eyebrows shot up, producing an effect Matheson found slightly comical. Not for the first time he wondered if his boss was up to the job. There was something so tame and harmless about Trent.

"Tell me more," said the plump little man. "I want to know all about this matter."

Nightmare Spawn

Epilogue: Lost and Found

"I'm going to go out on a limb, here," said Gould, "and ask what might sound like a stupid question."

"No such thing as a stupid question," Denny shot back. "Only stupid answers. I think you told me that, not long after we met."

Gould smiled and nodded.

"And we met because of Benson," he pointed out. "Benson took over the Romola Foundation, an obscure outfit that dabbled in psychic research, and put it on the trail of the Interlopers. Then he recruited your team to investigate Malpas Abbey, and we discovered a major menace. True?"

"True," Frankie said.

"So whatever Benson was, he did us a favor – in a way," Gould went on. "Otherwise Interlopers would have operated under the radar, yes?"

"Excuse me if I don't feel grateful for being fed to a monster," Frankie said sourly. "But I get the general point. Benson was the driving force then, Trent is now."

Gould took a mouthful of beer and wiped his mouth.

"Which brings me to my question. Do we know that Trent is actually a threat? Or is he in fact on our side, but operating covertly?"

Denny bridled at the suggestion. She began to talk about the horrific sensation of cold, dark menace she had encountered when she had made skin-to-skin contact with Trent. Frankie, she could see, was on her side. But Gould, while not questioning what she had sensed, queried its significance.

"What you felt sounds monstrous, perhaps evil," he agreed. "But perhaps a truly alien being would come across as that, without actually being so? With the Interlopers, we know they're hostile through their actions. With Trent, and Benson before him – if they're different beings – we don't."

Frankie and Denny fell silent and exchanged a furtive glance.

He must be so desperate to get Zoffany back, Denny thought. *And he must know how unlikely it is that she'll come back fully human.*

"Ted," Frankie said finally, "I get your point. Maybe Trent's motives are good, if alien. Hell, for all I know he could be some kind of cosmic guardian, trying to help us dumb humans out. But we have precious little to go on, except that he's not being truthful with us."

Gould looked pensive, and he finally raised his hands in a helpless gesture.

"You're right, of course," he admitted. "It could be Trent is playing some kind of perverse game with us, the way a mischievous child might torture small animals. If so, we're in trouble. I suppose all we can do is keep alert, and try to find out what the hell he – or it – is up to."

Phew, Denny thought. *For a second there I thought he might just go marching up to Trent and demand answers.*

***

"You okay, pal?"

Matheson looked up to see Collier sitting opposite him. Around them, the canteen bustled with the usual lunchtime activity.

"Yeah, fine," Matheson replied.

Canteen, he thought. *How did I get here?*

"Need your signature on a report, yet again," Collier grimaced, putting a sheaf of papers in front of his superior. "You'd think they'd cut down on paperwork, being a secret outfit and all that, wouldn't you?"

"Yeah," Matheson said, scrawling his name along a dotted line. "Yeah, all this paperwork."

Collier retrieved the report, placed it in a see-through wallet, then looked quizzically at Matheson. He leaned forward, lowering his voice.

"So, how did it go?" he asked.

"How did what go?" Matheson asked.

Collier looked puzzled, then impatient.

"You know," he urged. "Trent. The panic room. Spent cartridge?"

Matheson tried to dredge up some memory that would connect three such disparate ideas.

Why would Trent be in the panic room with a spent cartridge? Like that murder mystery game.

"Don't know what you–" he began, then stopped.

Collier's face changed, his mouth protruding to become a fleshy muzzle, his nose flattening, skin growing pale, eyes becoming tiny. Fascinated, aware that he should be afraid, Matheson stared as Collier became an Interloper, the hand resting on the file growing vicious claws.

"John, what's up with you? You look a bit – confused."

The creature's horrific mouth struggled to form the syllables. Matheson groped for his sidearm, then remembered that he was not wearing one. He glanced around, instinct telling him to check exits and other potential threats.

The canteen was full of Interlopers. They queued patiently at the counter with trays. They sat chatting over coffee. One was reading a copy of the *Daily Mail*, frowning at the sports section.

Oh my God, we've been infiltrated.

He looked back at Collier, and saw the familiar, amiable face of his comrade. A human being. Collier was picking up the report Matheson had just signed, looking annoyed.

"If you can't tell me, that's fine," Collier said. "But you might at least have said it in plain English."

As Collier stalked away, Matheson saw Trent enter the canteen, the Task Force leader chatting and joking amiably with everyone who crossed his path. Trent got himself a coffee and a Danish pastry, then made his way over to Matheson's table and sat down opposite.

"I really shouldn't," said Trent, gesturing at the pastry. "But they're so tempting."

"Yes, I suppose they are," Matheson said numbly.

"Still trying to process it all, eh?" Trent said, casually. "Struggling to make sense of a baffling situation?"

"It makes no sense," Matheson protested weakly. "They can't all be – but if they're not, that means I'm – I'm not sane."

Trent took a bite from the pastry and laid it precisely back on the plate. He leaned forward, just as Collier had done, but without any sense of the furtive.

"Take it from me, old chap," he said. "You're perfectly sane. You're just seeing things a little differently, that's all. You're seeing potential betrayal, threat, infiltration. We're not dealing with a normal threat. This is a paranormal conflict, and we are in the front line."

"Yes, sir," Matheson said, "but I'd still like to be checked out by the medical officer."

"No," said Trent. "I don't think that will be necessary."

And the little man waved a plump hand over his pastry, as if shooing away a fly. At the same instant, Matheson lost all desire to speak to the MO about his hallucination.

"There we are," Trent said. "No more troublesome visions. For now, at least."

"Thank you, sir," Matheson said. "Very reassuring."

"We have our special project to worry about," whispered Trent. "And nobody else must know. You must be my eyes and ears. And I will protect you from the deceivers, the traitors."

Matheson felt a sense of relief. He could not be sure of his own senses, that was clear enough. But Trent was wise, powerful, possessed of special knowledge. This much was clear.

A thought occurred to him, a niggling question requiring his notice, worrying at him like a tiny pebble in his shoe.

"Was Collier part of your special project, sir?"

Trent smiled and raised a delicate eyebrow. Matheson lost all interest in Collier.

***

Harriet Zoffany awoke, flinching when she opened her eyes. She was in a room with blank, whitewashed walls, a single door, and no windows. She sat up, groaning at the throbbing in her head. A dim light illuminated the bleak space.

Chloroform, she thought. *Old school, but effective.*

She was lying on a low camp bed, still wearing the clothes in which she had been abducted. A plastic jug of water and a beaker stood on a low table, close at hand. She swung her legs off the bed, tried to stand, and fell back.

Give it time, she told herself. *That's what you'd tell a patient.*

After a couple of minutes, she stood up again and walked carefully to the door. It was not, she realized, a cell door. She was shut in a regular room, possibly in a house or an office complex. That gave her slight encouragement.

It might not particularly be secure, she thought. *There could be a chance to escape.*

She reached for the door handle and tried it, a matter of reflex, as she was sure it would be locked. The handle turned smoothly, and the door opened. The room beyond hers was oddly like a hotel lobby, carpeted and with wood paneling. There were seats, low tables, and two long windows on either side of the room. She suddenly became aware of a slight vibration, and she touched the wall.

Something mechanical, she thought. *It must be an engine.*

The revelation that she was on a boat of some kind, and in motion, sent her rushing to the window. There was nothing outside but open sea, the waves a few shades darker gray than the sky.

"Ah, good, you're awake!"

Two people in blue coveralls had entered the room via large double doors. They were a man of about thirty and a gray-haired woman in her forties. Both had the slightly stooped look of controlled humans. They were smiling at Zoffany, walking slowly forward. The woman carried a tray with cereal, toast, and a cup of tea or coffee.

"Who are you?" Zoffany demanded. "Where am I?"

"I'm Ms. Lassiter," said the woman, "and this is Mister Fordyce. We're going to be looking after you."

"You abducted me," Zoffany pointed out. "People are going to be looking for me. The Task Force, police."

Lassiter shook her head, smile unwavering.

"We're well outside British territory by now," she said. "And I wonder how much information about us your Task Force will share with foreign governments?"

"Quite a lot, I think," Zoffany said, trying to sound confident.

"Anyway," Fordyce said, "we've brought you some breakfast. You must keep your strength up."

Lassiter put the tray down on a table and stood back. Zoffany felt no desire to eat. But she reasoned that keeping her strength up did make sense. She sat down and reached for the cup, which proved to contain tea.

"I normally have coffee, first thing," she pointed out.

Lassiter shook her head again.

"Too much caffeine is not a good idea," she said.

As she sipped her tea, Zoffany tried to recall if caffeine affected Interloper metabolism. She could not remember any experiments on the compound.

But they would know, she reasoned.

She ate as much of the breakfast as she could, all the while trying to solicit information that might prove useful. She learned that the boat they were on had been bought with money Cassandra diverted from Sir Charles Lanier's vast fortune. She wondered if anyone was trying to follow that money trail and silently hoped they were.

"Finished?" Lassiter said, and took up the tray without waiting for a reply.

"Now it's time to get down to business," Fordyce said, stepped closer to stand by Zoffany. "We have so much to do!"

I won't let them take me, she thought. *I'd rather take my chances in the sea.*

She stood up carefully and tried to give a reassuring smile. Her two captors stood to either side of her and ushered her out of the room, through the double doors, and into a corridor. She saw a door at the far end, and beyond it the line of the horizon. She braced herself, wishing she had used her gym membership more often.

"Here we are!" said Lassiter, indicating a steep staircase to the lower deck.

Now or never, thought Zoffany.

She thought she might make it. For a few seconds, she easily outdistanced Lassiter and Fordyce, but then she hit the door at the end of the corridor. It was locked. As she struggled with the knob, she began to moan in despair, twisting around to see her captors approaching at a leisurely jog. When they took her by the arms, they were quite gentle.

Nightmare Spawn

"No, going outside is not sensible," said Fordyce. "Far too chilly!"

"Please, please don't do this!" she begged.

"Sorry," said Lassiter, "we have our orders."

Zoffany started to struggle, but she soon realized she was in the grip of people who were used to overcoming resistance.

"Of course, you're nervous," Lassiter said. "But you have a great purpose to fulfill!"

"We believe that children are our future," added Fordyce.

"Right!" Zoffany responded, still digging her heels in. "A very laudable sentiment."

"The young ladies will be so pleased to meet you," added Fordyce, as he and his cohort lifted her off her feet.

"Young ladies?" she asked.

"Yes," Fordyce explained, "the young ladies are down in the luxury cabins."

Zoffany was manhandled down the stairway and taken along a passageway with a row of sliding doors. The first one was opened, and Zoffany found herself staring at girl of about six. The girl was sitting on the edge of a bed, eating what seemed to be a bowl of pasta. Then Zoffany realized what was actually in the bowl, a mess of bloody gray matter.

"Isn't she sweet?" asked Lassiter. "And growing so fast."

Zoffany felt too sick and frightened to speak. The girl-creature looked up, mouth bloody. Zoffany felt a crawling sensation in her mind, cool tendrils touching her thoughts, glancing at her memories.

Oh God, immature queens survived.

The girl-creature smiled, her teeth pale and sharp.

"Now," Lassiter said, sliding the door shut, "your role in this new phase is vital. Our final orders were to make sure we helped bring all your wonderful knowledge to the young ladies."

"Of course," Zoffany said, resignedly. "Very logical."

"I'm glad you see it that way," Fordyce said brightly, as he steered her into another cabin. This one was unoccupied, except for a small, dark egg in a bowl on a bedside table. Lassiter began to take off Zoffany's shirt as Fordyce picked up the egg.

"It's just ready," he told Zoffany. "Won't keep you waiting more than a couple of minutes."

Zoffany made one last effort to break free, but Lassiter quickly clamped a pad of cotton over her nose and mouth. As the fumes took effect, she felt the attendants lift her and lay her gently down, face to the wall. She was not quite unconscious when the sting of contact came, and all her detailed knowledge of the Interlopers, and their complex interactions with human biology, began to drain away.

* * *

Nightmare Rising
Nightmare Series Book 6

Nightmare Rising

Prologue: Morlocks and Medics

The nightmare always began in the same way.

Denny was walking in a forest, golden summer sunlight dappling the undergrowth. Birdsong and the hum of bees surrounded her. She glimpsed blue sky through the leaves, felt a gentle breeze on her skin. Small creatures clambered, leaped, or scurried through the bushes. A butterfly, wings richly patterned in red and black, fluttered in front of her face.

She almost smiled. But she knew the idyll would not last.

With dream-logic, she could suddenly see through the earth, foliage, the roots of trees. It was as if the ground was made of glass. Beneath her feet, she saw a vast network of burrows. Not tunnels, these were not engineered but dug with claws, their walls cemented with mucous.

It was a huge nest of Interlopers.

As the vision became clearer, she saw the inhabitants of the underground hive. Pale and naked, scuttling along like anthropoid ants, the Interlopers swarmed in their thousands. One passed directly below her, paused, turned its face up to her. Above its elongated muzzle, a blended mouth and nose, tiny black eyes gleamed.

The Morlocks, she thought. *Soon it will be time.*

Sure enough, the sirens began to sound, the wailing tone rising and falling. Suddenly she was no longer alone. All through the forest, people were walking, blank-faced, purposeful, heading the same way. The great multitude looked to be of all ages, all races. Mothers carried babies in their arms, old folk were supported by younger men and women.

"No," she said, as she had to, every time. "No, you don't need to go!"

Denny ran to the nearest man, tried to make him stop, but he ignored her, kept walking. She went through the same futile process again and again. But eventually, the crowd of vacant-eyed walkers grew so dense that she was simply carried along by it.

The sirens were very loud now. She did not want to see where the mesmerized people were going, but she had to turn, had to look. A great edifice of white stone stood on the margins of the forest. It was topped by a colossal head of an Interloper, fearsome maw ringed with vicious teeth, tiny eyes set in deep sockets. Beneath the massive stone head, humans trooped into the pedestal, vanishing into the shadows. From within Denny heard snarls, screams.

Eaten alive, she thought in despair. *All eaten alive.*

She was very close to the gateway now, and the sirens were blotting out all thought. She could see pale figures lurking inside the vast stone pedestal, pouncing on defenseless humans as they walked inside. And the crowd was still carrying her forward, so that Denny knew she would soon be in the killing zone. She looked down. Her bare feet were treading in patches of fresh blood. She battled against the human tide, but in vain.

Then she was inside. As soon as she had crossed the threshold the sirens stopped. The great gateway closed, trapping Denny and the other human cattle in twilight. Interlopers moved forward, crouching, predatory, masters of their dark domain. One by one, they pounced and fed, cracking open skulls, feasting on the bloody matter within.

And then, only Denny was left alive.

"No!" she cried. "You can't have me, you won't take me!"

She pounded on the metal doors that sealed her only escape route, knowing that it was futile. She waited for the attack to come. But she stood unmolested, untouched.

"You have nothing to fear," said a low voice.

Turning to face the semicircle of creatures, she saw that they had changed. They had all taken on human form. The same form, a specific female. Thirties, slim, average height, and a bright, inquisitive expression.

Each one had Denny's face.

"What is this?" she gasped. "Why are you doing this?"

The nearest fake Denny smiled, shrugged.

"You know why," said the creature. "You're one of us, now."

Denny woke abruptly, heart racing, her limbs tangled in bedsheets. For a moment, she wondered if Frankie would knock on her door, check on her. Then she remembered her roommate was in Fordham on Task Force business.

"Mopping up operations," Denny muttered.

She grabbed a notebook from her bedside table and tried to note down details of the dream before they faded. As it was a recurring nightmare, she had assumed that it was somehow connected to the surviving Interlopers. It was also, obviously, based on an old science fiction movie that had scared her as a kid. After she had finished the latest page of notes, she flipped back and saw that it was consistent with earlier attempts to summarize the dream.

Could just be my subconscious, being a jerk, she mused. *Or something else. Information leaking through. Thanks to Jabba.*

Denny threw back the covers and padded into the bathroom. She felt herself compelled to check on her symbiont several times a day now. The organism had become so short and narrow that it no longer merited its nickname. As she angled the mirror in her hand, she saw that the glistening tube of alien tissue had shrunk again. It was less than six inches long, and no wider than her finger.

"Once it was you and me," she murmured. "But soon it will just be us."

Again, she wished Harriet Zoffany were still around to consult. The biologist had established that symbionts slowly blended their genes with those of their human hosts. Zoffany's experiments on rats had also hinted at a merging of nervous systems. But what that might imply for humans, no one knew.

"But we're gonna find out pretty soon," Denny sighed, putting down the mirror. "In the meantime, Jabba, let's try and get some shuteye."

***

"So, what seems to be the trouble?" asked Doctor Khan.
"I seem to have a sort of growth. On me back."
The patient sitting opposite Khan was David Stainforth, currently employed at Fordham city hall. Stainforth was forty-three, stocky, rather pale, with a few gray hairs in his close-cropped hair and thin goatee beard. The doctor glanced at the notes on the screen. Before now, the man had a pretty clean

record. A detached retina a few years earlier had been treated successfully. There was nothing else of note.

"When did you first notice this growth?" asked Khan.

"That's the funny thing," said the patient. "Sometimes it isn't there at all. Then sometimes I can see it, and it's really big and horrible. You know, ugly like?"

"So it's a recurring problem?" Khan said, making a few notes on his pad. "Is it giving you any pain, discomfort?"

"No," Stainforth said. "But sometimes it – it kind of talks to me."

Khan fixed a smile on his face and moved his left hand below his patient's line of sight. There was a panic button under his desk. Security would be with him in seconds, or so he had been told.

"Talks to you?" Khan said, keeping his voice neutral. "In what sense?"

"At night, sometimes," Stainforth replied, unblinking and sincere. "When I'm on duty monitoring the CCTV, you know? And I hear this voice. It sounds a bit like a woman, or a girl. Sometimes more than one. I can't make out the words, but you kind of get the taste of it. You know?"

Khan nodded.

"Do go on," he said, left thumb poised above the panic button as he took more notes with his other hand.

"I get the feeling I'm supposed to do something for these people, these women," Stainforth said, frowning. "I feel compelled, you know? But this compulsion, it goes away real quick. And that's when I feel the – the growth. The thing on my spine. But then whole days can go by and I forget about it. Sounds crazy, but I forget it's even there. I can't explain it, doc. Do you want to see it?"

This could be above my pay grade, thought Khan. *But he doesn't seem dangerous. And it may be a genuine physical ailment with some psychiatric complications.*

"Okay, perhaps I'd better take a look at this – growth," he said, rising from his office chair. "Please, take off your jacket and shirt."

Khan had expected to see, at most, some kind of rash on Stainforth's back. But when the man removed his shirt and turned around, the doctor had to stifle a very unprofessional exclamation. A moment later, he felt dismay, tinged with panic. He had no idea what the problem was, but it looked serious. A dark greenish-brown streak of glistening tissue extended partway down the man's spine. It was about eight inches long and roughly an inch wide.

"Well," Khan said, trying to sound calm and well-informed, "you certainly have picked up something."

He reached out tentatively, then stopped, took a pair of disposable latex gloves from a box on his desk. He felt a sudden, irrational desire to do anything other than touch the slimy-looking tissue. But Khan could hardly back off, not with a patient awaiting his verdict. He put his right index finger onto the weird growth. It yielded with a quiet squelch. Khan jerked his hand back as the patient gave a little gasp.

"Is that painful?" the doctor asked.

"Painful?" Stainforth asked, as if puzzled. "Oh, the pain. The pain of separation."

He's afraid it might need surgery, Khan thought. *Not surprising. But look at it, that thing needs to come off.*

"I think you need to see a specialist about this," the doctor said, putting on his most reassuring tone. "I'm going to refer you to the university hospital."

"University," murmured Stainforth. "So much knowledge."

"Yes, very knowledgeable people!" Khan said brightly, stepping behind his desk again. The barrier between him and the patient, however symbolic, seemed suddenly important. "Please, sit down again, and you can put your shirt on."

As Khan typed a hasty message to a colleague at the hospital, he noticed that Stainforth had not moved. Instead, the man seemed to be mumbling something, the words inaudible.

Oh, God, Khan thought, standing up again, *psychiatric problems always complicate things so much.*

"David?" he said tentatively, wondering if a less formal approach would help. "There'll be an ambulance along in about ten minutes to take you to the hospital. Please, put your shirt on and take a seat."

The patient stared at Khan as if seeing him for the first time.

"They're calling me!" moaned Stainforth. "The sea, the sea is so wide, and they are so young, so small. I should go to them. But I can't."

Khan suppressed the urge to push his panic button. Instead, he gave in to curiosity and examined the weird growth again. It seemed to be worm-like. Khan ran a finger down where the pale human flesh joined the gray-green tissue. Stainforth gasped again, twitched slightly.

"I'm sorry," he said hastily. "Did that hurt?"

"No," breathed Stainforth. "It's not pain, exactly. It's this terrible sense of – of loss. I was part of something, I'm sure. Something beautiful. Something amazing. And now I'm so alone. Alone!"

The man spun around, grabbed the doctor by the lapels of his jacket. As he jabbed the panic button, Khan noticed that Stainforth's pupils were dilated.

Maybe there's something in his system, the doctor thought. *But what kind of growth secretes a mind-altering drug?*

"Please try and calm down, David," he said, attempting to sound firm.

Stainforth let go, still staring at Khan.

"The beautiful ones are too far away," he said, mournfully. "They left us behind."

Khan was about to suggest that Stainforth put his shirt back on when the man's head jerked around.

"They're coming!" he said, looking alarmed for the first time. "The enemy!"

Oh crap, thought Khan, taking a step back.

***

"We've got another one."

Frankie Dupont looked inquiringly at Ben Collier.

"General practice, other side of town," the agent explained. "The doctor emailed an expert on parasites, guy at the university hospital. A couple of keywords got flagged up."

"Slimy?" Frankie hazarded. "Creepy?"

"No, 'spine'," Collier corrected, as they left their safe house and headed for their unmarked van. "And also 'baffling'."

As Collier put the black van in gear, Frankie puzzled over what she had just heard.

"We go to red alert if a doctor admits to being baffled?" she asked, incredulously.

Collier guffawed as he swung out into the mid-morning traffic. It was a bright day in late March, and he put on a pair of sunglasses before answering.

"You'd be surprised how rarely doctors admit to not knowing what the hell they're seeing," he remarked. "As a profession, they have to maintain a show of – what's the word?"

"Omniscience," put in Hattersley, the third member of the team.

"Keep your eye on your fancy gadgets," returned Collier. "See if we get a signal. Security has detained the guy, but he's still on the premises."

"This Code Nine detector is a Heath Robinson contraption at best," Hattersley grumbled.

Frankie twisted around in her seat.

"Heath Robinson?" she asked. "Here's me thinking Gould invented it."

Hattersley looked smug.

"You would say Rube Goldberg," explained the technician. "Wacky inventions that are more elaborate than useful."

Frankie gave Hattersley her most withering stare.

"Ted Gould did a damn good job," she said. "It worked okay when he was using it."

Collier laughed as Hattersley reddened and turned to the controls of the detector.

"Bad workman blames his tools," Collier remarked. "And here we are, H-man. Got anything?"

Collier swung the van into a small car park next to a low, red-brick building. A sign proclaimed it the Thornhill Medical Practice. A loud beeping sound came from the back of the van.

"A definite blip," Hattersley said, grudgingly. "Could be a Code Nine."

A man burst out of the front door of the building. He was naked to the waist, his eyes wide. Behind him came another man in a jacket bearing the label SECURITY.

"I'm guessing it's the first guy we want?" Frankie said, unbuckling her seat belt.

It took them a couple of minutes to restrain and sedate David Stainforth, then bundle him into the back of the van. Doctor Khan objected strongly to his patient being 'grabbed by some randos'. He was somewhat mollified when Collier showed him his security clearance.

"He'll get the usual visit from Scotland Yard, be told some stuff about national security," Collier explained as they drove away. "It usually works. Most professionals don't want a black mark on their file."

"Do you think this one is the last?" Frankie asked.

She was in the back with Hattersley, making sure Stainforth remained laid on his side despite the van's swerving through mid-morning traffic.

"I doubt it," Hattersley said gloomily. "Cassandra enslaved a lot of locals via her little cult. Even if most of them left town, there could be plenty of Code Nines left."

Frankie checked Stainforth's pulse and breathing. The Task Force medics back at the nearby military airbase would perform more elaborate tests. Then he would be taken back to headquarters in London. He was the seventh controlled human detained so far. She agreed with Collier's assessment, that only the most valuable people had been taken when the Interlopers had fled.

Valuable people like Zoffany, she thought ruefully. *God knows what they're doing to her, exploiting her for.*

"You think they'll figure out a way to cure them?" she asked Hattersley.

"You're assuming it's an illness," the technician pointed out. "Some might see it was a different state of being. Evolution, in fact."

Frankie felt herself growing resentful of the Englishman's perverse way of looking at things. But she kept her voice level when she responded.

"I reckon being enslaved by monsters from another dimension doesn't count as progress."

Hattersley's mouth twisted up in a crooked smile.

"It is from the Code Nine viewpoint," he said. "Know your enemy, Frankie. Put yourself in his place. Or in this case, its place. For them, converting us into slaves and food animals makes sense, but it's a huge task. A human antagonist would probably balk at the scale of it. But–"

Frankie nodded reluctantly.

"But they're not human," she finished. "And they could give it a try. Take us over. Turn us into cattle."

They fell silent as Stainforth moaned and fretted under the anesthetic. The black van stopped briefly at the airfield gates, then headed out onto the runway. Soon they would be back in London.

We'll be back under Trent's supervision, Frankie thought. *I wonder if Hattersley would be so cool and theoretical if he knew there was more than one non-human threat?*

"Cheer up, Frankie!" said Collier. "We're winning, one day at a time. We'll get them all eventually."

***

"I do not care what your papers say, *Herr Kapitan*," said Andreas Schliewe. "Your vessel cannot use our facilities. No spaces are available."

The British captain standing in front of Schliewe looked blankly at him for a moment. Then the man smiled, and the German harbormaster felt oddly relieved.

Why did I fear he might attack me? Schliewe wondered. *Such a thing is unheard of.*

The two were standing on the busy docks at Hamburg, the picturesque backdrop of the medieval city barely visible beyond cranes, trucks, and warehouses. The captain of the large, London-registered motor yacht had been very persistent about requiring a place to dock. But, as Schliewe had pointed out, he could not conjure up a space that did not exist.

"I appreciate your position, Herr Schliewe," the captain replied, his tone friendly. "But our circumstances are somewhat unusual. Perhaps if you came aboard you might change your mind?"

Schliewe frowned. His keen sense of propriety was always alert to the possibility of bribery. Smugglers offered thousands, sometimes millions, to humble functionaries so that they could bring drugs, arms, and trafficked individuals through Hamburg. Since he had taken charge, Schliewe had enforced the regulations assiduously.

"I pride myself on my professionalism," he warned. Then a thought occurred to him. "Are you claiming that you require to dock at once for emergency reasons?"

The captain's brow wrinkled in thought, then he shrugged.

"We have passengers who are – let us say, celebrities? One of whom wishes to come ashore. But this – celebrity – would rather do so discreetly."

Schliewe frowned, checked the passenger roster of the yacht. He saw no names that he recognized. Noticing this, the captain admitted that several passengers were traveling under assumed names. Schliewe raised an eyebrow, back on familiar territory – that of clear rules, properly enforced.

"I must inspect these persons' passports before I can consider allowing them ashore," he said. "And of course, I will have to contact my opposite number in German Federal Customs."

"Of course," the captain said. "Procedures must be followed. But first, please come aboard the Fulmar and meet our VIPs."

Schliewe was about to refuse when the captain reached out and took his hand. The German pulled back, but not before he experienced an odd, tingling sensation.

As if someone had tickled the inside of my head, he thought. *Most peculiar.*

"Herr Schliewe," the captain said quietly. "I think I can trust you. The persons I am referring to are members of a certain singing group that is very popular with pre-teen girls."

When the captain named the group, Schliewe thought of his twelve-year-old daughter, and her reaction if he got the autographs of her favorite singers. He made an instant bargain with his conscience. He would inspect a luxury yacht applying to use the harbor facilities and meet its famous passengers.

And if this perfectly sensible procedure results in some autographed pictures for little Julie, so much the better.

Ten minutes later, Schliewe climbed up the ladder from his launch to board the *Fulmar*. He had inspected many vessels in his time, and at first, the yacht seemed ordinary enough. It was only as he was shown below deck by the captain that he began to wonder at the absence of other crewmembers, and the silence.

Normally there would be music playing. Crewmen shouting. A general bustle as people prepare to go ashore.

However, Schliewe shrugged off his concerns, as the captain led him along a passageway to a large, furnished lounge. Seated on a couch he saw three young women dressed in expensive-looking clothes, attended by a couple of adults dressed as wait staff. Even Schliewe, with his limited interest in pop, recognized the famous faces.

"Here he is, girls!" said the captain.

Schliewe fixed a smile on his face and advanced across the lounge, already wondering how he could get such famous celebrities through the dock area without too much fuss. The three girls stood up, beaming dazzling smiles at him. He was about to say what a pleasure it was to meet such stars when the captain and one of the waiters grabbed him by the arms.

"What? Please, gentlemen, ladies," Schliewe protested. "This is most irregular."

The other waiter stepped forward and sprayed something from a small bottle into Schliewe's face. It stung his eyes, produced an acrid, burning sensation. He coughed, spluttered, protested some more. Then his captors led him to a chair and lowered him carefully into it.

"This is outrageous!" he exclaimed, tears streaming down his cheeks. "Serious charges will be brought, I assure you!"

Schliewe tried to stand, but felt dizzy, could not lever himself upright. The stinging sensation in his eyes faded, but was replaced by a strange humming noise that grew rapidly louder. A sensation of numbness spread over his face, down his chest, into his limbs.

"Help me!" he croaked.

He reached up for one of the men standing over him, then stopped to gaze at his hand. Schliewe's vision was dimming, but it seemed as if the flesh of his fingers was darkening, becoming purplish-black. Just before darkness closed in, he saw his thumbnail fall off, the exposed flesh beneath looking like rotten fruit. There was an iron taste of blood in his mouth.

The last words he heard were in English. They were spoken in a cool, measured voice by a woman.

"A qualified success," said the unknown woman. "But with a few more adjustments we will be able to start testing on a larger scale."

Nightmare Rising

Chapter 1: Deceit and Detection

Never be alone with him, thought Ted Gould, glancing at the short man walking just ahead of him. *That's what we agreed. But it's not easy when he's your boss.*

"Good morning, good morning!"

Trent, the Task Force leader, was full of effusive bonhomie. The staff at the children's home greeted him familiarly. He was clearly a regular visitor. This made Gould resentful, confused. He had only seen Lucy half a dozen times since Denny Purcell had rescued her over a year earlier.

She's my sister. I should see her more often, get to know her better. Despite the obstacles.

They were ushered down a corridor by a member of staff. The walls were decorated with bright murals of tropical islands, forests, mountains. Amiable creatures swam or ran or flew, and none preyed upon one another. Monkeys in trees looked benevolently down at lions, mice peered up at comical owls, smiling dolphins cruised amiably past schools of multi-colored fish.

Propaganda, Gould thought. *We prettify nature, play down the violence. Is that wise?*

The attendant showed them into an observation room. Gould steeled himself to ask her to stay, but did not need to. Instead, the woman stood between Gould and Trent while they watched the children play. Sometimes a little boy or girl would look directly at the one-way mirror. Even though he knew all the child could see was its own reflection, Gould still felt uncomfortable.

"Of course," the woman said, "this room would normally only be used by child-care professionals and such. But Lucy – well, we all know there are special circumstances."

"Quite so!" Trent responded with his usual chirpiness. "And we are most grateful to all of you for being so accommodating."

At that moment, a fresh group of children ran into the playroom. Lucy was among them, talking eagerly to another girl. Gould was not good at judging children's ages. To him Lucy looked about six or seven, though medical opinions varied. The fact was that she had been born three years after Ted, but they were now nearly fifty years apart.

"All that time away," Trent murmured. "So sad."

Gould looked round sharply at his superior. The cover story was that Gould was Lucy's uncle, a long-lost relative. Paperwork had been contrived to fit the story. But the looks that staff members sometimes gave Gould led him to wonder if they thought he was actually the girl's father.

They might think I disowned her, then regretted it. But how can I insist that the nicer lie is the true one?

It was a minor complication. The central fact was that Lucy Gould had been abducted and kept in the Phantom Dimension for a few weeks, by her reckoning. Decades had passed in the human universe. After her rescue, she had been almost unable to speak, severely traumatized. But looking at her now, Gould saw a normal child dragging a large, stuffed rabbit around behind her.

"She never lets go of that bunny," the attendant remarked. "Sleeps with it, insists on having it with her at bath time. It's looking a bit battered now."

"Her one constant in a baffling, chaotic world," Trent remarked.

A pager beeped and the woman excused herself. Gould looked at the door as it closed behind her, took a faltering step after it, then realized he could not justify leaving the observation room.

"Don't be afraid, Ted, old chap," said Trent. "Your precious mind is quite safe with me."

Gould turned to see Trent looking at him benignly. The plump little man was leaning against the far wall, thumbs in the waistband of his slacks.

Could anyone look more harmless?

"We need to have a chat, Ted," Trent went on. "About the serious problems we both face. You've been involved with this from the start. You've sacrificed a great deal. A glittering academic career. People you love, lost to you."

Trent levered himself upright and Gould flinched involuntarily.

"You seem rather jumpy, old chap," Trent said, face a picture of concern. "I shouldn't have mentioned work matters in this situation. Very insensitive of me. Forget it – just forget it for now."

The female attendant came back into the room at that moment, apologizing for being called away. They resumed their observation of Lucy. Every smile, every gesture, was painful to Gould. He and Harriet Zoffany had tentatively planned to adopt the little girl, despite formidable bureaucratic obstacles. Now he might never see Zoffany again, and Lucy seemed likely to be raised by strangers.

They watched for another ten minutes or so, then Trent declared that they had a long drive back to London. Fortunately for Gould, Trent always used a chauffeur. They made awkward conversation on the return journey.

"You're aware," Trent put in during a lull, "that the life sciences team has finished their analysis of the egg fragments?"

Gould was not and said so.

"Yes," Trent went on breezily. "Judging by the remains of larger shells, it seems that three females were hatched. The daughters of Cassandra, out there somewhere."

Trent gestured at the sunlit English landscape as it rolled past.

"Three potential queens," said Gould. "Three females that can produce dozens, maybe hundreds of new Interlopers. And we have no idea how to find them."

Trent looked around, eyebrows raised in quizzical amusement.

"Don't be downhearted, old chap!" he said. "I'm sure with such a brilliant team I'll be able to report success very soon. We have the money trail, plus your detector, and of course the addition of Ms. Dupont to our squad of agents–"

Trent talked on, but Gould found it impossible to listen to the upbeat monologue. Instead, he wondered what Trent might really be. And whether, without his knowledge, the being masquerading as an overweight little bureaucrat had already tinkered with his mind.

With luck, he thought, *Denny will be able to tell me.*

***

"We've got another one – missing German harbormaster," said Tania. "Andreas Schliewe vanished after setting off on a train from Hamburg to Switzerland."

"And you're telling me this because?" returned John Matheson. "Thousands of people go missing every day in this country alone."

The researcher wagged a finger at the security chief.

"We're looking for possible Code Nine activity, and this one gets three red flags." She counted them off on her fingers. "One, a person in authority, two, based on an international frontier, and three, the disappearance followed unorthodox behavior."

Matheson nodded, then followed Tania out of his small office and into the operations room. Three rows of desks accommodated the Intelligence Section. This consisted of six non-combatant agents whose time was largely devoted to combing the internet. Officially, their brief was to look for unusual activity. Informally they described their activity as 'weird watch'. Tania da Silva was their team leader. For her birthday, she had been presented with a coffee mug bearing the title Chief Weirdo.

"This the guy?" asked Matheson, pointing at a photo on Tania's monitor.

"You deduced that from the mass of German words on the screen?" she asked. "Yes, that's him. Family man, clean record, very punctilious. Well, obviously, he's a German official. But his wife reported that he seemed strange, rather distant, for a few days before he disappeared."

"On a train to Switzerland," Matheson mused. "If it was a Code Nine, what's so special about Switzerland, as opposed to any other European country?"

Tania enumerated a few more facts on her fingers.

"One, a fiercely neutral country that we can't operate in very effectively, at least compared to NATO member states, and two, it's famously home to a lot of secret bank accounts."

Matheson nodded.

"Including some of the Lanier fortune?" he suggested.

"I wouldn't be surprised," Tania replied. "And the one thing everyone needs, human or otherwise, is hard cash in some form."

They discussed the situation some more. It was obvious that, if an Interloper had come ashore in Hamburg posing as the harbormaster, it must have arrived by sea. While Tania set out to identify suspect vessels, Matheson got in touch with a sub-contractor in Geneva. It was a long-shot, but he could at least offer to send over one of Gould's Code Nine detectors. The Task Force also had the ability – not strictly legal – to track unusual financial activity online.

"You can expect the detector to be flown in via private charter," he explained. "Of course, it should automatically bypass Customs at the airport, but remember – remember–"

Matheson found himself struggling for words. Somehow, he could not articulate the straightforward procedures he had in mind. For a brief second, as he groped for a phrase, a piercing pain jabbed him behind the eyes, and he winced. He saw Tania turn around, mild concern on her delicate features. Matheson grinned weakly, and mimed drinking a pint of beer. She shook her head in mock disapproval.

But I only had two pints last night, he thought, as he managed to finish the call. *Slept like a baby, felt fine this morning. What just happened?*

For a moment, he considered consulting the Task Force's chief medic. But then Matheson dismissed the idea. He had taken over as security chief after the shocking demise of Comstock, an old comrade. Matheson had always enjoyed the role of second-in-command. Now he faced the burdens of leadership, which ranged from life-and-death decision making to signing off on agents' expense claims.

If I have any more problems, I'll see the MO, he told himself. *But it was probably just one of those things.*

***

"Ready for your close-up, Mister De Mille?"

Gould tried to smile at Denny's attempt to lighten the mood. The ends of his mouth curved up, but his eyes remained haunted, melancholy. Denny looked over at Frankie. The other woman got up and drew the blinds, plunging the apartment's living room into near darkness.

Like we're about to summon spirits, Denny thought. *And I suppose we are, in a way.*

"Okay," he said, extending a hand over the table. "Have a rummage around, on the house."

Denny took off one of her thin black gloves, flexed her fingers. The gesture was meaningless, a nervous habit she had acquired. This was the third time she had scanned Gould. She had taken to using the word 'scanned' not because it was especially accurate, but because Denny felt the term had the right sound for a scientist.

"Okay, Ted, here we go," she said, reaching out to grasp the tips of his fingers.

The first impression from the scientist was always the same. A sense of loss and loneliness that was very much at odds with his bluff, rational, British exterior. Denny had probed the emotions of many people during her career as a psychic. But they had been strangers. When she shared the emotions of friends, she tended to squirm with embarrassment, or worse.

Quick, get through the surface stuff, she told herself. *Drill down!*

Her telepathic ability was erratic, not easily controlled. Surface emotions and thoughts were easiest. But she forced herself to go deeper, resisting the urge to pull back, free herself from the torrent of complex, often dark emotions. As she had entered Gould's mind before she knew what to look for, and what to avoid. She skirted the painful memories of his sister's disappearance, the terrors of his encounters with the Interlopers. At the same time, she tried to avoid the more intimate details of his relationship with Harriet Zoffany, but still caught cringe-making glimpses.

Full speed ahead, she told herself. *Get back to the crucial moment, that day when all hell broke loose on the London Underground.*

Denny saw the cluster of memories she needed, reached for them, tried to grasp them. The memories proved elusive, as before, darting away from her grasp. It was a kind of safeguard, she suspected. Because the memories, when she finally caught them again, were like nothing she had seen in a normal human mind.

She was looking out of Gould's eyes, as he stood in the conference room on the top floor of the Romola Foundation. At first, the room was empty. Gould looked around, then decided to leave. Suddenly, the room was full of tall, cadaverous figures in smart business suits. And they were all identical.

Even though Denny had reviewed the memory several times, the multiple Bensons were still startling. The word 'clones' had occurred to her, but it was insufficient. Cloning was something that made a kind of sense, a fringe scientific feat. This was very different. The Benson being seemed to multiply itself at will, as if by magic.

What the strange beings said to Gould she could not discover. But what they did was clear enough. This incident had been suppressed by some bizarre method. Cassandra, the Interloper Queen, had broken through whatever screen had been put in place by the Benson-beings. As well as revealing the memory, this had allowed Denny to identify what she thought of as the 'flavor' of suppressed memories. There was something bland, overly-neat, about regions of memory that had been manipulated. And this meant that she could scan her allies to see if their minds had been tampered with.

"Okay," she sighed, letting go of Gould's hand. "You're still clean. Just the original example, Benson's tinkering – nothing more recent."

"So far as you know," Gould pointed out. "We're making a lot of assumptions about Trent."

Denny did not reply. She had spotted a few other trace thoughts in the scientist's mind. Gould was fearful and suspicious of Trent. But at the same time, he nourished a wild hope that the being might be benevolent. To Denny, who had touched the cold, dark void that lurked in the core of Trent, it seemed a forlorn optimism. But she did not want to condemn Gould's fragile hope.

"Me next," said Frankie, matter-of-factly. "Let's get psychic."

Denny found it easier to scan Frankie. Their long-term friendship held firm at the subconscious level. Compared to Gould's tortured, convoluted persona, Frankie was straightforward, almost simple. The only surprise Denny had encountered was Frankie's fierce loyalty to her, which was another cause of embarrassment.

"That's okay," Denny said, pulling back. "No sign of fakery."

Frankie got up and opened the blinds again. While they had no reason to believe they were being spied upon, they had gotten into the habit of hiding any unusual activity. Between them, Frankie and Gould had obtained the tech needed to sweep the flat for bugging devices. But, as Gould had sourly observed, they had no real idea of Trent's capabilities. For all they knew, the plump little man could read their minds all the time, making conventional surveillance obsolete.

"Which is why," Gould had remarked, "we need to test his limitations."

Denny reminded the scientist of this as they tucked into their post-scan pizza, a ritual they had developed to defuse inevitable tensions.

"I assume," Denny said, "that your Loper detector doesn't work on him?"

"I conducted a discreet test – got no reading at all," Gould confirmed. "But that's not surprising. Whatever Trent and Benson are, they're nothing like Interlopers."

"'Nomads' is what Cassandra called them," Frankie pointed out through a mouthful of melted cheese and pepperoni. "That's kind of suggestive."

Gould nodded as he opened a can of warm British beer.

"I'm sure there's a link between these Nomads and the portals," he said. "Perhaps they actually create them, and spend their time hopping between worlds. Observing. Interfering."

"Why?" Frankie asked. "I mean, what's their deal? Are they just explorers, or out to conquer us, or what?"

Gould sighed and shook his head.

"I'm inclined to shelve that whole issue," he admitted. "I still think the Interlopers are the more serious threat. Yes, we should find out more about these so-called Nomads. But they're not overtly hostile, so much as keen to remain undetected."

Frankie waved a slice of pizza to raise a point.

"Is there any evidence that Trent, and Benson before him, are based on actual human beings? I mean, if they replaced actual human beings, the way Lopers do, the original men would have left electronic trails – right?"

Gould nodded.

"Benson left a paper trail – passport, birth certificate, driver's license. And all the corresponding online data. However, every attempt I made to find a relative, or someone who simply had known him outside the foundation, I ran into a brick wall. If there ever was a real Benson, he was a man with no friends or family."

"But Trent is running a top-secret government outfit, not an outfit that investigates spooks," Denny pointed out. "Surely they'd do more than a basic background check?"

Gould nodded again.

"MI5, Scotland Yard, all of those guys dig very deep," he admitted. "Either there was a real Trent who got replaced at some point, or Trent's powers of manipulation are amazing."

They paused to consider the possibilities. Then Denny spoke.

"If he has woven some elaborate web of deception, mind-control, what have you, it must take a lot of effort. I mean, okay, he might have godlike powers. But if so, why does he sneak about using humans like us? Why not just say 'Alakazam,' kill off the Lopers, and go home?"

"Wherever that is," added Frankie. "Maybe the planet of the happy little fat guys?"

"Nothing happy about whatever is inside that little fat guy," Denny said, closing her eyes for a moment. "Every time I think of it, I get chills. Me and poor old Jabba. I think he was traumatized."

Gould gave a little snort.

"I know," Denny smiled. "Sounds dumb. But that's fear of the unknown for you."

"Quite," Gould agreed. "What we need is information. So, while we have to focus on the Interlopers, maybe I can find some way of analyzing Trent. He can't be a perfect simulacrum of a human being. There must a scientific way of showing what he really is."

"Knock yourself out, professor," Frankie remarked. "But what if he finds out?"

Gould shrugged. "He'll mess with my mind, I suppose. Make me forget the idea."

Let's hope it's nothing more drastic, Denny thought.

***

The tissue sample under the microscope consisted of dead cells. They had exploded from the inside, destroyed by a virus similar to the common cold. The virus had been cleverly tweaked by Harriet Zoffany. Despite her best efforts, the beings that had enslaved her had tapped into her knowledge, her creativity, and weaponized her. Then she had weaponized Interloper DNA.

"Doctor Zoffany!"

"Just leave it on the bench," she said, without looking up. She knew who it was. It was always the same person.

The man called Fordyce brought her lunch every day at the same time. It was always the same, a chicken sandwich. Fordyce and Lassiter, the other two controlled humans on the yacht, were like amiable robots. Incapable of much original thought, they operated to a routine and did their best to please the immature females. Given the hostility the sisters felt to one another, this was not easy. Rival demands often froze their slaves into immobility. However, the 'young ladies' in the luxury cabins never pushed the humans too far. Zoffany felt that the creatures understood that being able to closely mimic humans might not be enough, and that real people could be useful.

The yacht *Fulmar* cruised the North Sea between Britain, Scandinavia, Germany, and other maritime nations. Thanks to the sizeable Lanier fortune obtained by Cassandra, it could dock almost anywhere and take on provisions. Discretion over such matters, Zoffany knew, could be bought. Which was useful given the need for occasional consignments of animal brains from abattoirs.

Harriet Zoffany was torn between three tyrants. Three minds constantly tugged at hers, three powerful egos made inhuman demands. She did not really care. It was preferable to being controlled by one Interloper. The tug-of-war meant that, while she was never wholly free, her true self could occasionally surface and observe her circumstances. Because she needed to think in the abstract, she had more intellectual freedom than the other humans on board. But not much more.

It was hard to keep track of time. Zoffany suspected that she had been on the *Fulmar* for over a month, but was unsure. All that time, the juvenile queens, via her symbiont, had urged her to add creative input to the knowledge extracted from her. Zoffany was the only top-flight biologist who had studied the Interlopers, albeit not as much as she would have liked. Now she was able to do vast amounts of research– so long as it was to further the Interloper cause.

That cause, as always, was survival. The plan, as she had grasped some of its details, was suitably monstrous. Zoffany had no idea how she was going to fight against her captors. If she was too overt in her resistance, they would instantly detect it. Whatever she did had to be subtle. But now, she was stumped as to what kind of sabotage she could successfully pull off. She could hide some thoughts from the immature queens, but deeds were another matter.

In the meantime, she analyzed the remains of the hapless German harbormaster, now replaced by one of the fully-grown Interlopers. Mind-control meant that any pangs of conscience Zoffany might have felt were suppressed, and she felt perversely grateful for that. The victim had not died pleasantly, though at least it had been quick.

Too quick, she thought, preparing samples of Schliewe's tissue. *Something that virulent would tend to burn itself out.*

At the back of her mind, she knew that one of the queens struggled with the concept of a weapon that was too effective.

Zoffany knew better than to try and instruct the creatures. Instead, she waited as a second juvenile female rummaged in her mind and assessed the argument. She felt the pressure of the two queens' attention lift, a moment.

Deep down, out of reach of the immature females, a shard of the real Harriet Zoffany survived. A sliver of the biologist's individual free will remained untouched by the 'young ladies'. Zoffany recognized the conflict as typical of social insects, in which several females were gestated, but only one could survive to breed. In bees, the first queen to hatch killed the others. Zoffany had not been able to discover how the Interlopers handled sibling rivalry. Part of her hoped all three potential queens would wipe each other out. But it seemed a forlorn hope.

Lopers don't kill Lopers.

The next thought was dangerous, but it recurred with monotonous regularity. The death of Andreas Schliewe, in which Zoffany had been powerless yet complicit, made it more urgent.

Humans do kill Lopers. I should at least try.

Nightmare Rising

Chapter 2: Captives and Cattle

"We can't keep them locked up forever," said Frankie. "Or maybe we can? Is there something in English law that lets you do that?"

Matheson shook his head. They were in the canteen along with Collier and Hattersley, discussing the problem of their 'guests'. The term prisoner was never used in the Task Force. This was despite the seven men and women in the holding cells who definitely didn't want to be there. Stainforth, the latest captive, had been sedated since his capture the previous day. When he came around, he would begin demanding his rights, just like the others.

"We can hardly send them to a secure psychiatric facility," Collier explained wearily. "Like I said before, the first thing the staff would do is spot the symbionts. So, we can only wait until the damn things are fully absorbed."

Frankie nodded, frustrated. She knew that removing a well-embedded symbiont endangered the victim's life. She had only avoided enslavement by killing the creature within moments of its hatching. But it went against the grain to simply wait while alien creatures merged with innocent humans, presumably to enslave them forever.

"You think we should experiment on them, whatever the risks?" asked Collier.

The bluntness of the question caught her off guard. She found herself questioning her own motives.

Would I be okay with seeing a stranger die if it helped free Denny from Jabba? That would make me a monster.

"No!" she protested. "I just think letting them alone, not trying to help, could be a fate worse than death. It's – it's a goddam impossible situation, is what it is."

John Matheson joined them. The security chief had obviously caught the drift of their conversation.

"All those people have got families, friends," he pointed out. "In the movies, you can just take out the bad guys. In real life, we're going to get a ton of pressure from politicians, the media, human rights organizations, the UN. Short version – we can't just disappear people in this country. And not one of them has broken the law."

It took Frankie a moment to grasp what Matheson meant.

"You mean, we have to let them go?"

Matheson shrugged.

"We get them to sign the Official Secrets Act, making them liable to a stiff prison term if they talk about what happened. Not that Code Nines are likely to care, but it's procedure."

Frankie was about to protest, but then saw Collier smiling faintly.

"What's the secret?" she asked. "What am I not getting?"

Collier reached into the breast pocket of his dark blue uniform and took out a small glass tube. Frankie took it, examined the tiny object inside. It looked like a shard of metal.

"Hey!" she exclaimed. "This looks like the ID chip they put in my aunt's cat. You've been micro-chipping controlled humans?"

"Bingo," said Collier, retrieving the chip. "It's a very advanced form of RFID chip, and it means we'll be able to track our guests once they're free. Which will be soon."

Matheson dug a fork into his food, gazed at it in distaste, then put the fork down.

"Well, we can start the more difficult task," he said, without enthusiasm. "Trying to determine just how many kids in Fordham care homes were replaced with Code Nines. And how many have already been adopted, or fostered."

Frankie decided not to ask how many children might have been killed and replaced. There were some things she simply did not want to know unless it was absolutely necessary.

And maybe not even then.

***

The routine in the laboratory of the *Fulmar* was interrupted by an insistent command. Zoffany's symbiont urged her to leave her research at once, and go to the main saloon of the yacht.

The young queen Zoffany had dubbed Alpha was slightly larger, perhaps older, than the other two. As she entered the lounge, the scientist felt a surge in the power emanating from Alpha. The relative influences of Beta and Gamma, still below deck, declined.

Alpha had taken on the appearance of a beautiful, pale-skinned, fair-haired girl. The being was clad in a white dress, her small feet in glittering sandals. Zoffany thought she resembled a medieval princess from a Victorian painting.

"You have done well," said Alpha. "The man died swiftly, and in terror. That is good."

Her voice was that of a teenage girl, its lightness of tone radically at odds with her words. Zoffany was grateful that the juvenile female still needed to speak. Mind-to-mind communication was clearly an adult ability. It gave Zoffany some hope that the young queens could not probe every part of her mind.

"I will be leaving you soon," Alpha went on. "I have a purpose to fulfill elsewhere. Soon I will be ready."

Zoffany was surprised, then tried to stifle her exultation. The most powerful of her tormentors was going. She tried not to think of possible consequences, instead maintained a bland façade of compliance.

"You will continue with the project," Alpha commanded. "You will perfect the virus, so that we may prevail in chaos."

"Of course," said Zoffany, inclining her head.

It was irrational, but Zoffany did not like to meet an Interloper's gaze for long. She had no evidence that the creatures' powers were linked to their unblinking stare. But the effect was too disconcerting.

Alpha stood up, and walked over to Zoffany. Despite her small, slight frame, the Interloper was still intimidating. At close range, Zoffany felt the creature's intense hunger, not merely for power, but also for food. With a sinking sensation, she realized that Alpha needed to feast before her journey.

Surely, I am safe? At least for now.

Alpha reached up and ran a finger along Zoffany's cheek. The scientist tried not to flinch.

"You are safe," Alpha said. "But remember, clever one – no human is irreplaceable."

Zoffany realized with a sense of panic that Alpha could read her thoughts in detail via physical contact. The queen was no longer a juvenile, she concluded. The creature was ready to mate.

"Quite correct," Alpha murmured, turning away. "Copulation is necessary."

The slender being gestured to Fordyce, who had been standing by, his expression blank. Fordyce, a sturdily-built man, walked forward and stood facing Alpha. The queen put a tiny finger against the side of the man's head, and he moved over to the couch, began to take off his clothes. As he did so, Alpha removed her dress with a casual gesture, and stood naked before Zoffany.

Oh my God, the scientist thought.

The body of the creature was perfect, an idealized version of the nubile girl. But Alpha radiated a cool, confident power that no human girl had ever known. After Fordyce had disrobed, she casually pushed him down onto the leather couch, then climbed on top of him.

The clinical precision of her movements reminded Zoffany of a praying mantis. There was no sign of arousal or passion on Alpha's part as she took what she needed from the enslaved human. Fordyce showed no emotion at all, and Zoffany concluded that he was now merely an extension of Alpha's will.

This is the opposite of love-making.

Zoffany wanted to look away, knowing what must come next. But scientific curiosity conspired with horrified fascination, and she continued to watch.

Alpha raised her small, delicate-seeming hands above her head. In a few minutes, the tips of the creature's fingers grew into black, ferocious claws. Alpha plunged the vicious talons into the sides of Fordyce's head. Zoffany flinched at the sounds of flesh and bone being penetrated. The man jerked, gasped, flailed his hands for a moment. Then Alpha had lifted the upper half of his skull away, revealing the bloody gray matter within.

Zoffany felt her half-digested lunch coming up as Alpha plunged her hands into Fordyce's brain, tore out gobbets of neural tissue. The female Interloper's attention was now entirely focused on her post-coital feast. As a result, waves of inhuman pleasure washed over the scientist. She vomited, falling to her knees in a mockery of obeisance as Alpha tossed aside fragments of smashed skull.

Zoffany stopped heaving long enough to see Alpha stop plucking lumps of tissue out of the remains of Fordyce's head. The queen's human visage blurred, distorted, elongated into a funnel-like mouth. Alpha shoved her now-hideous muzzle into the ruined skull and began slurping up the last of her victim's brain.

"Oh dear, have we had a little accident, Doctor?"

Zoffany looked up to see Lassiter standing over her with a mop and bucket.

"Never mind, dear," said the tall woman. "We'll soon clear that mess up. Just move back a bit, so I can get at it, eh?"

"Of course," croaked Zoffany.

She crawled backwards a few paces and Lassiter began clearing up the vomit, fragments of scalp and bone, plus stray gobbets of brain tissue. The controlled woman worked with the bland energy of an untroubled soul. Lassiter was just squeezing out her mop when Alpha finished her repast, and her face resumed its familiar, angelic appearance. She gazed over at Zoffany and smiled thinly.

"I hope," said the young queen, "that your researches will ensure a decent food supply for us all. Get the balance right, scientist."

With that, Alpha put on her white dress, which was now speckled with little dots of red, and walked out of the yacht's lounge.

"Isn't she marvelous?" sighed Lassiter. "So sad she's going away. But at least we have the other young ladies to take care of."

Then the woman laid out a plastic sheet and rolled Fordyce's body onto it.

**

"We were wrong, people!"

Trent was his usual cheery self as he delivered the news.

"About what, chief?" asked Matheson.

Trent explained, at length, smiling benignly all the while. The Task Force had assumed that the children replaced by young Interlopers were being fostered or adopted by controlled humans. This made sense, as a way of ensuring the creatures blended in to human society. It was, as Trent observed, a logical assumption.

"But it seems the Code Nines had a different idea," he said, triumphantly, as if he was somehow being vindicated.

If he was a genuine human being, Frankie thought, *I'd want to punch the guy.*

Gould cleared his throat.

"So what's happened with the Code Nine kids? I mean, they must be somewhere."

Trent nodded sagely.

"Some are probably still in care homes," he said. "We have placed some people in Fordham social services to keep a lookout. Your detectors will come in handy, there, Ted."

"Fine, glad I could help," said Gould tersely. "But if most of Cassandra's offspring aren't in Fordham any more, where did they go?"

Trent jabbed at his keyboard, and a large wall screen lit up. It showed what Frankie recognized as a flow chart. Different colored lines intersected, diverged, merged. Two names leaped out – Fordham, Lanier. There were also the names of several businesses she did not recognize. Along the bottom of the diagram, where most of the arrows ended, she saw names. One name was preceded by the term 'Rt Hon', which she knew was the abbreviation for Right Honorable. The term signified a high-ranking British politician.

"I'm guessing corruption in high places?" Frankie said. "Some kind of adoption racket?"

"Got it in one, Ms. Dupont!" Trent exclaimed. "What we've uncovered is a well-funded effort to supply apparently perfect children to wealthy couples eager to adopt. Remember, most people who want an off-the-shelf child don't want damaged goods. Brutal, perhaps, but true. And when the couple is rich and privileged, they become even more exacting. A wonderful opportunity for our enemy to infiltrate the upper echelons of society."

Matheson looked puzzled.

"Okay, I see how they've done it," he said, "but I don't see why it would make sense to place Code Nines with normal human families of any kind? Sooner or later they'll be revealed – medical checks, that sort of thing."

Trent made a tent of his fingers and continued to beam at his subordinates. As time ticked by, Frankie found herself wanting to punch the little man again. Finally, Gould broke the silence.

"Later obviously doesn't count," he sighed. "That's the only reasonable conclusion. These Interlopers are not sleeper agents, they're time bombs, designed to go off very soon. A matter of months, maybe only weeks"

"Precisely!" Trent said, making a finger-pistol gesture at the scientist. "Dozens of adorable children, many quite tiny, just waiting to rip their adoptive parents to shreds, then disappear. Causing alarm and confusion at high levels, of course. They can kill their new mummy and daddy and then change appearance. To the police, it's a horrific child abduction that entailed the vicious murder of the parents. We've seen it before, haven't we?"

Frankie balked at the idea, and not merely because it was horrific.

"Seriously?" she demanded. "It sounds kind of random. I mean, just getting close to a few dozen influential people and killing them? That's old-school terrorism, right?"

"Yeah, and that means they're learning our ways," Matheson responded at once. "Adopting our methods. Disruption, assassination, and as you say, terror. They've gone from being the boogeymen lurking in old houses to unconventional warfare in a very short time. Code Nines evolve fast."

They all stared at the screen. Frankie imagined government ministers, top executives, senior bureaucrats, all jumping the adoption queue. It was easy to sympathize with their motives.

"They're going to pay a high price for sketchy dealings," she observed. "But I notice we've got some names already. How come?"

Trent explained that Tania's team included some competent hackers, and that some shady adoption agencies used did not have especially robust cyber-security. However, only a few adopters had been identified so far.

"It seems unlikely that we will get them all before whatever the Code Nines are planning takes place. But of course, we will get to the families we know about – won't we, John?"

"We will, chief," replied Matheson.

"Okay," Frankie said, raising her voice. "Am I the only one who wants to know what we do when we catch a Loper – sorry, Code Nine? Are we really going to kill a very influential person's newly-adopted child in front of them?"

The team fell silent. Nobody had a simple answer. Eventually, Frankie spoke up.

"I have a friend who might be able to help."

***

"I don't have to go anywhere near Trent?" Denny asked. "I'm not going to take orders from that – person."

Frankie assured her that she did not.

"You don't have to go near headquarters at all," put in Gould. "You are technically still a part of the Task Force, though you may not feel like it. That means there are no official hoops to jump through, we can just get on with it."

Denny pondered her friend's proposal. If Gould had come up with the idea, she might have rejected it out of hand. The scientist had often been more imaginative than reliable. But now it was Frankie who had suggested a way Denny could help save innocent lives from Interlopers. It was risky, but it was more humane than crashing into someone's home throwing nets over their screaming 'children'.

Denny looked down at her gloved hands. Gould and Frankie sat on the couch, looking at her anxiously. Denny had to smile at the ill-matched pair. Frankie, wiry and compact, was built to the same scale as the cramped apartment. Gould seemed too lanky, almost like an adult in a child's playhouse.

"We make quite a team," she said, managing a smile. "Okay, I think it is time we got the band back together."

***

Zoffany was dozing, lying on her side, a cushion propped behind her. One time she had rolled over onto her symbiont in her sleep. She had learned the lesson. Whenever she slept aboard the *Fulmar* her dreams were a mixture of the mundane and bizarre. On this particular night, she had been walking through a devastated city, most of its buildings in ruins, a few still had plumes of smoke emerging from them. Wrecked vehicles blocked the roads. In the distance, she heard gunfire, an explosion. But it was not human violence she feared.

As it was a dream she could not behave sensibly. She knew that being in the open at any time was dangerous. But she continued to pick her way through debris, clambering over rubble, avoiding bomb-craters, driven forward by some impulse she could not define. To her left was a clothing store, mannequins scattered in the vast windows, bright fashions marred by dust and broken glass. She heard a stealthy movement, froze, stared into the dark interior.

Then one of the mannequins moved, jerkily at first, raising itself on its arms. Its featureless face turned toward her, and black eyes appeared. Other shiny, bald figures began to stir. Zoffany retreated, turned, ran. But her path was blocked by a line of children, incongruously neat in their school uniforms, faces clean, eyes bright.

Their claws sharp. The mouths too wide, smiling with dozens of fangs.

"Oh, God."

She jerked awake, glad to escape from the nightmare. At first, she did not remember where she was. Then the cramped cabin came into focus. She saw the remains of a basic meal on a tray, the foldaway desk, the porthole. And with that realization came the prompting of the young queens, Beta and Gamma asserting themselves more now that Alpha was gone.

The urging of the alien minds was like an itch Zoffany could not scratch. She dressed quickly, made her way to the laboratory, and saw one of the Interloper crew waiting. The creature was stationed there permanently since Alpha's departure, a clear sign that Zoffany was not entirely trusted. It also hinted that Beta and Gamma were unsure of their powers. The scientist had concluded that she was allowed just enough creative freedom to do cutting-edge research. This let her retain some semblance of selfhood. But she had yet to push the limits, see just how much autonomy she truly had.

"The virus," the Interloper said, needlessly. "Quickly."

As Zoffany prepared another spray capsule, she glanced out of the porthole. She could see land, what seemed to be a grassy hillside.

Not a major port, I'd guess, she thought. *A small harbor, out of the way.*

"Hurry," urged her guard.

Zoffany completed her task, then paused. The Interloper's face was beginning to change. Normally the ship's inhuman crewmembers had generic, blank features. A Google search for 'white European male' might have thrown up similar faces. But now the creature's mock-human visage was firming up, shifting. The process fascinated the scientist, for all its bizarre nature.

This one is preparing to replace whoever is coming onboard, she realized. *Just like that poor German.*

For a fleeting moment, her loathing of the Interlopers surfaced, stopped her from leaving the lab. Her guard stopped its transformation, drew itself more erect, hissed.

"All right," she muttered. "I'm coming."

The creature followed her up the stairway to the saloon, then waited outside, its face still changing. As she entered the luxurious saloon Zoffany saw Beta, Lassiter, and a stranger. Lassiter was dressed in smart-casual yachting clothes, rather expensive. Beta looked like a short, dark girl of about thirteen. It was clear from the snatch of conversation Zoffany heard that Lassiter was posing as Beta's mother.

All very innocent, nobody would ever guess.

The newcomer was in a neat, dark blue uniform. Zoffany guessed that he was a Coast Guard or harbor official of some kind. Again, her hatred of her captors surfaced, but was quickly suppressed.

"Ah," said Lassiter, playing her role of wealthy yacht-owner, "here's our ship's doctor. I'm sure she can explain."

The stranger looked at Zoffany, face expectant. He was a young man, clean-shaven, his hair very fair, his eyes very blue. Again, her instincts rebelled against her task. But she felt the prompting of Beta in her mind, knew that this female was almost as strong as Alpha had been. Any conflict would be short-lived.

"Good morning, doctor," said the young man, politely. His voice was accented, but he spoke English very well. "I was just explaining to this lady that passports must be presented before anyone can land. While we are a small town–"

"I'm sorry!" Zoffany blurted out. "I'm so sorry, I can't help you."

The foreign official paused, his kindly face puzzled. Then his eyes widened. Zoffany knew that the official was looking past her, seeing a man with his own face entering the room. She raised the spray and squirted a few droplets into the young man's face while he was distracted.

"I'm so sorry," she repeated, stepping back. "It will be quick."

"What – what is this?" gasped the man, wiping at his eyes.

Lassiter and the Interloper grabbed him, dragged him quickly to the couch, and sat him next to Beta. The queen was dressed incongruously in pastel colors, dark hair pinned back by a flowered barrette. Beta examined her victim closely, gazing into his pained, horrified face.

The man spoke a few words Zoffany did not understand, guessed they were Norwegian or perhaps Swedish. He coughed, chest heaving, eyes suddenly bloodshot. The scientist braced herself for the decay of tissue, the precipitate rotting of the body. But after a few more seconds had passed, she saw none of the telltale signs of viral death. The man's skin remained flushed but healthy. No blood emerged from nostrils or mouth.

Oh, God, she thought. *Could this be a double success?*

When Zoffany had first been enslaved by the juvenile queens, they had demanded the seemingly impossible. The viral plague that would slay uncontrolled humans had been bad enough. It combined the infectious power of a regular virus with the genetic quirk that caused dead Interlopers to disintegrate. But then Alpha had added another twist, a variation on the theme of infection. So far none of their victims had shown the extraordinary transformation that Zoffany had tried to key to a fairly common gene.

But this could be the first one, the first to transform rather than die.

The Interlopers were ahead of her. She saw the creature that had taken on the young man's appearance change back to the look of a generic crewman. There was no longer a need to replace this man. The young official stopped coughing and spluttering, and his breathing gradually settled down. Zoffany checked his pulse, which was rapid but not excessively so. His eyes opened, and he gazed down at Beta.

"Welcome," said Beta. "Go about your duties. We need supplies, including brain matters. Animal will suffice for now."

"I understand, mistress," said the official, standing up. "It will be done."

After the new slave had left, Beta interrogated Zoffany about what percentage of plague victims would become controlled humans. Zoffany answered truthfully that she could only guess, as testing had been conducted on such a small scale.

"About one in three or four, at most," she hazarded. "Perhaps one in ten."

"And how many humans might prove immune?" Beta demanded.

Zoffany felt the urgency of that question. The queens had tried to absorb all her scientific knowledge, but struggled to grasp the methods and principles she worked by. However, they had grasped one thing. They knew that no infectious disease was one hundred percent effective. They knew that their new weapon would spare some humans. And they considered that a good thing.

"One in ten, maybe a little more," she admitted. "Unless we dial down the lethality."

Beta nodded, apparently lost in thought. Then Zoffany felt the mental pressure from the queen decline slightly. She was about to be dismissed.

"No, this machine civilization must fall for us to prevail," said Beta, her voice the pleasant contralto of a well-mannered girl. "That means utter chaos, total devastation. Only a few basic humans will be needed as food animals. Breeding stock will be established. But we need to refine the dispersal method. Your virus dies too quickly."

"Of course," murmured Zoffany, and left to continue her work.

Chapter 3: Think of the Children

"Tommy?"

Alicia Petrie stood in her spacious living room and gazed around. It was a very neat, tastefully-furnished room. The French windows looked out onto a fine garden, beyond which were the Malvern Hills. Spring was in the air, sun slanted across the plush carpet, and Alicia was a mother.

I've got the family I always wanted, she thought. *The perfect package. So why do I feel there's something wrong?*

"Tommy?" she called again. It was a Saturday morning, a time that ought to have been pleasant, even joyful. After a week of work for the adults and school for the children, the Petries could be together as a family.

Alicia's husband Ralph had suggested going to a wildlife park, or perhaps an aquarium. His refrain was always 'get them out of the house, get them interested in nature, science, that sort of thing'. But he always assumed that Alicia would make the arrangements, ensure the children were ready. And now she could not even find them.

The woman walked over to the French windows to look out into the garden. Tommy, who was eight, might have been playing outside. But she could see no sign of him. Nor could she see Daisy, the family dog, who had been behaving oddly as of late. The animal had initially barked and snarled at the children, who had naturally reacted with fear. Ralph had had to grab the normally-placid dog and chain her up in her kennel.

It had been an unfortunate start to the exercise in building a family. Since that first day, Daisy had been kept outside. The Petries had even started to look around for a family that might take the pet off their hands. Alicia had suggested getting a cat instead, but when she had mentioned it to Katie, the fourteen-year-old had not been keen.

"I don't really like animals," Katie had explained. "And Tommy's scared of them. We never had pets, you see."

The girl could not have chosen her words more effectively. Katie, while remarkably polite and obedient for a teenager, somehow managed to guilt-trip Alicia on a regular basis.

Casual remarks from the girl reminded Alicia of her privilege, her wealth.

But that's no reason to feel nervous around children, she told herself. *It's a steep learning curve for them, too.*

"Alicia?"

She jumped. Katie, dark-eyes and pale-faced, was standing in the doorway.

"Oh, you always move too quietly," said the woman. "Have you seen Tommy?"

Katie nodded.

"I think something bad has happened," said the girl. "Tommy's very upset."

Alicia felt her heart begin to pound as she visualized a series of possible disasters. She started towards Katie, clasping her hands together, wishing Ralph was back from London so Alicia did not have to cope alone.

"What is it?" she asked, praying for some trivial, childish problem.

"It's the dog," Katie said simply. "I think it's dead."

A couple of minutes later, Alicia was weeping over the hideously mutilated body of Daisy. The dog was lying in a neglected corner of the old kitchen garden, half-covered with spring weeds. Daisy's head was a mass of bloody pulp, nothing remaining of the animal's eyes, the whole cranium apparently ripped open.

Tommy was standing nearby, crying. Alicia scooped the boy up in her arms, shielding him from the horrific sight. After a moment in which he hung limply like a doll, Tommy put his arms around her. At that moment, Alicia noticed something, a tiny spot of brown on the boy's small, gray hoodie. Tommy smelled of soap, his clothes were freshly-laundered.

A brown mark could be anything, she told herself.

***

"Hey," said Collier, sounding slightly too enthusiastic, "good to see you again. Looking forward to working with you on this one."

Can't blame relative strangers for being nervous, she thought. *Even my friends aren't too comfortable around me nowadays.*

Denny had been polite but cool when greeting Collier and Hattersley. She had reluctantly agreed to work with a couple of Task Force agents, just as long as Frankie and Gould were present, too. She had expected some obstruction from Trent, given that Gould was chief scientist. But in the event, all her demands were met. She was given effective leadership of what had been informally dubbed Team Childcatcher.

And Collier seems okay, she thought. *At least he's not some macho asshat.*

"Okay," Collier said, "council of war, guys?"

The team was meeting in a cheap hotel room on the outskirts of Worcester. The place had been chosen at random and not pre-booked. Collier explained this was in case the 'Code Nines' were attempting to track them in conventional ways. Seeing Denny's skepticism, Collier had conceded that they were not involved in a conventional covert operation.

"But," he argued, "it doesn't hurt to be careful."

Now they were seated around the room, eating takeout and checking phones, tablets, pulling a provisional plan together. Denny, it was agreed, had to 'take point', using her abilities to scan the adoptive parents. She would have immediate backup from Frankie and Gould, while Collier and Hattersley would hold back.

"We'll come in if a more aggressive solution seems necessary," Collier explained.

"Shooting them, you mean?" Frankie asked.

"You know that's what he means," Denny chided. "Let's hope we can avoid traumatizing these people."

Hattersley snorted.

"Care to share with the rest of the class?" Collier asked sweetly.

The junior agent shrugged, poked suspiciously at his carton of noodles.

"I'm just saying, taking people's kids away for whatever reason – somebody will raise a stink."

Collier shook his head.

"Not one of these adoptions went through normal channels, mate," he pointed out. "That's our trump card. We spin them a yarn, flash security ID, talk about a wide-ranging investigation, and they will fold. Especially with Denny giving us a steer on just how to proceed."

Frankie looked over at her friend, seemed about to speak, then apparently thought better of it.

"It's okay, Frankie," Denny said firmly. "I got this. I faced Cassandra and survived. Her offspring don't scare me."

She held up her gloved hands, flexed her fingers, and looked around at Team Childcatcher.

"I'm ready."

**

The police were initially baffled, but called in a wildlife expert. His considered opinion was that Daisy had somehow got out into the road, been hit by a car, crawled back home, and died. A neighbor at a house about a hundred yards away said they had heard the dog barking, then a yelp. How Daisy got off her kennel chain was a mystery. But clearly, she had put herself in harm's way somehow.

"Post-mortem," the expert said, "predators and scavengers like crows could have accounted for the – the subsequent injuries."

"You mean the missing brain?" asked a police officer, then looked embarrassed when he saw Alicia's expression.

"It's all right," she told the policeman, and thanked the expert.

Privately, Alicia did not think the man had sounded too confident. But she clung to the explanation, not wanting to consider any other possibilities. The little brown blot on Tommy's clothing might have been blood. But she wanted to believe it was not.

It was just as the police were leaving that Ralph arrived from London. His silver Mercedes had to back up to allow the patrol car to leave the Petries' drive. When her husband finally got to speak to her, Alicia could see he was worried about security. She did not really understand his job, and he could not talk to her in detail about it. She only knew that it was important, and that he was relatively young to be entrusted with a matter of national importance.

"It was just Daisy," she explained, gesturing to the patch of crushed weeds where the dog's corpse had lain. "They took her away. She was hit by a car, they think."

"Oh, God. Do the children know?"

She nodded, and explained what had happened. But she omitted to mention the brown spot.

***

"Wow," Denny exclaimed. "This is some beautiful country."

Gould was driving the Americans in his rental car, while Collier and Hattersley followed in the unmarked van.

"Yes," the scientist said. "This is officially an Area of Outstanding Natural Beauty."

Seeing Denny's skepticism, he grinned.

"No, really, that's what we call the Malvern Hills. Officially beautiful bit of landscape. Quaint, I suppose. Blame Wordsworth and all those other nature poets."

Denny looked out at small farms, quaint cottages, the occasional large manor house. They passed what Gould said was a pre-Roman fortress, a series of stepped terraces leading up to a high summit. It dated from the second century before Christ, he explained.

It looks like someone had tried to sculpt a hill into a huge wedding cake.

Frowning, Denny recalled her nightmare, imagined the picturesque landscape riddled with Interloper tunnels. They were on their way to deal with two monsters. But she found the vision of England as a vast, Loper nest all too convincing. She tried to express something of this to Gould and Frankie.

"They'd have to kill a lot of us to be able to take over like that," Frankie pointed out. "Do you really think your dream might be a, I dunno, a prophetic vision?"

Denny hesitated. She had often wondered if Interloper powers included some kind of precognition. They were paranormal creatures. And in her encounters with Cassandra, she had gained a distinct sense that the queen, at least, had some ability to foretell the future.

But if Cassandra had precognition, she thought, *she would still be alive, surely?*

Denny shrugged off the question and tried to enjoy the landscape, the simple pleasure of a drive in the country. She checked the satnav, saw that they were less than a mile from their destination. Denny found herself envying the Petries, prosperous enough to live in such a beautiful part of the world. Then she saw the patrol car.

"Looks like something's already happened," Gould muttered.

"Whatever it is," Frankie put in, "looks like it's over."

The police vehicle had pulled over to the side of the road to let their car and Collier's van pass.

"Maybe it's nothing to do with us," Denny suggested.

Frankie's Task Force radio crackled into life. Collier asked if there was any change of plan.

"No," Denny called over her shoulder. "We're still going in. But let's be subtle. Get onto headquarters and find out why the cops were there."

There was a pause, then Collier spoke again.

"Could take a while. Your call."

Denny suspected that her unique status made Collier unwilling to challenge her.

After all, I'm a Code Nine who just happens to be on his side. Must be tricky.

"We give HQ an hour, then follow the original plan."

***

Tommy was playing video games while Katie was in her room, listening to music. The faint strains of bland, rhythmic pop drifted down the stairs while grunts and explosions emanated from the television room. As she moved around the kitchen, Alicia felt slightly reassured by the normality of the children's behavior. After the police had left, the youngsters had simply asked to be left alone for a while. A significant look from Ralph told her that talking things over could be done another time.

Why should they be traumatized? They've had it rough, seen terrible things. And, as Katie said, they don't like dogs. Only ones they encountered were probably vicious brutes used by drug dealers.

Alicia tried to shake off such bleak thoughts and concentrate on the meal she was preparing. The children were picky eaters, favoring quite bland if nourishing food. Rice seemed to be acceptable, as did mushrooms and chicken. So Alicia was working on a risotto recipe one of her old college friends had sent.

Garlic? No, probably not.

She had everything under control, and allowed herself half a glass of white wine as reward. But try as she might, she could not dispel the feeling of wrongness that went far beyond the terrible death of Daisy. The spot of what might have been blood loomed so large in her mind that she felt an urge to go and look at Tommy's hoodie, which was hanging up in the hall.

What kind of little boy hangs up his clothes so sensibly?

Such thoughts kept surfacing, no matter how often she told herself she was being silly. She knew all children were individuals. What was more, those who had been institutionalized might well be as neat as, say, army veterans. She recalled her own father, his bed always neatly made in the care home, shoes shining though he could only walk a few steps.

Alicia walked out of the kitchen and along the hall. The light gray hoodie was just visible, nestled between bigger grown-ups' coats. She would have to lift it off its hook. Her mouth felt dry as she moved closer and reached out to grasp the light fabric.

"Mummy?"

Alicia felt guilt and panic, spun around as she dropped the hoodie. Tommy instantly crouched down, picked up his garment, then stretched up on tiptoe to put it back on its hook.

"Oh, dear, you startled me, sweetie!" Alicia gasped.

I shouldn't be afraid of my own children, she thought. *And they are mine. I must truly believe that. They are well-behaved, intelligent, a credit to any family.*

"Sorry, I didn't mean to scare you," Tommy said, with a child's directness. "But there are some people outside. Are they the police?"

The doorbell rang. She heard heavy footfalls as Ralph left his study. Tommy darted back into the TV room and shut the door.

"Who is it, darling?" her husband shouted from the landing.

"Just going to see," she replied.

As she opened the door, she noticed that Katie's pop music had stopped, as had Tommy's video game sound effects.

Outside were two women and a man. The man looked somewhere between fifty and sixty, tall, balding, with an intelligent face. The women were much younger, and looked vaguely familiar. One, who was slightly taller than the other, with fairer hair, spoke. Alicia was slightly surprised to hear an American accent.

"Mrs. Petrie? We're sorry to call unannounced, but this is a security matter."

Though Alicia meant to ask Ralph to come down and talk to the strangers, somehow the three were already in the hallway by the time he appeared.

***

"I don't understand," said Ralph Petrie.

Sure you do, Denny thought. *And we don't have time to mess around with phony outrage.*

She had shaken hands with husband and wife, skin to skin contact allowing her to sample their immediate emotions and surface thoughts. Alicia Petrie was worried, confused, and much of her unease focused on the children. Ralph Petrie was more confident, as befitted an official with his clearance. And it had been quite a revelation to find out what his job was. Now Denny and her companions were sitting with the couple in their kitchen, hoping to shield them from what was to come.

"Let me make it clear, sir," said Gould, adopting a hearty, man-of-the-world manner. "You adopted two children who had been in state care. Nothing wrong with that, your motives are unimpeachable. But you cut corners by dealing with a private agency that is less than scrupulous in its methods. And I think you both knew that?"

Alicia Petrie started to cry.

"The waiting lists were all so long!" the wife wailed. "And after the IVF failed, we were – it was so bad–"

Her husband grasped her hand, urged her to stop. Denny was glad she could not feel their emotions at this point. Observing them was hard enough.

"We understand," Gould pressed on. "But I must emphasize that these are trafficked children. They have families, relatives who might well be fit guardians. Wrenching them away from all that is not morally or legally justifiable, is it?"

Denny gave Gould a discreet nod. She knew that this was the correct line to take with two basically good people. Alicia Petrie, in particular, had a strong moral sense. The woman had never been comfortable with the idea of rigging the system to cheat other childless couples.

"If you're worried about any collateral damage to your reputation or career," she said carefully, "you can rest assured, nothing will happen. This is one part of a much wider investigation."

Denny had been about to add more reassurances when a door opened into the hallway. A small face peeked out, withdrew, and the door slammed. Denny wondered if the Interloper had recognized her on such a short viewing. It seemed likely. What one knew, all knew.

"That was Tommy?" Frankie asked gently. "Kind of shy, isn't he?"

Alicia Petrie nodded, sobbed some more, blew her nose into a tissue given by Gould.

"It might be best," Denny said, standing up, "if we just took them now. Made it quick, a clean break."

Ralph Petrie looked up, bafflement giving way to outrage on his square-jawed face. He was a big, athletic-looking man of about forty-five. It occurred to Denny that he might be as much a problem as the Interlopers. Frankie seemed to have the same idea, producing her radio.

"Collier?" she said, in a low, urgent voice. "We need you in here now."

"What are you doing?" Ralph Petrie demanded. "What gives you the right to just walk into our home and take our children? It seems to me that you are the ones operating outside the law."

The man was standing up, now, and Gould was pushing back his chair. Denny made placatory gestures, stood between the two, knowing that Gould and Frankie both carried a Taser. Alicia Petrie looked on in tearful distress as the men tried to shout over each other.

"I've had enough of this," Ralph Petrie shouted. "Get out of my house! All of you!"

Before anyone could react, a fast-moving figure appeared in the hallway. It was almost a teenage girl, except for the talons and the elongated mouthparts. Alicia Petrie screamed, while Gould cursed, groping for his Taser. Denny threw herself forward, between the men, and collided with the Interloper.

The creature jumped back, hissing, its face now utterly inhuman. Ralph Petrie was staring aghast as the monster tried to shove past Denny, lashing at the man with vicious talons. But Denny had been right. Interlopers did not kill their own, and thanks to Denny's symbiont, the creature hesitated to injure her.

"She might change her mind, guys," Denny shouted, struggling to pinion the flailing being. "Bit of help."

Frankie shoved her Taser into the side of the creature, and Denny felt the Interloper stiffen. A spasm of movement followed as it recovered enough to resume the struggle. Gould tried to grab the entity's arms and secure them with plastic ties, but the confined space in the kitchen thwarted him. Denny's hand brushed against the creature's claws and she felt the full intensity of its cold, alien fury. The lust to destroy humans was so intense that Denny recoiled, had to force herself to retain her grip. She had anticipated this problem.

Alicia Petrie had been screaming almost continuously during the fight, but now she yelled in panic. Denny snatched a glance behind her and saw a second, smaller Interloper had come in from outside. It leaped onto Ralph Petrie's back, claws seeking his eyes. The man bellowed in pain and fear, spun around, failing to throw the monster off. Frankie lunged at the creature with her Taser, but Petrie's flailing arms knocked the weapon out of her hand.

Denny felt her Interloper knocked off balance by Gould's efforts, and seized the moment to slam the monster's head against the refrigerator. Dark blood gushed from a wound, but the creature did not collapse. Gould lunged with Taser, this time ramming the weapon into an eye socket. The nightmare being screeched and leaped back into the hallway, clutching at its face. At the same time, Ralph Petrie threw himself backwards into the wall, and the smaller assailant fell to the floor.

The front door gave way as Collier burst in, followed by Hattersley. Collier shot the first Interloper with his pistol, and it fell inert. As Collier stepped over it, the entity's flesh was already beginning to darken and bubble with rapid decay. The agent took a shooting stance, yelling at the Petries to get out of the way. But the smaller monster was already scrambling out of the back door and across the garden.

"Bugger," said Collier, rushing after his quarry. "Come on, Frankie."

Hattersley was already crouching over the dead 'Code Nine', trying to scoop some fast-rotting tissue into a glass tube. Gould was checking on Ralph Petrie, whose face was bloody. Frankie set off after Collier, her Taser drawn.

It will probably get away, Denny thought. *But it won't get another chance at its target.*

"What was that? What were they?"

Alicia Petrie's plaintive words broke an uneasy silence. Gould looked at Denny.

"I'll get the First Aid kit from the van," said Hattersley, putting the glass tube into a plastic baggie. "Nothing else to do here."

The place where the slain Interloper had disintegrated was stained with a brownish gunk, and a foul stench had filled the house. Brightly-colored clothes lay in the puddle. Ralph Petrie sat down by his wife again and stared at the place where the impostor had fallen.

"If we'd told you the truth," Denny said evenly, "you would never have believed us. Sorry, we lied, but you can see why now."

The couple stared at her, at a loss for words. Hattersley returned with the First Aid kit. After watching the agent's bungling efforts, Denny took over. Ralph Petrie was going to have scars, she felt sure, but had been lucky not to lose an eye. Again, as she touched the man's skin, she got confused, chaotic impressions of his life beyond his home.

Emergency planning executive, she thought as she dressed Petrie's wounds. *One of the guys who make sure this country could survive a natural disaster, nuclear strike, killer asteroid. Or a plague.*

***

"We can't try that again," Denny stated firmly. "It nearly went pear-shaped."

Team Scooby were back in their cheap hotel, planning to move on the next day. Nobody disagreed with Denny's assessment. Collier covered his face with his hands and spoke through them.

"We could so easily have ended up shooting the parents," he groaned. "It was a complete mess."

"True," Frankie said. "But it was still better than the original plan – throwing a net over people's kids without warning."

They were eating Chinese take-out. Collier had failed to hunt down the smaller Interloper. The Petries were now in protective custody in a safe house, well away from the Malvern Hills. And the team was now struggling with what to do next.

"The real problem," Denny opined, "is simply turning up might trigger an attack, every time."

"So you're suggesting we don't turn up?" Hattersley demanded, a sneer in his voice. "How could the Code Nines stand that kind of punishment?"

You jerk, Denny thought. *I could do without you and your attitude.*

"I mean," she said patiently, "we don't turn up waving official IDs and demanding to know where the children are. Instead, we surveille the parents, check out the Lopers without being detected. Then we bluff our way using a cover story."

Gould, who had been eating in silence, looked up from his carton of noodles.

"What kind of cover story? Charity collectors? Interior designers?"

"No," Denny smiled. "I was thinking of posing as a reporter, with Frankie posing as a cameraperson."

Gould grinned at that. They discussed the idea and concluded that providing standard video recording gear would be easy. In a pinch, they could simply buy some on expenses.

"It might just work," Collier conceded.

Frankie, mouth half full of chicken, asked what sort of cover story they would come up with.

"I thought we could ask them kind of an obvious question," Denny said. "Something we've done a hundred times before."

Seeing the puzzlement on all her companions' faces, she stood up and mimed holding out a microphone.

"Good morning, generic English person! Did you know your house is haunted?"

Nightmare Rising

Chapter 4: The Terror

"One down, several dozens to go," said Matheson.

"Quite," Trent replied, turning to the third person at the meeting. "Tania, how many adoptive families have we identified?"

The Intel chief referred to a printed sheet.

"Four definite, seven possible."

There was a pause, then Matheson spoke again.

"We're not going to win this one, not like this. We have only the one team that can tackle Code Nines effectively, and we don't know how many of the little buggers are out there."

Another pause, this time broken by Tania.

"Is it possible," she asked hesitantly, "that you could simply take the parents into protective custody, put the kids elsewhere? That might work, backed by high-level mandate, and of course a plausible story."

Trent shook his head.

"If we were dealing with ordinary citizens, scaring and bullying them to part with their children might be possible. But these are influential men and women. Some are very wealthy, all are clever and articulate. Imagine the media fuss."

"But their own kids are going to kill them!" protested Matheson.

"They'd never believe that," Tania pointed out gently. "Which is why we are struggling to fabricate a convincing lie. No normal security scenario fits this one. The Code Nines have been pretty clever."

Matheson settled back in his chair, frowning. The security chief found himself struggling to concentrate, distracted by a nagging sense that something was wrong. He looked over at Trent's avuncular features, then at Tania, cool and professional. He was aware that Trent was speaking again, and tried to focus on what his boss was saying. Something about Denny Purcell. A question.

"Sorry," Matheson stammered, "I was miles away. Sorry."

"I said," Trent repeated patiently, "that we should try to get Ms. Purcell to use her powers on our guests down in the holding cells. They might provide her with some useful data."

Matheson grunted. He admired Denny's courage, and after the skirmish in Fordham, he felt she could be trusted. But he also knew that Denny did not trust Trent, and would never willingly go near him.

Trouble is, I don't know exactly why.

For a moment, the nagging doubt that had plagued him for weeks almost took form. He was sure it concerned Trent in some way. He also had a vague memory of a problem concerning Comstock, his predecessor. But every time he tried to focus on the issue his memory betrayed him.

"John? Are you still with us?"

"Yes, boss!"

"As I was saying, perhaps you could persuade Ms. Purcell to rejoin our happy little band?"

Matheson nodded emphatically.

"I'll give it my best shot," he promised. "But in the meantime, what do we do about all those adoptive parents?"

Trent shrugged.

"I will alert my superiors in the ministry," he said. "And I'll try to spell out the nature of the threat. No doubt some sort of security alert will be sent out. But I'm afraid the political landscape is shifting. Some familiar faces are out, some new faces are in. And there's a general skepticism in high places about the Code Nine problem."

"So, they'll wait until something really bad happens," Tania said sourly, "then they'll try to cover up the fact that they were warned. Isn't that the usual pattern?"

Trent raised his hands in a gesture of helplessness.

"What can I say? I didn't make the world. In the meantime, I'm open to suggestions."

Matheson took a deep breath.

"There is one really obvious way to solve the problem, to show the parents they have not in fact adopted children at all," he said carefully. "And I think we all know what it is."

***

Sir Lester Byng strolled out of the Houses of Parliament and got into his ministerial Daimler. Byng had just endured a long, tedious debate about fishery quotas and related matters. He was ready to relax over the weekend at his country place.

"Good evening, sir," said his bodyguard, opening the rear door of the limousine. "A long day, it seems."

"Thank you, Stamford," replied the politician. "Another day, another dollar, as they say in our rebellious colonies."

The Special Branch officer was a fixture in the Byng family's life. Despite a recent downturn in terrorist activity, a member of Her Majesty's Government was a prime target. The Daimler was armored, the chauffeur a skilled police driver, expert at out-thinking potential attackers.

I'm as safe today as I was yesterday, he thought. *Those twits at the Home Office are just getting their knickers in a twist again. Happens every few weeks.*

Byng opened his briefcase and checked the alert he had been given at the cabinet meeting that morning. It was maddeningly vague, full of official jargon that further obscured its point. But Byng, with years of experience at hiding meaning in a forest of long words, grasped the essence.

Why would recently adopting children be a risk factor? What kind of sociopaths would target prominent people for that?

Byng was sixty-two, and had three grown-up children from two marriages. His youngest, Jessica, had always wanted children but was sadly unable to conceive. She had recently adopted a delightful little girl. Byng had done his best to oil the wheels, intervening a couple of times, just to make sure the bureaucrats didn't stand in his favorite daughter's way.

Byng checked his phone, scrolled through the organizer. He had remembered correctly – Jessica was bringing little Sara down from Edinburgh for the weekend. Byng was not sentimental about children, but Jessica's adopted daughter was charming, well-behaved, and very intelligent.

One couldn't ask for a sweeter granddaughter, he thought, looking at a picture of adoptive mother and child.

"Looking forward to a relaxing couple of days, sir?" asked Stamford.

"Quite so," Byng said amiably. "A quiet time with the family. We might go for little walks, but I suspect we'll spend most of our time around the fire, playing games with the little one."

"Very cozy," Stamford said.

Byng felt a slight twinge of guilt, recalling that Stamford and several of his colleagues spent their weekends guarding him and his family.

But that's what they're paid for, he reflected. *And they will give me peace of mind. If anyone wants to attack me and mine, they'll have to come through competent men. With guns.*

***

"I think I screwed up," said Gould. "I'm not a field agent. I should go back to headquarters and get on with my research."

They were driving to their next destination, having kitted themselves out as a fake documentary team. Denny tried to persuade Gould to change his mind, but the scientist was adamant. In Gould's opinion, he had simply gotten in the way at the Petries, possibly making a tricky situation worse.

"And," he pointed out, "you don't need me to operate the detector. All you need to do is turn the damn thing on. Even that arsehole Hattersley can do that."

"Yeah," Denny conceded, "I guess he can. And if you feel you'd be more useful in London, by all means, go. But remember, we're doing the fake film crew thing. You've got credentials as a paranormal investigator. So, sticking with me and Frankie would be useful."

And I'd feel a lot more comfortable with you nowhere near Trent, she thought. *I don't have many friends, and I don't want their minds getting messed up.*

"Also," Frankie put in from the back seat, "you're a Brit, we're not. It helps if the team has a native speaker, you know?"

Gould smiled at that, but remained silent for a few moments as he overtook a line of big, European trucks.

"Okay," he said finally, "I'll give the ghost hunter gimmick a try. It's a good idea. It has potential, anyway, if people go for it."

Frankie's phone chimed and she checked for messages.

"Looks like we have our next three targets, all in this area. Every couple has adopted a kid, age range six to twelve."

"Or so they think," Denny added.

They discussed the best way to get close to the suspected Interloper targets. They settled on a straightforward, open approach. Gould would phone each couple, asking if they could check out the family home for 'ghostly phenomena'. The cover story was that they were making a series about little-known hauntings.

"In each case it will be an entirely fictional haunting, of course," Gould added. "But I'm sure that between us we can dream up a few telling details, so that it sounds convincing."

They agreed to call the families that evening, and try to arrange meetings as soon as possible. If they were rebuffed, they would have to try a different approach, one devised by Matheson, with Trent's approval. It was brutally direct, the product of a military mind. But, as the agent had pointed out, it would 'provide irrefutable evidence' to the parents.

We might have to go that far, Denny thought. *But let's hope not.*

***

On Saturday morning, after a light breakfast, Sir Lester Byng threw on some jeans and a sweatshirt and went out for his morning walk. As always, he was shadowed by Stamford. The politician's route did not take him outside the extensive garden of his home. The gardener, a local man who had been cleared by security, turned up to do some work and Byng chatted with him for a few minutes. Then he went back inside, having given his daughter time to get up.

"Morning, my dears!" he said cheerily. "It seems set to be fine. Perhaps Sara would like to play in the garden? Get some fresh air?"

Byng's daughter, sitting at the breakfast table, looked dubious.

"Sara looks a little ill," said Jessica. "Perhaps she should stay in today."

Byng looked at the little girl, sitting quietly, peering down into her cornflakes. Sara did seem pale, but then she always had been. The child was quiet, but this was nothing new.

"Are you not feeling well, Sara?" he asked, lowering his voice. "Perhaps you've got a cold? Running a temperature, are we?"

Byng put a hand on the little girl's forehead. Sara flinched, and Byng jerked his hand away. He laughed nervously, not quite sure what had just happened. The child's temperature was normal, even a little cool. But when his hand had touched the girl's skull it seemed, for a moment, as if the flesh and bone had shifted.

As if it were fluid, or at least malleable, Byng thought. *What a horrible sensation. Must be overwork.*

Jessica was talking about putting her daughter back to bed if she continued to seem out of sorts. Clearly, Byng's daughter had not noticed anything wrong. The politician chatted for a while, then suggested putting Sara in the television room under a blanket.

"Now, dad," Jessica said sternly, "I've tried to limit the amount of TV she watches."

"Yes, I know," Byng said. "But if someone is feeling poorly, we make exceptions. Isn't that right, Sara?"

The child nodded, looking up at Byng with huge, dark eyes. Then Sara continued to toy with her cereal, having eaten only a few mouthfuls.

"Poor thing," said Jessica. "She was so looking forward to seeing you this weekend. When I mentioned we were coming over, her little face lit up."

***

One of the couples contacted by Gould had been very enthusiastic about the idea of 'being in a ghost-watching show'. They had agreed to allow the team to do some preliminary shooting on Saturday morning. The house in question was a former rectory in a small Worcestershire village. The team parked at the end of the lane, just out of sight of the house.

"I'll start filming as we go up to the gate," Frankie explained, hefting her new camera. "It'll look more convincing."

"And intrusive, of course," added Gould. "But at least we'll be invited this time."

As before, Collier and Hattersley stayed out of sight, but close. Denny led the way, admiring the quaint, ivy-covered house as they walked up the lane. It was hard to believe that anything monstrous might lurk in such an idyllic setting. Apart from birdsong, it was quiet, the village just starting to come to life.

It was when they reached the garden gate that Denny felt an odd tingling sensation between her shoulder blades. She realized that her symbiont was reacting to something. This was new. At the Petries she had not felt a similar sensation, at first.

But I did when the attack began.

"Guys," she said, "I think we should call in the others."

Frankie lowered her camera, reached for her walkie-talkie, urged Collier and Hattersley to move up. Gould walked off the path and looked in at the front window of the house.

"See anything?" Denny asked.

Gould recoiled from the window, retching. A moment later, the glass exploded and a pale, blood-stained figure hurtled through it. The Interloper was about one-third Gould's size, but it still fastened itself around his throat. Frankie dropped her camera and radio, groping for her Taser. Denny was already running forward, grabbing at the creature. Whatever the monster had looked like in its human guise, it was now in its true form, talons clawing at Gould's eyes while its hideous maw bit at the side of the man's throat.

"Get off him!"

Denny grabbed one thin, wiry arm. She felt the inevitable shock as the Interloper's emotions flooded her, and she struggled to stay in control as she yanked at Gould's attacker. As before, Denny's ambiguous status seemed to confuse the creature, and it jerked its head around. Tiny, sunken buttons of eyes regarded her, the bloody mouthparts hanging open. Denny saw shreds of raw flesh between the vicious teeth.

Between them, Denny, Gould, and Frankie managed to hurl the Interloper away, just as Collier and Hattersley appeared at the garden gate. The creature bounded upright and leaped straight at Collier. The agent brought up his pistol, but firing would have endangered Denny and her companions. As Collier hesitated, the Interloper leaped up and over the agents. Hattersley brought it down with a blow from a baton, and Collier shot it in the head as it writhed on the path.

"We triggered this," Denny said, as they watched the creature begin to disintegrate. "Just by arriving."

"We should have anticipated it," Gould said, his voice full of despair. "They must all have known what happened with the Petries. As soon as they spot us, they attack."

"Checkmate," said Hattersley, hunkering down over the bubbling corpse. "Damned if we do, damned if we don't."

"I'll check inside," said Collier.

Gould looked as if he were about to bar the way, but then relented, and Collier broke in the front door. They watched him go in, pistol drawn. Then a few moments later, they heard him retching. When Collier emerged, he was pale-faced, eyes downcast. Gould offered him a tissue to wipe his mouth.

"I forgot they had another child," Collier said. "Human child, I mean. Little girl, judging by the clothes."

The killings had to be referred to the local police, via headquarters, so a media blackout could be imposed. However, when the police arrived, they did not seem as surprised as Denny had expected. When she asked the senior officer why they were so well-prepared, he looked at her oddly.

"You've not been following the news?"

Frankie was already checking her phone, Gould looking over her shoulder. Denny guessed what they were seeing in the news feed. When Gould spoke, her suspicion was confirmed.

"We didn't just trigger this," he said quietly, gesturing at the broken window of the rectory. "We triggered it all."

***

Sir Lester Byng stood still, listening intently. The attack had come suddenly, out of nowhere, leaving him frightened and confused. One minute he was checking official emails in his study, the next he had heard screaming from downstairs. It took him a moment to recognize his daughter's voice. He had never heard Jessica in such terror.

"Sara! No!" she screamed. "No!"

Jessica's voice was cut off by a horrific gurgling sound, followed by a loud crash, and the shattering of plates and furniture. Byng was already on the landing by then, acting on instinct. Then he recalled the security alert, and forced himself to retreat and go back into his study. He took out his special pager, a panic button that would summon Stamford and the other Special Branch officers.

"This is a warning, we are armed officers!"

The voice came from the hallway. Byng imagined the armed police moving with practiced stealth. He knew that one had given his position away deliberately while the others were presumably flanking the terrorist, or terrorists. What worried Byng was that his daughter and granddaughter might already be dead.

"In here!"

Byng recognized Stamford's voice, heard heavy footsteps running down the hall. There were muffled exclamations, then what must have been an order, Stamford's voice urgent and low. Byng remembered his security briefings, and locked the study door.

Find a secure place, stay there quietly until the house has been cleared of attackers.

Byng considered shoving his desk against the door, then thought better of an improvised barricade. The sound of furniture being moved would reveal his presence. He wished his bodyguards would clear the house, tell him the job was done. Instead of a reassuring shout from the security team, though, there was nothing. For what seemed like several minutes, Byng heard no sounds from below. He became aware of his own rapid breathing, his elevated heartbeat.

The shots sounded like cannon fire when they broke the silence. Three rapid shots at first, then two more. They were followed by a yell of pain in what Byng felt sure was a man's voice. Another couple of shots sounded, confused sounds of yelling and crashing, and then silence fell again.

Oh, God, maybe I won't get out of this.

Fear for his life overwhelmed Byng's other feelings. The fact that his daughter and her adopted child were probably dead no longer counted. Always ambitious, he refused to believe that this was the end of his career.

Why don't those bloody cops let me know what's happening?

As if in reply to his furious thought, there was a gentle knock at the door. Byng hesitated, afraid to speak. The knock came again, slightly louder, a little more insistent. Then he heard a voice.

"Granddad?"

There was a muffled thud, not too close. Byng imagined that it was someone moving in the hall, or on the stairs. Meanwhile, little Sara was outside, knocking a little louder still.

She'll attract the terrorists' attention!

"Please, let me in granddad!"

Byng unlocked the door, fearful that the child had already given away his position. The tiny figure in its pastel clothing looked up at him with huge, frightened eyes.

"Get inside sweetie!" he hissed, grabbing Sara by the arm and pulling her into the room.

He shut the door quickly but quietly, locked it again. The scrape and click of the lock mechanism seemed louder than a gunshot. But when he listened for a few moments, he heard nothing. There was no stealthy movement, no subdued voices. No indication of how the skirmish outside had gone.

Perhaps they all killed each other?

Byng moved away from the door, still staring at the wooden rectangle. Eventually, he backed into his study chair, sat down heavily. Something forced itself into his consciousness, something he had glimpsed as he had let Sara in. He frowned, panic and confusion blurring his mind's eye.

What was it? A shape, a figure on the stairs.

It had been a man in a suit, lying on the stairs, faced down. A big, dark patch had stained the biscuit-colored wood. Byng was almost sure it was Stamford. His chief protector, probably dead, certainly incapacitated.

"Oh, God," he moaned.

"God isn't here, granddad."

The words came from the brightly-clad figure on the bed, who was sitting watching him in the half-light. The girl had her knees up to her chin, arms around her legs. There was something different about her. At first, Byng thought it was fear making Sara's face seem paler, her eyes darker.

"Nobody's here except you and me."

This time Sara was speaking in a clear, concise voice, remarkably like that of an adult.

"Shh!" Byng hissed, gesturing wildly at the door.

The child stood up on the bed, walked bouncily down the mattress, jumped down onto the floor. She still had to look up at his face, although he was sitting down. Now she was so close Byng could see what was wrong with her face. It was not only pale, but also oddly deformed, flowing like melting plastic.

"I know what scares you," said the Sara-creature.

Byng shoved his chair back, collided with his desk, tried to get up. The little monster bounded sideways, crouched low, cutting off his escape route. Far too late Byng realized that locking the door the second time might have condemned him to death.

No! It can't end like this, ambition cried. *I will survive this.*

"No, you won't," said the hideous entity in child's clothing. "You're afraid of nothingness, zero, nonexistence. That the great, brilliant Lester Byng will be flushed round the U-bend of history."

The phrase almost made Byng forget his fear. It had been used in private by an angry prime minister when Byng had crossed his boss. The insult had stung; he had never mentioned it to anyone.

"This is a nightmare!" he said desperately, clinging to a rational explanation. "That's how a child becomes a monster. That's how you know things nobody possibly could. I'm dreaming."

The hideous creature tittered.

"You're not the first to think that," it hissed. "But this nightmare is real. You're so afraid of nothingness. Well, nothingness is here. You are nothing. You never were anything. Just another hack, another interchangeable part in a political machine."

Every word, every turn of phrase, were spoken in a perfect imitation of Byng's voice. His own self-doubt, his own fear of failure, his deep-rooted insecurity, was revealed and used against him. He knew what was happening, but could not resist. Tears rolled down his face. He protested feebly.

By now, no trace of the child remained inside the pink dungarees and Peppa Pig tee. Which were, Byng now realized, spattered with blood … the tiny, delicate hands had sprouted talons. Worst of all, the face had vanished, no trace of any features remaining. The front of the creature's head was a blank oval, apart from two tiny black eyes and a small, round maw. The mask of colorless flesh reflected the emptiness – the ugliness – within Byng. The realization robbed him of the little courage he had left. He slumped off his chair, hands raised in front of his face.

The diminutive figure gathered itself, a predator about to spring. In the distance, Byng heard sirens. But they brought no sensation of hope. Now he knew he was nothing, no one.

How can nothing die? Impossible.

The leap, the slashing of claws, and the pain were quickly followed by merciful oblivion.

✳✳✳

Team Childcatcher disbanded itself as the demoralized group headed south, back to London. There was no need for discussion. Attempting to stop the Interloper 'children' was pointless. Throughout the long drive, they listened in silence to news reports of atrocities. The media kept ratcheting up the number of causalities, kept speculation about motives, kept asking questions that could never be answered in conventional terms. Eventually, Gould turned off the radio.

"Dozens," Denny pointed out. "Not hundreds, so it could be worse. They didn't have time to place too many spawn with influential people."

Gould glanced over at her.

"It could become worse. A lot worse. They could do it again. There are up to three Loper females out there, remember."

The idea brought Denny's train of thought to a halt. She had been wondering what the Loper spawn would do now that their adoptive families were all dead. She had wondered if Gould's detector could be mass-produced, and the Task Force expanded. This might allow Cassandra's lethal offspring to be hunted down.

But if they just keep breeding killer kids, we'll never catch up.

"So, what the hell do we do now?" asked Frankie.

Denny twisted around and looked at her friend. Every time she felt self-pity about the symbiont gradually blending its tissues with her, she reminded herself how much Frankie had suffered. And how little Frankie had complained. Now the camerawoman was sprawled in the back seat, surrounded by video and sound equipment.

Her comfort zone. She's always happier when she's working, or at least feels like she could be soon.

"I don't know," Denny admitted. "But if you can keep that little bugger Trent away from me, I'll try and scan those poor bastards in the cells. They might be linked to one or more of the young queens."

Frankie nodded, looking out at the sunlight landscape they were speeding through. There were signs of an early spring, Denny noticed, with bright green leaves decorating tree after tree.

"Where there's life, there's hope," she ventured.

"Yeah," Frankie said quietly. "But the way things are going, you gotta wonder just what kind of life there's hope for?"

Nightmare Rising

Chapter 5: Prisoners

Throughout the day, reports of horrific murders rolled in from around the country. The fact that most of the victims were linked to the government in some way led to major security alerts. Suspects of various political stripes were raided, detained, questioned. But as the catalog of slayings grew, no one could suggest a reasonable explanation. The emergency meeting of the Task Force top brass took place against a steady accumulation of horror. And every new report spoke of missing children.

"I think," said Trent, "it would be fair to say that there is no upside to this."

Tania Da Silva was slightly shocked to see her boss looking downcast. For the first time, Trent was at a loss for positive words. She had expected him to talk of regrouping, a counterattack, and a new strategy. Instead, he looked gray, washed out, as if he had suddenly lost all his energy.

Maybe he sees his pension evaporating, she thought. *If he gets fired over this, he's unlikely to ever stage a comeback.*

Trent met her eyes, and she looked down in shame. The little man could easily have guessed her thoughts.

"I note," Trent said wearily, "that the mainstream media have said nothing about any – paranormal factor."

"No, they are playing it fairly straight," said Tania, "though of course, the internet is awash with lunatic claims."

"Any of them accurate?" asked Matheson quickly.

Tania paused, accustomed to Trent's witty interjections. But instead, their leader remained slumped in his desk chair. For a weird moment, she thought he looked like a dummy or mannequin, something fashioned in the likeness of a man. He seemed too inert. Then she saw Matheson's inquiring expression and ordered herself to focus.

"Yes, of course," she said tersely. "If you throw enough crap at a wall, some of it will stick. Same with internet speculation – *some of it* will be near the truth."

Without speaking, Matheson took out his phone, tapped the screen, held it up. The title of the video was 'WEREWOLF CHILDREN – A COVER UP?' The actual clip was just a few seconds long. It showed a pale form with long, slender limbs scrambling over a wall. The Interloper moved with its characteristic speed, darting off into some undergrowth.

From the context, it was impossible to tell where the footage had been shot. It was also shaky and out of focus, facts Tania was quick to point out.

"It could so easily be fake," she said. "All that lousy found horror footage has done us a favor."

Matheson shook his head.

"There are dozens of comments referring to Denny's old videos," he pointed out. "People are making the connection. It might take a while, but somebody is going to have to officially acknowledge the Code Nine situation."

"Sooner rather than later, I fear."

They looked at Trent, who had again spoken in a weak, colorless voice. Tania felt a pang of sympathy for him. He had never treated her unfairly, and always acknowledged her talent, her hard work. She wondered if his replacement would be half so amenable.

"Perhaps it would be a good thing to put the facts before the public," Tania said, surprising herself.

My entire working life has been based on the opposite assumption, she thought. *But this is new territory. The old-school mentality just isn't working.*

Trent nodded slowly, then a flicker of his old smile moved across his visage.

"Perhaps you could leave us, now, Tania?" the little man asked. "We have some sensitive operational matters to discuss."

She nodded, rose, left the office. Now she was slightly offended. Not for the first time, Trent and his head of security were in secret conclave, excluding her. But, she reflected, from a career viewpoint it might not harm her to be a little further from her current boss.

If he's going down, no reason why I should go with him.

Tania returned to work, ordering her team to keep track of all the possible Code Nine references. Soon the intelligence gatherers were struggling with a volume of data they had never expected. It was clear that, for thousands if not millions of people, Denny's claims had been confirmed.

Tania sampled some of the comments. One theme kept emerging, until inevitably a very simple question went viral.

'Where is Denny Purcell now?'

***

Trent led Matheson out of his office and through the flock of busy Intel agents. As they passed shirt-sleeved colleagues, Matheson noted that few, if any, looked directly at him. Even Tania, normally willing to chat for a moment, barely acknowledged the two men.

I've already got career leprosy, he thought. *They don't want to catch it.*

As they reached the elevators Matheson hesitated, suddenly unsure where they were going, and why. Seeing his hesitation, Trent guided him into the elevator when the doors opened.

"Sorry, boss," he said. "Why do we need to go to the panic room? You think the Code Nines could attack headquarters?"

Trent did not meet Matheson's eyes. Instead, he continued to stare at the steel walls of the elevator.

"It's not out of the question," Trent said. "They are clearly more audacious than ever before. But that's not the reason I'm taking you down to the emergency bunker."

Matheson waited for an explanation, but none was offered. The lift reached the basement and they stepped out. Matheson felt the need to question Trent, ask him again why he was being taken underground. But when he tried to find the words his mind grew fuzzy.

"We'll soon be there," said Trent, with a touch of his old ebullience. "Then all will be made clear."

That sounds good, Matheson thought. *Clarity. I could do with some of that.*

The security chief followed Trent through the emergency control room, into the sleeping quarters. As they stopped amid the rows of bunks, Matheson almost recalled something significant.

Collier pointed something out to me down here, only the other day. What the hell was it?

"You look puzzled, my friend," said Trent, amiable but still sounding weary. "A problem shared is a problem halved, they say."

"It's just – this place," Matheson said hesitantly. "I remember we were going to investigate – some kind of an anomaly."

Trent nodded, took Matheson's arm and led him between the bunks to the right of the door.

"Something about Comstock, perhaps?" Trent asked.

"Yeah!" exclaimed Matheson. "Do you know what it was?"

"Oh, I can guess," Trent said. "Now, turn to face me, John. That's right. A little to the left – good."

Matheson felt impatient at being made to stand just so. It reminded him of parade ground drill when he had been a young soldier. He was about to demand that Trent simply tell him what was going on when the little man surprised him. Trent raised both hands and shoved Matheson hard, in the chest. Caught by surprise, the agent grabbed for the nearest bunk to steady himself, missed, and fell. He turned in mid-air, planning to roll and minimize any injury.

But he did not hit the floor.

Instead, Matheson found himself floating, limbs flailing, in a blank void. There was nothing but whiteness, a colorless light that came from all directions and cast no shadows. The bunkroom had been blotted out. Panic seized him, but he forced himself to stop thrashing around. He was clearly in weightless conditions, with no way to orientate himself.

Observe, find a way out, he ordered himself. *This can't just be a blank nothingness.*

But it was. After a few moments of carefully rotating himself in free fall, he saw no hint of any imperfection in the pearly glow around him. He could form no idea of scale. He might be inside a relatively small, opalescent sphere or adrift in some unimaginable alien cosmos. Matheson felt panic terror rise again, struggled to suppress it.

"Keep calm and carry on, eh? That's the British spirit!"

Suddenly Trent was floating beside him.

"Where the bloody hell am I?" demanded Matheson.

He tried to grab Trent but the unfamiliar conditions simply made him spin around his center of gravity. He instructively grabbed for a handhold, had to remind himself there was nothing there. Nothing apart from him, and Trent.

"Excellent question!" exclaimed Trent. "I do so love an inquiring mind. Where the bloody hell are you?"

The plump man was back to his old, cheery self, Matheson noted as he slowly stopped spinning.

"What the hell did you do?"

Trent did not reply at all. Instead, he multiplied like reflections in a funhouse mirror. Where there had been one little man there were now six, seven, eight. Matheson lost count as the white void filled up with Trents, all identical, all beaming cheerily at his confusion.

"How – what?" Matheson stammered.

"It is rather confusing," said one Trent.

"Not for us of course," said a second.

"We're used to it," chimed in a third. "It's your weird singular identities that we find strange. But needs must, and so we make the best of it."

Matheson's reeling mind seized on one obvious point.

"You're not human!"

Several Trents laughed. Then the various little men started to change. Their smiling faces froze, like humanoid robots that had been switched off. Plump flesh grew brittle and dry, like old plaster. Cracks appeared in hairless scalps. As Matheson gaped in horror, the Trents began to split open. From the man-shaped shells, black feelers emerged, rustling, waving in Matheson's direction. They reminded him of cockroach antennae.

The security chief expected some kind of huge insects to appear, but instead, the feelers multiplied, intermeshed, the revolting contents of each Trent-body combining to form a black ring of shifting tendrils. The last remnants of the desiccated Trent-bodies shattered into drifting fragments.

The ring of writhing, living blackness started to constrict, closing in on Matheson. He screamed in pure terror, now, all self-control gone. The nearest feelers took advantage of his panic, and plunged into his mouth. A cold, stinging sensation pierced his throat, and he fought for air. He heard a voice in his head, realized it was his own.

Is this death?

The whiteness around him was extinguished by a roaring void that flowed into him, a Niagara of freezing energy. Again, the voice inside him spoke. This time he could not be sure if it was his own.

No, not death. Something far worse.

"You okay, boss?"

Matheson was standing in the bunkroom, his phone in his hand. Collier's voice spoke from the cell, bombarding his superior with facts, questions. Something about Denny Purcell, the prisoners, finding the Code Nines. A sensation of intense cold made Matheson shudder, but then it was gone. Everything seemed to slip into place, and he felt normal again, his mind clear.

Wow, he thought. *My granny would say someone just walked over my grave.*

"Sorry," he said to Collier. "Bad connection, I'm in the panic room. Let me get back upstairs and I'll call you.

***

Beta went ashore at a small fishing port in Scotland. Zoffany did not need to see the fecund monster go. As the juvenile queen left the yacht, the mental pressure on Zoffany eased appreciably. Then she felt Gamma, the youngest and weakest of the trio, seeking out her mind. The psychic tendrils that gripped the scientist did not seem strong. Zoffany tried to hide a sense of exultancy, suppress a single, simple thought.

I could break free of this one, if I'm right about the serum.

With Beta went a small retinue of Interlopers, each one taking the appearance of a parent, or a sibling. To all intents and purposes, the group of monsters was a prosperous young family taking leave of their fancy yacht, heading inland. Where they were going, Zoffany did not know.

Left behind with Gamma and Zoffany on the *Fulmar* were the two controlled humans, plus three Interlopers. Zoffany had wondered in passing if the complement was enough to man the vessel. Then she cursed her stupidity. Not only did the Lopers work with virtually no sleep, they also possessed all possible seafaring knowledge. They had sucked it out of several first-rate brains during their voyages. Brains which had then been eaten.

How long before Gamma is sexually mature and as voracious as the others?

Zoffany shrugged off the thought and continued to work. She had the knack of thinking in purely abstract terms, which she knew confused Interlopers. The scientist had observed that the creatures favored well-defined thoughts, images, and emotions. The cold rationality of science was deeply alien to them. Hence their need for her skills. Taking her knowledge was not enough. It needed a human mind to put the knowledge to effective use.

Zoffany moved along her untidy laboratory bench. She felt a familiar flicker of resentment at the way she had been driven by Alpha to do so much, with such meager resources. She had achieved results that would have been spectacular in normal circumstances. If she had not been in thrall to the most powerful queen, she would never have produced the virus. But now she had it, she was determined not to let it be released.

Or at least, not in its present form.

Viruses tended to mutate rapidly. She had taken advantage of this, and produced a new variant. Zoffany had decided to dub her illicit, modified virus Nemesis, knowing the idea behind the word would satisfy the Interlopers. Secretly, she hoped it would prove to be the nemesis of her captors. She had, in effect, reversed the effects of the disease.

Only one little problem.

She placed a tissue culture under a microscope, watched cells reproducing rapidly in nutrient gel. Then she added a droplet of saline solution containing the Nemesis strain. Within seconds, she noticed cells start to change as the virus particles attached themselves. Hijacking the cellular machinery, Nemesis rapidly reproduced, breeding more copies of itself. Zoffany felt grim satisfaction as, one by one, infected cells burst. Soon the tissue culture was a mass of decomposing tissue, as the original sample rotted as rapidly as slain Interlopers.

Great. Maybe needs a few more tweaks. That rapid onset is not ideal.

There were two reasons why she did not want Nemesis to kill infected creatures as soon as possible. A virus needed time to spread, and live bodies were better disease vectors than dead ones. The second reason was less scientific, but just as compelling.

The cells she had just watched being destroyed so efficiently were from her own body. She had failed to devise a way for the virus to kill Interlopers alone. Nemesis would also destroy any human with a symbiont.

The soldier-boys would call this collateral damage, she mused grimly.

***

"Trent's out," said Matheson. "Finished. Gone."

"What?" blurted Frankie. "You mean they fired him?"

Matheson shrugged.

"What else could the politicians do? He was supposed to prevent this kind of carnage. He failed."

Denny was half-listening to the conversation while looking around the main office of the Task Force. A few people at desks gave her curious glances before returning to their screens. She felt ill at ease, despite Matheson's surprise revelation.

"So he's actually cleared his desk?" asked Gould.

"Yep, just stole away," Collier confirmed. "Left a message saying how much he'd enjoyed working with us, didn't say where he was going. I've seen this happen before. The more covert the operation, the more likely the boss man is to vanish overnight."

"They're sending some bureaucrat over to replace him," Matheson added. "Eventually. In the meantime, seems like I'm acting Task Force leader. So, come to my office!"

"I'd rather – take a look at the prisoners," Denny said, catching herself about to use the word 'scan'. She was unsure how much the regular personnel knew about her abilities.

"Right, right," Matheson agreed, turning to Collier. "You take her downstairs, okay? Rest of you guys, let's have a post-mortem on this latest – well, let's talk about it."

A short walk and an elevator ride took them to the sub-surface part of the small complex. As Denny stepped out into the corridor, there was a sudden, deafening blast of sound. As well as the siren flashing lights assailed her senses. Collier mouthed an apology and used an electronic key fob to turn off the alarm.

"Sorry," he said. "You triggered one of Gould's Code Nine detectors. He said he had recalibrated them all to ignore your particular energy signature. No idea what he meant by that, but he clearly screwed up."

"You think?" said Denny, her ears still ringing. "Okay, let's go."

Even before they saw the prisoners, Denny knew it would be bad. There was a stench of excrement, coupled with inarticulate noises. She was shocked to see that the controlled humans were in a bad way. Some were naked, smeared in their own filth, eyes staring blankly. The cells were cramped cages.

"You can't keep people like this!" she exclaimed, outraged. "A zoo treating animals this way would be closed down, for God's sake!"

Collier looked appalled, embarrassed.

"I had no idea it was this bad," he insisted, and started questioning the guards.

Denny, meanwhile, forced herself to go closer to the prisoner in the first cage. At first, she did not recognize the half-naked woman. But then she recalled the face half-hidden beneath straggling, greasy hair.

"Laura? Laura Bell?"

The woman's eyes focused on Denny for a moment, then she stared down at the floor.

"I don't know who Laura is," said the woman.

"Sure you do," Denny said, moving closer to the bars. "We met in Fordham. You worked for the newspaper there. Remember? We investigated the children's homes. The cult. The old factory? You must remember Cassandra."

Again, there was a flicker of recognition, rapidly fading. Impulsively Denny reached through the bars, grasped Laura's hand. Contact brought a torrent of confused thoughts, or half-thoughts. The symbiont nestled between the reporter's shoulder blades was struggling to remain in touch with the juvenile queens, and with the rest of the Interloper community. But it seemed that there was no strong, central mind directing Laura, or any of the other prisoners.

God, what a mess.

All Denny sensed was a jumble of conflicting emotions. The human personality wanted to be free, the symbiont yearned to exert control but had no set purpose. The conflict rendered the victim insane for all practical purposes. Denny struggled to connect with the real Laura, the individual submerged beneath a morass of futile alien impulses. But the person she had known seemed to have retreated into a kind of mental cocoon.

Leaving Laura Bell, Denny worked her way along the other cages. Some captives reacted violently to her presence, others refused to come near the bars. Those that did allow her to touch them were in as hopeless a state as the reporter. When Collier asked her what she had found, she replied, testily, that these people were too badly damaged to help anyone.

"You should get them help," she insisted. "They're no real threat to us so long as there's no single, controlling influence. If there's a real Loper queen out there, she's too far away to control them."

Collier nodded, nose wrinkled in distaste at the foul air.

"I'll get onto it," he said. "Like I said, this should never have happened."

Casualties of war, she thought, as she followed the agent away from the cells. *How many more people are going to end up mentally wounded before this is through?*

***

While Denny went downstairs with Collier, Frankie joined Gould in his office. The scientist's desk was laden with issues of scientific journals. Frankie remarked on this, having assumed today's researchers did all their work online.

"Sometimes it helps to read something in the old way," Gould said, with an odd smile. "But, yes, my research is mostly floating out there as electrons, digits. But not all of it."

Frankie plumped herself down in Gould's chair and swiveled around to face him.

"Okay, spill the beans," she told him. "You're being enigmatic. I hate that."

"This mean anything to you?" asked Gould, offering her a book.

Frankie picked up the slim hardback, examined it. It was obviously not new. The title meant nothing to her, nor did the name of the author. Both were in French. The volume had the familiar, musty smell of libraries or second-hand bookstores. The pages were yellowed.

"Andre Maurois?" she asked. "Favorite of yours?"

"I don't read French," Gould said. "Do you?"

She shook her head.

"My Creole grandma taught me a few choice expressions, but that's about it. Okay, what's so special about this particular bit of processed tree?"

Gould took the book back, held it up.

"I found it on my office desk when we got back," he explained. "Just lying there. I asked if it belonged to anyone else on that floor, but nobody owned up. And nobody saw who left it."

Frankie frowned.

"Sounds like a Trent-thing, in the absence of Lopers."

Gould flipped through the book, stopping at particular pages, brows furrowed.

"I agree," he said. "I just can't work out its significance."

"So you think the book is, what? A threat of some kind?" asked Frankie. "Like a horse's head, only in the form of obscure French literature?"

Gould snapped the book shut, put it down on the table next to his pint of bitter beer.

"I did some research, and found out that it's a minor classic of French literature. Science fiction, of a kind. Written in 1927, predicts a second world war, and suggests that our destructive tendencies could one day wipe out the human race. Unless ..."

Gould paused, looking expectantly at Frankie. She smiled, shook her head.

"Unless we all play nicely together?" she suggested.

Gould laughed, abruptly and with a hint of bitterness.

"No," he said. "That's been tried and failed a few times. No, what Maurois suggested was much simpler. He suggested we turn our aggressive impulses outwards. Against another intelligent species. In the book, a group of press barons manufactures a threat from space. Maurois has his newspaper magnates invent stories about beings from the Moon destroying remote villages so people get scared and angry. This softens them up so a kind of world government can be imposed to end the threat of war between nations."

"Fake news!" Frankie exclaimed. "He was way ahead of the curve, ol' Andre."

Gould gave her a very British, disapproving stare.

"Sorry," she murmured. "Couldn't resist."

Frankie picked the book up again, flipped through it.

Like knowing what it's about suddenly means I could read French, she thought, laying it down again.

"So what happens?" she asked, starting to become genuinely interested in the plot. "Does the cunning plan actually work?"

"Oh, a scientist invents a kind of death-ray that can actually blast chunks out of the Moon. And when they do that, it turns out that the Moon *is* inhabited, the natives are annoyed at being shot at. Then a genuine war begins."

"Oh, those wacky French satirists," Frankie said. "But I still don't get why somebody–"

The idea dawned on her so suddenly that she laughed aloud, despite its implications.

"Oh, God, no!" she exclaimed. "Really? Because that would be amazing. And creepy as hell."

"It would explain a lot of the things we know about Trent, and Benson – assuming they are two different people. Or non-people. Anyway, Cassandra called them Nomads. We should stick with that."

Gould was about to continue, but she held up her hand to stop him. She enjoyed the sensation of solving an intellectual puzzle that Gould had struggled with.

"The Lopers were forced to migrate here," Frankie said slowly, "because the portals connecting our dimension to theirs caused disruption. These Nomads planned it all. The Lopers had to adapt to our world, and engage in covert attacks, manipulation, and so on. And me, and you, and Denny all did our best to draw attention to the threat, in our different ways."

"They're the ideal external menace," Gould pointed out. "At least, they are at this stage. They're not sufficiently numerous or powerful to launch a full-on war against us – yet. They're not really comfortable with a technological world. But if left unchecked, they could adapt more successfully and, given time, replace us."

Frankie raised a hand again.

"And this outbreak of terrorism is leading to revelations," she pointed out. "People are making the link between these new killings and what happened at Malpas Abbey, Hobbs Lane, and so on. Sooner or later, most of the facts we know will come out."

"And there'll be a hell of a row," added Gould ruefully.

Frankie nodded, ideas churning in her mind.

"Fighting the Lopers appeals to just about everyone, when you think about it. The military get to shoot at monsters. Scientists like you get to analyze weird stuff and dream up amazing gadgets. Ordinary folk get to be paranoid and report their neighbors for acting strangely. Lots of investment in new weapons and other stuff. Even religious leaders could get in on the act – the Lopers are a lot like demons."

"Don't forget the politicians, and the media," Gould put in. "Twenty-four-hour rolling news coverage, most of it flabby speculation. It would be like a Third World War, but going on indefinitely, and with minimal casualties."

Frankie pondered the idea.

"So, you could argue that Trent and Benson had our best interests at heart?" she said finally. "That they aren't just a different brand of monster, but some kind of benevolent super-beings?"

Gould made a helpless gesture. He threw himself onto an old couch that stood against one wall of the cramped office.

"I want to believe it," he said, putting his hands over his eyes. "God, how I want to believe. For reasons that are all too apparent."

Frankie spoke quietly.

"They might save Harriet."

Gould sighed.

"Chances are, the Nomads have their own agenda, one just as destructive and inhuman as the Interlopers. But I'm clinging to the remote possibility that, yes, they might be on our side."

He held up the French novel.

"But of course," Gould went on, "if they are evil bastards, this is just the sort of convoluted mind game you'd expect them to play."

Frankie mused on the idea that they were all simply pawns in a vast game. She had always valued her freedom, but knew that in reality everyone was limited in so many arbitrary, unjust ways.

"Could you stand to be just a piece on a cosmic chessboard?" Gould asked.

"Nah," she replied. "If some smug player reaches down to pick this particular piece up, at least I want the chance to bite his fingers."

***

Matheson buttoned up the collar of his shirt.

"Is there something wrong with the central heating in this place?" he asked, slightly irritable.

"Not that I know of, John," said Tania, looking puzzled. "Seems warm to me."

The others made negative noises. It was an odd question, Denny thought, given that the Task Force complex felt like an American office building. Which meant it was several degrees warmer than the average British workplace.

"Never mind," the security chief said, "let's move on. Are there any positives from this bloody fiasco?"

Denny waited for somebody else to speak. Frankie was gazing at her interlaced fingers. Collier looked uncomfortable. Gould seemed to be gazing into infinity, his mind presumably on scientific matters. Tania, who Denny did not know, was scrutinizing an iPad.

"Okay," she said, "maybe it's time the world did know the truth. So far, the Lopers have only attacked this country. But they could be spreading out, starting new nests around the world. Surely, it makes sense for governments to co-operate to fight the threat? And they can hardly do that without people finding out."

Gould and Frankie exchanged a glance. Not for the first time, Denny wished her psychic ability extended beyond direct physical contact.

"We might," Gould said carefully, "have a fresh perspective on just that question. Now that Trent is gone, we have a few things to tell you about him. And a chap called Benson, who also disappeared in odd circumstances."

As Gould outlined his theory about the mysterious Nomads, Denny saw a variety of responses in her colleagues. Tania looked skeptical, Collier confused, while Matheson seemed almost indifferent. Denny herself, having touched the bleak nothingness inside Trent's human form, felt Gould was far too neutral.

"Seriously?" Tania asked after Gould had finished. "Trent is some kind of alien? But not a Code Nine?"

"Nothing like them at all," Denny said emphatically. "Very different. The Lopers have a few things in common with us – emotions, the need to survive. These Nomads seem utterly different from any form of life. As we know it."

Tania mulled that over, then asked Gould a question.

"You seem to think these Nomads might not be our enemies?"

Gould hesitated for a moment, obviously choosing his words.

"The Nomads have an agenda," the scientist said finally. "It might not be entirely hostile, in my opinion."

"I hope," Tania said tactfully, "that we're not assuming our enemy's enemy is our friend?"

"No," Frankie put in firmly. "More likely both sides want to screw us over, just in different ways."

"Now that I can relate to," said Collier, looking pleased. "Sounds like the world I know."

Chapter 6: Revelations

"You realize I'm not a doctor?" Gould asked, as Denny pulled her shirt over her head.

Three days had passed since the terror attacks. The Task Force was in limbo, awaiting some sort of directive from up high. In the meantime, Frankie had continued to train with Collier, while Gould pressed on with his research. Denny had overseen the transfer of the prisoners to civilian hospitals. Then she had turned to Gould, demanding a medical from the physicist despite his protests.

"I don't care," she said firmly. "I don't know any of the medical team here, and I certainly don't trust them. But I need a second opinion on Jabba. Do tests like Zoffany would – do your science stuff. Tell me what's going on."

Gould clucked and tutted as he examined the symbiont, which was now like a dark thread of glistening tissue, a fraction of an inch across. After insisting that he was indulging in 'educated guesswork' and that 'Harriet would know exactly what to look for', he asked Denny to put her shirt back on.

"So, what's the verdict?" she asked. "Will I ever sing at Carnegie Hall, doc?"

"Very much doubt it," Gould replied with a weary smile. "But you seem to be in excellent health. And your little friend is very nearly gone. What remains is mostly Interloper protoplasm, with very little in the way of nerve cells."

Denny looked dubiously at the scientist.

"But I can sense emotions, read thoughts, the way I could before," she said. "So Jabba and I are one now, I guess?"

"Very much so," Gould said, looking slightly evasive. "Of course, we don't know if your psychic abilities will last. As I keep saying, and I know it's tedious, Harriet would have a solid hypothesis on the matter. I am blundering around and guessing."

Denny stood up and laid a hand on Gould's sleeve.

"You're doing a damn good job, Ted," she insisted. "She'd be proud of you. And she'd say she taught you everything you know about biology."

Gould nodded, seemingly only half-listening. Denny recalled that she had not scanned her allies for nearly a week. When she suggested it to Gould, he agreed and held out a hand. Denny removed a glove and touched Gould's fingers.

As before, deep sadness and frustration over Zoffany's fate colored all the man's thoughts. Denny felt pity, but also frustration. She could tell that Gould had been distracted from his research by his lover's abduction. While this was perfectly natural, she wished her could focus more on the big picture.

God, I'm getting Loper ruthless, she thought, half-remembering an old quotation from a college professor. *Fight with monsters, become a monster – something like that.*

Gould, who had been looking down at Denny's ungloved hand, suddenly flinched, stared at her. His expression was comical, but she did not laugh. Gould's horror coincided with a weird, crawling sensation all over her body. It was like the tingle that Jabba emanated when the creature was hurt or excited. But this time it seemed to emanate from her face, rather than her spine.

"What's wrong Ted?" she asked.

Gould did a double-take, shook his head.

"Sorry," he said. "It was just – for a second there, while we were touching, you looked a lot like Harriet."

It took a moment for the scientist's words to sink in.

Oh, Jesus Christ, Denny thought. *Oh, God, no. That can't be happening.*

"I won't mention this to the others," Gould said, his voice lower. "I might have been mistaken. We've no proof."

Denny stared at the scientist.

"I felt the proof," she said. "I felt the change beginning."

A couple of Task Force agents passed in the corridor outside, talking loudly. Gould put a finger to his lips.

"We need to talk about this in private. This, and maybe some other things."

***

The *Fulmar* was anchored outside the mouth of a large harbor. At night, Zoffany saw a constellation of electric lights from her cabin. She did not know if they were anchored in the British Isles or some other nation. But she guessed that a chance to escape might be about to present itself.

Since Gamma had taken over, Zoffany had discovered even greater freedom to think for herself. The third queen was, she felt sure, the runt of the litter. Gamma's mental tendrils tried to drive the viral research forward, but the creature seemed to have little grasp of what science was, let alone advanced biology.

However, the scientist was careful not to let slip any of her innermost thoughts. She had tried to master the art of working on a problem in a serene, detached way, while ostensibly thinking of someone else. Whenever she felt Gamma's clumsy mental probing, she threw up a kind of smoke screen, by reciting a nursery rhyme or nonsense poem. It had taken a while to perfect the art, but after a few days, she had become adept at running two trains of thought at one time.

"Mary had a little lamb," she said to herself, as she loaded a needleless injector. "Its fleece was white as snow."

She put the cylindrical injector carefully onto the laboratory bench in front of her.

"And everywhere that Mary went, her lamb was sure to go."

Lassiter, the female controlled human, entered the lab, carrying the usual midday meal. The two humans did not acknowledge one another. There was no possibility of conversation. Lassiter and her male counterpart were kept on a tighter rein. It seemed as if Gamma devoted most of her efforts to Zoffany's guards, preferring to watch the scientist via human eyes rather than directly via symbiont.

"Thank you," said Zoffany as Lassiter set the tray down.

The unexpected gambit led the woman to pause, and look puzzled. For a moment Zoffany thought Lassiter was about to reply. But then Gamma's mind reasserted itself. Lassiter's expression became blank, and the woman spoke in a dull monotone.

"Is your work done yet?"

Zoffany smiled, still running a nursery rhyme in her head.

"It is nearly complete. I can demonstrate upon this human if you wish."

Lassiter's face still showed no emotion, but the pause suggested Gamma was thinking.

"What are you suggesting?" said the slave, eventually.

Zoffany held up the injector, and began to mentally recite 'Little Boy Blue'.

"I will show that the virus cannot harm a human when it is linked with a helper," she explained. "Let me inject Lassiter. There is no significant risk."

Another pause, this time running to several seconds. Zoffany almost forgot the rhyme, felt rising panic. She became convinced that Gamma would refuse, was onto her. But then Lassiter stepped forward and rolled up the sleeve of her coverall.

"Very well," said the woman's mouth. "You may test your refined virus on this subject."

Zoffany struggled not to feel any exultation as she picked up the injector. Without ceremony, she pressed the business end of the device against Lassiter's wrist, pushed the button at the other end. There was a sharp, mechanical hiss. Lassiter did not flinch. When Zoffany withdrew the injector, the woman rolled her sleeve down, turned, and walked out of the room without another word.

Zoffany leaned against the wall of the improvised laboratory. The room suddenly seemed hot, the noise of waves lapping against the *Fulmar* very loud. Her heart was racing. She looked at the injector, a basic plastic tube, its glass reservoir now depleted.

It will take a while, she thought. *If it works at all. In the meantime, I'd better look busy.*

She began to centrifuge some blood samples she had taken from herself and the other humans on board. It was a pointless exercise, if she was right about the latest viral mutation.

"Baa baa black sheep," she sang quietly to herself. "Have you any wool?"

She sent the centrifuge spinning, the electric motor startlingly loud in the confined space.

"Yes sir, yes sir, three bags full."

***

"You still feeling the cold, boss?" asked Collier.

Matheson looked up from his computer monitor, mumbled a vague affirmative.

"I can ask them to turn up the heating," Collier went on, sitting down opposite the security chief. "Couple of degrees? Everybody else will be in swimwear, though."

Matheson did not react to the weak joke.

He's looking older and a lot more tired than usual, Collier thought. I'd had *thought he'd cope better with being in charge.*

"Anything I can help with, John?"

Collier seldom used his old comrade's first name. During their years of service in the army, they had gotten used to surnames, and stuck to that after moving on. Until now, Collier had felt their friendship had not changed. But now he wondered if being acting leader of the Task Force had finally proved too great a burden for Matheson.

I can't just blurt that out, though, he thought. *Be tactful.*

"Just say if there's anything I can do," he reiterated. "It's a right bloody mess, but you didn't make it. We're all in this together. We're a team, right?"

Collier ran out of platitudes, feeling foolish. Matheson stared up at him, his expression unreadable. Then the security chief nodded and spoke in a low, clear voice.

"There is something you can do," he said. "Step up the routine checks on Denny Purcell, and her associates – Gould and Dupont."

"That's not what I had in mind, boss," Collier said, surprised. "Do you think there's a problem with them?"

Matheson shrugged, swung round in his chair, punched up a picture of Harriet Zoffany on the wall screen.

"One of them has definitely been compromised," he said. "Seems likely this has affected Gould's judgment. We're up against a very manipulative enemy. Purcell has that parasite thing on her back, technically she's a Code Nine, right? And Dupont always stands by her."

Collier nodded uncomfortably.

"I can see the logic, I just don't feel too comfortable spying on people I work with. But okay, you're in charge, I'll arrange it."

Matheson continued to stare at the picture of Zoffany. Collier was about to ask a more detailed question on the proposed surveillance. But he suddenly felt the urge to leave the room. There was an odd atmosphere, and he felt as if he were being watched.

"Check with you later, boss," he said quietly, as he closed the door.

In the main office, he caught Tania's eye, forced a smile. The feeling of being watched had gone.

All that talk about spying, he thought. *Got the jitters.*

***

As expected, Zoffany was summoned to the presence of Gamma the day after she had injected Lassiter. The human slave had shown no sign of illness. Zoffany had been almost certain her viral strain would have no immediate effects, but there had been an element of doubt.

I'm a damn good scientist, she told herself as she prepared another injector. *Now all I need is to keep it together, and take my chance.*

The virus was needed because yet another hapless human had boarded the *Fulmar*. Zoffany had felt the bump as a smaller vessel came alongside, then heard unfamiliar voices. Gamma was preparing to leave, after one of her Interlopers replaced this latest victim.

"Four and twenty blackbirds, baked in a pie," she sang under her breath as she climbed the narrow stairway to the ship's saloon. "When the pie was opened, the birds began to sing ..."

Zoffany kept reciting her nursery rhymes, putting out interference, as she approached the third queen. Gamma was mentally the least impressive of Cassandra's daughters. But physically, the juvenile was the best developed. Cassandra had harvested some comparatively rare genes to create Gamma. As she entered the saloon, Zoffany felt a slight shock at how much Gamma had grown in the last few weeks. The creature was a shade under six feet, dark-skinned, with wavy brown hair. The young queen's face was strikingly beautiful, though the eyes were as cold as those of a shark.

"Ah, doctor," said Gamma, smiling. "This gentleman is the local harbormaster. He seems to think we must either fill out some paperwork or move on."

The man standing in front of the reclining queen was a gray-haired, sturdy-looking man of about fifty. As she exchanged greetings with the man, Zoffany admired his direct gaze and firm handshake. She guessed he might react well in a crisis.

"I was just explaining to the young lady," the man said, clearly uncertain of Zoffany's status, "one can't simply drop anchor where one likes, no matter how fancy this boat might be."

Zoffany noted that the man's accent was northern English, placing the yacht somewhere off the British coast. She made a helpless gesture.

"Well," she said, trying to sound playful, "this young lady is used to getting her own way."

Behind the harbormaster, the Interloper that served as the *Fulmar*'s captain was already changing. The creature's face was flowing like slowly melting wax, taking on the square, weather-beaten look of the unsuspecting human.

"I can see that," said the harbormaster, "but I'm afraid we must all obey the regulations. It's for the common good, you see."

Zoffany felt Gamma urging her to strike. The young queen was impatient to go ashore. She took the small injector from her pocket, stepping forward between the man and the female Interloper. The harbormaster looked puzzled, then alarmed. Behind him, a creature that had expertly copied his face grimaced and gestured at Zoffany.

"Finish it!" hissed Gamma.

The harbormaster tried to retreat, was grabbed by his double, and started to struggle. Zoffany raised the injector, striving to keep her mind blank, a nullity. She was all action, suppressing thought, as she carried out the deed she had planned for so long.

"No!" shouted the harbormaster.

Zoffany spun around and jabbed the injector into the side of Gamma's neck. The creature screeched, hit out at Zoffany, and sent the scientist reeling across the room. Gamma rose, clutching at the spot on her neck where the spray had penetrated her skin. Zoffany felt waves of anger, confusion, and fear radiating from the monster.

If I'm right, it should work almost at once.

Zoffany's refined virus was designed to harm only Interlopers, sparing all humans. The genetic traits that had made the original virus so effective had been reversed. Zoffany doubted whether the infection would prove lethal, but had banked on it having a tremendous impact on an Interloper's metabolism.

Even as she watched, Gamma's skin began to break out in patches of grayish brown. The juvenile queen collapsed on all fours, making a hideous gurgling noise. A gush of greenish-yellow vomit sprayed from Gamma's maw onto the splendid carpet.

As always happened, the queen's followers were affected by her distress. The Interloper holding the harbormaster let go and staggered back, clutching its head. Lassiter burst into the room, face pale, mouth agape. Zoffany felt exultation, an almost childish delight in her own cleverness. Her own mental techniques shielded her well from Gamma's mental chaos. The core of self she had preserved and nurtured could emerge, now.

"Come on," she said to the baffled harbormaster. "They can't stop us. We must get away now!"

Zoffany grabbed the man's hand and half-dragged him away from the writhing Lassiter. They burst out onto the deck, ran over to where the harbormaster's launch bobbed alongside the yacht. An Interloper, face in flux, stumbled onto the deck as they started to climb down onto the launch. There was a helmsman on the smaller vessel, looking up from the wheelhouse in puzzlement.

"Go, go!" urged the harbormaster, as he untied the launch. "Just get away, man!"

A moment later, Zoffany was looking back at the *Fulmar* over a wide vee-shaped wake. She heard the harbormaster shouting into his radio, something about criminals, terrorists, the need for assistance. She turned to look ahead at the city beyond the harbor, and anticipated her return to the human world.

Maybe I got them all, she thought. *But even if I didn't, I struck a blow. I showed them what a human can do.*

Zoffany checked the other container that she had shoved into her jeans pocket before leaving. This was a small, sealed glass tube containing what she thought of as 'concentrated Nemesis'. She intended to refine it further, so that she could be sure it would kill every Interloper on earth.

We're about a mile away now, she thought, looking at the *Fulmar* again. *Well out of range.*

"I will never have to feel any of their filthy minds again," she said quietly.

At that moment, she realized that her time aboard the yacht had transformed her utterly. A timid scientist had become a vengeful fanatic, determined to exterminate the cause of her suffering. Zoffany felt a qualm at the corruption of her objective, scientific worldview.

"Can you tell me what the hell is going on?"

The harbormaster was standing beside her, a picture of irate officialdom. Zoffany laughed, then apologized, calling herself hysterical.

"You see," she began, "I've decided to save the world. In a rather messy way."

The sturdy man looked at her in puzzlement and concern. Zoffany guessed he would turn her in to the police.

Well, they'll soon find out who I am, she thought. *And then I can get back to the Task Force and spread the good news. A virus that's harmless to humans, spreads rapidly, kills Lopers.*

"Nemesis," she said quietly to herself.

***

"I don't think I can control it," Denny said. "It seems to be triggered by strong emotion in whomever I'm in contact with."

They were sitting in the apartment Denny shared with Frankie. Gould was slumped on the couch, looking washed out. He had spent much of his day trying to understand Zoffany's research notes. He had reached a few tentative conclusions. The main one, he admitted, was that 'I should have listened to her more carefully when she talked about molecular biology'.

"I believe you," Frankie said, perching on the arm of the couch. "I mean, it's crazy, but it makes sense. Cassandra clearly had something special in mind for us. She was so keen to enslave us rather than kill us. Maybe this was her idea of punishment?"

Denny was startled by the idea. It had never occurred to her that her symbiont might have been unusual in some way. But now that Frankie had expressed the notion, it was quite persuasive.

"But what if all the controlled humans end up like this?" she asked. "Maybe it happened quicker with me because Ted zapped Jabba, gave him a lobotomy?"

The women looked to Gould, who shook his head wearily.

"It's possible," he said, "but I think Frankie has a point. Cassandra conducted experiments on her victims, in various ways. I think you were one of those experiments. There's no sign of any of the prisoners we held showing shape-shifting abilities."

They fell silent for a moment, and the dull roar of London traffic from the street filled the small room. Denny thought of the teeming city outside, and looked down at her black gloves.

Never to be able to touch another human being, she thought. *Because if I did, I could become their worst nightmare. Or their most cherished desire.*

"I guess it's irreversible?" she said. "I mean, this is being fused at the genetic level with the Lopers. There's no shot to cure it?"

Gould started to talk about retroviruses, genetic amplification, and a lot of other things Denny did not understand. Eventually, the Englishman ran out of words, and energy. He put his head into his hands.

"I'm sorry," he said quietly.

"Not your fault, Ted," Frankie said gently, patting his shoulder. "Hey, we'll get through this. We always do."

Denny saw Frankie's expression. Her friend was as confused and scared as Gould, as Denny herself.

"Hey," she said, "maybe what happened in the lab was a freak incident. Maybe it's not so bad. We can try it out, this power."

She took off her right-hand glove.

"Frankie? You wanna go first?"

Denny extended her hand, and Frankie reached out tentatively. Then Denny pulled back, and stood up.

"Let's do this in front of the mirror," she suggested, leading the way. "The one in the hall."

The tiny hallway seemed very crowded. Gould lingered near the living room door, clearly uneasy. Frankie was tense but met Denny's gaze, gave her a slight nod. Denny faced the mirror, held out her hand, and Frankie gently gripped her fingers. This time there was no shock, no sudden impressions. But Denny felt her face grow warm, her skin crawling, a peculiar feeling that her flesh was growing less dense and shifting over her bones.

She saw her mouth widen in the mirror, her eyes growing larger. The line of her cheek shifted slightly, making her face heart-shaped. Frankie was thinking of Cassandra, and Denny was becoming a fair facsimile of the dead queen.

"That's enough," Denny said, breaking contact. "I think we got a clear result, right Ted?"

"Right," he admitted. "You're a new human species, first to evolve in a few million years. Congratulations."

"I guess there won't be a parade," Denny said, heading back into the living room. "Are you going to tell Matheson I'm an even bigger freak than he thought?"

"No, definitely not," Gould said instantly. "He's not a bad man, but he's military, and they don't like complications. He'll see you as a kind of tame Interloper, lock you up, maybe hand you over to biological warfare experts over at Porton Down. We want you to stay free. Obviously."

Denny nodded. She had had her doubts about Gould in the past, but he had come through several times. Frankie, she could never mistrust.

Two people in the world I can count as friends, she said. *More than some have had.*

A thought struck her, then. Something Gould had said when he had examined her that morning.

"You said you wanted to share a couple of things, Ted? What was the other one?"

The scientist opened his briefcase and took out a black book with a blank cover. It looked like a notebook or diary. Its pages, Denny could see, were somewhat frayed and discolored.

"I'm guessing this is not a poetry reading?" Frankie asked.

"It's the story of an obsession," Gould said, handing the book to Denny. "A man fixated on death, and the possibility of other worlds. And it tells us something about the Nomads. The ones who seem to be responsible for everything that's happened so far."

Chapter 7: The Second Book

"Where'd it come from?" Frankie asked, as Denny examined the black book.

"I brought some documents and other material from the Romola Foundation," Gould explained. "Most of it was of academic interest only. Accounts of hauntings, attempts to investigate psychic powers, that sort of thing. But there was one item that piqued my interest. Take a look."

"I need some more coffee before I plunge into Victorian spiritualism and all that jazz," Frankie said, heading out to the kitchen. "Get reading, girlfriend, I'll catch up."

Denny opened the book and found a beautifully handwritten title.

The Journal of Sir Algernon Romola

She flipped to the first entry, found that the narrative began after the sudden death of Romola's young wife. Romola's grief, confided to the pages of the journal, was profound and enduring. While he put on a brave face for the world, he admitted to being heartbroken, and resentful. He rejected the traditional comforts of religion and became obsessed with the paranormal.

> *I find myself increasingly preoccupied with the question of survival – the survival of the human soul. I know that an English gentleman should seek solace in faith, but the comforts of conventional religion do not help. I cannot accept the cold words of the priesthood as the final verdict. I cannot await the Last Trump to meet my Elizabeth again.*
>
> *Since my beloved wife was taken from me, I have attempted to ascertain the value of so-called spiritualism. I have invited several advocates of this new and dubious science to my home. I was at first impressed. Tables rose, shook, overturned. Voices spoke in the darkness.*

I had a vision of a white-clad specter that, in my desperation, I saw as my dear departed love.

But it was all a tissue of lies. Deep down, I think I always knew.

Ironically, I first became suspicious of the spiritualists when they endeavored to impress me even more. The 'messages' they delivered from Elizabeth were, at first, bland and general in nature. They talked of a happy afterlife, a place of eternal joy, devoid of suffering. Eventually, I became bored with this, and the charlatans duly noted this. Then their 'Elizabeth' started to hint that I should reward the kindly mediums who had reunited us.

Denny was about to skim ahead, wondering if the journal was as significant as Gould seemed to think. A Victorian's account of his futile quest for his wife's ghost seemed irrelevant. But then something caught her eye, and she started reading more closely again.

It was the arrival of a strange gentleman, Mister Clay, that finally disillusioned me of my obsession with séances. This man, superficially rather commonplace, turned out to be a remarkably wise and insightful person. He appeared, without any formal introduction, at my door one day in late autumn. His card merely stated that he was Thaddeus Clay, and gave his address as a rather good London club. But on the obverse of the card, he had written, in a neatly-formed hand, the following phrase.

'I also seek the truth.'

I was by this time very wary of any stranger claiming to be interested in truth, as I had become skeptical about my flock of tame spiritualists. Not once had I heard 'Elizabeth' speak more than platitudes about happiness and love. I had also noted that, without financial incentive, the table-turners became markedly less able to perform. What were deemed 'gifts' to mediums has quickly become salaries.

However, prejudice prevailed in this case. I reasoned that Clay, whatever else he might be, must at least be a gentleman. Once the servant had admitted him to my study, I saw that he was short, bald, rather plump, and with an amiable expression. Quite the contrast to the intense and somewhat ingratiating manner I had become accustomed to in spirit-believers.

Trent! Clay must be Trent, thought Denny. That can't be a coincidence. Did he choose the same appearance twice, at times over a century apart? Or can Nomads only take on one human form?

She read the next few entries closely, wondering just how Trent had manipulated Romola, and why?

I bade my visitor sit down by the fire. After some conventional small-talk, I moved on, perhaps a little rudely, to ask Clay why he had called on me?

"Firstly," he said, "to disabuse you of the notion that sitting in a darkened room with a confidence trickster can summon your dead wife's spirit."

This blunt statement caused me to bridle slightly at the man's presumption. Seeing my expression, he smiled ruefully.

"Perhaps I spoke harshly, Sir Algernon," said Clay, in emollient tones. "But I wanted to be clear about what I am not. I concern myself with reality. With a different realm, yes, and one where psychic energy is strong. But this paradise the mediums talk of – it is all mere tommyrot."

It may be perverse of me, but hearing mediumship dismissed in such brutal terms upset me. It is often the way – we resent it when another man expresses an opinion we are unwilling to voice. Clay seemed to sense this.

"Yes," the little man said, "it is not easy to hear the truth. But remember, I can show you the reality. Or rather, a different reality. A whole world of strange beings!"

A question formed on my lips, but I could not speak the words. I did not dare ask Clay if I would be reunited with my beloved Elizabeth. Again, however, the perspicacious little man seemed to read my thoughts. He inclined his head, a rather grave gesture for such a cheery character.

"You will see her again," he said. "If that is your true desire. I will show you a realm where the dead can live, not merely as shimmering phantom, but as flesh, bone, sinew, and blood."

"Sir," I exclaimed, standing up. "You insult my intelligence!"

"No, Sir Algernon," Clay replied quietly. "I admit that I promise you the seemingly impossible. But it is a promise that I can and will keep."

Denny felt a chill run up her spine. The last, slender remnant of her symbiont quivered, reacting to her emotion. She could guess what Clay was going to show Romola. It would be trivially easy to give the hapless aristocrat a reunion with his dead wife. Or at least, a very good facsimile of one.

Sure enough, the next few pages dealt with Clay's careful manipulation of his victim. Romola was prevailed upon to buy Malpas Abbey, then in a near-ruinous state. Denny read on, anticipating the next phase in Romola's indoctrination.

I found myself in the lair of the depraved Lord George Blaisdell, who had supposedly been whisked away by the devil one dark night in 1792, along with his guests and servants. Only one man survived the alleged Black Mass – a Scots journalist who was blinded and died in Bedlam. I have always scoffed at such Gothic excesses, but now I was not so sure.

The underground temple – a vulgar and contemptible place, decorated with obscene murals – had been sealed up by Blaisdell's heirs. But despite this precaution, the house had such an evil reputation that it was abandoned, and therefore easily acquired.

Once the temple was reopened, Clay told me to simply go to the one serviceable bedroom in the house and wait. He would send my love to me. I found this ridiculous, and said so. However, the little man was persuasive as always. Besides, we were in the middle of nowhere, and I had little choice but to go to bed or seek a room at the village inn.

As midnight chimed, I was nodding by the fire. I had taken a little port wine to fortify myself against the chill autumn air. But despite the soporific effects of the drink, I was instantly alert when the door creaked open. A foot appeared, small and pink-toed. It was followed by a bare leg. Then a woman entered the room.

It was Elizabeth! Perfect in every detail, her pale body standing before me, her modesty preserved by the long tresses of her golden hair. She looked at me, and her face lit up with recognition. Then she grew serious, and extended her lovely arms, and began to walk toward me.

Right up to the last moment, I refused to believe that she could be a creature of flesh and blood. But then she settled herself on my lap, and ruffled my hair, and ran a delicate hand over my cheek. She kissed me, and spoke words to me that only Elizabeth could have known. She spoke in detail of our first meeting, and so much more.

> *Decency forbids me from describing the rest of that night.*

Yeah, wouldn't want to be indecent, she thought. *Let's just assume there was non-stop Loper action. Poor guy.*

"You've gotten to the sex scene, I take it?" Gould asked.

Denny sighed.

"So Algernon here becomes Clay's best bud. But how did Clay stop the Loper from simply killing Romola? I mean, that's what they'd usually do. Appear as the beloved, deceased wife, lull the victim into a false sense of security, then bam! Out come the claws and teeth. Violent sadism is their MO."

"Perhaps the Interlopers had a better use for him," Gould suggested. "They immediately sensed his emotional need, and his fixation on the paranormal."

Denny conceded that the idea made sense. She returned to the journal, and found Romola waking up alone the next morning.

> *I was bereft! The vision of pulchritude that I had embraced was gone, vanished like a phantom. Naturally, I suspected that I had been the victim of some imposter. Had I been drugged, mesmerized? Or had I simply dreamed of the encounter, as I slept uneasily in a supposedly haunted chamber?*
>
> *No, there was abundant proof that my night of bliss was real. I shall describe this in some detail for the benefit of posterity, as I believe important discoveries should be properly documented.*

"Ew!" Denny exclaimed. "Some of these Victorians, not so strait-laced."

"You might want to skim a bit," Gould observed. "He does go into quite a bit of detail. The next part is interesting. Clay turns up again."

I could not deny that Clay had, by some arcane means, shown me that which I had believed impossible. The dead can live. Perhaps death itself is mere illusion, and we all exist eternally in some strange otherworld. If so, it would disprove conventional religion, but I have long since despaired of priestly sententiousness.

What is more, Clay claims to have a scientific explanation for my experience. He says that there are doorways, or portals, to other worlds. That these can be discovered by judicious research. And, most importantly, that all manner of marvelous beings can emerge into our mundane world from these wondrous gateways.

Whatever else he may be, Clay is no charlatan. He offers me no whispers in the dark, no elusive phantoms. Instead, he proved that there are forms of existence hitherto unsuspected by mystic or scientist. I should be grateful to him. I am, in fact, to some extent.

But I do not trust him. There is something too pat, too convenient, about the way he came into my life. When something seems too good to be true, it usually is.

"Smart guy," Denny remarked. "He felt there was something weird about Clay."

She skimmed the next few pages, which dealt with Romola's plans for a foundation that would conduct further research. At the same time, he continued to follow Clay to what the little man called 'sites of paranormal significance'. Denny was startled to see that one such site was 'not far from a small town in the Welsh border region, a place called Machen'.

"Yes," said Gould, when she remarked on this. "It seems the portals were known to Romola. Which struck me as rather puzzling, as when I was recruited to the foundation, their existence was controversial. We didn't know any of the stuff in this journal."

"What happened?" Denny asked.
"Read on," Gould suggested.

> I found that the natives of Machen practiced a bizarre kind of child-sacrifice, seeking good fortune for their community in return. Whenever crisis threatens, they take one or more newborns to a mystic wood, where odd, pale creatures with tiny dark eyes whisk away the offerings.
> This appalled me, of course, and I was all for intervening to stop the monstrous rituals. I was convinced that simply publishing an account of the scandal would force parliament to act. But Clay persuaded me that to do so might cause more harm.
> "They are," he said, "liable to react violently if thwarted. They might well massacre the entire population of the town."
> While I was skeptical of this claim, what I had seen of the eldritch creatures made me think twice. I asked Clay whether they were the so-called Good Folk, or faeries. He answered in the affirmative, but qualified his answer by saying that they were nothing like the fey beings of folklore.
> "The one thing the legends get right," he said, "is that time in their world runs far more slowly. A year in their world might be a century in ours."
> This gave me pause for thought. It sounded rather like one of the fantastical tales of Lewis Carroll. But I had no reason to doubt Clay, merely vague misgivings. He had shown me that, from such a 'portal', my own dear departed wife could emerge.
> I had not considered what motives he might have for involving me in his arcane world.

"I take it things went wrong?" Denny asked, frowning up at Gould.

"Read on," the scientist said. "You may find it interesting. I got a sense of déjà vu."

She turned the page, but found a sudden shift in tone and content.

> *Now is the time to act. I will establish a scientific foundation, bearing my name, that will put my fortune to worthwhile use. My good friend Clay will bring his considerable expertise to help build this organization. He has many interesting ideas.*
>
> *My foundation will act to dispel the confusion and mystery surrounding the so-called metaphysical realm, and strive to get at the facts. Instead of 'things that go bump in the night' we will shine the light of science upon hauntings, finally determining the truth about ghosts and such. And, I hope, we may find evidence that will prove the existence of an afterlife.*
>
> *Of course, my motives are not primarily scientific, for all that I hope to further the cause of progress. I yearn for my lost love. I often feel that, despite the failure of our investigations so far, my dear Elizabeth is sometimes close to me. She truly haunts my dreams, and I have often awoken imagining that she has just left my side. Fantasy? Perhaps. We shall see.*

"Hang on," Denny protested, skimming forward and speed-reading, "he went from gaining first-hand knowledge of Lopers to what looks like total ignorance? Oh, I get it, Trent did a number on him."

Gould nodded sadly.

"Clouded the poor chap's mind, just as Benson clouded mine. Romola stopped keeping a journal shortly afterward and seems to have stashed this one away with other family papers.

That's how it ended up in the archive at the Foundation. I don't think anyone had bothered to look at it for over a hundred years."

Denny handed the faded book to Frankie, who examined it casually.

"Well, we know Trent was around in the Victorian era," Denny said. "Which suggests that these Nomads live for very long. Maybe immortal?"

"Or time travelers," Frankie murmured. "Slipping between dimensions, moving through time faster or slower."

Gould made an affirmative noise, and reached for his briefcase.

"There's something else," he said. "Another bit of trivia from the archives. There are hardly any photographs from the early days of the foundation, but I found a few. I wasn't that interested in them, at first. But then I looked more closely."

He handed Denny a small, sepia-colored photo, curled at the edges. It showed a group of men in antiquated suits. The unsmiling faces might have been any group of Victorian gentlemen. But one was startlingly familiar, despite the faded image. It was a long, cadaverous face, bare of the usual mustache or whiskers. Its expression was devoid of any obvious emotion.

"That's Benson!" she exclaimed.

"Sure is," Frankie said, peering at the photo. "Exact opposite of Trent, appearance-wise. Except for the baldness, of course. Those guys don't do hair, for some reason."

Gould smiled.

"Quite. Check the back of the picture."

Denny turned over the photograph and saw a few handwritten words, plus a date – 1892.

"I guess it says 'Romola Board of Trustees'," she concluded, after struggling with the badly faded ink. "Are you saying Benson was in charge all that time? Somebody would have noticed, surely?"

Gould shook his head, and handed over another photo. This one was in better condition and larger. Dated 1932, it had a printed title, 'Romola Foundation – Board of Trustees'. Conspicuous in the center was a familiar, plump figure. Trent, or whatever he had called himself at the time, was the only one smiling. Denny studied the photo more closely, but could see no difference between the Trent she had encountered and the one in the picture.

"So they alternated control of the foundation?" Frankie asked. "Why? I mean, what was their game plan?"

Gould pointed at Frankie.

"Precisely! Game plan, like we said before. Pieces on the cosmic chessboard. The manipulation, the trickery, the roundabout approach. We tend to see this in terms of politics or warfare, the way human conflicts occur. But what if this is in fact, a game between two powerful, inhuman players, Benson and Trent?"

Denny looked at the pictures again, thinking of a sequence of events spanning many decades. The Nomads had posed as human for a century and a half. They had contrived to bring humans and Interlopers together more closely. Trent had begun the process by targeting the grief-stricken Romola. Several generations later, Benson had manipulated Denny and her original production team into a confrontation with the monstrous beings.

"You think we're literally being played?" she asked, surprised at how angry she felt. "That all this death and suffering is just an amusement for them?"

"Us and the Lopers," Frankie added. "If it's a game, they're victims, too."

Guess that makes me a victim twice over, Denny thought.

"There's something else you should know, Frankie," she said. "Something Ted found out this morning. Kind of a secret."

"Fun secret?" Frankie asked.

"Not for me," said Denny.

Then she tried to explain.

Nightmare Rising

Chapter 8: A Departure and a Return

"You're not changing into a monster," Frankie said decisively, her voice strained. "You're still the same person I've known for, what, eight years? Best friend I ever had. Never a Loper, never one of those things."

Denny felt conflicted, unsure of how to respond. Gould had reverted to Englishman mode, looking uncomfortable at this display of emotion.

"We've got to face the possibility," she said carefully, "that I'm a botched experiment. Ted and me, we think Cassandra wanted to create the perfect hybrid – a real human being, born and raised, but with Loper powers. If they can convert people, it would give them a huge edge."

Frankie looked puzzled. Gould, safe on purely scientific grounds, took up the narrative.

"Relying on females to produce spawn could never produce significant numbers," he pointed out. "But if you can turn a full-grown human, complete with all their knowledge and memories, into an Interloper, it would be a game-changer."

Frankie nodded and took a gulp of her Jim Beam. The remains of ice cubes clinked as she set the glass down clumsily.

"Yeah, I get it," she said. "And I nearly became – one of these amazing experiments. Okay. But do we really know that you'll become a full-on Loper? They've screwed up before."

Denny tried to find reassuring words. But she was also struggling against another problem, one that she had not expected. Every few minutes her vision became distorted, and she was punished with a grotesque view of the world. At this moment, she saw Frankie and Gould as an Interloper would. They were huge-eyed, clumsy creatures. Their mouths were tiny slits, their skins blotched and mottled. Beyond them, the other patrons of the pub were a gallimaufry of similar aberrations.

A pang of revulsion struck Denny just before her vision returned to normal. She took a deep breath, and tried to explain to her friends what had just happened. Frankie was wide-eyed, horrified, shaking her head. Gould was typically curious, asking questions, speculating about the nervous system.

"The eye is a very inefficient camera," he added, sounding pleased with himself. "About ninety percent of what we see is edited and modified by the brain. So, if you see humans as monstrous, it's because your brain ..."

Gould trailed off, realizing too late what he was saying.

"Monster brain," Denny said, raising her drink to her lips. "Better enjoy the booze while I can. I kinda doubt Lopers get drunk. Doesn't seem like their kind of thing."

"The more we know about this," Gould insisted, "the better. We should try to determine just how far the change has gone."

Denny was getting a slight buzz from the alcohol. She nodded at a tall, strikingly attractive girl who was leaning on the bar, surrounded by admirers. Denny thought she was probably a model or actress.

"See her?" she said.

Gould and Frankie both turned to look. Frankie was the first to turn back and face Denny.

"What's so special about her – oh my God."

Denny caught sight of herself in a mirror above their booth. She had managed to approximate the pretty girl's high-cheekbones and wide-mouthed look.

"The eyes are a little too close together," she admitted, "but I'm not sure I can move them around – not much, anyway. And I've no idea if my hair can change at all."

In the mirror, she saw a man at another table staring across at her, open-mouthed.

Crap, she thought. *What a dumb thing to do.*

She looked down, letting her hair curtain her face, and allowed her features to return to their familiar conformation. When she looked up, she saw the gawping man was already talking to some friends, laughing.

"People tend to dismiss things that are obviously impossible," said Gould. "And that goes double for things glimpsed in pubs after dark."

***

The following morning, Collier stopped Denny and Frankie as they entered headquarters. He led them aside to an interview room and closed the door carefully behind them. Gould was already waiting, and clearly impatient.

"What's this about?" the scientist demanded. "Why the cloak and dagger stuff? Isn't this complex secure anymore?"

"I can't answer to the second question," said Collier soberly. "But I can tell you what it's about. Police up north picked up a woman who came ashore at Tynemouth from a yacht called the *Fulmar*. She's very confused, but from what she said, and the description, it could well be Doctor Zoffany."

Gould jumped to his feet, as if his lover were about to walk through the door.

"Emphasis on the 'could'," Collier said firmly. "We asked a discreet Royal Navy doctor to examine her at the port. He'll be checking her now, and he should be able to send a picture. Then we'll know."

"If it is her, how did she get ashore?" Frankie asked. "Did she escape somehow? Or did they let her go?"

Collier shrugged.

"Point is, if she's with us, she's not with them," he said. "And no, I don't know what the procedure is for an agent who's been attached to a symbiont."

The security man looked at Denny.

"As you'll have noticed, we just make this stuff up as we go along, then give it a clever name later."

For a moment, Denny considered telling Collier about her nascent Loper abilities. But once more, she decided against it.

He's one of the good guys, probably, she thought. *But even the good guys can get things badly wrong. And even I don't really know what I am, now. Why should anyone else cut me some slack?*

"Okay," said Collier, opening the door. "Let's get along to the official meeting, where Matheson will tell you what I just did. I wanted to give you guys a heads up, since – well, since this particular case is really personal to you."

Gould shook Collier's hand gravely before they left the interview room. The scientist seemed unusually intense. As they walked along the corridor, Denny brushed against Gould, making brief contact through their clothing. She sensed a wave of apprehension mixed with hope.

I'm getting more sensitive to feelings, she realized. *Absorbing Jabba hasn't ended the process.*

A moment later another thought occurred to her.

If this is not the end of my conversion, maybe it's just the beginning?

***

Matheson had an electric small heater in his office, which was stiflingly hot. The acting leader of the Task Force seemed tired and distracted as he stumbled through the meeting. The agenda was not long, but Matheson had to be reminded of items by Tania.

Maybe he's got the flu, Denny thought. *Or maybe it's something else.*

Tania was speaking now, going over the course of the *Fulmar*. It seemed that the yacht had docked in several European countries before returning to Britain. There was a brief discussion about whether Interlopers were now operating internationally. Gould pointed out that there was evidence of the sightings in America, as well as other parts of the world.

"But we've assumed that only one group survived the collapse of the Phantom Dimension," the scientist concluded. "The handful of creatures led by Cassandra."

"So far as we know," Tania retorted. "But assuming you're right, the group that infiltrated the UK might now be spreading out. They're not numerous, so operating in small groups like infiltrators or terrorists would make sense."

The debate continued, but Denny was focusing her mind on Matheson. The man did not merely look ill, he looked slightly deranged. His expression changed from moment to moment, ranging from slightly manic joy to abject misery. Denny wondered if she was the only one picking up on this. Looking around, she saw concern on Frankie's face, and Gould's.

Maybe the guy's had his mind tampered with? Denny wondered. *It's the sort of thing Trent might get up to.*

Denny began to try and think up a reason to stand up and move closer to Matheson. There was an office desk between them, but behind the security chief was a window with a fine view over the Thames. There was a lull in the discussion, after Gould said something about the amount of damage Interlopers could do if they bred in sufficient numbers. She slipped the glove off her right hand.

"That's right," Denny said, trying to sound natural. "They could devastate a great city like London. Imagine them, becoming people's worst fears, spreading panic."

She stood up, ignoring Tania's frown and Collier's puzzlement, and strode past the desk to the window. As she got closer to Matheson she felt an odd chill, as if walking into a cold draught. The sensation lasted for just a moment, but it was clear and disturbing.

"Yeah," she said, gesturing out the window at the dome of St Paul's Cathedral. "They could do as much damage as Nazi bombs. Imagine whole areas in flames, mass panic."

"Very interesting," Tania began. "But I think in light of recent events we're all aware of the danger to society Code Nines represent."

"What do you think, Matheson?" Denny said, and laid a hand on the man's shoulder. "You've seen some terrifying sights, back in the day–"

She stopped, forgetting the cliché she was about to deliver. Even though she had touched Matheson through his clothes, a piercing chill ran up her hand, and with it came a surge of emotion. It was a kind of psychic scream, the despairing cry of a mind in torment.

'Help me!'

"Matheson!" she shouted, jerking her hand away. "Oh, God!"

The others were rising to their feet, shouting questions. Collier told her to back off, Tania looked confused and scared. Denny barely heard them, however. She was retreating to the far corner of the room, staring at Matheson. The chief agent was quivering in his chair, shaking like a man exposed to intense cold. His skin seemed blue, now.

It was the cold void, Denny thought. *The thing I sensed inside Trent, it's inside Matheson now.*

"Boss?" Collier asked tentatively, leaning over the desk.

Matheson turned his head and looked up at Collier. His lips opened, and for an instant, it seemed as if he were about to laugh. Then he gagged, his eyes rolling back in their sockets. Tania screamed as a gout of blood erupted from Matheson's mouth and splashed over Collier's face and jacket. Collier reeled back, wiping his face with his sleeve. Gould was hesitating, while Frankie was dragging Tania toward the door.

"Get out," Denny urged them all. "It was trying to hide, now it's got nothing to lose."

As the group retreated, Matheson's body began to shake even more ferociously. More blood spurted from his mouth, and trickles of red ran from his white, sightless eyes.

"Lose," said a thick, gurgling voice. "Lose. Nothing to lose."

"That's Trent!" cried Tania. "How can Trent be speaking through him?"

"He's inside him," Denny said bleakly. "Possessing him. A neat way to avoid losing control of this outfit."

"Control!" bellowed Matheson's distorted mouth. "Control you all!"

A black tendril appeared, weaving its way into the air from the depths of Matheson's throat. Denny saw a pulsing and swelling in the man's throat, and more blood spilled from every visible orifice. After weaving hesitatingly back and forth for a couple of seconds, the feeler seemed to identify Denny. It pointed, rigid, then shot toward her. Denny flinched, raising a hand to ward it off. But the weird limb did not quite reach her, protruding just over a yard from Matheson's face. The door was open now, and only Frankie and Collier remained with Denny inside the office.

"What the hell is happening?" Collier demanded, drawing his sidearm. "What is it?"

"The real Trent," Gould shouted from behind him. "Just get away."

At that moment, Matheson's jacket began to bulge, then more black tendrils burst from it, blindly flailing. Denny saw shattered bones and bloodstained entrails spill onto the desk as the Trent-being emerged from its ill-fated victim. Collier fired, the gun loud in the confined space. She was about to rebuke him for a pointless gesture. Then she saw the neat hole in Matheson's forehead. She realized Collier felt he was putting a friend out of his misery.

"How much of the damned thing is there?" Gould whispered.

The network of thick black stems demolished what was left of Matheson's body, expanding to fill half the office. It made no noise other than hissing and crackling. Denny, last to leave, peered into the roiling mass. But she could see no nucleus, no actual body to which the ever-questing limbs were anchored.

Truly alien, she thought, as she slammed the door. *No organs, no brain, no body as we understand it.*

By now several armed agents had appeared, among them Hattersley, who looked terrified. Someone asked if the door and office window would 'hold that bloody thing'. The question had already occurred to Denny.

And the answer is almost certainly no.

She turned to Collier, who was still gaping in horror at the fate of his old comrade. Denny grabbed him by the arms and got a wave of panic and confusion.

"Snap out of it, Ben!" she hissed. "Take control of this. Get these people out of here first. That thing could start moving any second."

As if to underline the point, one of the pointed black tendrils struck the door. Someone screamed and the small crowd moved back. One armed agent took aim with a sub-machine gun. Collier looked at Denny, then spoke to the motley group.

"All unarmed personnel evacuate the building," he snapped, then gestured to the man taking aim. "Hold your fire unless it comes out. Then let it have the lot."

"Bullets won't stop that!" exclaimed Hattersley. "We're done for if we stay here."

"Shut up, dumbass," Frankie said, punching Hattersley on the upper arm. "You'll scare the women."

More blows landed on the door and window. The office now seemed to be full of monstrous, twisting tubes of alien protoplasm. Denny could see no sign of Matheson's remains. Another blow starred the window glass, and the remaining agents fell back a few more paces.

"Hold your fire," Collier said, his voice firmer now. "Look for a clear target. Anything like a face, a body."

"It doesn't have those," Denny insisted. "It's just a network of limbs. If it has a brain it must be distributed through the whole fabric of the creature."

Now Denny was becoming aware of a new sensation. It was the same intense coldness, the sense of a starless void that she had encountered before. But along with it came something more familiar. She felt Interloper emotions, predominantly rage, coursing through her mind. The feelings were intense, oddly tinged with fear and doubt. It took her a moment to realize they were distinct from her own reactions.

They're tuning in, she thought in confusion. *Somehow, they've connected with me again.*

There was a response, a powerful thought forcing itself into her mind. It reminded her of Cassandra, but was subtly different in tone. The voice that spoke in her head was not threatening. But its message was still unwelcome.

'You are more like us with every day that passes. Eventually, we will be one, as it should be.'

"No!" she shouted, causing heads to turn.

At the same moment, the Nomad lashed out at the office window and smashed it. Black tendrils spilled into the main office, flailing. Without waiting for orders, an agent opened fire, emptying his pistol into the monster. This signaled a general fusillade from the security team. Bullets tore into walls, shattered glass, but seemed to have no effect on the coiling mass of limbs.

"Fall back!" Collier yelled, vaulting over a desk.

Most of the squaddies retreated, still firing. Then Denny saw Hattersley, standing transfixed, simply staring at the Trent-creature. Frankie started pulling at the agent's jacket, trying to haul him away, but it was too late. A tendril shot out and pierced Hattersley's belly, then emerged from the other side.

Now that she was closer to the limb, Denny could see that it had sprouted thorn-like barbs. As Hattersley screamed in pain, the Nomad pulled him into its forest of tendrils, easily overpowering Frankie. There was a confused thrashing. Gunshots punctuated a horrific crunching and rending sound. Gobbets of bloody flesh were flung across the office.

"I think Trent's pissed about his cover being blown," Frankie said, as she and Denny turned over a desk and crouched behind the improvised shield.

"You think?" Denny remarked. "This isn't going to protect us. We need to go."

The Nomad lashed out again, the sharp tip of a tendril opening the face of an unwary agent. The man fell, crying out in pain. Now the bulk of the alien entity was in the main office, rolling slowly forward. It reminded Denny of a vast, black tumbleweed. The agents, two supporting the wounded man, were in full retreat now, no longer firing.

Denny and Frankie stumbled out into the corridor, and Collier slammed the door behind them. There was a rustling and crashing. Denny imagined more desks being overturned, thick black feelers reaching into every corner.

"It's growing, somehow," she pointed out. "No way was all that crap inside poor Matheson."

"It's dimensionally transcendent," Gould said, his voice a mixture of wonder and fear. "It isn't restricted by our conceptions of size. For all we know, it could engulf the entire city."

There was a brief silence, broken by the sound of shouts and doors slamming in the distance. The evacuation was obviously underway.

"Nah," Frankie said, gesturing at the locked door. "That thing is a game player, remember. If it wanted to simply destroy humans, it would have been upfront from the start. We broke the rules, that's why it's angry."

"Yes!" Gould exclaimed. "It doesn't like it when the pieces on the chessboard misbehave."

Collier had been trying to follow the conversation.

"That thing in there is Trent?" he asked.

"Yes, it is," Denny said. "No time for explanations now, let's just keep moving away from it. Maybe it'll calm down in a while."

They were already near the main entrance when Frankie raised a hand.

"Listen!" she hissed.

"I don't hear anything," said Collier, after a pause.

"Exactly!" put in Gould. "It's stopped thrashing about."

They waited a couple of minutes, but no more sounds came from the office. Eventually, Gould asked if there was a security camera they could check. Collier produced a pad and took a few seconds to summon up a feed. Then he gasped, holding up the small screen for all to see.

"It's gone!"

***

"So, you're in charge, now?" asked Frankie. "Sorry, Ted, that came out way too incredulous."

"Nobody could be more surprised than me," admitted Gould, adjusting a high-tension power lead. "Chief science officer, apparently that gives me seniority. But they're sending some bureaucrat over, so my glorious reign won't be very long."

Nearly two hours had passed since the Nomad had revealed its true form. A biohazard team was completing the clean-up of Trent's old office. The remains of Matheson and Hattersley had been recovered, though it was hard to tell which was which. There were plenty of bullet holes. But no 'anomalous biological material' had been found, according to the chief biologist. The Nomad masquerading as Trent had vanished without a trace.

"While we're waiting for my replacement," Gould went on, "we can at least try and determine if the Nomad vanished through a portal. I've been wanting to try this thing out for weeks. Never could have expected I could do it right here in headquarters."

Denny looked at the mass of electronic equipment occupying the center of the main office. According to Gould, it would detect any unusual electromagnetic phenomena. She had enough faith in the physicist to feel hopeful. Collier, Tania, and the rest were still so shocked that they went along with anything Gould suggested.

"I recommend everyone withdraw from the area," the scientist said loudly. "Just in case."

"Just what we need," muttered Tania, as they filed out. "A wacky experiment that might go seriously wrong."

Denny stayed behind. Gould seemed about to object, then smiled.

"I suppose you're not too worried about the risks from mere earthly technology, eh?"

"Not really," she said, wryly. "Some mad scientist stuff could be just the relaxing interlude I need."

Gould retreated with his laptop behind a transparent, toughened glass shield. Denny joined him and watched as the Englishman turned on the equipment. Gould had tried to explain what the experiment was supposed to achieve, but once he got into 'eleven-dimensional spacetime', she had given up.

"Okay, professor," she declared. "Fire up the crazy."

Gould gave her a mock-disapproving stare, then tapped the screen of his laptop. Nothing seemed to happen. Then Denny heard, just at on the very edge of hearing, a rising hum. On Gould's computer screen, a red line traced an upward path. Denny felt her heard racing and clenched her hands inside their gloves.

"What do you expect to happen if–"

She never finished the question. Between the mass of equipment and the wreckage of Trent's office, the air started to shimmer. Fascinated, Denny watched as a rough globe formed. It was about three feet across, its edges gleaming in the disturbed air. She felt hair standing up on the back of her neck.

"Ted, you're a genius!" she exclaimed.

Then the portal changed. The rippling, mirage-like effect gave way to cloudy gray, then black. A lightless globe hovered a couple of feet above the bloodstained office carpet. The globe began to expand, its edge pulsing, and Denny suddenly felt an intense chill.

"It's the Nomad's world, through there," she shouted. "Turn it off, Ted!"

Gould was already jabbing at his screen, but it had no apparent effect. The globe was now at least five feet across. Denny stared into the void, trying and failing to tear her eyes away. Despite the utter blackness, she sensed movement, a presence that knew she was there. It might have been Trent, Benson, or some other Nomad. All she could be sure of was that it was vast, devoid of compassion, and fiercely intelligent.

An elongated black shape emerged from the globe, wove back and forth, then started to extend toward the glass screen. Gould threw his laptop aside and dove sideways toward the main cable. The black tendril was poised above him, jabbing down toward his back, when he pulled the connectors apart. There was a screeching noise, so high pitched that Denny felt it in her teeth more than heard it. Then the black tendril was falling to the floor, and the globe of darkness had vanished.

They stood looking at the severed Nomad limb. It twitched for a few seconds, then stiffened. Its black, glossy surface became pale, turned ash-gray, and then started to crack. Gould looked around, grabbed a coffee mug, and scooped up some of the desiccated tissue.

"Dust to dust," said Gould, looking into the mug. "Okay, that was bloody terrifying. But also, highly significant. It may be that there are latent portals everywhere, and with a more compact form of equipment, we can open them. Or maybe, with more refinements, we could block them, close them off."

"Great," said Denny. "But can we destroy the Nomads with this gizmo?"

Gould looked surprised at the question, then pensive.

"It's possible," he mused. "If they are linked to the portals, it could be a way to disrupt their activities, if not actually eradicate them. But that's pure speculation."

Frankie appeared, leading the rest of the Task Force team back into the room. They talked about what Gould might have achieved, and how useful it could be. Then Collier received an urgent call. Denny saw Gould become tense, all his attention focused on the new security chief.

"Yes, Ted, you're right," Collier said as he hung up. "She'll be here in a few minutes."

***

"Harriet!"

Gould rushed forward as the woman stumbled into the interview room. She was between two agents, under Collier's supervision. At first, it seemed the security men would stop Gould, but Collier waved them back.

"It's okay," Collier said. "She's one of ours, no matter what she's been through. We've learned our lesson."

It was the first time Denny had seen people literally fall into one another's arms. Gould and Zoffany almost collapsed to their knees. The woman was weeping, her lover stroking her hair, making consoling noises.

"Ted, I know it's Harriet," said Denny. "But you should still be careful."

Frankie was already moving carefully around the couple so that she could get behind Zoffany. Denny nodded to her. They were on the same page. The doctor who had examined the biologist had reported an unusual growth on her spine. There was a major risk that Zoffany was controlled, and might try something.

Seems unlikely, Denny thought. *She's got no weapons, and doesn't look too strong. But still, Lopers are full of tricks.*

Zoffany looked up at that moment, and laughed. She stood up and raised her shirt, showing the greenish-black tissue between her shoulder blades. Despite her own experience of symbionts, Denny still recoiled at the sight.

"Don't worry, the organism can't influence me, not anymore," she said. "I broke the hold they had on me, you see! That's how I escaped."

"That's amazing!" Denny said, trying to sound enthusiastic. "But let's get you checked out, eh doc? You've been through a lot."

Denny could sense brief flashes of neural activity from Zoffany's symbiont now. But the creature did seem weak, as if asleep or somehow comatose. It was certainly less active than those of other controlled humans she had encountered lately.

Perhaps she did beat them, Denny thought. *We need some good news. But maybe something else is going on.*

"She had a container with her," Collier said. "It's down in the lab now, being analyzed. She seems to think it's some kind of potent Code Nine killer."

Zoffany snorted, laughing again. She sounded a tad unbalanced to Denny, but not necessarily unreliable. Gould coaxed Zoffany to a chair and sat down next to her, contriving to always hold her close.

"It's Nemesis, Ted," Zoffany babbled, putting a pale hand on Gould's arm. "I devised it, created it, despite them. Alpha, Beta, Gamma – the three queens, they were distracted, preoccupied, so I had time to work. I fooled them, and made Nemesis. Their Nemesis!"

Zoffany looked up at Collier.

"It *is* a Code Nine killer, Ben," she said emphatically. "Works on the Typhoid Mary principle. The carriers – we humans – don't develop any symptoms. We spread the virus to them, the bastards, and it kills them all. They only have to come near us, attack us, and they die! Easy peasy!"

Denny felt her heart skip a beat. She thought of her own status, stuck in the shadowy realm between human and Interloper.

What if there's a blurred line, she thought, *between 'us' and 'them'?*

Gould was gazing at Zoffany, now. His expression showed doubt, confusion.

"Harriet," he said slowly, "you were on that yacht for weeks, and somehow you devised a surefire way to kill the Lopers? That sounds – very implausible, you must agree."

Zoffany became even more animated, grabbing her lover, talking rapidly.

"Yes, but I had all the genetic material I needed, you see," she said. "They'd done a lot of preliminary work. Clearly, they had absorbed information from some people with scientific training, not to mention a great deal of medical knowledge."

Gould nodded, patting her gently on the arm.

"I understand," he said, in a placatory tone, "but, Harriet, why would they let you create something that endangers them, for any reason? They must have known what you were thinking. You were so close to them, all the time. How could you possibly hide something as complex as genetic engineering? The weaponizing of a virus?"

Zoffany looked puzzled, then frightened.

"Mary had a little lamb," she said suddenly, brightening. "I worked out ways to trick them, you see! Little rhymes, nonsense, deception. Humpty Dumpty, you see? That's how I made Nemesis. Behind a smokescreen of nonsense and banality. I fooled them all!"

"Maybe we should get her to the sick bay," Collier suggested. "She could do with some rest, I think."

Gould started to get up and tried to raise Zoffany to her feet. The biologist kept talking, the words tumbling out.

"I created the virus to destroy them," she said, but her voice was uncertain. "I know I did. It's real – you can analyze it here!"

"I know it is," Gould said, soothingly. "The science team is on the case. I think Collier's right, what you need is some rest, Harriet. Let's just get you checked out in the sick bay–"

"Wait," said Denny firmly. "There's something we can do to clarify this."

She looked over at Collier and his guards.

"Ben," she said, "if you trust me, take your guys outside, close the door behind you. It's for the best."

Collier hesitated, then jerked his head at the two security men.

"Rules are made to be broken," he muttered as he left. "Especially around here."

"Good idea, Denny!" said Zoffany in a stage whisper. "Don't let the brass hats know too much about it! Military minds, all famously limited!"

She looked up at Denny, her tone half-pleading. Her eyes were wide and bloodshot.

"You see, I worked out a way to trick them, the young ones! They were stupid, and always vying for power. That made it easier. And their powers hadn't fully developed. And – and this is vital information – they just don't understand science, Denny! That gave me a huge advantage, that lack of creative thought."

Denny pulled up a chair to sit at Zoffany's side, then took off one of her gloves.

"Are you willing to let me scan you, Harriet?" she asked. "You remember how that works?"

Gould looked stunned, started to protest.

"Ted," Denny cut him off. "We're used to Lopers employing brute force methods. Mind control, fear, violence. But we also know they're evolving. And they know about the Nomads' methods. They're adaptable."

"Oh, sweet Jesus," breathed Frankie, who was leaning against the door, a fascinated spectator. "If Lopers have started messing with our memories, too, we're royally screwed."

"Not necessarily," Denny snapped. "And it might be something else entirely. Let me try and find out. Harriet?"

The biologist shook her head, leaning away, clutching at Gould. The physicist made soothing noises, gently holding Zoffany, and looked into her eyes.

"I know it's frightening," he said. "But Denny's on our side. She's one of us, remember? She doesn't want to hurt you, just find out what happened after the Interlopers kidnapped you."

It took several minutes of coaxing, and Denny began to expect Collier to return. But eventually, Zoffany relented and held out a white, quivering hand. Denny smiled reassuringly and took the biologist's fingers in hers.

And she was sitting in a different room entirely.

Nightmare Rising

Chapter 9: Nightmare Visions

Denny was looking through Zoffany's eyes, hearing the manic echo of her thoughts, feeling her emotions. The biologist was working with frantic speed, surrounded by laboratory equipment. Zoffany noted that the room had portholes, and realized that it was a cabin on the yacht *Fulmar*.

Another person entered carrying a tray of food. The meal was basic, chicken and some vegetables, along with a glass of water. Zoffany ate and drank hastily, barely acknowledging the man who brought and took away her tray. The scientist was thinking about DNA, her theories and conclusions suddenly clear to Denny.

When I'm in her head like this, I know what she knows, Denny thought. *Cool.*

Time passed, days and weeks melting away as Denny roved along the timeline of Zoffany's memories. At first, nothing seemed wrong. The kidnapped scientist had a symbiont urging her to work against the human race. But Zoffany had devised a way to hide her true self, a shield against the weak and bickering minds of Alpha, Beta, and Gamma.

Kind of convenient, Denny thought. *Okay, Harriet is very smart and mature, and human adolescents are notoriously erratic. But the juvenile Queens aren't human.*

Denny began to search for signs of inconsistency, evidence that Zoffany's memories might have been tampered with. She tried to find the same true memories lurking within false ones that she had first detected in Gould. But she detected no evidence of Nomad-like tampering.

As far as Denny could tell, Zoffany had produced a small amount of a human-killing virus. This had been tried out on a few unfortunate individuals, to convince the Queens that their weapon was effective. But in fact, the biologist had sabotaged that virus, making it incapable of surviving for long outside the lab. Meanwhile, she had perfected a virus that exploited the unique qualities of Interloper DNA.

Maybe Zoffany is right, she thought. *Perhaps she really did fool them. Nemesis could be real.*

Denny moved forward, approached the time when Zoffany staged her escape. She saw the scene in the luxurious lounge of the *Fulmar*, with the unsuspecting harbormaster about to be replaced. She saw Zoffany attack Gamma, driving the injector into the creature's neck. Then came the confused escape as the Queen thrashed around, vomited. The other Interlopers and controlled humans lost control, sharing their leader's confusion and distress.

Something wrong here, Denny thought. *Zoffany was hardly affected.*

She examined the scientist's memories more closely. Zoffany was convinced that her tricks had shielded her from the suffering the virus had supposedly inflicted upon Gamma. It was hard to credit that improvised mental defenses, such as nonsense rhymes, would work so well.

But Zoffany had to get away, Denny reasoned. *Which means she couldn't collapse and writhe around on the floor. The escape was rigged. I'm almost certain.*

Denny went back along Zoffany's timeline, checking times when the scientist had supposedly shielded herself most effectively. Now that she was focusing on particular moments, she spotted the first deception almost at once. Zoffany created her human-killing virus, put samples carefully into a small fridge. Shortly after, Zoffany began to work on the Interloper-destroying variant. Or so she thought.

Appalled, Denny watched as Zoffany's hands systematically disobeyed her mind. The scientist labeled containers as if they contained a new virus, but in fact, they were simply fresh cultures of the original. All the routine acts of a professional scientist, things Zoffany did automatically, were hijacked. Often it was as simple as mislabeling a glass vial.

They weren't weak or divided among themselves, Denny thought. *The three were always nudging Zoffany in their chosen direction. They let her think she was free of them, at least sometimes, so that she would work harder.*

While the biologist was thinking of complex, theoretical problems, her body had always been under subtle, near-total control. Denny was shocked and dismayed to see that the three Queens were very knowledgeable about scientific methods. And

Gamma, it seemed, was also a good actor, one who could apparently puke on command.

"We have many hidden talents," said a cool, clear voice in Denny's head. "Come, link with our minds. Now that you know the truth, you must decide what your response will be."

***

The shock was immense, dislocating reality. The lab aboard the *Fulmar* vanished, and Denny felt the sudden scrutiny of several monstrous minds. Interloper minds.

Oh, God, she thought. *All Three Queens.*

She felt the minds of the creatures, knew them at once as Alpha, Beta, and Gamma. And Denny knew something else. Harriet Zoffany believed she had given the creatures those names, but in fact, the juvenile females had devised them for themselves. It reflected their order of birth, not the hierarchy Zoffany had assumed.

What appeared to be three young girls sat facing Denny. On the right was the tallest, Alpha, with a voluptuous figure, a sensuous mouth. To the left sat Gamma, darker than the others, and still with some trace of the cute child she had so recently seemed to be. Beta fell partway between her sisters in looks and manner. She was, Denny felt, the middle child, confident and secure.

They might have been three ordinary teenagers, except that the chintzy sofa they sat on was not indoors. Instead, the three queens reclined casually amid chaos and devastation. It was a world of shattered buildings, flames, clouds of smoke, and distant gunfire.

"Not real," Denny said defiantly. "This is what you want, not what will be. Your dream, our nightmare."

"Brave words," said Alpha. "For such a freak. Neither human nor like us. Tainted, a mongrel, a half-breed."

"How long would you live if Collier knew you were almost one of us?" asked Beta. "And even if you persuaded him to trust you, what of your politicians, your generals, the media you worked for? They would, at the very least, imprison you for the rest of your life."

"You're going to have to make some big decisions, Denny," added Gamma. "Most, if not all, of your human friends will certainly die in the pandemic. It has already begun. You can still survive. Join us. Complete the process. Finish your journey."

"Never!" Denny exclaimed. "I'm human, despite everything you've done to me. I won't become one of you."

Alpha laughed humorlessly and waved a slender hand. The bleak background rippled, faded, and was replaced by a very different vista.

"Abracadabra," Alpha said. "I believe that's the conventional thing to say when conjuring things up."

Denny looked out in puzzlement at an idyllic world. They were on top of a low hill looking out on a river valley. What might have been the Thames meandered across meadowlands. Clumps of trees dotted the rolling countryside. Above was a beautiful summer sky dotted with a few fluffy clouds. There was no trace of the half-ruined city, no sounds of violence. Only birdsong, and a breeze ruffling the grasses.

"This is what many of your people desire," Beta said, looking around in apparent curiosity. "Very simple, of course, but then a lot of humans are."

"I don't see any people," Denny objected. "It looks like the human race is extinct in this particular fantasy."

"Oh, there are people, Denny," said Gamma. "Look."

Denny followed the pointing finger and saw that this world was inhabited. The people she saw were dressed in simple clothing, with something vaguely medieval about it. She guessed that everything worn or used in this world was hand-made. The people approaching were a small family group. There were four adults. Denny guessed their ages at between twenty and forty. There was also a little girl of around ten, and a boy a few years younger. One of the women was obviously pregnant.

The little group were carrying baskets, and as Denny watched the children gather berries from bushes, while the adults dug up roots and tubers. It seemed there was no agriculture in this world, just foraging.

They look happy, I guess, she thought. *But kind of dumb.*

"These are your ideal humans?" Denny asked. "Peasants out of the Dark Ages?"

"Such cynicism," said Gamma, mildly. "This is a world without war, oppression, exploitation. People just live out their lives. They can tell stories, sing, dance, do all the things that come naturally to humans."

Denny recalled her dream of the Morlocks, and reflexively looked down at her feet. The earth beneath them seemed solid enough.

Beta laughed.

"You think we want to live in warrens?" she asked. "We are not insects, no matter how often you liken us to ants or bees. No, when we take over, we will walk among you. Look again."

The small family group had stopped foraging and were all staring downhill, toward the river. Walking up toward them was a white-robed figure, tall, majestic, moving with liquid grace. As the person got closer, Denny could see that it was a dark-haired woman with a pale, beautiful face, smiling benevolently. She was crowned with a garland of wild flowers.

"A goddess," said Alpha. "One of many. This is a world of complex mythology, the way humans like it."

The explanation was superfluous. The adults had all fallen to their knees, and were chanting what was presumably some kind of hymn or prayer. Denny could not make out the words. The language was not familiar, but seemed simpler, gentler than English. The two children remained standing, gawping up at the preternatural being. The so-called goddess raised her hands in a benevolent gesture, then indicated the older child.

Oh, God, no, Denny thought.

"I don't want to see this!"

"You must," Gamma insisted. "It is the new covenant."

The little girl looked frightened, clinging to the pregnant woman. But the woman patted her daughter, clearly reassuring her. The girl walked forward, hesitantly. The false goddess reached down and took the child's hand, then led her away, towards a small clump of trees.

"A sacred grove," Beta explained. "A place no human would dare to go."

As the two figures vanished into the shadows, Denny felt disgust and anger welling up. She could guess the child's fate.

"If humans did venture into your sacred grove," she said, "they'd find a big heap of bones, right?"

The vision froze. The depleted family group stood, statue-like, gazing after the girl. Silence fell as the drifting clouds stopped moving, the breeze-stirred grass became still.

"A small sacrifice, for a peaceful world," Gamma insisted. "The percentage of humans killed to sustain us would not be large. Trivial, compared to your own brutal activities."

"Heard that before," Denny sneered. "End justifies the means, can't make an omelet without breaking a few eggs. Just because humans are screwing up this world does not give you the right to enslave them and turn them into fatted cattle."

There was a pause. Gamma smiled, as if she had just won a point.

"Don't you mean 'enslave us'?" asked the Interloper.

Alpha nodded sagely.

"You are already finding it hard to identify with homo-sapiens," she observed. "There is a distance, hard to bridge, even with those you care for."

"No!" Denny insisted. "I'm not like you, I don't see people your way."

Ignoring her, Beta chimed in.

"That distance will only grow greater as you evolve."

Denny shook her head emphatically.

"If all you offer the human race is this," she said, gesturing at the hapless worshippers, "then I'd rather die fighting you."

Alpha shook her head, smiling as if in pity.

"You misunderstand," she said. "There are many possible futures. This one is sedate, idyllic, stable. It is one we would prefer, with only the most basic technology, and little chance of so-called progress."

"After you've wiped out most of the human race!"

Denny looked from one serene face to another, but saw no hint of remorse or doubt. She had hoped, desperately, that this generation of Interlopers might have acquired some finer qualities. They had incorporated a vast array of human thoughts and feelings into their hive-mind, after all.

"No," said Beta. "We use such knowledge, we do not let it pollute us."

"Then there's no point to this!" Denny cried. "Let me go! Let me go back to my people."

Denny made a tremendous mental effort, lashing out at the vista of ruins. The image wavered, started to fade. But then she felt the queens assert their dominance. Together she could not defy them, not in their psychic realm.

"We have more worlds to show you," Gamma said, as if offering a treat. "So many possibilities, once the human world of swarming crowds and cruel machines is ended."

***

"This doesn't seem right," said Frankie.

Denny had been clutching Zoffany's hand for about thirty seconds. Frankie reached out, then hesitated. She did not want to break the connection prematurely, before Denny could find out what they needed to know.

But maybe, Frankie thought, *this is not a regular scan.*

"What do we do?" asked Gould.

Frankie recalled Denny's courage, the way her friend had come for her in the Phantom Dimension. Denny had braved very real monsters as well as psychic attacks to fulfill a promise.

Surely, she'll be okay just probing Zoffany's memories? I've got to have faith in her.

"We wait a while," Frankie decided. "If this lasts another minute or so, then we intervene."

Gould nodded dubiously.

"I hope you're right," he said. "For both their sakes."

***

The three Queens had conjured up a new vista for Denny to observe. This time they were in a city. It was nothing like a modern metropolis, though. Instead, it reminded Denny of virtual reality reconstructions of Rome or Babylon. Stately buildings stood on all sides, made from stone blocks. One especially elaborate structure had a fine portico with marble columns. They were in some kind of market square, with merchants crying their wares, as people walked along, perusing items laid out on stalls. Denny saw chickens, baskets, bales of cloth, and many items she could not identify. It was noisy and dusty, but the people seemed less miserable than modern Londoners.

"More advanced than our first version," said Gamma. "A basic model of what you call civilization."

This time the Interloper females were sitting on the rim of an ornamental fountain. Denny stood in front of them, and kept dodging out of the way of pedestrians who obviously could not see her. Eventually, she gave up, and let an old woman walk through her as if she were a ghost.

"So you went from Stone Age to what, Bronze Age? Big deal," she remarked.

"We can preserve much of what you call your culture," Beta pointed out. "Literacy, agriculture, metalworking, roads, a system of laws. And of course, religion."

"One geared to our purposes," added Alpha. "Observe."

A group of men in white robes appeared from the fine building, lining up in front of the marble columns. Denny guessed that it must be a temple of some kind. Already a small crowd had gathered, and there was an air of anticipation. Denny heard sounds from beyond the square, shouts, screams, and the sound of people marching in step. Men on horseback appeared, wearing elaborate armor and plumed helmets. They were followed by a column of soldiers carrying spears and shields.

"Conquering heroes," Gamma said coolly. "Come to honor their deities for helping them defeat their foes. They're bringing home many captives."

Now Denny saw a group of tired, ragged men and women hemmed in by the troops. A few soldiers chivvied the prisoners along with spears, forced them to the steps of the temple. Denny had a sick feeling, knowing what would happen next.

By now, all the civilians were jostling for position. The most elaborately clad of the military leaders dismounted, then bowed to the waiting priests. The victorious general made a speech and drew his sword. One of the male captives was dragged forward, held so that his head hung over a large bronze bowl. Without further ceremony, the general decapitated the man. Blood gushed down the temple steps.

"Another brain for your kind to munch on?" Denny asked, disgusted. "How many heads do you guys need?"

"With at least one of us in every temple, in every city, we would need to keep your silly little wars going," Alpha replied. "As before, we take the guise of local gods. See!"

A towering figure emerged from the shadowy interior of the temple. Everyone, even the general, fell to their knees, foreheads in the dust. The Interloper was in the form of a half-man, half-reptile, complete with alligator-like jaws. It was at least eight feet tall, Denny estimated, and hugely muscular. The creature strode forward, picked the severed head from the sacrificial bowl, and cracked it between its jaws like a walnut. Brains and gore slathered down the enormous body. In a few moments, the Interloper was satisfied, and retreated into its lair.

"This is your idea of civilization?" Denny said in disgust.

"Is it so very different from yours?" Beta challenged. "Many thousands of innocents die in the name of some higher purpose every day – you have so many causes to kill for, along with many good reasons to let your fellow humans perish. Under our system, the numbers would be far smaller."

"That doesn't win you any points with me," Denny spat.

"Very well," said Alpha.

The city, the temple, the splashes of blood and tissue, all vanished.

"You are not satisfied with simple worlds," Alpha went on, gesturing at a featureless black void, "you want to see another possibility?"

***

"Denny?"

Frankie reached out, hesitantly, and laid a hand on her friend's shoulder. Denny's hand was still clutching Zoffany's. Normally such a scan took a second or two, but nearly a minute had passed. Denny and Zoffany were both motionless, staring blankly. A trickle of drool ran down the biologist's chin.

Some kind of trance, Frankie thought. *Maybe they're in some kind of feedback loop, trapped in each other's minds?*

"This is not good," Gould lectured. "We should separate them."

Zoffany slumped over as soon as the link was broken. After some shouting and confusion, the scientist was put on a stretcher and taken to the sick bay. It took a few minutes for Denny to recover. Then she started talking so fast Frankie had trouble keeping up. She begged her friend to slow down, form thoughts, speak clearly.

"I've seen what they want to do with us," Denny said. "They're going to wipe out most of us, enslave the rest. God, it's horrifying!"

"What? What's their plan?" Frankie demanded.

"They tricked Zoffany," Denny said, grabbing Frankie by the arm. Frankie tried not to flinch at the unaccustomed contact. "They played her. She's carrying a virus. Quarantine her now, and get the medical team on the case. You've got to tackle this quickly, or it will spread."

Collier was quick to respond, and Zoffany was soon in quarantine. The security chief also demanded answers and Denny tried to provide them. She struggled to explain how she had linked with the three Queens. But she was on firmer ground when she stressed that Zoffany had been an unwitting Interloper pawn. Gould, meanwhile, was only just beginning to grasp the implications of the altered virus.

"They took the world's leading expert on their biology and turned her knowledge against us," Gould said, staring wide-eyed at Denny. "With Harriet on board, literally, they could be sure their virus would spare them. Bloody clever."

"Typhoid Mary, that was a good analogy," agreed Denny. "But the disease she's carrying will kill humans, or most of them. Wiping out ninety percent of our species and taking down our high-tech civilization is the Lopers' best chance."

Collier looked skeptical.

"Biological warfare? That's for disaster movies," he said. "There are so many measures in place–"

"And half the guys who are supposed to oversee those measures are now dead," Gould cut in. "Don't you see? This is the Interloper end game! They damaged our capacity to fight a pandemic, then started one."

"How many people might she have infected already?" Denny demanded.

Now Collier looked horrified.

"They had no reason to suspect infection," he whispered. "She was passed from the harbormaster to the police, then taken to a doctor for examination. They brought her down by chopper, so there's the pilot, then the detail that brought her from the airport."

"Don't tell us, tell them!" Frankie urged. "Come on, Ben, we need to lock this place down, and isolate everyone who might be carrying the virus. Starting with us."

They made their way upstairs to a small emergency control room, already crowded with Tania and her Intel team. As soon as she saw the main monitor screen, Denny knew it was too late. There were more 'terrorist attacks', again killing government officials and other senior figures.

"Too much news," Tania said, looking stressed and confused. "Reports coming in from all over this country, and other parts of Europe. It's not clear exactly what – oh, God, what now?"

The screens had gone blank. NO INTERNET CONNECTION messages flashed up. Tania's people went into a collective meltdown, while Frankie checked her phone. She had no service. Looking around, she saw Gould and Collier were in the same boat.

"They cut off our communications, somehow," Collier said. "Just when we need them most."

"Switzerland," said Gould. "Remember, Tania? That German we suspected of being replaced headed for Switzerland. In Zurich, there's a global internet node – vital, and probably quite vulnerable to Interlopers. There's one in London, too. The redundancy that makes the system resilient. But if they've hit several key points at the same time, it will mean total gridlock."

"And mass panic," added Frankie. "People will just complain when they can't get stuff on their phones, but when they realize it's nationwide, they'll start looting, rioting, all the usual stuff caused by the usual suspects."

Collier stared at her, then rushed out of the room without another word.

"He has a wife and kids," Tania said. "Most of us have families."

Crap, Frankie thought. *But he'd have worked it out himself in a minute or so.*

"Okay, most people here will want to go help their loved ones," she pointed out. "But if anyone leaves, they'll risk spreading the virus, making the Lopers' job easier."

"We've only gotten very flimsy evidence that there *is* a virus," Tania responded, already heading for the door. "Nobody has died yet. And yes, I am going to my kids, and nobody's going to stop me. Everything that's happened today proves this organization is finished."

Frankie held up her hands and stepped aside as Tania's move signaled a general exodus. Soon all the agents had fled, leaving Frankie alone with Denny and Gould.

"To be honest," Gould said, "locking the place down was never an option. Not after what happened to Matheson. Morale was obviously shot to buggery."

"So what do we do?" Frankie asked. "Sit here and wait till we develop boils, or however this plague works?"

Gould hesitated.

"I don't want to leave Harriet," he said finally. "I'm going down to the sick bay. She might be able to tell us something useful now."

Frankie thought that unlikely, but did not want to crush Gould's hopes.

"Okay," she said. "But let's arm ourselves. And yeah, I know, you don't know how to fire a gun, British guy. I do, so let's find one."

***

Nightmare Rising

Tania da Silva abandoned her car about a mile from Task Force headquarters. She had tried to make it out of central London by road. She cursed her naivety as she grabbed her bag, locked her BMW, and joined the throng on the sidewalk. People seemed to be heading for the nearest Underground station, but Tania reasoned that the network would be overwhelmed soon, if it wasn't already.

No, she thought. *I'm going to walk out of the heart of the city, then see if I can get a cab to the suburbs.*

It was a cold, sunny day in early spring, and Tania was wearing flats. She calculated that it might take her an hour and a half to get out of the roiling mass of confused humanity. It did occur to her that things might not be better in the suburbs, but pushed the thought aside. She tried her phone again, but cell service was still down.

Sabotage by the spawn was far more effective than we ever anticipated.

Tania had a pepper spray in her bag, a brown belt in Tai Kwon Do, and a determined attitude. She felt reasonably confident as she navigated the crowded pavement, dodged between stationary vehicles, and kept an eye out for troublemakers. On one occasion, she saw a gang of youths fighting police, and on a couple of occasions, she heard shots fired in the distance. But in general, people seemed more excited or annoyed than actually panicked or angry.

Score one for the British stiff upper lip, she thought.

After nearly two hours, she had reached the edge of the historic City of London. Behind her lay the various royal palaces, the Tower of London, and the heart of government. Ahead of her was the way home. She thought of her children, her husband, and their pleasant house in its quiet, leafy avenue. Every few minutes she tried her phone, cursing when it failed. But then she caught sight of something in a side street that gave her hope.

The old-style public phone booth was one of a handful still left in London. Tania was surprised to see that there was no queue waiting to use it. Then she reasoned that most people were so used to cell coverage that using an old-style landline would not occur to them. She raced forward, pulled open the door, and slammed it behind her. The phone was modern enough to take cards, and she started to search for hers.

Where is everybody?

The thought was unwelcome, but hard to ignore. She looked around, peering through the small glass panes. Not a single human being was in sight. Yet only a few minutes earlier she had been dodging through a confused throng. She had somehow ventured off the main drag, away from any hope of help. She waited for someone to appear, but not a single pedestrian walked into view. Then a car sped by, screeching as it turned the corner.

Means nothing, she told herself. *Just make the call.*

She slid her Visa into the slot and punched out her home number. The phone began to ring, the purring sound slowly becoming maddening as she waited. Then she heard her own voice, startlingly clear.

'Hello! You've reached Tania, Roj, Mabel, and Jake. We can't come to the phone right now, but if you–'

She hung up, trying to suppress dark fears. There was an ad for a taxi company in the booth, but when she tried it, she ended up in a queue. Tania slammed the handset down, fumbled the door open, and tried to reorient herself. It occurred to her that getting a cab without a working phone would not be easy. She looked at the houses lining the quiet cul-de-sac, and wondered if she should simply knock on someone's door to ask for help.

If somebody did that to me, I'd pretend not to be in, she thought, ruefully. *So much for community spirit.*

A scream split the cold air, making her jump and retreat toward the phone box. The noise seemed to come from nearby. Tania took out her pepper spray, and continued to back away, out of the side street. Then a figure burst out of one of the gardens and fell into the road. It was small, dressed in pale clothing, with bloody wounds on its back.

A child, she thought, feeling sick with shock and fear, *it might be Code Nines hunting a child!*

The small figure got up, turned a round face in Tania's direction. It was a little girl, her corn-colored hair held back by an Alice band, eyes wide with fear. The child was crying. The girl wailed when she saw Tania, an inarticulate noise, but still eloquent.

"Come on!" Tania shouted, taking a few steps forward. "Come to me! I'll keep you safe!"

The girl hesitated, glanced behind her, then started toward Tania at a limping run. As the child got closer, Tania saw a jagged wound on one leg, oozing dark blood. Then two more figures appeared, adults this time. Both men were carrying improvised weapons, and were red-faced with exertion. One pointed and shouted, raising what Tania thought was a machete. The second man, fatter and slower, was carrying a massive hammer.

Tania grabbed the girl's hand and dragged her along toward the main road. She heard the men shouting, could not make out the words. All she knew was that the girl looked a lot like Mabel, if Mabel had been a little younger, and dressed in more old-fashioned clothes. She snatched the girl up and ran, surprised by her own speed and strength. Glancing back, Tania saw they had widened the gap, and within another minute, they had lost sight of the men completely.

"All we need to do is find a police officer," she gasped, her lungs burning. "Then you'll be safe."

Tania put the little girl down, holding out her hand to hold. The girl looked up at her blankly. Tania wondered why she had not noticed before how dark the child's eyes were, and how pale her skin.

Oh, God, she thought, terror seizing her.

"Thanks, Tania," said the Interloper. "I got plenty of useful data while we were running. Now I can finish you."

The monster crouched, gathering itself for a spring, its human features melting away. Tania struck out, hitting the small creature on the side of the head, and sent it staggering sideways. When the Interloper came at her again, she had her pepper spray, and the noxious fluid caused the creature to screech and put its paws over its tiny eyes. Tania turned to run, and saw the two men heading straight at her. She felt immense relief, but it did not last. The Interloper had recovered, moved fast, and leaped onto her shoulders. She landed heavily, struggled to roll over onto her assailant, tried to tear the vicious talons away from her throat.

As she battled for survival, Tania saw the two vigilantes approaching, hoped they would prove a match for the monster. Sure enough, the Interloper screamed as the machete came down. Tania felt the impact of the blow, then a much more severe impact. The creature stopped moving, and she rolled over to see that its head had been bashed in.

People aren't so bad, she thought. *Here I was imagining widespread mayhem, crazy behavior.*

"Thanks, guys," she said, looking up at the panting men. "Sorry, totally misread the situation back there. Do you have a First Aid kit? I've got a couple of scratches on my neck."

The men looked at each other, then down at her.

"Too late," said the fat one. "It broke skin. She might be infected."

The other man nodded, raised his machete.

"What?" Tania shouted. "What do you mean? It's not like a zombie movie, you don't turn into one if they bite you! That's not what's happening here! Believe me, I know, I work for the government, you've got to believe me—"

She was still protesting when the blade came down.

Nightmare Rising

Chapter 10: Desperation

A handful of Task Force scientists and medics had stayed at their posts.

Zoffany was inside a plastic bubble, all her air processed, filtered, recycled. An intravenous line kept her heavily sedated. While Gould was checking on her, Collier and Frankie went to the arsenal and distributed weapons. Then they made the Task Force canteen their temporary headquarters. As Denny pointed out, at least it had plenty of food and water.

"Hey, check this out," said Frankie, as they were grabbing something to eat.

The regular television in the canteen was carrying something called the Emergency Broadcast Network. An announcer, his face and voice familiar from BBC news bulletins, was saying something about a major crisis, and 'staged evacuation of London and other urban areas'.

"They're not mentioning disease," Gould observed, "but people must be able to figure that out."

"What about foreign governments, media?" Frankie asked. "Is anyone offering to help? Or trying to exploit the crisis in some way?"

She looked around at blank faces, then recalled hearing pop music in the canteen sometimes. She went over to the counter and looked behind it. Sure enough, there was a small digital radio on a shelf. Frankie picked it up, turned it on. It was set to BBC Radio Two, which she knew generally broadcasted classic pop interspersed with news. Now it was simply replaying a recorded message.

'... *advised to wait for instructions from civil defense authorities. Do not panic, do not hoard food and water, do not go to National Health Service facilities unless you are seriously ill...*'

Frankie took the radio back to the table, switched from digital to analog and started to search wavebands. Sure enough, there was chatter from foreign media. The first voice she heard sounded Dutch, which nobody understood. Then came an accented voice speaking in good English.

'... international flights canceled, all European airports closed for the duration of the emergency. The situation in London remains unclear, and reports of further outbreaks around the world are so far unconfirmed. The nature of the virus continues to be a subject debate, with some claiming...'

"The Lopers have done a number on our entire global civilization, and they did it on a deadline, to a budget," Frankie said, switching off the radio. "You could almost admire the bastards' work ethic."

"So what do we do?" Collier asked, between mouthfuls of survival rations. "Sit here and guard a half-empty building? Or go out and risk getting killed?"

"If any of us are infected," Gould said grimly, "where we go doesn't' matter much. But, as Tania said, we can't be sure how lethal this putative virus might be."

Denny thought of the way Gould had hugged Zoffany close when she had arrived just a few hours ago.

"Do we know how the virus is spread?" she asked.

"Airborne, according to Harriet," Gould replied. "Like flu, or the common cold."

"How long before symptoms appear?" Denny continued. "Hours, days?"

Gould looked at Zoffany, lying pale and motionless inside her bubble.

"Ted?" Denny asked, suddenly anxious.

Gould looked at her and shrugged.

"Based on my own symptoms, I'd say hours," he said. "I'm experiencing some disorientation, elevated temperature. Like a bout of flu coming on."

Before he had finished speaking, bio-suited medics were supporting him, leading him to a chair.

"It's started," Frankie said, resignedly, as they watched Gould having blood drawn and swabs taken. "I don't see what we can do. Guess I should stay here and wait to see if I'll get it."

Denny nodded, not trusting herself to speak. She had not told Frankie about the visions shown to her by the Interloper Queens. The third vision she had only glimpsed, before the contact had been broken. But, judging by the little she had seen, the third possibility was the worst of all.

And it could be the most likely future for this world.

"Okay," Denny said, raising her voice. "We need to do a whole lot of things. First, help find some counter to this virus. I can get to Zoffany's memories, her knowledge, try and convey stuff to the team here. Then there's locating the Queens, helping the authorities track them down. There can't be that many Lopers. Killing them all is possible. They can't kill all of us."

The medics and researchers did not demur, but she noticed a few sidelong glances. The biohazard team was busy putting Gould into a sealed bubble. A group of scientists and lab techs were gazing at Denny. Their expressions might have been hard to read. But they were only a few feet away, and Denny could sense their hesitancy.

They want to make a difference, and they don't mind me taking charge, she thought. *But they know what I am. Or at least, they think they know. Now's not the time to tell them the whole truth.*

"True," Frankie said. "We still have numbers on our side, and firepower. But the Queens could be anywhere. How can we track them down?"

Denny thought for a moment, then shook her head.

"They might not be just anywhere – their powers don't have unlimited range," she pointed out. "Cassandra's influence extended over a few miles, maybe a little more. So, if any Lopers are attacking London, there must be at least one Queen in the capital, now."

This theory did not thrill the Task Force personnel. Denny could sense several becoming more anxious about their families. She wanted desperately to be more imposing, more leader-like. Without thinking, she felt the odd sense of displacement as her body adjusted. She had grown taller by at least an inch, and she felt her features had become harder, nobler.

"We can beat this, if we work together," she declared. "Millions of people need us. More importantly, there are scientists around the world who need to know what we know, so they can help crack the virus, develop some kind of countermeasures. So, everyone who isn't working on the disease, please find ways to communicate what we know, and what we'll know very soon."

One technician raised her hand.

"There's a special government comms system," she said. "Buried cables, designed to keep NATO working in the event of a nuclear attack."

"Glad you're on board," Denny said, with a brief smile. "Tap into that, find someone in authority who sounds smart, get them up to speed. Anyone got any questions?"

There were none, and the motley band of experts was soon busy with various tasks. Denny and Frankie went over to Gould, in part simply to try and reassure him. But when Denny began to ask the physicist about specific matters, he could not answer clearly. Gould had become delirious. Formby, the doctor in charge, explained that antiviral drugs were in short supply. Yet the drugs represented their only hope of arresting the progress of the disease.

"Where do we get more?" Denny asked. "No, of course we can't go outside and risk spreading the damn virus. And I'm guessing nobody could bring them to us, not with central London gridlocked."

She paused, a thought occurring to her.

"Hey," she said quietly to the doctor. "Suppose a person had a natural immunity to the virus? Could that be useful?"

"Absolutely!" Formby replied, then realization dawned. "Oh, you mean – you think you might – because of your symbiont?"

"Doc," Denny said, leading the medic to one side. "I'm pretty sure they don't want to kill controlled humans. Something the symbionts put into your system must provide protection. Could you find it in time?"

At that, the doctor shook her head decisively.

"The biochemistry is far too complex," the woman said. "It would be the most reckless experiment imaginable."

Denny sensed despair, a bleak fatalism that blossomed inside the doctor's mind like a dark flower. It was chilling, and Denny knew she had to offer some hope right now. A shocking thought came to her.

"Okay," she said. "Use that biochemistry. We retrieved some symbiont eggs from Cassandra's island, and from the factory in Fordham. They're in cold storage, right? Use them."

The doctor turned to look at Gould in his sterile bubble. The scientist was unconscious, now, his face ghastly pale, his breathing loud and labored.

"That would be massively unethical."

"I know," Denny said urgently. "Believe me, I know that in every molecule of my being. But what else have we got?"

***

Ben Collier did not waste time trying to drive through central London. He guessed rightly that the roads would soon be gridlocked. Instead, he went to his car, got out his gym gear, and set off at a brisk jog through the streets. He planned to get out of the congested, chaotic heart of the city, and either hire, commandeer, or simply steal a vehicle further out. It was a vague plan, but it was all he had.

He tried not to think of his wife and children. He had always striven to keep their world separate from his. Now that barrier had come crashing down. The job had expanded to become his entire world, because the Code Nines were now an immediate threat to everything that mattered.

But I know more about them than most, he told himself, as he dodged between abandoned vehicles. *I've got knowledge, and knowledge is power. I can protect my loved ones. I can do this.*

As Collier jogged along, switching from road to sidewalk and back as suited, he tried to gauge the mood of the people he passed. At first, he saw confusion and dismay, as dozens simply stared at their phones, unable to believe there was no signal. Then he noticed anger, resentment, heard raised voices. Snatches of conversation told him people were variously blaming terrorists, foreign powers, even alien invaders.

Well, he thought, *they're half-right.*

He was passing through the Camden area when he heard the first gunshots. Collier instinctively dodged into cover and assessed the threat. The shots had been fired by a handgun, he decided. Sound carried deceptively amid tall buildings, but he was sure the shooter had not been close.

Gangsters, he thought. *Some little toe rag settling a score, maybe, knowing the police have got their hands full.*

As he set off again, he recalled that he had seen only a handful of police so far, and all were standing by cars stuck in the city-wide jam. Collier reflected that everyone had been taken by surprise. Soon real panic would set in. He glimpsed a small child, crying, being dragged along by an impatient adult. He thought of all the children in the capital, seeing their world totter.

Got to think of my own kids first.

"Excuse me!"

Collier slowed, almost stopped. A gray-haired man pushing a frail-looking woman in a wheelchair was waving urgently at him.

"My wife, please help, she is very ill, she needs—"

But Collier, hardening his heart, had already sped up. He never heard what the sick woman needed. He doubted he ever would. A few moments later, he turned into a street where the looting had begun. He nearly collided with a couple of youths carrying a huge TV. Collier swerved and turned into a side street, glad he had abandoned his quasi-military Task Force gear.

Central London was behind him now, and he began to look around for transport. One of his Special Forces skills was breaking into and stealing cars. But the roads were still useless, so he continued jogging. Then he saw several bicycles chained to a rack outside a London University building. His car thief's tools were easily adapted to bike theft. Within a minute, he was cycling north.

Twenty minutes later, he was nearing his own neighborhood when a car swerved around the corner and nearly hit him. He was so shocked, and so busy dodging the hatchback, that he did not recognize it at first. It was his wife's car, heading south.

Susie decided to come to me, he thought. *God, I hope she brought the girls.*

He discarded his bike and ran after the car, waving his arms. The little Honda was already stopping, and now that he was closer, Collier could see two small faces looking out of the rear window. He ran to the car, wrenched open the front passenger door, and started to get in.

"Oh, God, darling, I was so—"

Collier broke off, staring in bafflement. It was not Susie in the driver's seat. It was a strange man, someone Collier did not recognize at first. He took in the man's slightly humorous expression, the untidy hair, the round, undershot jaw, the day's growth of beard. Then he saw the small scar just above the left eyebrow, and recognized the clothes the driver wore. The truth dawned. The face looking back at Collier was his own.

"Hi Ben," said the Code Nine. "We were just coming to get you. Nice of you to meet us halfway."

Collier hesitated just a moment before he tried to get out and slam the door. But already the diminutive figures in the back seat had leaped forward, fastening eager talons on his shirt, his flesh, his scalp. As he tried to beat off his attackers in the too-confined space, he saw the faces of his children already fading, like all his hopes.

***

Formby, the acting chief medic, had second thoughts about using symbionts several times. On each occasion, Denny, with Frankie's support, had talked her round again. Eventually, Formby and her team had a small, dark egg ready. What remained was to put it inside Gould's sealed bubble. The scientist, now delirious, could not understand what was happening. Denny took the egg and went through a small airlock, reasoning no harm could come to her from more exposure to the virus.

"Desperate times need desperate measures, Ted," Denny said, as she turned Gould over onto his side. "That's a British saying, isn't it?"

"Denny?" Gould asked weakly. "What are you doing?"

"Trying to save your life," she replied, trying to sound confident. "It's a wacky experiment, you'll love it."

"Wacky is not a recognized term in physics," Gould grumbled. "Why are you taking my shirt off? I am a married man. Well, not married, but Harriet and I have talked about it–"

"Hope you've got me and Frankie down as maids of honor," Denny put in, keen to distract him from what she was doing. "I just love frilly pink dresses, preferably with puffed sleeves."

Gould laughed at that, but then went into a paroxysm of coughing. Denny saw specks of blood spot his pillow. She positioned the egg next to Gould's back. She could already sense the stirring of the creature within. Though the entity was almost mindless, it could still sense the presence of a human organism. It had been genetically programmed to perform one task. Denny stepped back as the egg's leathery shell split. A gray-green, slug-like creature emerged, its eyeless forepart waving in the air.

This is obscene, she thought, surprised at her own revulsion. *Perhaps the Queens are right. Perhaps I am becoming a monster.*

The symbiont wriggled out of its shell with startling speed and clamped a row of suckers onto Gould's spine. The man quivered, moaned, reached around as if to try and swat the creature away. Denny grabbed Gould's arm, easily holding it back as the symbiont nestled into place.

Is he really weak now, she wondered as she gazed at the creature nestling into place, *or am I getting stronger?*

The creature pulsed, and Denny felt a wave of crude, animal pleasure radiate from the rudimentary nervous system. The symbiont was fully attached. There was no obvious change to Gould's condition, except that he stopped moaning and struggling. Now he lay very still, his breathing regular, wheezing slightly.

An intercom squealed, startling Denny.

"His vitals are unchanged," called Formby, her voice distorted by a small speaker above Gould's cot. "But we wouldn't expect an instant cure. It could be that once a person contracts the virus, nothing can reverse the process."

Denny resisted the urge to yell a rebuke at the doctor, knowing the woman was struggling in almost impossible conditions. Instead, she leaned over Gould, put a hand to his perspiring forehead. The contact brought a flood of suffering, as she stared at his mental state. He was in pain, an ache that seemed to embrace his entire body. Delirium brought Gould hallucinations, so that Denny glimpsed herself as an Interloper, complete with beady eyes and horrendous fangs.

Part of him sees me as inhuman, she realized. *He can't help feeling like that. Maybe they all do.*

"Okay," she called to Formby, "I'm going to come out, no point in me waiting around if it's going to take–"

She stopped, peered at the symbiont. The creature was writhing, rippling, the slimy body apparently trying to break free. At the same time, Gould gave a gasp, and Denny sensed his pain grow intense, unbearable. Then he lost consciousness, while Formby started shouting at her team. Medical alarms sounded, but were swiftly silenced. Denny gathered that Gould was suffering some kind of heart problem, that some kind of injection was needed.

"What is it?" she shouted through the plastic. "What should I do?"

The medical team were too busy to answer, or too panicked. Formby was fixing the headpiece of her biohazard suit in place, ready to enter the bubble. Denny looked down at Gould, the man who had unwittingly set her on the road that led to this moment. He was gray-faced, wheezing, dying, and she had only one crazy idea as to how to save him.

"Ted," she said, grabbing one of his hands in both of hers. "Ted, I won't let you go."

This time she went deep, not merely skimming the surface of Gould's mind but delving into the essence of his being. It was a world in chaos, fragments of the scientist's life drifting like icebergs of random thought, disconnected from any thread of experience. The most important moments in his life were, naturally, the most prominent. Denny saw Gould's childhood juxtaposed with his time as a student, his feelings for Zoffany mixed up with the terrible loss of his sister, Lucy. She looked for something positive, a way to make Gould fight for his life. She focused on Lucy, but Gould's memories of her were tainted by boyhood guilt over her abduction.

Come on Ted, she urged, trying to send the thought into his mind. *We can do this. We can find you something to live for.*

Suddenly she became aware of another mind, a presence all too familiar. It was Gamma, the Interloper observing the man's struggle for life with mild interest. Denny realized that the symbiont had finally formed its link with the hive, connecting Gould's mind with his would-be controllers.

'Clever trick,' Gamma said in Denny's mind. 'One of your human experiments, I assume?'

Denny tried to lash out at the creature, push the alien mind away from Gould's. The burst of anger seemed to surprise Gamma, and Denny felt the inhuman consciousness retreat. At the same time, thoughts began to cohere in Gould's mind. Denny saw images flash by, all of the encounters with the Interlopers. Gould was suddenly focused on the enemy, the beings he had always hated and feared.

Well done, Gamma, Denny thought. *You reminded him of something worth living for. Wiping out you guys.*

She sensed Ted's pain diminishing, his mental confusion replaced by a steely focus. The scientist's mind was returning to something like normal. Thoughts and memories were no longer adrift, confused, but cohering into a view of the world that made sense. Denny let go of Gould's hand and suddenly became aware of Formby saying something about 'condition stabilized'.

"I think we got this, Ted," she whispered. "But this next bit won't be pleasant. I'm sorry, I have to do this."

She had already found the right memory in Gould's mind, knew what he had done to her back on the isle of Holyhaven. The hasty act had saved Denny from enslavement by Cassandra. Now she picked up a Taser and held it at the upper end of the symbiont, rerunning in her mind the mutilation Gould had inflicted on a similar creature.

Almost mindless, she thought. *But not quite. Just enough of a brain to count.*

Taking a deep breath, she pushed the Taser against the symbiont's slimy tissue and pushed the button. The device gave its distinctive buzz, and Gould screamed, arching his back. Denny had to grab him to stop him from falling onto the floor.

At the same moment, she felt the intense psychic pain of the creature she had maimed.

Discarding the Taser, she held onto Gould as he writhed in pain, his nervous system flooded by the agony of the symbiont. After a few moments, Gould's mind seemed to cohere again, his familiar personality emerging from a mental fog of suffering. Denny searched for Gamma, for any Interloper mind observing Gould. There was nothing, so far as she could tell, beyond the man's own consciousness.

"Sorry, Ted," she said again. "But I think we did it."

Gould croaked something, his eyes still shut, lips barely moving. Denny leaned closer, asked him to repeat the words.

"They must ... be ... close."

For a moment, she did not understand. Then Denny cursed loudly. Gould, in his pain and confusion, had spotted something obvious that she had missed. She looked over at Frankie, who was standing close by the other side of the sterile plastic wall.

"God, I'm such an idiot!" she shouted. "They must be in London. We can still beat them."

After she left Gould's bubble, Denny explained to the team what she meant.

"I sensed all three of them, all the female Code Nines. Their powers have limited range, we know that. So they can't be far away. In London, certainly. That gives us a chance. If we can get to them and kill them, it would be game over."

Looking around at the medical team, Denny saw a mixture of enthusiasm and bafflement. She quashed rising frustration, knowing how tough keeping it together must be for the motley group.

"I get it," said Frankie. "But London's a big place. Did you get any sense of where they might be? Is there any way to detect them?"

Denny looked over at Gould.

"Ted's detector works at short range," she mused. "He's improved it a lot, though. If we can bring him around—"

Doctor Formby started to protest, but Denny cut her short.

"I know, your patient, your rules," she said. "Just do your best, but remember – he is your superior, so if he orders you to let him out of that bubble, you'll pretty much have to."

Denny led Frankie out to the canteen where they could talk with fewer distractions. As they walked down the corridor, she noticed her friend looking up at her with a curious expression.

"You gonna stay like that, now?" Frankie finally asked.

There was a mirror behind the counter of the canteen. In it, Denny saw a taller, more imposing version of herself. Her jaw was firmer, suggesting greater determination. Her features in general, seemed harder.

"I didn't know," she said finally. "But I guess it's kind of externalizing how I feel."

"Cool," said Frankie, but Denny could sense it was not.

She feels I'm not the person she used to know, Denny thought. *And she's right.*

Denny turned up the volume on the TV. The emergency broadcast was now mentioning infection. A different announcer was trying to keep calm, advising people on ways to avoid catching 'an unspecified virus'. From talk of evacuation, the official line now was that people should stay in their homes and wait for help to reach them.

"Yeah, right," Frankie said. "They've lost it, I guess. London has fallen, or as good as."

They got something to eat and began to discuss ways to find Alpha, Beta, and Gamma. The first plan they formulated was to install one of Gould's detectors in a helicopter and fly low over the city.

"The only problem," Frankie concluded. "Is that we ain't got a chopper and nobody is going to give us one."

"Okay," Denny said, smiling ruefully, "what else have we got?"

Frankie toyed with the limp salad on her plate for a few moments before speaking.

"We've got a link to the Queens," she said. "Way you tell it, it's a two-way connection with no way for them to shut it off, right? So it's kind of like when the cops talk to a kidnapper, and then they analyze the background noise and say 'Yeah, he's near an airport, just under the flight path'. Could you do something like that?"

Denny saw what her friend was getting at. The thought of deliberately seeking to share the thoughts of the inhuman trio horrified her.

But that's why she thought of it, and I didn't, Denny thought. *It is obvious, a resource we should use.*

***

"If you won't let me out, bring my work to me," Gould ordered. "Get me a computer, at least. Connect me to the Task Force Intranet. Also, I need the emergency comms network – if we've got that?"

A technician gave a thumbs up gesture through the transparent plastic.

"Great," Gould said, pausing to cough, doubled over on his cot. "Do we have any security people at all? Any armed agents?"

This time there was no thumbs up. Formby shook her head.

"They all left, along with most of the Intel team," she explained. "Your people and mine – about half stayed."

Score one for science, Gould thought. *But it leaves us almost defenseless.*

He felt weak as a kitten, and his head was pounding. But he was eager to get to work. Connecting with Denny and Gamma had set his mind racing, despite his illness. He could feel his new, modified metabolism fighting off the virus, sharing the symbiont's instinctive desire to repair its host. He wondered if he, too, would be changed still more, perhaps become like Denny?

God, I hope not.

After taking a mouthful of water he lay back, almost exhausted by the simple exertion of raising the cup to his mouth. His brain, however, continued to work. If the Interlopers were in London, it meant they must have some purpose beyond merely causing chaos. The virus was enough for that.

So, what are they planning? Is there something we don't know?

A suited nurse appeared, carrying Gould's laptop to the airlock. His fingers twitched as he thought of the data he needed, the picture of events he had to build up. He glanced over at Zoffany, lying sedated, apparently serene in her own sterile bubble. He felt a pang of guilt at involving her in a field operation which had put her at risk.

Benefit of hindsight, he thought. *Also, classic case of mixing work with personal life. God, what a mess.*

The nurse plugged in his laptop and rested it on his lap. Gould thought the woman seemed stressed, her face pale and drawn inside her airtight suit. As the nurse went back into the airlock, he logged on and began to search through Zoffany's files. The biologist had speculated about the Interlopers at great length, trying to formulate a comprehensive theory of their social order as well as their bizarre physiology. Some of her ideas were fascinating, but he was soon struggling with basic terminology.

I can't concentrate on this, Gould thought after a few minutes. *I'm still too sick. Damn.*

He closed his eyes, leaned back, and began to drift off into a doze. Then a sharp pinging noise jerked him awake. An unfamiliar icon had appeared on the taskbar and was flashing at him. He clicked on it. It was a message from the government. The Home Secretary's office was keen to know what was happening, and what resources the Task Force might need to stop it.

Two excellent questions, he thought, as he began to slowly type a reply. He was just finishing when Denny and Frankie came back into the sick bay.

"Great news," he called, dismayed by his croaky voice, "we're back in touch with the politicians."

"The day just got better," replied Frankie.

Gould noticed Denny being assisted through the airlock into Zoffany's bubble. He looked a question at Frankie, who nodded.

"Yeah," she said. "Sorry, but Harriet's our direct line to the bad guys. Denny thinks she can get their location, maybe. It's a long shot, but we had to try it. Or rather, she did."

Gould stared at Denny as the woman stood over Zoffany. The young American TV presenter he had known was almost gone, now. Denny's face had matured, become almost timeless.

And this is after a few months, he thought. *What will she be like after years as a hybrid human-Interloper? Will she look human at all, unless she chooses to?*

Gould tried to suppress dark, disturbing thoughts. He wanted to return to his work, trying to find more worthwhile tasks for his political masters. But he could not tear his gaze from the other sealed bubble, as Denny stepped close to Zoffany, and laid one of her long, pale hands on the unconscious woman's forehead.

Nightmare Rising

Chapter 11: The Great Game

It took only a moment for Denny to find herself once more in the court of the Queens. Alpha, Beta, and Gamma sat facing her, expectant, their energy focused. Behind them, a strange vista swirled and rippled, as Denny struggled against the nightmare they sought to impose on her mind.

"Don't fight it," Alpha warned, with a hint of contempt. "You're not strong enough."

"No human could be," Beta added. "Not even a freak like you."

"Accept the vision," Gamma went on. "See the world we plan for your kind. Then choose your side. Time is short."

The shifting patterns of color settled, resolving into another cityscape. This one was not the scene of devastation Denny had been shown before. Nor was it like the primitive metropolis with its temple of false gods. Instead, she saw an industrial city, buildings blackened with smoke that also stained the air. She heard the pounding of machines, felt vibration through her feet.

The inhabitants were pale, unhealthy-looking people, dressed in drab clothes that looked uncomfortable and dirty. Denny thought of old photos of Victorian workers, people racked with tuberculosis, and malnutrition, poisoned by pollution. She looked up, saw huge iron gantries above her, thronged by more dispirited workers. The inhabitants were shuffling between dark towers that seemed to combine elements of the factory and the apartment block. Denny saw no smiles, heard no laughter. In fact, everyone seemed to be silent, as nobody was having a conversation. There was no sign of any stores, no hint of entertainment.

"What's this?" she demanded. "Some kind of hell on earth?"

"You rejected our previous suggestions," Alpha pointed out. "So we created something a little more like your modern society."

"We simply removed all the trimmings," Beta added. "The bits that make people feel free, in control. They are not needed."

"We'll be in control," Gamma said, with a hint of smugness.

A streetcar, rusty and rattling, moved past, sparks falling from the overhead power line. Suddenly a woman, her face contorted with despair, broke free from the horde on the sidewalk and hurled herself under the trolley's iron wheels. There were some desultory screams accompanied by an ear-splitting squeal of brakes. Denny looked away as the woman fell under the car, but had to look back. Most of the inhabitants were already walking away, with only a handful of bystanders gazing dully at the mess.

"Great," she said. "You want life to be meaningless for everyone. Quite an achievement."

"Not meaningless," Gamma chided her. "Merely grim and oppressive. But look! Here are some people with a sense of purpose."

A small van appeared, engine sputtering out a cloud of blue smoke. It pulled over and three blue-uniformed figures got out. These men were much more energetic than the citizens Denny had seen so far. She noticed that they seemed slightly hunchbacked and guessed they were controlled humans. They rushed over to the scene of the accident, shoving the gawkers aside, ordering them to 'go about their lawful business'.

"They speak English!" Denny exclaimed.

"Well, of course, they speak English," Alpha said. "This is London, after all."

Denny looked up, peering at the cityscape. A half-ruined, gray-flecked dome was just visible in the dirty haze. St Paul's Cathedral was barely recognizable. She looked back at the uniformed men, who were dragging the mangled remains of the woman out from under the streetcar. One took out a saw and began cutting open the victim's skull. Denny looked away again.

"Waste not, want not," Beta said coolly. "The brains were undamaged."

"Why?" Denny demanded, almost forgetting her purpose in coming to this vile no-place. "Why inflict this on anyone?"

"Population size," Gamma shot back. "The more basic societies we showed you could feed only a small number of people, therefore could only feed a small number of us. But technology, even if it is only steam-powered, can keep hundreds of millions alive on this planet. In such a society we could flourish, evolve more rapidly."

"What makes it particularly delightful," Beta added, "is that the most utopian human society will inevitably develop into an urban hellhole of some kind. It's in your nature to be cruel, oppressive, to exploit one another. So why wait?"

"We just have to take away some of your more dangerous toys," Alpha said. "And then we can have a nice, quiet utopia. Our utopia."

Denny sensed that something was being withheld, some other purpose that the trio was not going to reveal. She was tempted to try and snatch at it, mentally, but remembered her purpose. She lashed out at the grim vista, focusing all her energy on disrupting the Queens' possible future. The dark buildings, the shambling workers, froze and faded. Silence fell. But after a couple of seconds, the cityscape returned, the noise of machinery as loud as before.

"Really," Gamma said. "You think you're a match for all of us? You're as foolish as Doctor Zoffany."

Denny did not reply. She was still straining, inexpertly, to break through the Queens' well-crafted illusion. She tried a different ploy, imagining graphic deaths for each of the females. She pictured bullets ripping Alpha apart, an explosion shattering Beta's delicate frame, an incendiary bomb incinerating Gamma. She poured all her hatred of the Interlopers into the violent fantasy, and for a moment, it seemed to work. She felt her antagonists flinch, and caught a glimpse of blue sky, light-colored structures, dense crowds in bright clothes.

Of course! Denny thought. *How dumb not to guess it straight away.*

She sensed anger, dismay from her enemies, and pulled back from the contact. She knew where the enemy was.

And it was too late.

***

"Collier's back!" said Formby.

Gould looked up, surprised. The security chief had left so quickly he had assumed the man would be home by now.

Or dead, he thought grimly. *But if he's back, he could be a lot of help.*

"Where is he?" Gould asked.

"Stuck at the main entrance," Formby explained. "Security lockdown. We need your code to let him in."

Gould gazed dumbly at his laptop, wondering if he could remember the relevant code. He had once had a superb memory for detail, but now his mind was woolly, struggling with problems he would once have regarded as trivial. He was aware of medics watching him, and played for time, calling up the video feed from the security cameras.

Sure enough, he's there.

Gould saw Collier's round face peering up into the camera, then glancing behind him. The man seemed nervous, his eyes wide, stepping from one foot to another, pushing at the door buzzer impatiently. Gould wondered if the agent had had a change of heart, or simply been unable to escape the heart of the old city.

Either way, I must let him in.

He remembered three of the four numbers of the code needed to end the lockdown.

"Gould?" Formby said, voice small in the speaker above his head. "He could be in danger right now."

"I know!" Gould snarled. "Don't you have clearance to let him in?"

That silenced the doctor, but he could still not remember the last digit. Frustrated, he jabbed at the camera controls, wondering if Collier was at risk. It seemed as if there was nobody in the street behind the agent.

No, there is somebody, Gould thought. *Lurking around that corner.*

As he watched, two small figures appeared, forms that an ordinary person might have mistaken for children. But their swift, stealthy movement, their pale features, the way their arms hung low, told him what they were. He clicked on the security interface and speedily punched in the first three digits, hoping muscle memory would find the fourth.

LOCKDOWN DISCONTINUED

Gould leaned back, sighing, and there was a small cheer from the onlookers. When he looked back at the screen the Interlopers were rushing forward. Now Gould could see some other shapes, moving too quickly to count.

Close the door after you, Collier, he thought, feeling sudden panic. *For God's sake.*

He moved the camera down, saw the first of the child-sized creatures vanish from view. It could only have come into the Task Force building. Too late, Gould remembered that he could restore the lockdown with the same code. By the time he had punched it in, at least half a dozen Interlopers had rushed by the camera.

"They're coming in!" he shouted.

"I know," said Denny's voice.

Gould looked up to see the American standing over Zoffany, gazing across at him.

"They were coming here all the time," Denny went on. "We represent the biggest threat to them. Of course, they want to deal with us. That's why they came to London."

The being Gould had thought was Collier burst into the sickbay. Doctor Formby and her team retreated, most of them cowering against the far wall. The Collier-face was already ill-defined, flowing like fleshy dough. There was a shot, and a hole appeared in the pale forehead. The creature fell face forward, frozen halfway in transformation.

Frankie was aiming a pistol, firing again. But Gould could see the attackers were moving fast, and too numerous for her to deal with on her own.

***

Denny realized what was happening a few moments before Gould. She moved quickly to leave Zoffany's biohazard bubble, and was just emerging from the airlock when Frankie was overwhelmed by three smaller Interlopers. For a moment, Denny feared for her friend, but the creatures showed no desire to kill Frankie. Instead, they dragged her upright and held her.

Denny darted sideways to the sickbay's inner door, which connected to the main office via a short passage.

She had just reached the doorway when Alpha appeared.

Seeing the female in real life for the first time, Denny was struck by how young and fragile the creature looked. But there was nothing weak about Alpha's expression as she examined the captive humans.

"No resistance," she said clearly to the medical team. "Do as you are told and you won't be harmed."

Beta and Gamma both appeared and stood just behind their older sibling. Denny assessed the intruders' strength. All of the fighters the Queens had brought were not yet fully grown. The fake Collier had been the only one that could have masqueraded as an adult male. But there were six juveniles. All the youngsters were in their true, horrendous form, wielding fearsome teeth and talons.

Don't like those odds, Denny thought.

"Denny, now is the time for you to choose," said Alpha. "Your human world totters. Join us, help us. We will not harm you. Humans would."

The three females radiated psychic energy, their mental force suddenly focused on Denny. She felt her will weakening as the Queens filled her with yearning to belong, coupled with distrust and fear of the human race. Visions of persecution and torment filled her mind. She saw herself in a padded cell, fastened to a steel chair, white-coated figures conducting tests. She felt the sting of a hypodermic, saw scientists cutting open her sedated body.

"They might dissect you," Beta warned. "To find out what makes you tick."

Denny reeled, groping behind her for the door handle. More horrific images, false memories tailored to her worst fears, almost overwhelmed her. She looked down and saw her belly bulging, realized she was pregnant. Masked nurses held her down while a doctor slit her open, removing by Caesarean something that was not a human child. The bloody thing squalled, its mouth a mass of fangs, its already open eyes tiny and black.

"They might use you as breeding stock," Gamma said. "To create a new race of slave-soldiers. Just imagine the damage your offspring could do, the oppression, misery, and injustice they could enforce for one human regime or another."

Denny felt the cold metal of the door handle, shoved it down, and felt the door give behind her. She fell out of the room as two small Lopers darted forward. Denny managed to slam the door against the pursuers. The Queens sent more nightmare images, this time showing Denny transformed into a Loper breeding female. Her lower torso was massive, a shapeless bulk of semi-transparent tissues. This time white coated tormentors were coaxing eggs from her, inserting probes and stimulators into her body to boost fertility.

"Or you could become just like us," Alpha hissed.

"No!" she shouted.

She stumbled down the passageway, crashing into the door of the office. For a moment she was afraid it was locked, but then it yielded and she was inside the big, open-plan space. The desks and chairs were still arranged around the walls, with Gould's experimental gear occupying most of the room. She ran to the power supply and switched it on, then snatched up the laptop Gould had used.

I can remember what he did, she told herself. *I was in his mind, I gathered his thoughts, I remember doing this as Ted. Now I'll do it as me.*

The mental pressure from the Queens had dwindled, but now four Interlopers had entered the room. They formed a rough arc in front of her and began to advance. She knew that they could not kill their own kind, but was sure they could grapple her to the ground and hold her.

"Stay back!" she warned, jabbing at the laptop screen.

There was a low hum from Gould's equipment, and the Lopers paused for a moment. But they did not hesitate for long, and soon they were within a couple of yards. Denny struggled with Gould's memories, increased the power, hoped she had not overloaded the system. A slight ripple in the air appeared in the center of the room.

"Look!" she said, pointing.

Surprisingly, all four creatures did turn to look. Then they froze, gazing at the shimmering sphere. Denny felt their fascination, and their fear.

Portals are scary for them, too, she thought. *Makes sense.*

"Okay," she said, putting down the laptop. "That's my ride, kind of."

The Interlopers reacted too slowly to stop her as she ran a couple of paces and then leaped straight at the portal. She closed her eyes just before she crossed the edge of the sphere. Instantly all trace of the three Queens' mental influence vanished, turned off like a light. She braced herself for impact, expecting to hit ground of some sort.

After a couple of seconds, she felt herself still falling.

***

Denny opened her eyes and saw a pearly radiance that seemed to come from everywhere at once. She was weightless, and felt her stomach lurch as she flailed in the colorless void.

Well, I escaped, she thought. *Now all I have to do is un-escape, somehow.*

She waited, turning slowly in the bright nothingness. She had gambled everything on a hunch, an educated guess based on all Gould's theories about the Nomads and their attitude to other life-forms.

If I'm right, they can't just ignore me. If I'm wrong, they might just kill me.

"Well, well, who have we here?"

Trent made a little tent of his plump hands, balanced his chin on his fingertips. He was sitting at one end of a long conference table. Denny was seated halfway along. She glanced around in surprise, saw another figure at the opposite end to Trent. She recognized the lank, cadaverous form of Benson. The room, she realized, was the conference chamber of the Romola Foundation, where Benson had tampered with Gould's mind.

"A nuisance," Benson said, evidently answering Trent.

"No," said Denny. "A piece that has moved off the board."

Trent adopted his familiar look of boyish enthusiasm.

"She is right, you must admit, my friend," he said.

Benson inclined his head slowly in a lugubrious nod.

"Yes," he admitted in his sepulchral voice. "But only because you were sloppy. You made a false move. You revealed our existence. You know what the rules say about that."

For the first time, Trent's face lost its cheerful expression.

"No!" he protested. "This game must go on. We can't stop now. Think of the concatenation, of how many other games would be affected—"

Trent paused and peered at Denny.

"We could simply remove this particular piece," he said. "Replace it with something more conventional – a regular human, without any of these odd hybrid qualities."

Benson shook his head decisively.

"Too late," he declared. "This unit is entangled in the timelines of hundreds, if not thousands, of others. We were both remiss in not foreseeing her bizarre conduct. We have no choice but to end the game."

"It's not a goddam game!" Denny yelled, leaping to her feet and bringing both hands down flat on the table. She cursed out the Nomads, spewing obscenities at the game players. Everything she had heard had confirmed her worst fear. The Nomads had no grand, higher purpose for human or Interloper. They were merely gamers enjoying a complex, violent spectacle. Now they were dismayed at the way the game had developed, and might be about to abandon it.

"You can't just cause this much suffering and destruction and then walk away!" she screamed at Trent. Turning to Benson, she went on, "You've no moral right to spend centuries making a flawed world even worse, adding to the sum of human misery!"

Eventually, she exhausted her reserves of outrage. The fact that she still seemed to be in a very ordinary, corporate conference room did not help. She sat down, glowering at each Nomad in turn. The two man-shaped creatures regarded her silently.

"Well, go on," she taunted Benson. "Put this piece back in the box."

Still, neither Nomad spoke, and a glimmer of hope formed in the back of her mind.

"But you can't, can you?" she went on. "You said it yourself, I'm too important, and getting rid of me will foul up your stupid, cruel game."

This did prompt a reaction in Benson. For a second, the ugly human visage rippled, became unfocused, and Denny glimpsed a mass of writhing tendrils. She flinched, expecting the creature to attack her in its true form. But the change only lasted for a split second, and Benson's familiar human face returned, still devoid of emotion.

"It is not," said Benson, "a stupid game."

"No," said Trent, "it is the most beautiful of art forms, the most wonderful of creations. But you cannot grasp it, limited as you are to a primitive space-time continuum."

Denny's anger flared again.

"Oh, right," she sneered. "Your game is so goddam wonderful, so cosmically brilliant that I literally can't grasp how amazing it is. How convenient. Right up there with 'you don't know him, he goes to another school'. You may have all sorts of incredible powers, but that doesn't stop you from being shallow, selfish assholes!"

"Enough!" said Benson sharply, holding up a large, bony hand. "See the game as we see it."

"You can take your game and shove it up–"

Denny did not finish her insult. The bland conference room had vanished, along with Benson and Trent. She was once more adrift in a void, but this time it was alive with strands of light. All around her, myriad threads of multi-colored radiance interwove, flickered, converged into shining nodes of light. Sometimes flashes dazzled her, sometimes entire regions of the huge glowing fabric grew dark. Everywhere she looked was movement, the contrast of light and darkness, a sense of vibrant energy. And her psychic sense told her that myriad minds were at work in this extraordinary place, busy working at schemes she could not grasp.

It could be another fake, she thought. *But I don't think so.*

"It's beautiful," she said grudgingly. "Is it the universe?"

"No," said Trent. "It is many universes. All interacting, merging, splitting apart. Not unlike life itself, it is ever-changing, yet somehow remains the same."

Trent was drifting beside her, still appearing as an overweight little man in a dark blue business suit. He gestured at a greenish skein of energy that flickered, became ragged, then faded to a few dull strands of radiance. Then orange light flared, and more threads grew, fanning out into a vast, elaborate web.

"It's all alive," Denny breathed. "I'm impressed. And confused."

"This is our game board," Benson said, appearing just beyond Trent. "The only one there is. All others are mere imitations, shadowy reflections of the true game."

Denny turned weightlessly, almost losing herself in the vast tapestry of infinite creation. Finally, she looked at Trent.

"You're not gods," she said flatly. "Though I've wondered if you might be demons."

"True in the first instance," Trent enthused, "but the jury is still out on the second point."

"The real point," Benson interjected, "is that what we are and what we do is vastly greater than a mere mortal being can comprehend. You cannot judge us, any more than a microbe can judge the scientist who eradicates it."

Denny laughed, bitterly. The beauty of the game suddenly vanished.

"Microbes don't answer back," she pointed out. "And I do judge you. And I guess that, if you're not gods, you have to answer to someone, or something. And I want to lodge a protest with the big boss. You know? Register a complaint with your head office."

Trent giggled as if Denny had made a slightly dirty joke. Benson remained expressionless.

"I don't get to complain?" Denny went on. "Okay, how about I get a free turn, or something? Another roll of the dice? Because no matter how fancy your friggin' game is, no matter how much vaster than my tiny little mind it is, I'm sure at least one of you guys has cheated, or screwed up in some other way."

"This has gone on too long," Benson said.

"Matheson," said Denny, and waited for a response. When none came, she felt grim satisfaction.

"Yeah, Matheson. The guy you killed, Trent. You didn't nudge him down a particular path in life, did you? Nothing very subtle about that."

"Irrelevant!" snapped Benson. "You do not know what you are saying."

Denny sensed uncertainty, though she could not read the creatures' emotions.

"Oh, I think she does," Trent responded. "And she is at least half-right. I did make – let us call it a mistake. I acted hastily. Things were not supposed to go like this."

The wondrous vista of interwoven universes vanished, to be replaced by a view that was both startling and yet oddly familiar to Denny. She was hanging in space, looking down on the Earth. The planet was in full sunlight, great swathes of white cloud obscuring much of the oceans and continents. But she could just make out Europe, and the British Isles off the continental coast.

"The true essence of the game," Trent said, "is to make the greatest possible changes by the most gentle and subtle of interventions. The art is always to conceal the act."

"Yeah, I kind of guessed that," Denny said, struggling not to be impressed by the vista below. "You work through people, plant ideas in their minds, stuff like that."

"It would be grossly inappropriate," Benson intoned solemnly, "to interfere more directly. Against the spirit of the game."

"What's happening down there?" Denny asked, ignoring the urge to swear at Benson some more. "How bad is it?"

Trent made a slight gesture with stubby fingers, and the Earth rose rapidly toward them. Denny saw London appear, laid out like a map. Then they got closer, and she saw chaos. The heart of the city was gridlocked. Fires were burning, smudging the sky with drifts of smoke. Here and there, blue flashing lights showed that police, ambulances, or firefighters were failing to battle through the traffic jams.

"What about the virus?" Denny asked. "You know, the plague that wouldn't exist at all if it weren't for your goddam game?"

"Over thirty thousand infected, so far," Benson said bleakly. "Estimated global impact, at least one hundred million deaths. Containment measures in other countries are surprisingly effective."

"In Britain," Trent added, "not so much. At least one-third of the population will die."

"You callous bastards!" Denny raged. "I thought you might have some sense of shame, some vague idea of responsibility –"

She broke off when the two Nomads began to change, their human forms bulging and splitting. Tendrils of glistening black emerged from the discarded shells, growing until they blotted out the sky and the world below. Denny spun around, near panic, as the network of weird growth merged into a rough globe that enclosed her. A few glimmers of light were still visible through the interwoven strands.

'We will send you back, now. Prepare for further adversity.'

The cold thought pierced her mind. Behind it, she sensed mental power far in excess of any Interloper.

"Gee, thanks guys," she murmured, as the space enclosed by the writhing tendrils began to shimmer like heat haze. "Adversity. Who could've guessed?"

'We will grant you one temporary advantage. Use it wisely.'

***

"Who is least valuable here?" asked Alpha.

Doctor Formby looked down at the Interloper and shook her head silently. Frankie could see that the woman was terrified. But despite her terror, Formby was refusing to cooperate. Behind the doctor, the medical team were hemmed in by a semicircle of juveniles, hissing and snarling.

They need brains, Frankie thought. *Or at least, they're going to take some.*

"Hey!" she shouted.

Alpha and the other Queens turned to look at Frankie.

"Plenty of brains out in the streets," she went on. "Why waste an expert you might use?"

Alpha titled her head on one side.

"You are pretending to be stupid," said Alpha. "You know that there is danger outside. Individuals with firearms, rioters, some danger of buildings collapsing. We require brain matter, we will take it here, in safety."

Frankie lunged forward, blinded by rage. The two Lopers that were holding her almost lost their grip, but then sank talons into her arms through her shirt. She yelped at the pain, felt the warm sensation of blood flowing, staining her sleeves.

"Very well," Alpha said, walking towards Frankie. "You are probably the least useful in terms of knowledge. And you have thwarted us before."

Frankie struggled more frantically against her captors, indifferent now to the pain. But she was held firm as Alpha drew close, looked her in the eye. Frankie tried to see some evidence of the alien monster inside the human façade. She saw only the face of an intelligent young woman.

"We could use surgical instruments, I suppose," Alpha remarked, running a sharp fingernail along Frankie's hairline. "But the traditional method is probably just as effective."

Frankie tried to kick Alpha in the knee, but the creature anticipated the move, dodging successfully. Alpha waved an admonitory finger.

"I can read your surface thoughts, emotions. You think your friend, the freak, will return to save you. Yes, she once rescued you from our world, now lost to us. But she cannot save you in this world, which will soon be ours."

Alpha's face was losing definition, becoming distorted, ugly. The beautiful eyes darkened, shrank, retreated into deep sockets. The full, sensuous mouth grew, became a grotesque maw lined with needle-like fangs. Frankie felt the fingernail running along her forehead become sharper, steel-hard. A stinging sensation was followed by a warm trickle. Blood flowed down her face, into one of her eyes, half-blinding her.

"We will crack this one open slowly," Alpha hissed, her voice still bearing a slight trace of the feminine. "All the rest, observe as we feast. Disobey us, even in the smallest matter, and this will be your fate. Do not–"

Frankie felt the vicious talon stop, withdraw, saw Alpha spin around. A shimmering in the air seemed to embrace the wall behind Formby and her team. The medics, shouting in panic, ran to the far corner of the sick bay. The entire far wall, including the doorway leading to the main office, simply vanished. Chunks of plaster and brickwork fell into the vastly expanded portal, the debris disappearing in its turn.

My God, the whole ceiling could collapse.

Denny appeared, moving fast, seeming to fall out of the air and landing on all fours. Two juvenile Interlopers sprang forward, hands reaching out to grab her. Frankie's feeling of optimism vanished when she realized that Denny on her own would simply provide the Queens with another prisoner.

"If only we could take her brains," mused Beta.

"But we must not kill our own," Gamma insisted. "Even a mongrel is one of us."

"That's good to hear," said Denny.

Except that her lips didn't move.

Frankie thought she was going insane. Another Denny had materialized, falling out of nothingness, landing right behind the first. There was a gasp from the human onlookers; hisses of surprise and rage from the Interlopers. The creatures holding Frankie let her go and dashed forward. But before they reached the second Denny, a third had appeared, then a fourth, and a fifth.

"Impossible," Frankie breathed.

The second Denny pounced on the nearest Interloper, grasped its neck, and twisted. There was a sickening crack and the creature flopped to the tiled floor. A confused melee began, Interlopers trying to restrain the multiple Dennys, while the latter went for the kill. As Frankie watched, she saw the five versions of her friend transform into quasi-Lopers, faces distorted by fanged muzzles, fingers growing talons. They began to fight in a vicious, frenzied fashion.

"Exterminate them all!" shrieked the first Denny.

There were squeals of pain and confusion as the juveniles tried to withdraw only to be taken down. The three Queens had already retreated to the outer door, Alpha spreading her arms as if to shelter the two younger females cowering behind her. The slaughter became sickening, with chunks of pale flesh ripped from maimed bodies, black eyes gouged, limbs broken. By now, the Dennys were unrecognizable as human, each one a slavering, misshapen monster, clothes soaked in dark blood, dark eyes wild with a killing rage.

"Stop!" begged Alpha as the last squealing juvenile was ripped apart. "Do not come closer!"

The group of Dennys ignored her and kept closing in. Frankie felt a mixture of exultation and disgust, tinged with shame at her own response. Then she spotted Beta taking something out of her jeans, recognized the gun that had been taken from her.

"Denny!" she shouted. "Look out!"

Five hideous faces turned to look at her. At the same moment, Beta fired from behind Alpha. A gaping hole appeared in the side of one Denny's head, a red spatter spraying over Zoffany's bubble. The other Dennys screamed, staggered, and Beta fired again, but this time her bullet struck her target in the torso. Before Beta could take a third shot, the three uninjured Dennys had leaped at the Queens.

A moment later all Frankie saw was a confused tumbling, clawing mass. She grabbed a pair of scissors from a surgical trolley, rushed forward, and was about to plunge it into the neck of a monster when she realized that it was wearing Denny's shirt.

Frankie threw the scissors aside, retreated, and covered her face with her hands so she did not have to look at the hideous spectacle.

Monsters, she thought. *The monsters have won. Whatever happens, the monsters have won.*

Epilogue: Monsters

"They gave me another award," said Gould. "Well, a medal."

"Really?" exclaimed Frankie. "Cool, let's see it."

The scientist took a small, blue box out of his pocket, put it on the pub table. Frankie opened the box, and saw a silver star with a red and white ribbon. She lifted the medal, tried to read the inscription.

"Hungarian?" she guessed.

"Polish," Gould said, with fake smugness. "I'm now an honorary member of the order of the Polar Star. For some reason."

"Maybe they overstocked," Frankie suggested. "But hey, you could go into the scrap metal business."

Gould smiled as he closed the box.

"I'd give them all if she could be here with us," he said, quietly.

"Harriet's in good hands," Frankie said quickly. "And she's not going to be charged with any crime, that's a plus. I heard that the new antiviral drugs–"

"I'm not talking about Harriet," Gould cut in.

Frankie fell silent. She glanced around the pub, noted the shabbiness of most of the clientele, the stylish duds of a small minority. The latter consisted of confident, loud-talking men and their showy girlfriends.

Black marketers, she thought. *People who can get you extra ration cards, little luxuries. Some things never change.*

"Can't say the food has improved," Gould said, pushing away his plate of cod and chips. "And the choice of beers is fairly atrocious."

Frankie had to smile at that. Like a lot of Brits, Gould was now a constant complainer. Nearly two million people had died in the pandemic, half of them in the UK. But containment measures followed by radical treatments had curbed the Interloper virus. The disease itself had rapidly lost momentum, helping the experts to defeat it. Zoffany, for all her genius, had done a hasty job, and so-called Nemesis had lost much of its virulence after only a few weeks.

"What the hell happened, Ted?" she asked finally.

The Englishman took his time gulping a couple of mouthfuls of pale ale before answering.

"You want a different answer from last time? Or the time before that?"

Frankie shook her head in despair. After the military had arrived at the Task Force headquarters, they had found body parts. All had been provisionally classified as human. Statements from Formby and the others had been confused, hard to credit. Some spoke of monsters whose corpses melted, decayed so rapidly that all that remained was a pool of foul slime. A form of collective hysteria akin to cabin fever had been diagnosed.

Payments had been made, generous pensions promised, general silence bought.

"Okay," Gould sighed. "I think she contacted the Nomads and somehow persuaded them – or bullied them, more likely – into giving her one of their bizarre powers. That allowed her to multiply, like Benson and Trent, and finish off the Interlopers. But we both saw Beta shoot one part of the multiple being. And she died. We're on the same page, so far?"

Frankie nodded. She recalled Denny's funeral in Baltimore, the weeping parents, the strange charade. The coffin had been open, and Frankie had lingered by the corpse. It was the Denny she had known, not the hideous being she had seen take down the Interlopers. Denise Purcell was lauded as a brilliant journalist whose career had been cruelly cut short by terrorists, or possibly violent looters.

"I watched the video footage again today," said Gould. "Still got my security clearance, might as well use it. I know you don't want to hear this but I'm still not sure if she got all of them. I think maybe one of the three got away."

"No evidence for that," Frankie shot back quickly. "You know you shouldn't speculate. Especially not in public."

She glanced around, unsure if they were being overheard. Since the state of emergency had been imposed, saying anything too controversial was dangerous. Elections were supposedly due next year. But at the moment, much of Britain felt like it was under military occupation, albeit by its own forces.

To break another silence, she asked Gould about his 'back trouble'. This was their code for the scar caused when the symbiont had been absorbed. He shrugged and shifted in his seat, still reluctant to lean right back in his chair.

"Sometimes I wake up and imagine the little bugger is still there," he admitted. "But the theory goes that, with the Lopers all gone, the symbionts simply decayed for lack of stimuli. The good part is that the immunity they conferred on us is still there. Just in case."

They talked some more, but the conversation kept veering back toward those who were absent. Eventually, they said goodnight, and each set off on their journey home.

***

The tunnels were dark, deep, seemingly endless. The great city had lost power during the first days of the plague, and the underground trains had not run for months. By the time the government had restored order and reclaimed London, much of its infrastructure had been wrecked. Rioting, vandalism, theft of copper wires, had all made the Tube useless. It was slowly being restored, but in the meantime, the tunnels were silent by day and night.

The creature that had once called itself Denny survived on rainwater, rats, and the occasional feral dog. The latter, it could only hunt at night, when great swathes of the capital were under curfew. The rats, it could get any time. The animals it preyed upon, usually made the mistake of seeing the creature as human. They were deceived by form, by voice, by scent. When they realized their mistake, it was much too late.

The creature knew that it had once been human. It did not care. It shunned humans as any wild thing must. It knew more than a mere animal, but ignored any thoughts that did not concern immediate survival. Above all, it suffered. Its pain was not merely material, though it ached in every bone and sinew. It spent every waking moment repenting a loss it could not understand, could never come to terms with.

Part of it had died. Part of it was always dying. Part of the creature's mind was perpetually in a white room, too brightly lit, too full of people and beings that were not people. Part of it was always falling to the floor, blood gushing from its jaws. No matter whether it traversed a dank, cool tunnel under the metropolis, or loped from shadow to shadow on the surface, it suffered.

Sometimes its routine was disrupted in a way it did not quite understand, in a fashion that both excited and hurt it. A strange impulse led it to the surface when it did not need to hunt. On this night, it scrambled up, from the great tunnels through a drainage system, then up to a sewer. It lifted a manhole cover, knowing that it was night, and used its dark-adapted vision to scan the street. It was drizzling, and the scene appeared deserted. Light, painfully bright, flared as a car passed the end of the street, making the creature drop the cover.

The noise of the engine faded. Silence fell. Then footsteps sounded, walking fast.

The creature's heartbeat quickened. It lifted the steel cover again, peered through the narrow gap. A small figure was just visible, passing by. The creature waited until the human had rounded the corner, then climbed out and rushed to the nearest shadow. It wore a few ragged garments it had found on its hunts, modified its form to that of human.

It kept tracking the small human by its steps, loud in the empty streets. It did not understand the need to be close to the being. But it could not resist the impulse, any more than it could ignore hunger when it burned in its belly.

***

"A psychic?" said the waitress. "Really?"

Denny smiled up at the girl and nodded politely. She handed over one of her new business cards, told the waitress to tell her friends. Already she was imagining the next few months. So many people had suffered during the plague and subsequent chaos, so many scars that she might help to heal.

As the waitress went back to the counter, Denny looked out of the little tea shop window. This seaside resort was a little shabby, its glory days long past. But the views over the bay were beautiful on a clear, calm day.

I can live here in peace, for a while. Try to make sense of it all.

A dark van stopped outside the café, blocking the view. The shadow of the bulky vehicle turned the wide window into a mirror, and Denny saw herself. Her new face, carefully crafted to seem bland, amiable, unthreatening, was familiar now. She could use her Interloper powers almost unconsciously, only losing her new visage in sleep.

So, I'll be sleeping alone for a good while.

She could hear the waitress chatting to her colleague at the checkout. Excited whispers told her that more customers would be coming her way soon. She smiled slightly to herself and lifted her teacup. But as she was about to sip the brown liquid, her hand began to quiver. She put both hands on the cup, set it down carefully. She checked her face swiftly in the window, just in case her new guise had faltered.

The attacks were less frequent now, but still unpredictable. They had been almost debilitating when she found herself wandering the streets of London at the height of the Emergency. She couldn't seek medical help, couldn't trust anyone now. But she did not really need experts to tell her what was wrong.

I'm incomplete, she thought. *I was divided, multiplied somehow, something no human should suffer. Something no ordinary human could survive.*

One of her selves had been killed outright. That much she knew, and the pain of separation was still acute. It throbbed inside her like a psychic wound. But there was something else, another sense of loss that was harder to pin down, more worrying. Sometimes she dreamed of darkness, of feral impulses, mindless urges. She dreamed of hunger and blood.

Is part of me still out there? Denny wondered. *Has it become a different version of me, the Loper I might have become?*

"Can I get you anything else?"

Nightmare Rising

The young waitress was back, inventing a pretext to talk to the psychic. Denny shook her head, skimming the girl's thoughts and feelings. There was something refreshing about the very commonplace hopes and fears she found. Denny resolved to do as much as possible to help people in this backwater, earn a modest living, lay low.

And if part of me is still out there?

As she paid her check, she tried to shrug off the thought that some alter-ego, another Denny, might be roaming. If she set out to find this, she risked exposure. She could not risk being caught, studied, experimented upon.

She walked out into the fresh, sea air, trying to forget London, and hoped that tonight she would enjoy a dreamless sleep.

***

Frankie stopped outside her apartment building and looked up and down the street. She saw nothing unusual, no sign of movement. But as she took out her keys, she kept glimpsing something in the periphery of her vision; the tail of her eye. She felt relief when she slammed the front door behind her, ran upstairs to her flat, and locked herself inside.

"Imagination," she told herself. "Paranoid times."

But I'm not turning on the light. Not yet.

Instead, she stood in the dark, looking out of a crack in the curtains. She had never seen anything, despite feeling herself being watched many times. Every time she told herself that this time, she would see it, whatever it was. But every time before she had looked out at a London street and seen nothing.

What's that?

Frankie held her breath, clutching the curtain, expectant. But the moving shape was only a dog slinking along. She assumed it was one of the hundreds of strays that had taken to living wild in packs after the crisis. Most had been dealt with, but there were still a few around.

Maybe the poor mutt followed me, she thought. *Some memory or instinct telling it a human might provide it with food and shelter, but not brave enough to come close.*

It was the rational explanation. Sighing in relief, she stepped away from the curtain and headed into the kitchen to make some herbal tea. She was just filling the kettle when a sharp, startling noise made her pause and turn off the faucet. She ran back into the living room and peered out, not trying to hide. The street was still deserted. She heard a faint, dull clang. Something metallic had fallen, or been struck.

Vandals smashing stuff up, she thought. *Maybe curfew wasn't such a bad idea.*

She went back into the tiny kitchen, set the kettle to boil. But later, as she lay in bed waiting for sleep to come, she thought back to the noise she had heard, wondering why it so preoccupied her.

It had been a brief, startled yelp. The sound of a dog in distress, cut short.

* * *

FREE Bonus Novel!

Thank you once again for downloading this book. I'd really appreciate it if you took a minute to leave a review, it helps tremendously!

Don't forget to download your **FREE full-length novel**. Let us know where to send it by signing up for our mailing list below. You'll also learn about upcoming releases, future discounts and giveaways:
www.ScareStreet.com/DavidLonghorn

See you in the shadows,
David Longhorn

CPSIA information can be obtained
at www.ICGtesting.com
Printed in the USA
LVHW031315220221
679637LV00004B/333